The Vagabond Clown

An Elizabethan Mystery

EDWARD MARSTON

Allison & Busby Limited
12 Fitzroy Mews
London W1T 6DW
allisonandbusby.com

First published in 2003.
This paperback edition published by Allison & Busby in 2015.

A CIP catalogue record for this book is available from
the British Library.

10 9 8 7 6 5 4 3

ISBN 978-0-7490-1841-2

Typeset in 10.5/16 pt Sabon by
Allison & Busby Ltd.

The paper used for this Allison & Busby publication
has been produced from trees that have been legally sourced
from well-managed and credibly certified forests.

Printed and bound by
CPI Group (UK) Ltd, Croydon, CR0 4YY

*To Lynn Farleigh and John Woodvine, friends,
actors and true Shakespeareans*

The grounde work of Commedies is love, cosenedge, flatterie, bawdrie, sly conveighance of whoredom. The persons, cookes, knaves, baudes, parasites, courtezannes, lecherous old men, amorous young men . . .

STEPHEN GOSSON: *Plays Confuted in Five Actions* (1582)

Chapter One

The trouble came when he least expected it. Nicholas Bracewell was, for once, caught completely off guard. Until that moment, the performance had been an unqualified success. *A Trick To Catch A Chaste Lady* was an ideal choice for a hot afternoon in the yard of the Queen's Head in Gracechurch Street and the spectators were highly appreciative. What was on offer was a riotous comedy that was played with such skill that it kept the large audience in a state of almost continuous hilarity. Waves of laughter rolled ceaselessly across the yard. In the role of a bumbling suitor, Lackwit, who fails time and again to win the hand of his beloved, Lawrence Firethorn led Westfield's Men superbly, setting a standard at which the others could aim, if only to fall short. The one actor who rivalled his comic genius was Barnaby Gill, the acknowledged clown of the company, a man whose facial contortions were a delight and whose sprightly jigs were irresistibly funny. Gill was in the middle of one of his famous dances when the shadow of disaster fell across the afternoon.

'Why do they laugh so, Nick?' complained Firethorn, who had just quit the stage and was standing beside the book holder. 'These are stale antics. Barnaby's jig has as much novelty as the death of Julius Caesar.'

'He's a born clown,' said Nicholas Bracewell admiringly, glancing up from his prompt book to watch Gill at work. 'He plays upon his audience as upon a pipe.'

'And produces dull music.'

'They do not think so.'

Firethorn inflated his chest. '*I* am the true clown,' he boasted. 'My touch is altogether lighter than Barnaby's. I play upon playgoers as upon a church organ.'

'Yes,' said Nicholas with a smile, 'and produce some very irreverent chords.'

Before he could reply, Firethorn was distracted by a huge roar of laughter from the inn yard. Envy surged through him at once. Annoyed that Gill was getting such a wonderful response onstage, he turned to look at his capering colleague. But it was not the comic jig that was provoking the explosion of joy. Gill, in fact, was standing quite still. Two young men had suddenly leapt up on to the makeshift stage from the audience and were grappling with each other. Assuming that the fight was part of the play, the spectators urged them on, shaking with even more mirth when Gill, outraged that his dance had been interrupted, made the mistake of trying to pull the combatants apart,

10

only to be set on by both of them. The hapless clown was pushed, punched, slapped, tripped up, kicked hard in the ribs then thrown unceremoniously from the stage.

Amused at first, the standees at the front of the pit lost their sense of humour when the flailing arms and legs of Barnaby Gill landed among them. Items of furniture soon followed as the two interlopers began to hurl various properties from the stage. A chair hit one man in the face. A heavy stool knocked another spectator senseless. Flung into the air, a wooden table caused even more damage when it landed simultaneously on three people. This was no trick to catch a chaste lady, still less a device to entertain the onlookers. It was a deliberate attempt to halt the play in its tracks. Protests were loud and angry. In an instant, the atmosphere in the yard was transformed.

Nicholas was the first to react, discarding his book to make an unscheduled appearance on stage and grab one of the miscreants in order to march him off. Firethorn came charging out to deal with the other young man but the latter jumped into the crowd and started to cudgel everyone within reach. A brawl developed immediately and the whole yard was soon involved. Stirred into action, drunken apprentices clambered onto the stage and tried to release the captive from Nicholas's hands. Other members of the cast came streaming out to assist their book holder, only to be ambushed by a second group of apprentices who had been roused to join in the melee. Violence was lifted to a new and more dangerous level. The noise was deafening. Above the roars of injured parties rose the screams of women and the yells of frightened men. There was a mad dash for the exits, producing such congestion that people began to buffet each other indiscriminately.

Nor was there any safety in the galleries. Viewing the disorder from above, those who had paid extra for a seat and a cushion were forced to duck and dodge as missiles were aimed at them from below. Half-eaten apples scored direct hits. Sticks and stones seemed to come from nowhere. One man scooped up fresh horse manure from the stables and flung it at the gallants and their ladies in the lower gallery. Panic reached the level of hysteria as spectators fought their way to the steps. Private battles broke out on every staircase. All trace of courtesy vanished. Rich apparel was badly torn in the commotion, wounds were readily inflicted. Shrieks, curses, threats and cries for help blended into a single ear-splitting sound. Chaos had come to the Queen's Head. Its morose landlord, Alexander Marwood, the bane of the theatre troupe, viewed the scene from the uncertain safety of a window, shouting himself hoarse and gesticulating wildly as the fighting intensified.

Nicholas struggled valiantly against unequal odds. Forced to let go of one man, he beat off three others who tried to overpower him then used his strength to dislodge an attacker, clinging unwisely to Firethorn's back. The actor was already wrestling with two other invaders of their stage before banging their heads together and sending them reeling. Nicholas looked around in despair. The play had been comprehensively ruined. Properties had been tossed into the crowd and the scenery had been smashed to pieces.

Barnaby Gill had disappeared under the feet of the fleeing public. It was a black day for Westfield's Men. They came out to support their fellows in the fight but only added to the general tumult. Dick Honeydew, the youngest and most talented of the company's apprentices, still in his costume, abandoned all pretence of being the beautiful Helen, object of Lackwit's wooing, and hurled himself into the fray. It was a grave error of judgement. Within seconds, his wig was snatched from his head, his dress was torn from his back and he was shouldered roughly off the stage.

Honeydew's cry went unheard in the turmoil but Nicholas had seen the fate of his young friend. Leaping from the stage, he went to his aid, lifting the boy to his feet with one hand while using the other to brush away a leering youth who was trying to molest the play's heroine. The book holder carried Honeydew quickly back to the tiring-house.

'Stay here, Dick!' he ordered. 'This is not your battle.'

'I'll do my share,' said Honeydew, raising a puny arm. 'Westfield's Men ever stick together. We must all protect our property.'

'It's beyond redemption. My job is to save our fellows from serious harm.' He indicated the cowering figure in the corner of the room. 'You stay here and comfort George. He needs your succour.'

'Oh, I do, I do,' wailed George Dart.

Dart was the assistant stagekeeper, a small, slight, timorous creature who all too often took on the role of the company's scapegoat. Though he had many sterling qualities, bravery was not among them. While others had rushed out to do battle, Dart shrunk back into the tiring-house with his hands over his ears. Honeydew took pity on him and put a consoling arm around the diminutive figure. Nicholas felt able to return to the battlefield. When he went out on stage, he was relieved to see that it had now been reclaimed by the actors. With a concerted effort, they had driven all the interlopers off their precious boards and were patrolling them to make sure that nobody else trespassed on their territory. Firethorn stood in their midst, bellowing at the audience to calm down but only succeeding in driving them into an even greater frenzy.

Nicholas glanced up at the galleries. They were rapidly emptying. Even their patron, Lord Westfield, was beating a retreat from his place of honour with the members of his entourage, scrambling through a door that led to a private room. The affray would do untold damage to the reputation of the company, making even their most loyal playgoers think twice before venturing into the Queen's Head again. *A Trick To Catch A Chaste Lady* had ended in catastrophe. There was worse to come. As the crowd continued to disperse, a familiar figure was revealed. Trampled in the exodus, Barnaby Gill was lying on the ground, clutching a leg and groaning in agony. Nicholas jumped from the stage and bent over him to protect Gill from any further injury. Firethorn also came to the aid of the stricken clown.

'What ails you, Barnaby?' he said, kneeling beside him.

'My leg,' replied Gill through gritted teeth. 'God's blood, Lawrence! How could you let this happen? They've broken my leg.'

'How do you know?'

'How do you *think* I know, man?'

Nicholas turned to the stage. 'Fetch a doctor!' he called and one of the actors ran off immediately. There were still many bodies milling about in the yard. 'Let's move him to a place of safety,' he suggested. 'We can use that table.'

Calling two more actors to assist him, Nicholas righted the upturned table that had been thrown from the stage. The powerful Firethorn, showing an affection for his fallen colleague that surprised them both, lifted Gill as gently as he could and lowered him onto the table. Four of them bore it slowly away with its passenger still writhing in pain. Only when they had manoeuvred the table into the tiring-house did they feel that he was out of danger. Gill was surrounded by the sympathetic faces of his fellows. They saw the implications at once. A clown with a broken leg would not be able to dance for a very long time. It was a bitter blow to a company that relied so much on the talents of the inimitable Barnaby Gill. Everyone tried to soothe him with kind words.

When they least needed him, Alexander Marwood came bursting in. There was no compassion from the landlord. He ignored Gill completely. His gnarled face was puce with fury and the remaining wisps of hair stood up like tufts of grass on his gleaming pate. He pointed an accusatory finger at Firethorn.

'See the mischief you have done, sir?' he howled. 'You've brought ruin down upon me. You and your knavish company have turned my yard into the pit of Hell.'

'Away, you rogue!' yelled Firethorn, rounding on him. 'Can you not see that Barnaby lies injured here? What are a few damaged pieces of timber to a broken leg? Take that ugly face of yours out of here before it makes me puke.'

'I demand recompense, Master Firethorn.'

'You shall have it with the point of my sword.'

'I'll not be browbeaten, sir.'

'No,' warned Firethorn, bunching a fist. 'You'll be hand-beaten, foot-beaten, cudgel-beaten, stone-beaten and axe-beaten until you look even more hideous than you are now. By heaven, if I were not so fond of dumb animals, I'd beat you into a pulp and feed you to the mangiest curs in London.' He raised an arm to strike. 'Begone, you foul wretch! You offend our sight.'

Marwood backed away in fear. 'Stand off, sir, or I'll set the law on you.'

'Not before I set my toe against your vile buttocks.'

Nicholas moved in swiftly to prevent Firethorn from carrying out his threat. Taking the landlord by the shoulder, he ushered him out of the room and onto the stage. He disliked Marwood as much as any of them but he knew the importance of trying to placate the egregious little man who, when all was said and done, provided them with their inn yard theatre. Westfield's Men enjoyed a precarious relationship with Alexander Marwood at the best of times. That relationship would not be improved by a violent assault upon him.

'I'll turn you out,' said Marwood, still pulsing with impotent rage. 'I'll not have Westfield's Men on my premises a moment longer.'

'Calm down,' said Nicholas. 'You are too hasty.'

'I was certainly too hasty when I let my yard to your troupe.'

'We've both gained from the arrangement.'

'I should have expelled you years ago, Master Bracewell.'

'And what would have happened to all the income that we have brought you?' asked Nicholas, appealing to his pocket. 'We not only pay you a rent, we fill the Queen's Head with happy people who are only too ready to drink your ale and eat your food. Come, sir, you have turned a handsome profit out of the company.'

Marwood looked balefully around the yard. 'Do you call this profit, sir? My benches damaged, my balustrades cracked, my shutters torn off their hinges. I dare not think what horrors that mob visited on my stables. This is a calamity!' he cried. 'I am surprised that my inn is still standing.'

'We regret what happened as much as you.'

'But you and your fellows are to blame, Master Bracewell.'

'Not so,' said Nicholas. 'We are victims of this affray, not progenitors.'

'Westfield's Men attract rogues and vagabonds into my yard.'

'We appeal to anyone who wishes to enjoy a play. Our spectators were filled with your ale, remember. Hot weather and strong drink worked against us this afternoon. Think how rarely it has done that,' argued Nicholas. 'No matter how rough and unruly an audience, our plays usually please them so much that their behaviour is above reproach. *A Trick To Catch A Chaste Lady* has always found favour before. Set this one bad experience against the hundreds of good ones that have taken place at the Queen's Head.'

'My mind is resolved, sir. We must part forthwith.'

'You forget our contract.'

'Its terms stipulate that my yard may be hired for the sole purpose of presenting a play. Not for encouraging the sweepings of the city to run riot. The contract is revoked.'

'Would you lose the income that it gives you?'

'I'd rather lose that than the inn itself.'

'The damage may not be as great as you fear.'

'No,' moaned Marwood, running his eye over the debris. 'It's likely to be far worse. Get your fellows off my property, Master Bracewell.'

'Not until we help to clear up the mess.'

'Westfield's Men will be the death of me!'

Clutching his head in despair, the landlord turned on his heel and scurried off to the taproom. Nicholas let him go. There was no reasoning with Marwood in a crisis. A confirmed pessimist, he preferred to luxuriate in misery. Nicholas took a quick inventory of the yard. Most of the spectators had fled now, leaving only the stragglers and the wounded behind. They limped out of the Queen's Head as best they could, glad to get away from the scene of devastation. Items from the play lay scattered on the ground alongside food, vomit, discarded tankards and a selection of hats that had been plucked from their owners' heads. Dick Honeydew's stolen wig floated in a pool of blood. Doors, shutters and balustrades had all been damaged. Some of the benches in the galleries had been upended and snapped in two during the headlong flight. It was a depressing sight.

Nicholas was about to call the others to help him clear up the yard when he noticed someone still up in the gallery. Slumped in his seat, the man was young, well-built and exquisitely well-dressed. What interested Nicholas was the fact that the last surviving member of the audience had been part of Lord Westfield's entourage, the exclusive coterie that occupied a privileged position in the gallery. The man's eyes were closed as if he had drifted off to sleep. Nicholas wondered if he had somehow been knocked unconscious as the spectators struggled to escape. Crossing to the nearest staircase, he went up the steps and made his way along the gallery to the lone figure. He shook him by the shoulder to see if he could rouse him. The man suddenly fell forward and the book holder grabbed him before he hit his head on the balustrade. It was only then that Nicholas saw the handle of a dagger protruding from his back. The man's days as a playgoer were over.

Chapter Two

It was almost an hour before Nicholas Bracewell was able to rejoin the others. Having summoned constables to report the murder of the anonymous playgoer, he helped them to carry the body to the waiting cart that would take it to the morgue. Nicholas then went off to give a sworn statement to a magistrate, describing the circumstances in which he had found the dead man but having, at this stage, no clue as to his identity beyond the fact that he was a friend of Lord Westfield's. Word of the riot at the inn alarmed the magistrate and he hoped that culprits could be found and arraigned, but Nicholas had doubts. Once they had started the affray, none of the youths lingered in the yard for too long. They escaped while they could. Nicholas feared that their crime might well go unpunished.

When he returned to the Queen's Head, he found that almost the entire company was helping to dismantle their stage and clear up the wreckage in the yard. There was a pervading air of sadness as they sifted through the remains of their property, acutely conscious of the severe blow dealt to their livelihood. Only two actors were missing. One of them, Lawrence Firethorn, soon came clattering into the yard on his horse. Reining in the animal, he dismounted and went over to Nicholas.

'This is the worst day in our history, Nick,' he decided. 'It will take us an eternity to recover from this. Barnaby injured, our scenery destroyed, our performance ruined and our audience put to flight. Truly, this is our Armageddon.'

'Did the doctor arrive?' asked Nicholas.

'He came and went. As soon as he set the leg in splints, I helped him to convey Barnaby to his lodging. We had to move him with great care.'

'How is he now?'

'Cursing his fate and trying to dull the pain with some Canary wine.'

'What did the doctor say?'

'The break was clean and it should heal in time.'

'How long will that be?'

'Months and months.'

'Meanwhile,' said Nicholas, 'we have lost his services.'

Firethorn heaved a sigh. 'Yes, Nick,' he agreed. 'I never thought to hear myself admitting this but we shall miss him mightily. Lawrence Firethorn may be the shooting star of Westfield's Men but Barnaby Gill can light up the heavens as well.' His gaze shifted to the litter-strewn yard. 'Why did this have to happen? What on earth was it about

A Trick To Catch A Chaste Lady that set them off?'

'The play was not to blame.'

'Then what was? Did Barnaby's jig cause such offence?'

'No,' said Nicholas. 'Whatever play we performed today was already doomed. This was no random act of malice. The brawl was planned.'

Firethorn blinked. 'You think that someone set out to spoil the performance?'

'I'm certain of it. Only two of them jumped up onto the stage at first but I fancy they had confederates in various parts of the yard. That's why the fighting spread so quickly,' said Nicholas. 'I think they were paid to bring us down.'

'By whom?'

'I have no idea.'

'But for what possible reason?'

'That's what we have to find out.' Nicholas cocked an eye upward to the gallery. 'We also have to determine why someone was stabbed to death here this afternoon.'

'That creeping insect of a landlord would have been killed as well if I could have got my hands on him!'

'Forget Alexander Marwood. We have worries enough to vex us.'

'Too true, Nick,' said Firethorn, running a hand through his beard. 'Murder takes priority here. It behoves me to give the poor man the tribute of a passing sigh. Do we know who the victim was?'

'Not yet. But I trust that our patron will furnish us with a name.'

'It's a pity that he cannot furnish us with some

money for we shall certainly need it. Much of what was damaged is beyond repair. And our reputation is badly besmirched. Come,' he urged, walking into the middle of the yard, 'let's help our fellows move the rest of this trash. The sooner we get away from this accursed inn, the better.'

'We need to stay away for a time until tempers cool.'

'Why so?'

'The landlord is upset.'

'That ghoul is *always* upset.'

'He's resolved to terminate our contract.'

Firethorn glowered. 'Let him try. I'll terminate the villain's miserable life!'

'He owns the Queen's Head,' Nicholas reminded him. 'If we are ever to play here again, we must win him over somehow.'

'Then that's an embassy I leave to you, Nick. I can't treat with the rogue.'

'He needs time apart from us.'

'But this is our playhouse.'

'We'll not perform here again for some while.'

'But we must or our occupation dies.'

'I've a notion that might solve that problem.'

'Then let's hear it, man.'

'All in good time.'

Nicholas scooped up the chair that had been hurled into the audience from the stage. Its back had been cracked and one of its legs was missing. He held it up to examine it. Firethorn shook his head sadly.

'We can soon have a new leg put on that,' he observed with bitterness. 'It will not be quite so easy to repair Barnaby.'

The injury not only caused Barnaby Gill extreme pain. It had inflicted a deep wound on his pride. During his long career on the stage, he had never failed to captivate an audience with one of his jigs and invariably earned an ovation at their conclusion. This time, it was different. His art had been insulted, his dance interrupted and his humiliation completed by a vicious attack. As he lay on the bed in his lodging with a half-empty cup of wine in his hand, he was in despair.

'I am done for, Edmund!' he groaned. 'Barnaby Gill is no more.'

'That's foolish talk,' said Edmund Hoode, the resident playwright with the company. 'You're invincible, Barnaby. This is but a small mishap. A short and well-deserved rest from your labours on the boards.'

Gill snorted. 'Rest, do you say? How on earth do I rest when I am in agony?' he asked, pointing to the leg that was in splints. 'And well-deserved? Since when did I deserve to be set upon by two rogues who beat me black and blue?'

'I was merely trying to make a virtue of necessity.'

'Where's the virtue in losing my one source of income?'

'Your leg will heal in time.'

'Not for ages.'

'The doctor was full of optimism.'

'*I'd* be full of optimism if he'd broken *his* leg,' said Gill testily. 'The old fool had no idea how long it would take to mend or whether I'd ever be able to dance on it again.'

'Be patient, Barnaby.'

'When I'm in such torment?'

Gill drained his cup and tossed it aside. Hoode felt sorry for his friend. He could see the quiet terror in Gill's eyes. It was as if the clown's whole future had been broken in two along with his leg. There was no guarantee that his nimbleness would not be permanently impaired. He feared that he might go through life thereafter with a limp. Hoode felt a deep personal loss. Every play he had ever written contained a part that was tailored to Gill's unique comic gifts. Performances of those works without him would be gravely weakened. Hoode was a kind man with a moon-shaped face that was now creased with concern. He bent solicitously over the bed.

'Is there anything I can get you, Barnaby?'

'Only a gravedigger to bury me.'

'You are still very much alive.'

'My art is dead and, without it, so am I.'

'Away with such thoughts!'

'Look at me, man,' said Gill, grimacing. 'You see a corpse before you.'

'I see the finest clown in London,' replied Hoode loyally. 'You are a trifle battered by life at the moment, that is all.'

It was true. In addition to the broken leg, Gill had sustained other injuries. His face was heavily bruised and one eye had been blackened. Having been trampled on by dozens of feet, his whole body was a mass of aches and twinges. He had aged visibly. Hoode had never seen him looking so haggard and miserable. It was very worrying. He did his best to cheer up his friend.

'In a month's time, all this will be forgotten,' he said.

'Never! This day is graven on my heart in perpetuity.'

'New triumphs lie ahead of you, Barnaby.'

'What use is a one-legged dancer?'

'I foresee a complete recovery.'

'Then you are a poor prophet, Edmund. How can I recover from such ignominy?' he cried, tears beginning to roll. 'It was torture out there on that stage today. I was in the middle of my jig when the rogues set upon me. In front of all those people, I was torn to shreds. When they had finished their sport, they tossed me into the pit like a child's doll. The wonder is that I've lived to tell the tale.'

'Nothing can keep you down, Barnaby.'

'It can, it has, it will.'

Gill wiped away the tears with the back of his hand and went off into a reverie. Hoode felt a surge of sympathy for him. The broken leg would not simply interrupt a brilliant career on stage. It would have a disastrous effect on Gill's private life. Most of the actors in the company seized their opportunity to impress and attract female admiration among the spectators. Following the example of Lawrence Firethorn, seasoned in that particular art, they learnt how to catch the eye and set a heart aflame. Gill, too, relied on his performances to excite an audience but, in his case, young men were the intended target. Alone among Westfield's Men, he preferred male company and his

26

performances were his chief means of winning new friends and gaining new conquests. Exiled from the stage while his broken leg slowly mended, he would hardly be in a fit state to seek consolation in certain discreet London taverns. He was also inordinately proud of his appearance, dressing in flamboyant attire and continuously preening himself. Such vanity was now superfluous. Gill would not dare even to look in a mirror.

Hoode did not approve of his friend's private life but that did not stop him from understanding how deprived he must feel. At a stroke, Gill had lost the two sources of pleasure in his life. He was cruelly separated both from his profession and his recreation. Hoode made one last attempt to offer him comfort.

'All is not lost, Barnaby,' he said. 'Though you may no longer prance about a stage, you can still earn money with your songs. You can still raise a laugh.'

Gill was sour. 'Yes, *everyone* will laugh at me now.'

'You have given song recitals before.'

'Only when I wanted to sing, Edmund. The case is altered. All that I wish to do now is to curl up in a corner and die of shame. How do you think I will feel when the rest of you strut boldly at the Queen's Head while I suffer here?'

'We shall never know.'

'Why not?'

'There'll be no strutting at the Queen's Head for a long while,' explained Hoode. 'It was badly damaged during the affray and renovations will be needed. But our main enemy, as ever, is that morose landlord of ours. Alexander Marwood vows that we'll never set foot across his threshold again.'

'Hold him to his contract.'

'He claims that it was revoked by what happened today.'

'What does Lawrence say?' asked Gill.

Hoode gave a wry smile. 'If it was left to Lawrence, the landlord would be hanged from the roof of his inn and set alight until he burnt to a cinder. Fortunately, wiser counsels have prevailed. Nick Bracewell has come to our rescue yet again.'

'Oh?'

'As you know,' Hoode went on, 'we were due to quit the city in ten days' time on a tour of Kent. Nick has suggested that we leave almost immediately. It will have the virtue of keeping us employed and putting distance between us and the landlord of the Queen's Head. The hope is that he will soften towards us while we are away and be more subject to reason by the time that we return.' Hoode saw the other's face darken. 'Is this not the solution to our predicament?'

'No,' growled Gill.

'But it's our salvation.'

'And what about *me*? At a time when I most need my fellows, they will be cavorting around Kent without me. How can you desert a friend like this?'

'It's not desertion, Barnaby. It's a means of survival.'

'Your survival – not mine.'

'The company takes precedence over any individual.'

'Even when I suffered grievously on its behalf?' urged

Gill. 'I was the one who was attacked. I was the one who was flung to the ground and stamped on. It was an ordeal. Show me one person who endured more than I did.'

'I will,' said Hoode softly, 'though I have no name to put to him.'

'No name?'

'In the heat of the affray this afternoon, a man was stabbed to death in the gallery. He came to see a play and forfeited his life. We all regret your injuries, Barnaby, but we must reserve some sympathy for a murder victim.'

Gill was cowed. 'Who was the man?' he murmured.

'That remains to be seen.'

Nicholas Bracewell finally tracked down Lord Westfield early that evening. Their patron was about to leave his house on his way to visit friends. Nicholas caught him as he was in the act of stepping into his carriage. Lord Westfield was still shaken by the events of the afternoon and he was even more disturbed when he heard of the murder that had taken place at the Queen's Head. He gave an involuntary shiver.

'Dear God!' he exclaimed. 'And he was sitting so close to me. That dagger could have finished up in any of our backs. Even mine!'

'Happily, my lord,' said Nicholas, 'that was not the case.'

'This is disgraceful. A play is supposed to provide pleasure, not endanger life.'

'It was a most unusual occurrence.'

'So I should hope.'

'But I'm surprised that this is the first you heard of it, my lord,' said Nicholas. 'The man was in your party. Were you not aware of his absence when you fled?'

'No,' replied the other with irritation. 'We were trying to escape an affray. In those circumstances, you do not pause to count heads. Once outside the inn, we went our several ways. I assumed that Fortunatus was safe.'

'Fortunatus?'

'That is his name. Fortunatus Hope. An ill-favoured christening, if ever there was one, for the fellow had appalling fortune and but little hope.' He stepped down from his carriage. 'Yes, from what you tell me about his appearance, it has to be Fortunatus.'

'Did you know him well, Lord Westfield?'

'No,' said the patron. 'He was a newcomer to my circle, a lively fellow with a turn of phrase that amused me. I looked to become better acquainted with him but that, alas, it will not now be possible.'

'Is there anything you can tell me about him?' asked Nicholas.

'What sort of thing?'

'Did this Master Hope have any enemies?'

Lord Westfield became pensive. He was a short, plump, red-faced man of middle years in a doublet of peach-coloured satin that was trimmed with gold lace. His tall green hat sported an ostrich feather that curled down mischievously over his right temple. Though Nicholas was unfailingly polite to their patron, he was more than aware of his shortcomings.

Lord Westfield was an epicurean, a man whose whole life was devoted to idle pleasures, usually at someone else's expense. His love of the theatre encouraged him to retain his own troupe but it existed as much to add lustre to his name as to achieve any success on its own account. Lord Westfield liked nothing better than to loll in his chair in the lower gallery at the Queen's Head and bask in the praise of his hangers-on as he showed off his company to them. That joy had been taken summarily from him during the afternoon's performance and the memory of it still made him bristle with disapproval.

'It was an appalling scene,' he recalled. 'Utterly appalling!'

'I agree, my lord.'

'There were ladies in my party. They might have been injured.'

'Luckily, they were not,' said Nicholas. 'Others did not escape, I fear. There were a number of casualties, Barnaby Gill among them.'

'Master Gill was grossly abused. How does he fare?'

'Not well, my lord. He suffered a broken leg.'

'Poor fellow!'

'It may be months before he is fully recovered. He'll be unable to join us on our tour of Kent. That is the other thing I came to tell you, my lord,' he added. 'Since we have worn out our welcome in Gracechurch Street, we mean to leave London sooner than planned. I believe that you intended to be in Dover when we played there.'

'Indeed, I do,' said the other. 'Lord Cobham is a friend

of mine. I've promised him a stirring performance from Westfield's Men. Let me know the dates of your stay in Dover and I'll contrive to be there at the same time.'

'Thank you, my lord,' replied Nicholas, trying to guide him back to the more important matter. 'Before I do that, however, I would like whatever information you can give me about Master Hope. I asked if he had enemies.'

'None that I know of. Fortunatus was such an amiable character.'

'Someone had a grudge against him.'

'Evidently.'

'Where did he live in the city?'

'I told you. He only recently befriended me.'

'He must have a family. They need to be informed of this tragedy.'

'Fortunatus hailed from Oxfordshire,' said Lord Westfield. 'It will take a louder voice than yours to reach the ears of his family. I doubt that even Lawrence Firethorn's lungs would be equal to that task.'

'Perhaps another member of your circle could give me an address,' suggested Nicholas, annoyed that he was getting so little help and wishing that Lord Westfield would take the murder more seriously. 'I need urgent assistance, my lord.'

'Why? This is a matter for the law.'

'It also concerns us. And I fancy that we may be able to make more headway than some local constables who were not present at the time. We were there, my lord.'

'Do not remind me!'

'There has to be a reason why Fortunatus Hope was killed at the Queen's Head.'

'More than one person drew a weapon to defend himself,' remembered the older man. 'Could not Fortunatus have been the victim of a chance dagger?'

Nicholas was firm. 'No question of that, my lord.'

'How can you be so certain?'

'I used my eyes.'

'But the place was in uproar.'

'That was the intention. The affray was started with the express purpose of distracting attention so that a man could be murdered. Cunning was at work, my lord,' insisted Nicholas. 'Someone set out to strike against you, your company and your friend.'

'Saints preserve us!' gasped Lord Westfield, a flabby hand at his throat. 'Do you tell me that *I* am in mortal danger as well?'

'We have a common enemy, my lord,' said Nicholas, 'and we need to unmask him with all speed. Every detail I can glean about Fortunatus Hope is vital. Otherwise, the person or persons who have shown such ill will towards Westfield's Men may soon strike again.'

Chapter Three

The meeting took place in Lawrence Firethorn's house in Shoreditch, a sprawling, half-timbered dwelling with a thatched roof in need of repair. Situated in Old Street, the house was presided over by Firethorn's wife, Margery, a formidable woman with a homely appearance that belied her strength of character and her iron determination. Not only did she cope with a husband whose roving instincts were a continual threat to marital harmony, she brought the children up on true Christian principles, provided bed and board for the company's apprentices and ruled the roost over her servants. The place was never less than clean, the food never less than delicious and the hospitality never less than warm. When the first guest, Edmund Hoode, arrived, Margery gave him a cordial welcome and wanted to hear all about his visit to the ailing Barnaby Gill. The second person to knock on her door was Owen Elias, the spirited Welsh actor, and she accepted his kiss with a girlish laugh. But it was for Nicholas Bracewell that she reserved her most affectionate reception, wrapping him in a tight embrace and chortling happily. Firethorn had to call his wife to order.

'Let the fellow in, Margery,' he scolded, 'before you squeeze all the breath out of him. You have three thirsty guests in the house and your husband's throat is also dry.'

'Say no more, Lawrence,' she replied, bustling off to the kitchen.

Nicholas went into the parlour to be greeted by the others. Ordinarily, Barnaby Gill would have been present at such a gathering. There were other sharers in the company but he, Firethorn and Hoode made all the major decisions, assisted usually by Nicholas, who, as the book holder, was only a hired man but who was included in discussions about future policy because of his cool head and resourcefulness. Gill always objected strongly to his presence at such meetings but he was overruled each time by Firethorn, the leading actor and manager of Westfield's Men. Nicholas was pleased to see that Elias had replaced Gill at the table. Unlike the troupe's clown, the Welshman was a firm friend. He was also a person with firm opinions that were expressed with characteristic honesty. There would be none of the petty bickering that Gill invariably brought to any exchange of views.

Taking the seat to which Firethorn waved him, Nicholas turned to Hoode.

'How is he, Edmund?' he asked.

'Barnaby is wallowing in self-pity,' said Hoode.

'No novelty there,' observed Firethorn tartly.

'Show some sympathy, Lawrence,' chided Hoode, shooting him a look of reproof. 'He's in great discomfort. The doctor gave him some medicine to ease his pain but it has no effect. Barnaby suffers dreadfully. The pain is not confined to his leg, I fear. It is seated in his heart and his brain as well.'

'He does not *have* a heart.'

'Shame on you! At such a time as this, Barnaby needs our support.'

'Then let us drink to his health,' said Firethorn as Margery entered with a tray that bore four cups of wine and a platter of cakes on it. 'Thank you, my angel,' he added, patting her on the rump as she passed. 'What would I do without you?'

'Find someone else to wait on you, hand, foot and finger,' she retorted before handing out the refreshments. 'Is there anything else you need, Lawrence?'

'Only peace and quiet, my dove.'

'I'll make sure that the children don't interrupt you.'

After distributing a smile among the three guests, she sailed out again and left the men to raise their cups to the absent Gill. Firethorn was anxious to begin the discussion.

'Well, Nick,' he said, taking a first sip of wine, 'did you see Lord Westfield?'

Nicholas nodded. 'Eventually.'

'What did he say about this afternoon's disorder?'

'He was shocked and disgusted. Fearing injury to

himself and his friends, he hustled them out so quickly that he was quite unaware of the fact that one of them was in no position to leave.'

'Did he identify the dead man?'

'Yes,' said Nicholas. 'His name was Fortunatus Hope.'

'I think he should have been called Misfortunatus,' said Elias with a grim chuckle, 'for he chanced on no luck at the Queen's Head. Who could have wanted to kill the fellow?'

'Lord Westfield could throw no light on that, Owen. Nor could he even tell me where the man lived. Master Hope, it seems, only recently came into his circle and was still much of an unknown quantity. What our patron has promised to do,' said Nicholas, 'is to make enquiry among his other friends to see if any of them were better acquainted with the fellow. At the very least, we should write to his family to tell them of the tragedy that has befallen them.'

'That office should surely fall to Lord Westfield,' said Firethorn.

'I fancy that we might perform it more readily.'

'Are our patron's feathers so completely ruffled, Nick?'

'His plumage is in danger of falling out. Because of what happened today, he thinks that his own life may now be in jeopardy. By the time I left him, he was shaking like a leaf.'

'Did you apprise him of that fact that we mean to quit the city forthwith?'

'I did. He thought it a sensible move.'

'What of our visit to Dover?' asked Hoode.

'Lord Westfield still intends to be there when we play at the castle. He'll send word to Lord Cobham that we'll reach

Dover earlier than expected.' Nicholas tasted his own wine. 'When he has to advise a distinguished friend of a change of date, our patron will reach willingly for his pen. But he is less ready to pass on news of a murder to the family of Fortunatus Hope. I'd have thought it simple courtesy.'

'Lord Westfield lends us his name, Nick,' said Firethorn briskly. 'Do not look for much else from him. He's a man of strict limitations. But enough of him,' he went on, slapping his thigh. 'The decision is made. We take to the road the day after tomorrow. All that we need to debate is whom we take with us.'

'As large a company as we may,' said Elias.

'A number of the hired men will have to be released, Owen.'

'It seems an act of cruelty to discard them.'

Firethorn shrugged. 'Cruel but necessary. Some of the musicians will have to stand down as well. We can only take musicians who can also carry parts, or actors who can play an instrument.'

Hoode finished eating his cake. 'Our main concern is how to replace Barnaby,' he said, brushing a few crumbs from his arm. 'Nobody can match his talent but we must find a substitute who will not let us down.'

'Is there nobody within the company?' wondered Elias.

'None, Owen. You can sing as well as Barnaby but I mean no disrespect when I say that you could never emulate his other skills. We must perforce look outside Westfield's Men.'

'What is the point?' asked Firethorn. 'The best clowns

are already employed elsewhere. We could hardly lure one away from Banbury's Men. Giles Randolph would not oblige us with the time of day, still less with one of his comedians. We'd meet the same rebuff from Havelock's Men. They'd sooner part with their teeth than help us.'

Elias frowned. 'There must be *someone* who meets our needs.'

'There is,' said Nicholas, 'and he is not attached to any company.'

'Who is this paragon?'

'Gideon Mussett.'

'Why, of course!' said Elias, jumping to his feet. 'The very man. Giddy Mussett can make an audience laugh until they sue for relief. He is the one clown who could fully disguise the absence of Barnaby Gill.' His face clouded. 'Yet, wait awhile. I thought that Giddy was contracted to Conway's Men.'

'He was,' agreed Nicholas, 'but it seems that he fell out with them.'

'Giddy Mussett falls out with everyone,' said Firethorn ruefully. 'Nobody can doubt his talent but it's allied to every vice in the calendar.'

'Barnaby is not exactly a saint,' Elias noted, resuming his seat.

'Perhaps not, Owen, but neither does he drink himself into a stupor, pick a fight on the slightest provocation and frequent the stews of Bankside.'

'If all who love fine ale and fine women are to be excluded, then half of us will stay in London. On those two accounts,' admitted the Welshman, 'Giddy Mussett is no worse than Owen Elias. I, too, am cursed with hot blood and find it difficult to walk away from a quarrel.'

'Mussett incites quarrels for the sake of it.'

'Not if he is kept under control,' argued Nicholas.

'No theatre company has so far managed that feat.'

'I believe it to be within our compass.'

Hoode was curious. 'Why do you say that, Nick?'

'For two main reasons. The first is simple gratitude. Every actor would rather be working than kicking his heels. Giddy Mussett is no exception. He would make an effort to show his gratitude to us. The second reason,' said Nicholas, 'is that we would be much more vigilant than some of our rivals. Let him out of our sight and he would surely go astray. Bind him to a contract of good behaviour and we may have a different result.'

'It sounds as if it is at least worth trying.'

'I believe so, Edmund.'

'So do I,' added Elias. 'Giddy is our man.'

Firethorn was sceptical. 'Something tells me that we are courting disaster here.'

'Not if we lay down strict rules,' said Nicholas.

'Mussett would not recognise a rule if it recited the Catechism at him. Besides, you are forgetting something, Nick. We seek a substitute for Barnaby and he would never allow Giddy Mussett to take his place. They are sworn enemies.'

'Need we *tell* Barnaby?' asked Elias.

'He would never forgive us if we did not.'

'True.'

'In any case,' said Firethorn, '*we* might stay silent but the truth would surely get back to him by some means. Giddy Mussett would make certain that it did. Nothing would content him more than to profit at Barnaby's expense. He'd crow like chanticleer and do his best to oust him altogether.'

'That would never happen,' said Nicholas. 'Mussett would only be engaged as a hired man for as long as we required. It would be made clear at the start.'

'I side with Nick,' decided Hoode. 'Giddy Mussett is our only hope.'

'He gets my vote as well,' said Elias.

'Give him *your* blessing, Lawrence.'

Firethorn downed the remainder of his wine in one loud gulp and pondered. Nicholas exchanged glances with the other two then waited for a response from the man with the real power in the company. Unless Firethorn could be persuaded, they would have to look elsewhere for a clown.

'I do not like the idea,' said Firethorn at length.

Nicholas was blunt. 'Suggest a better one and we'll gladly accept it.'

'Mussett is too troublesome a bedfellow.'

'Do not be misled by his reputation.'

'And what of Barnaby? He'll be mortified.'

'He'll come to see that we made the only choice possible,' said Nicholas. 'Granted, the two men share an intense hatred but only because they are keen rivals. Beneath their hatred is a deep respect for each other's skills.'

'That will only make Barnaby green with envy.'

'Which would you rather have, Lawrence?' asked Hoode. 'A green and resentful Barnaby or a pallid clown who makes a mockery of every comedy that we stage?'

'Edmund is right,' said Elias. 'We are in a quandary and there is but one way out of it. Bear this in mind. *We* make the decision – not Barnaby.'

Firethorn stroked his beard thoughtfully. 'Mussett is certainly a fine singer,' he conceded, 'and he is as vigorous as any man in a dance. Of his comic skills, there is no doubt. My worries concern his private habits.'

The Welshman chuckled. 'We all have those, Lawrence.'

'Employ the fellow and we may imperil the whole company.'

'That's a risk I'm prepared to take.'

'There's no risk if we keep Mussett on a tight rein,' asserted Nicholas, wishing to bring the discussion to a close. 'That will be my task. I'll answer for our new clown.'

Firethorn was still unconvinced. 'I have grave reservations,' he confessed. 'Besides, we do not even know that he will accept a place with us.'

'Oh, I assure you that he'll accept anything that's offered to him.'

'How can you be so confident of that, Nick?'

'Because I took the liberty of finding out where he dwells at present,' said Nicholas, 'and he'll be more than ready to leave his present abode. I'd stake my life on it. Giddy Mussett is languishing in prison.'

* * *

King's Bench Prison stood on the main road south out of London, close to the Marshalsea, another of the city's many jails. Stretching down through Southwark, the thoroughfare was noted for the number and size of its inns. There seemed to be a continuous line of hostelries with barely a few shops and houses to separate them. It meant that wretched prisoners were living cheek by jowl with places where pleasure and entertainment were in good supply. While they endured squalid conditions and meagre rations, customers nearby were celebrating their freedom by enjoying the comforts of the Bear, the George, the White Hart and all the other happy taverns that lined the route. Throughout the whole day, sounds of merriment drifted into the ears of the condemned and the convicted, reminding them of what they had lost and making their ordeal all the more difficult to bear.

King's Bench Prison, however, was not entirely lacking in jollity. Since he had been incarcerated there, Gideon Mussett had done his best to brighten up the lives of his fellow prisoners. He was not impelled by any unselfish concern for their welfare. His songs and dances were never offered freely in order to distract people from the misery of their situation. Mussett was engaged in a battle for survival. He performed for reward. The money that he earned from grateful spectators was spent on drink, tobacco and edible food. Imprisonment for someone as poor as him would otherwise have been a species of torture. Only those with something in their purse could stave off the hunger and despair that claimed so many victims.

Whenever he raised the spirits of his companions with some rousing songs or with a comical dance, he had an appreciative audience.

'More, Giddy. Please give us more.'

'Sing to us of Wild Meg again.'

'Aye, or of the Sweet Maid of Romsey.'

'Dance, Giddy. We've not had a jig today.'

'Up on the table and dance!'

Giddy Mussett raised both palms to still the outburst of requests. He was a short, angular man in his early forties with an ease of movement that made light of his age. His exaggerated features gave him a striking appearance. His cheeks were gaunt, his hooked nose unusually large and his chin pronounced. With the shock of red hair on his head, he looked in profile like a giant cockerel and he certainly had something of the bird's arrogant strut. Mussett bared his uneven teeth in a grin.

'My legs are tired today, my friends,' he said. 'If you would have them dance, they will need to be revived with a drink of ale or a pipe of tobacco.'

'You've taken every penny we have,' complained one man.

'Then there'll be no jigs this morning.'

'We'll not be cheated out of our entertainment,' said another man, tossing a coin to the clown. 'There, Giddy. That will buy us your legs again.'

Mussett winked. 'It'll buy you no other part of my body, Ned, I tell you that.'

Raucous laughter filled the cell. There were ten of them,

crammed together in a narrow cell with a long table at its centre. Sleeping arrangements were primitive and the only ones who managed anything approaching a peaceful night were those strong enough to fight for the best places in the filthy straw. A compound of revolting smells filled the room. Sun streamed in through a window high in the wall to illumine a scene of utter degradation. Most of the men were in rags and the two ancient women wore equally tattered garments. The stench of poverty intensified the pervading reek. The only thing that helped them to forget their dire predicament was a performance by their very own clown. But they were to be deprived of even that today.

A key scraped in the lock and the iron door groaned on its hinges. Putting his head into the cell, a brawny man with a greying beard fixed Mussett with a stare.

'Follow me!' he ordered.

'But we want our jig,' protested the man who had parted with the coin.

'Then we'll let you dance at the end of a rope,' said the jailer with a snarl. 'Did you hear me, Giddy? Follow me.'

'I'll not be long, my friends,' promised Mussett, waving cheerily to the others. 'I charge you all to stay where you are until I get back.'

He followed the jailer out of the room then waited while the door was locked again. A minute later, he was conducted into the prison sergeant's office and left alone with a tall, handsome, broad-shouldered man in his thirties. Wearing a leather jerkin, the visitor had fair hair and beard. Mussett studied him for a moment.

'I believe I know you, sir,' he said.

'My name is Nicholas Bracewell,' returned the other, 'and I'm the book holder with Westfield's Men.'

'Ha!' sneered Mussett, spitting on the floor with disgust. 'Then you are a friend of that vile toad called Barnaby Gill.'

'I'm pleased to number him among my fellows.'

Mussett was combative. 'Then we have nothing to say to each other. I despise him. Has he sent you here to mock my condition? Is that your purpose, sir? Do you treat the King's Bench Prison like another Bedlam where you may gain your pleasure by viewing the mad and the unfortunate? I am neither, Master Bracewell,' he went on, pulling himself up to his full height. 'Tell that to your crawling worm of a friend.'

'I would rather speak to you,' said Nicholas calmly, 'and if you have sense enough to listen, you may hear something to your advantage.'

'Not if it's coupled with the foul name of Barnaby Gill.'

'You deceive yourself. However, since you clearly prefer life behind bars to an early release from your detention, I'll trouble you no more and simply apologise for interrupting your leisure.' Nicholas turned on his heel. 'Farewell.'

'Hold there, sir,' said Mussett, grabbing his arm. 'Do you speak of *release*?'

'Only to someone who has the courtesy to listen to me.'

'A thousand pardons. Life in this sewer has robbed me of what few manners I possessed. Courtesy in not in request here.' He gave an obsequious smile. 'Tell me what has brought you here. I'll hang on every syllable.'

'Even if I mention the name of a man you detest?'

Mussett gritted his teeth. 'Even then, sir.'

'Thus it stands,' said Nicholas. 'During an affray at the Queen's Head, so much damage was caused that we have to depart on a tour of Kent while renovations take place. Master Gill was badly injured in the course of the commotion. A broken leg keeps him off the stage for months.'

'Amen to that,' said Mussett under his breath.

'We need a substitute and the name of Gideon Mussett came into the reckoning. There is, of course, a bar to your employment,' observed Nicholas, glancing around. 'You are imprisoned for debt and likely to remain here for some time.'

'For ever, Master Bracewell. How can I ever discharge the debt when I am in no position to earn money? What little I can scrape together is quickly spent on necessary items here in the prison.' He gave a hopeless shrug. 'My case is no worse than most of those who share that stinking cell with me. One man, Ned Lavery, incurred a debt of two hundred crowns and is like to spend the rest of his life under lock and key. The poor devil is so desperate for food, I caught him eating his own breeches yesterday.'

'Your own debt is much less than two hundred crowns.'

'A paltry six pounds, borrowed of a rogue I thought a friend.'

'I know the amount. I've spoken with the sergeant.'

'What did he say?'

'If the debt is discharged,' replied Nicholas, 'he has no

right to hold you here. Though, from what I hear, he will be sorry to let you go.'

'I earn a crust of bread by making the old walrus laugh.'

'How would you like to earn more than a crust of bread?'

Mussett put a hand over his heart. 'Teach me how, sir, and I'll be your most obedient servant. If I breathe this fetid air any longer, it will kill me.'

'You'd need to agree to a contract.'

'State your terms and I'll abide by them to the letter.'

'Then, first,' stipulated Nicholas, 'understand this. We do not discharge your debt by means of a gift. It is money on loan and we expect you to pay it back to us, by degrees, out of your wage.'

'I'd insist on doing that.'

'Next, we come to your reputation.'

Mussett sighed. 'Do I still *have* one worthy of the word?'

'Drunkenness and truculence are always linked to your name.'

'Not any more, I assure you. A month in this antechamber of Hell has made me see the error of my ways. You'll have no trouble from me, Master Bracewell.'

'If I do,' warned Nicholas, 'you'll answer to me.'

'I give you a solemn vow.'

'You are to do as you're bidden without complaint or hesitation.'

'All this, I accept willingly.'

'Then let me add one thing more. I'll hear no carping with regard to Master Gill. We hold him in high esteem.

You merely fill his place until his leg has mended. You gain from his misfortune,' Nicholas pointed out. 'That should make you thankful.'

'Oh, it does,' said Mussett solemnly. 'I'll even mention his name in my prayers. By all, this is wonderful! I never thought to get the chance to work with Westfield's Men,' he continued with growing excitement. 'They are the finest troupe in London. Lawrence Firethorn is a titan among actors and there's no better playwright alive than Edmund Hoode. Truly, it's an honour to be invited to join you.'

Nicholas was stern. 'Do not abuse that honour.'

'I'd not dream of it.'

'My eyes will be on you at all times, remember.'

'They'll see nothing untoward.'

'One more thing. Not all the members of the company share my faith in Giddy Mussett,' said Nicholas. 'They know your history too well. Prove them wrong. Show them that you can give of your best on stage and behave like a gentleman off it.'

'Have no doubts on that score,' urged Mussett, taking his hands to squeeze them. Tears welled in his eyes. 'You are my deliverer, good sir. I never thought to see an open road again, leave alone ride along it as one of Westfield's Men. This news restores my faith in God for it can be nothing less than Divine intervention. I swear to you that you'll have no cause to rue the day that you employed Giddy Mussett. I'll touch neither drink nor women and, whenever I meet provocation, I'll turn the other cheek. Will this content you?'

'Indeed, it will,' said Nicholas, taking him by the shoulders. 'Welcome to the company, Giddy. I'll need to conduct some business with the prison sergeant then we'll have you out of here for good.'

Tears of gratitude rolled down Mussett's cheeks and he adopted a pose of total submission. After giving him a warm smile, Nicholas let himself out of the room. The moment his visitor left, Mussett's expression changed. The tears gave way to a sly smile and the ingratiating manner to a surging confidence.

'Give up drink and lechery?' he said with distaste. 'Never!'

Chapter Four

Lawrence Firethorn had always flattered himself that he had the loudest voice in London so he was both surprised and disconcerted when there was such a strong challenge to his primacy. In volume and intensity, Barnaby Gill's exclamation was truly impressive.

'Giddy Mussett!' he roared.

'Calm down, Barnaby,' said Firethorn. 'You'll do yourself an injury.'

'I'll do Mussett an injury if he dares to usurp me. I'll tear that miserable impostor limb from limb then set his head upon a spike for all to see. How can you even *think* of such a stratagem, Lawrence?' he demanded. 'I'd never yield my place to him.'

'You're in no position to hold it yourself.'

'Then promote someone from within the company.'

'Who?'

'James Ingram, Rowland Carr, even Owen here.'

'None of us can hold a candle to you, Barnaby,' said Elias.

'I'd sooner George Dart acted as my shadow than let Giddy Musett within a mile of any role I call my own. God's blood!' howled Gill, unwisely smacking his injured leg for emphasis and producing a spasm of pain. 'Why treat me so barbarously?'

Firethorn looked across at Elias but said nothing. The two men had called at Gill's lodging to enquire after his health and explain that they would be leaving on tour the following day. They kept the mention of Musett's name until the end. It was received with frothing disbelief.

'It's a veritable nightmare,' said Gill, staring ahead with widened eyes. 'There is only one man in the world whom I detest utterly and you choose him to supplant me.'

'He merely helps us out of a dilemma,' said Firethorn.

'And what about *me*?'

'We hoped that this news might please you, Barnaby.'

'Please me!' spluttered Gill. 'Nothing is more certain to displease me. Imagine how you would feel if we replaced Lawrence Firethorn with Alexander Marwood.'

'Heaven forbid!'

'This is far more than a mere insult. It's a betrayal of everything that I have done for Westfield's Men. Do you not understand that?'

'What we understand,' said Firethorn with a soothing smile, 'is that we are about to take the wonder of our work to various parts of Kent. Our reputation goes before us,

Barnaby, and it rests just as much on our comic skills as upon anything else. How can we keep that reputation if we have no clown?'

'By finding someone else,' said Gill, 'but it does not have to be Giddy Mussett.'

'I fear that it does.'

'Nobody else is available,' explained Elias. 'Clowns of your quality are in short supply, Barnaby. And plays such as *Mirth and Madness*, *Love's Sacrifice* or even *A Trick To Catch A Chaste Lady* would have been impossible without a capable substitute for you. We scratched our heads for ages until Nick Bracewell came up with the answer.'

Gill was rancorous. 'Yes, I thought this might be Nick's doing.'

'He was the person who tracked Giddy Mussett down for us.'

'In which leaping house did he find him?'

'None, Barnaby. Giddy was keeping his art in repair by entertaining the other prisoners in King's Bench Prison. An unpaid debt led to his arrest.'

'Then how is he able to take up your invitation?' When both visitors looked uneasy, Gill's ire reached a new peak. 'You discharged his debt?' he asked with incredulity. 'When that mangy cur is finally locked in his rightful kennel, you actually pay money to get him out again? This beggars belief! Do the other sharers know that you plundered our limited funds in order to bring about this outrage? That you dared to replace me with a fornicating drunkard who'll brawl his way across Kent with you?'

Firethorn was shamefaced. He had anticipated a hostile response when he broke the news to Gill and he had taken Elias with him in order to deflect some of the anger that would be inevitably produced. What he had not expected was the white-faced rage that greeted his announcement. Propped up on his bed, Gill seemed to forget that he was an invalid and waved his arms violently whenever he spoke. In the confined space of the room, the clown's fury was markedly increased and he seemed beyond the reach of any reason. Firethorn sought to check the verbal assault by changing the subject.

'His name was Fortunatus Hope,' he said.

'Whose name?' grunted Gill.

'The man who was stabbed to death at the Queen's Head. Nick spoke to our patron about him though he got precious little help. Lord Westfield showed scant sympathy for his friend. He was more concerned about his own skin.'

'Be fair, Lawrence,' said Elias. 'Master Hope was a newcomer to his circle. Lord Westfield did promise to find out more about the fellow. Nick is due to see our patron again to learn what information has come to light.'

Gill curled a lip. 'Nick Bracewell *has* been busy,' he sneered. 'Searching the prisons of London for Giddy Mussett and poking his nose into a murder that is of no concern at all to him.'

'It's of concern to him and to all of us,' asserted Firethorn.

'I'll not lose sleep over it.'

'You should, Barnaby.'

'Why?'

'Because you were directly involved in the crime.'

'How could I be, Lawrence? I was myself a victim.'

'We all were,' said Firethorn. 'I did not realise it until Nick Bracewell pointed it out to me. The affray was not simply a means of wrecking our performance. It caused a commotion that served to hide a foul murder. The villain who killed Fortunatus Hope was in league with the devils who ruined our play.'

'Ruined our play,' repeated Gill morosely, 'and broke my leg.'

'Master Hope's fate was far worse than yours,' said Elias. 'Remember that. Which would you prefer – a broken leg or a dagger in your back?'

'Oh, I'd choose the dagger every time, Owen. At least, it would have saved me from the indignities you pile upon me. To be replaced by Giddy Mussett is a living death. Give me oblivion instead,' declared Gill. 'I'd suffer no pain and disgrace in the grave.'

Anne Hendrik was not looking forward to the morning. A night of shared tenderness in the arms of Nicholas Bracewell had left her feeling vulnerable. She always missed him sorely when he was away from London and this time his absence promised to be longer than usual. Knowing that he would only be in Kent, she had toyed with the notion of travelling to the county herself to watch one or more of the performances but the demands of her work were too pressing. Anne was the widow of a Dutch hatmaker, who developed a business in Southwark because the guilds prevented him, along with other immigrants, from operating within the city boundaries. When Jacob Hendrik died, his English wife not only took over from him, she discovered skills that she did not know she possessed. In the early stages, however, before her prudent management led to increased prosperity, she took in a lodger to defray expenses. Nicholas Bracewell soon became much more than a man who slept under her own roof yet he never threatened her independence or forfeited his own. It was an ideal relationship for both of them.

'Will you be sorry to leave?' she asked him.

'I'm always sad to leave you, Anne,' he replied, slipping an arm around her, 'but there's no remedy for it. The Queen's Head is closed to us and we have no other playhouse in London. We are fortunate to have invitations that take us to Kent.'

She snuggled up against him. 'You have an invitation here as well.'

'True, but I could hardly share that with the whole company.' Anne laughed and he kissed her gently on the forehead. 'There is, I confess, another reason that makes me want to tarry.'

'Am I not reason enough?' she said with mock annoyance.

'You are the best reason I ever met in my life, Anne.'

'Then I'm content to let you go.'

Nicholas became serious. 'What irks me as well is that I'll be unable to look more closely into the murder that took place. For the sake of Westfield's Men, it's a crime I would dearly love to solve.'

'But the victim has no link with the company.'

'Master Hope was a friend of our patron.'

'From what you told me, he sounds more like an acquaintance. Someone who was on the very fringe of Lord's Westfield's entourage.'

'It matters not,' said Nicholas. 'He was murdered during our performance.'

'That does not mean you have to be involved in finding the killer, Nick.'

'I believe that it does. We are implicated here. I'm certain that the riot and the murder were linked,' he went on, sitting up in bed. '*A Trick To Catch A Chaste Lady* was not merely interrupted to provide cover for a sly murder. It was stopped with a purpose. Someone wanted to inflict harm on us as well as on Fortunatus Hope.'

'How do you reach that conclusion?'

'Look at the situation, Anne,' he suggested. 'Master Hope is singled out an enemy who means to kill him. Why choose to do the deed in broad daylight at the Queen's Head? It would have been so much easier to dispatch him quietly in some dark alley or while he slept at night. Do you follow my reasoning?'

'I think so.'

'Why go to the trouble of setting up that array? Those lads who started it were no doubt paid well for their work. Why take on such an expense unless there was a double intent?'

'To strike at Westfield's Men as well.'

'They struck with cruel accuracy,' noted Nicholas. 'Our

performance was abandoned, our property damaged, our actors injured. Hundreds of spectators were demanding their money back. And to add to our woes, the landlord expelled us from his inn and vowed that we'd never play there again.'

'He has done that before, Nick, on more than one occasion.'

'My argument holds. Someone was definitely trying to wound us.'

'A rival, perhaps?'

'We shall never know until we find the motive behind Master Hope's death.'

'I thought that Lord Westfield offered to help you there.'

'He did,' said Nicholas. 'He undertook to speak to someone who might give us more detail about the dead man. But all he learnt was that Fortunatus Hope had a wife and family in Oxford, whom he neglected shamefully in order to pursue his pleasures in London. Master Hope, it seems, was a pleasant individual, popular with friends and agreeable to strangers. Since he went out of his way to avoid an argument, it's difficult to see how he could have upset someone enough to make them contemplate murder.' Church bells nearby began to chime the hour. 'Forgive me,' he said. 'Six o'clock in the morning and all I can talk about is the stabbing of a playgoer. What kind of conversation is that with which to depart?'

'You do not have to go just yet, Nick.'

'I'll not stay abed much longer.'

'Long enough to answer me this,' said Anne with a smile.

'Remind me of the play that was so brutally foreshortened. I have forgotten its title.'

'*A Trick To Catch A Chaste Lady*.'

'Do you know of such a trick?'

Nicholas grinned. 'Why? Is there a chaste lady at hand?'

'That's for you to find out.'

'The play is a comedy.'

'I'll not object to laughter.'

'What *will* you object to, Anne?' he asked, taking her in his arms.

'Only your departure.'

And she kissed him on the lips as evidence of her sincerity.

On previous occasions when they were about to quit the city, Westfield's Men assembled as a rule at the Queen's Head but that was an inappropriate meeting place this time. Evicted from their home in Gracechurch Street, they instead gathered across the river in Southwark, choosing the White Hart as their point of departure. Wives, children, friends, relatives, mistresses and, in some cases, even parents, came to send them off. Three wagons had been hired to transport the company and some, like Lawrence Firethorn, brought their own horses. The fine weather over the preceding week meant that they could expect hard, dry, rutted roads that would bruise a few buttocks as they rumbled along, but which was far preferable to being at the mercy of driving rain on muddy tracks. The omens were good.

Having walked with Anne Hendrik the short distance from her house, Nicholas Bracewell was touched to see that the small crowd included some of the hired men who would not even be taking part in the tour yet who had come to wish their fellows well on the journey. It had been the book holder's task to inform the actors of their fate and it was a sombre experience. Talented men had been left behind because economies had to be made. Reduced in size, the company would be discarding some who would not work again until Westfield's Men returned to the capital. Actors were not lone victims. Thomas Skillen, the stagekeeper, was too old and frail to cope with the exigencies of travel and there was no place either for such loyal souls as Nathan Curtis, the carpenter, and Hugh Wegges, the tireman. Their functions would fall to other, less practised, hands.

Margery Firethorn had made the long trip from Shoreditch so that her husband would have a wife and children to wave him off. Her face was set in an expression of quiet resignation but she brightened as soon as she saw Nicholas approaching. After rushing across to hug him, she kissed Anne in greeting and nudged her playfully.

'You have chosen the handsomest man in the company,' she said.

Anne smiled. 'We chose each other, Margery.'

'That's how it should be. You are blessed in her, Nick.'

'I'm in no danger of forgetting that,' he assured her. 'Anne reminded me of it only this morning. But you must excuse me,' he said, as new faces arrived. 'I must make an inventory of who is here and who is yet to come.'

Margery watched him go then stood close enough to Anne to whisper to her.

'I'm surprised that you two have never wed,' she confided.

'How do you know that we have not?' teased Anne.

'Because I would see it in your face. If he were mine, I'd drag him to the altar.'

'Nick is not a person to be dragged anywhere.'

'He dotes on you, Anne.'

'Would marriage secure or spoil his devotion?'

'An apt question,' conceded Margery, glancing at her husband. 'Lawrence's passion has never waned but I can only count on it when we share our bed. Let him venture outside London and he becomes a lusty bachelor. You'll have no cause to doubt Nick but I'll not be able to show a like trust in my husband.'

'You should, Margery. Whenever they are abroad, Nick says, Lawrence never ceases to mention your name with fondness.'

'Only when his guilt stirs.'

'Yes,' said Anne, 'he's guilty at having to leave you behind.'

She looked across at Firethorn and saw him enjoying a few last moments of fatherhood. His two sons were sitting astride his horse while he chatted with them. Anne's gaze moved to Edmund Hoode, who was talking earnestly with Owen Elias, then on to Nicholas. He had taken control with his usual efficiency. After counting heads, he was helping George Dart to check the list of scenery, properties and costumes that would be making the journey to Kent. Anne's surge of pride was matched by her sense of loss. It was inspiring to see Nicholas at work with the troupe. He was in his element and everyone treated him with respect. When she remembered that she would not be seeing him for some weeks, a tremor ran through her. Margery's hand went to her arm.

'Be brave, Anne,' she urged. 'The first night is the worst.'

Nicholas himself was not looking that far ahead. He had a more immediate concern. When he was satisfied that the wagons had been correctly loaded, he turned to look for missing persons again. Three had been absent at the first count and he was relieved to see that both James Ingram and Rowland Carr had now appeared. However, he was disturbed when there was still no sign of the latest addition to the troupe. He was not alone in being worried about Gideon Mussett. Hoode came anxiously across to him.

'Where *is* he, Nick?' he asked.

'He'll be here,' said Nicholas with conviction.

'And if he does not come?'

'Then I take the blame squarely on my shoulders, Edmund.'

'I feared that this might happen.'

'Have faith. He gave me his word.'

'Only when he was sober,' said Hoode, glancing around. 'And how long will sobriety last when he has so many taverns in which to get drunk? If he is here, I suspect that he's lying in a stupor in the Bear, the George or the Tabard. This street is a very heaven for a thirsty man. Have you searched the taprooms yet?'

'There's no need of that. I warned him to avoid ale.'

'Then he will drink sack or Canary wine instead.'

'He's no money to buy either,' said Nicholas, 'and he's been bound to a contract that obliges him to curtail his pleasures. If he refuses to obey, he'll end up back in the jail from which we plucked him.' He pointed to prison buildings nearby. 'That may be the answer, Edmund,' he continued, his spirits reviving. 'I should have used more care before I nominated the White Hart as our meeting place. What man would wish to return to the very shadow of the place where he was imprisoned? That's why Giddy is not here. He'll meet us further down the road where ugly memories are not so easily revived.'

'*We* will be the ones with ugly memories, if he lets us down.'

'That will not happen. He needs work.'

'Perhaps he's gone to seek it elsewhere.'

'I put my trust in him, Edmund.'

Hoode gave a nod. 'Then I put my trust in your judgement.'

No sooner had the playwright moved away than Firethorn strutted across. He was beaming regally at all and sundry but his eyes were darting nervously. Grabbing Nicholas by the arm, he took him aside.

'What time did you tell the rogue to be here?' he asked.

'Upon the stroke of eight.'

'It's almost half an hour past that.'

'Something has, perchance, delayed him.'

Firethorn was scornful. 'Some fat whore in red taffeta no doubt!'

'No,' said Nicholas. 'Giddy has not gone down that path. We must remember all those nights he spent in prison when he could barely snatch an hour's sleep, and that in the greatest discomfort. If anything delays him, it's pure fatigue.'

'Where did he lodge?'

'He said he would stay with a friend.'

'What friend?' demanded Firethorn. 'Where does he live? Giddy Mussett is as slippery as a wet ferret. You should not have let him out of your sight, Nick.'

'He swore to me that he'd be here.'

'Then where, in God's name, is the saucy rascal?'

The answer came from behind him. Shutters opened on the window of an upstairs room in the White Hart and a startling figure was revealed. Giddy Mussett was dressed from head to foot in bright yellow garments and wore a blue hat that rose up in a point until it reached the tiny bell at its extremity. In case anyone was not aware of his sudden appearance, Mussett put a fist to his mouth and blew a token fanfare. All eyes turned to look up at him and he revelled in the attention.

'Good morrow, friends!' he called. 'Giddy Mussett is sorry to keep you waiting. He had important business to complete within the tavern here but he is now ready to join you on your wondrous journey into Kent.' He swayed slightly. 'I'm privileged to be a member of Westfield's Men and I hope you'll welcome me with open hearts.'

Nicholas was both pleased and alarmed to see him, reassured that the clown had actually turned up but distressed by the way that he was slurring his words. Firethorn looked on with disgust.

'The fellow's drunk!' he protested.

'I think not.'

'Look at the way he is swaying.'

'He's here and we should be grateful.'

'Get him down, Nick.'

It was a pointless command. Before Nicholas could even move towards the tavern, Mussett contrived his own dramatic exit from the establishment. After waving happily to the crowd below, he seemed to lose his balance and fall headfirst through the window. There was a gasp of horror from all those below. Had they lost their new clown at the very moment they had been introduced to him? Would his blood be spattered all over the ground? Their fears were unfounded. Turning a somersault in the air, Mussett landed on his feet with catlike certainty. He doffed the hat that had stayed miraculously on his head and grinned wickedly at his audience.

'Giddy is not quite so giddy, my friends,' he announced in an unwavering voice. 'I'm as sober as the best among you and ready to share in your great adventure.'

Elias led the applause. 'It was all a jest!' he shouted.

Nicholas did not join in the general laughter. Relieved that Mussett was there, he was quietly angry at the way they had all been kept waiting so that the clown could make an impact on his first appearance. He resolved to make his feelings known to Mussett when they had a chance to speak alone. Firethorn, on the other hand, had no such reservations about their new clown.

'Welcome to the company,' he said, striding forward to shake Mussett's hand. 'We are pleased to have you with us, Giddy.'

'Not as pleased as I am to be here, Master Firethorn.'

'You were born to entertain.'

'Laughter is meat and drink to me.'

Replacing his hat, he executed a little dance then did a handstand to show off the two bells attached to his heels. After clicking them several times to pick out a simple tune, he rolled forward and sprang to his feet. Another round of clapping broke out and he bowed to acknowledge it. Mussett had achieved an instant popularity. Other members of the company gathered around to offer their own welcome. Some, like Elias and Hoode, already knew him but most were meeting the newcomer for the first time. Mussett's gratitude was obvious. While others were still locked away in the filthy cell at the King's Bench Prison, he was about to set out with the most celebrated theatre company of them all. His commitment to Westfield's Men seemed wholehearted.

Nicholas was keen to be on the way. There was a long journey ahead of them and a protracted leave-taking would only produce more sadness among those left behind. After giving Anne a kiss of farewell, he called the others to order and told them to clamber aboard the wagons that had been allotted to them. A flurry of embraces with loved ones followed before the departing actors were ready. Nicholas signalled to Mussett to join him on the first wagon and the four apprentices were delighted to have the clown beside them. Firethorn, Elias and James Ingram mounted their horses. For reasons that remained undisclosed, Hoode had decided to travel on a donkey. They were all sorry to be leaving the comforts of London and the security of their playhouse at the Queen's Head. Travel would be arduous and it was uncertain how well they would be received in the various towns where they intended to play. Unseen hazards might lie ahead. Subduing their individual fears, they put on a brave face for their departure.

At the last moment, however, it was unexpectedly delayed. Out of the stream of traffic that had been rattling south over London Bridge since dawn came a small cart that was moving at some speed. The driver, a stout man in his fifties, yelled aloud and waved to them with his whip. When he reached the wagons, he took his cart in a circle before bringing it to a halt. Lying on straw in the rear and propped up on a leather trunk was Barnaby Gill, his broken leg still held fast between splints.

'Wait!' he called. 'I'll come with you.'

'That's madness, Barnaby,' said Firethorn.

'I insist. If someone else is to take my roles, I wish to be there to make sure that he does not abuse them.' His eye flicked over the assembly. 'Where is the knave?'

'Here, Barnaby,' said Mussett, standing up to give him a cheerful wave. 'It's good to see you again.'

'I take no delight in seeing *you*,' said Gill sharply. 'Now, help me, someone. Get me and my baggage off this cart and onto the most comfortable wagon.'

'Is it wise to travel in that condition?' asked Nicholas.

'If both my legs were broken, I'd happily endure the pain.'

'No,' said Firethorn. 'We'll not let you suffer so, Barnaby. We're actors. We have no skills as nurses. You need care and attention.'

'I need to be sure that no threadbare clown will try to displace me.'

'You will only be in the way, man.'

'That's my intention, Lawrence.'

'Do not be so perverse,' said Hoode, bringing his donkey alongside the cart. 'Why give yourself further grief? You'll get no pleasure from what you see, only the anguish of hearing another being applauded in your stead.'

'You penned those roles for me, Edmund. I want to protect my property.'

'It would be more sensible to protect your injured leg.'

'My mind is made up.'

Hoode and Firethorn tried to persuade him of the folly of his decision but he was adamant. As a leading sharer with the troupe, Gill had rights that he was not prepared to cede to anyone. When the argument reached its peak, it was Mussett who ran across to join in. Alone of those present, he offered encouragement.

'Welcome, Barnaby,' he said. 'Travel beside me in my wagon.'

'Anywhere but that!' snapped Gill.

'But we could discuss the roles I have to play.'

'Never!'

'I could explain to you how I'll outshine you in each and every one.'

68

'Keep away from me, Giddy.'

'Would you not like to have me as your nurse?'

'I'd sooner eat your night soil!'

Mussett cackled. 'A herbal remedy that cures all ills, I do assure you.'

Nicholas intervened to separate the two men, sending Mussett back to the first wagon then trying his best to make Gill reconsider his decision. It was all to no avail. The company was forced to accept an additional member on its tour. With the utmost care, Gill was carried across to the last of the wagons with his baggage and made as comfortable as was possible. He sat there with a grim smile on his face. Firethorn had profound misgivings. He turned to Nicholas.

'I spy danger ahead,' he confided, rolling his eyes. 'There is only one thing worse than having no clown.'

'I know,' said Nicholas. 'Having *two* of them.'

Chapter Five

Progress was slow on the first stage of the journey south. Driving the first of the wagons, Nicholas Bracewell set the pace, making sure that the horses were not pushed too far or too fast as they hauled their heavy loads over uneven roads. There were frequent stops to rest and water the animals, and to allow the travellers to take refreshment or relieve themselves. Moods varied considerably in the three wagons. Thanks to the presence of Giddy Mussett, the occupants of the first were in a state of almost continuous delight. George and the four apprentices, in particular, laughed at everything he said or did. Nicholas was amused by some of the comments he heard over his shoulder but he had not forgiven Mussett for delaying their departure and giving them all an unnecessary fright. Had they left at the appointed hour, Nicholas reflected, they might have avoided the embarrassment of having to include Barnaby Gill in their number.

Rowland Carr was in charge of the second wagon. As well as much of their baggage, it also contained several of the actors. Carr was a sharer with the troupe, a slim, sharp-featured man in his early forties with a reputation for being dependable. While he would never be capable of stealing a scene on stage, he could always be relied upon to offer a sterling performance in a supporting role. Like the others around him, Carr was a married man who was sad to part with his wife and children, fearful that they might not manage easily without him. Owen Elias rode beside the wagon and tried to cheer his fellows with humorous comments but a mood of quiet sorrow prevailed. They were already missing the joys of family life.

It was in the third wagon that Barnaby Gill held court, stretched out in the middle of the remaining actors and pouring scorn on the hated rival who had replaced him. His remarks were a compound of envy, malice and sheer disgust. They did nothing to lighten the atmosphere in the wagon. Lawrence Firethorn brought his stallion alongside and attempted once more to convince Gill that he would be better off in London.

'All you will do is prolong your misery,' he said.

'It's my decision, Lawrence.'

'A foolish one, at that. Why force yourself to watch something that you know you will despise? And there is another aspect here. How can Giddy Mussett give of his best if you are leering at him from the audience?'

Gill smirked. 'I'll do more than leer at him, I warrant you!'

'Think how that may damage our performance, Barnaby.'

'Mussett is my only target.'

'But you'll trouble the whole company.'

The others in the wagon said nothing but their expressions showed that they agreed with Firethorn's observation. Gill was already proving a disruptive influence. He was a prickly travelling companion with a score to settle. Serious problems would ensue.

Summer sunshine bathed them every inch of the way and it was only when evening shadows began to dapple the fields around them that they started to look for shelter. Nicholas selected a wayside inn called the Shepherd and Shepherdess because it was large enough to accommodate them and well over halfway to their first destination. Its brightly painted sign depicted two rustic lovers, each in a smock and equipped with a crook, holding hands as they stood amid their sheep. After leading the troupe into the yard, Nicholas brought them to a halt for the day. As soon as the book holder jumped down from the wagon, Firethorn beckoned him over.

'Barnaby is set on causing an upset,' he warned, dismounting from the saddle.

'That must be prevented at all costs.'

'How has Giddy behaved?'

'Like an angel,' said Nicholas. 'Dick Honeydew and the others love him already. He made a long journey seem very short.'

'Barnaby made it seem like an eternity. If I broke my leg, Margery would not let me stir from the house until it mended. He should do likewise. The doctor advised it. Whatever drove Barnaby to force himself upon us like this?'

'His pride.'

'And sheer stubbornness.'

'Something of both, I fancy.'

'Keep the pair of them apart, Nick,' implored Firethorn. 'The last thing we need is a duel of words between two vicious tongues.'

'A plan has already been devised.'

'Even you cannot watch both of them at the same time.'

'No,' agreed Nicholas. 'I'll keep guard over Giddy Mussett. Someone else will make sure that he does not get too close to his rival.'

'Someone else?'

'George Dart. I've told him to fetch and carry for Barnaby.'

'Is he equal to the task?'

'He'll not let us down.'

Ostlers came out to take charge of the horses. While the others got out of the wagons and unloaded their belongings, Nicholas and Firethorn went into the inn to speak to the landlord about accommodation. It was soon arranged to everyone's satisfaction. Nicholas was responsible for deciding on the sleeping arrangements. Having put Mussett in the room that he would occupy himself with six others, he assigned Gill to a chamber as far away as possible. A tiring journey made supper especially welcome and the actors ate and drank with enthusiasm. Though he provided a deal of merriment, Mussett refused to touch any ale and Nicholas was duly impressed. Gill, by contrast, seated at the other end of the table, consumed too much food and drank far too much wine. The meal did not improve his bad temper. He glared at Mussett.

'They should have left you in prison where you belong,' said Gill harshly. 'A rat-infested cell full of the lowest criminals is your natural home.'

Mussett responded with an amiable chuckle. 'You've committed some heinous crimes yourself, Barnaby,' he said. 'I've watched you at the Queen's Head and found you guilty of a murderous assault on every part you played.'

'Enough of that!' said Nicholas over the laughter. He suppressed Mussett with a cold stare. 'I thought we had an agreement, Giddy.'

'Barnaby put it out of my mind. But you are right, Nick,' he went on, exuding penitence. 'My comment was cruel and unfair. I offer Barnaby a sincere apology.'

Gill was not appeased. 'Then I throw it back in your teeth.'

'If only I had some!'

Mussett bared his few remaining fangs and raised another laugh. Firethorn brought the brief exchange to an end by drawing Gill into conversation about their mutual triumphs during former tours of the provinces. It was a successful distraction. Gill slowly mellowed. Nicholas, meanwhile, repeated his warning to Mussett to avoid any more clashes with the man he had been hired to replace. The rest of the evening passed without any further outbursts. One by one, the actors drifted off to bed. Mussett was among the first to leave and Nicholas was struck by the way that he ignored a parting jibe from

Gill. Time rolled on until a mere handful of them still lingered in the taproom. Deputed to stay close to Gill, the exhausted Dart could barely keep his eyes open. He was grateful when his charge finally struggled from his seat with the aid of a wooden crutch.

'Let me help you upstairs, Master Gill,' volunteered Dart.

'First, take me outside, George.'

'Willingly.'

'Let me rest on your shoulder.'

Steadying himself on the crutch and the shoulder, Gill hopped across the floor on one foot with painful slowness, wincing as he did so but bearing the discomfort bravely. Dart was a patient assistant who escorted him all the way to the privy in the yard.

'Thank you, George,' said Gill, opening the door.

'Am I to wait?'

'No, take yourself off to bed. I can manage alone.'

Dart withdrew gratefully and Gill closed the door of the privy behind him before loosening his breeches. It was no easy task when he could only stand on one leg. He began to regret the amount of drink that he had taken. It made him light-headed. Still in pain, he refused to let his disability get the better of him. It took an age for him to lower himself gingerly onto the seat. He soon lapsed into a reverie. So preoccupied was he with thoughts of wreaking his revenge on his rival that he did not hear the stealthy feet that approached outside nor even the gentle scraping noise against the timber. Five minutes later, he was ready to leave and begin the laborious climb up to his room. But there was an obstacle to overcome first. When he tried the door, it would not open and, no matter how hard he pushed against it, he could not budge it. Gill was enraged. He was trapped in a foul-smelling prison. He seethed, he shouted, he banged on the door with his crutch but nobody came to his rescue because he was out of earshot. While the rest of the company bedded down happily for the night, Gill was shut away in the Stygian gloom of the privy.

It was an hour before someone finally let him out by removing the stake that had been jammed against the door. Gasping for air, Gill hopped out into the yard on his sound foot and made a solemn vow.

'As God's my witness, I'll *kill* Mussett for this!'

Nicholas Bracewell's hopes of a swift departure after breakfast next morning were soon dashed. The actors were roused from their slumber, the wagons loaded and the horses harnessed. All ate heartily until the sorry figure of Barnaby Gill came in with the aid of his crutch. Everyone had heard of his plight in the privy and the sniggers were loud. Respected for his talent, the clown was never liked by the majority of the company because he was too vain and disdainful to mix freely with them. In the short time he had been with them, they found Giddy Mussett a much more pleasant companion. When Gill saw his rival, talking to the others with easy familiarity, his wrath was kindled once more.

'You, sir!' he challenged. 'You lousy, beggarly, God-forsaken, flea-ridden cur!'

'Good morrow, Barnaby!' said Mussett cheerfully.

'That was *your* doing, was it not?'

'What crime am I supposed to have committed now?'

'Locking me in the privy.'

'Is that what happened?' asked Mussett with a look of innocence. 'It was not my jest, I promise you. I wish that it had been. If you were trapped in there, you had some idea of what it was like in prison. You were sitting on your own King's Bench.'

'Silence!' bellowed Firethorn, cutting the laughter dead. 'Eat your breakfast, Barnaby. Life always feels more irksome on an empty stomach.'

'I demand that you punish Mussett first,' said Gill.

'Why?'

'Because of his outrageous behaviour towards me.'

'He denies it.'

'I do,' said Mussett with vehemence. 'I'd never strike a man when he is down. Your injuries earn you my consideration, Barnaby. Why not take the weight off your foot and join us at the table?'

'Join us?' echoed Gill with indignation. 'Join us? Do you dare to claim a place among Westfield's Men? *You* are the interloper here, Giddy.'

'Granted, but that does not mean I played a trick on you last night.'

'Do you have any proof that it was him?' asked Firethorn.

'Who else could it be?' replied Gill.

'Any one of a dozen people, Barnaby. You have hardly endeared yourself to us since we left London. Be more tolerant.'

'I'll not tolerate this! Giddy deserves to be arrested for this.'

'Why not report me to the Privy Council?' taunted Mussett.

Even Firethorn's booming command was unable to stem their mirth this time. It was so humiliating for Gill that Nicholas took pity on him. Moving across to him, he slipped an arm around his waist and almost carried him to a seat, lowering him carefully down. He looked around the table with a stern eye and the laughter gradually died away.

'If you have finished,' he said quietly, 'there is nothing to detain you. When Master Gill has been allowed the privilege of eating his food in peace, he'll join you and we can all set off.'

They took their cue and rose from the table. Nicholas's gentle rebuke achieved more than Firethorn's angry yell. Most of those who withdrew to the yard were slightly ashamed. The apprentices were completely cowed. Accustomed to being bawled at by Firethorn, they no longer feared his rage quite so much. The last thing they wanted to do, however, was to arouse Nicholas's displeasure. When the others had dispersed, Mussett remained behind, standing at the end of the table like a prisoner before a magistrate. Gill scowled at him and Firethorn glowered. Nicholas then came to the defence of the clown.

'I think you are mistaken,' he said. 'Giddy could not have been the culprit.'

'He must have been!' cried Gill. 'Who else would stoop so low?'

Mussett gave a shrug. 'Not me, Barnaby.'

'That's an arrant lie.'

'Giddy is speaking the truth,' said Nicholas. 'I left here at the same time as you and found him asleep upstairs. It was impossible for him to steal away and play that trick on you. I'd surely have heard him leave.'

'There's your answer, Barnaby,' said Firethorn, relieved to hear that Mussett was, after all, innocent of the charge. 'It must have been one of the others. Or someone quite outside the company. Have you considered that?'

'No,' retorted Gill. 'It was a vindictive act. I accuse Giddy.'

'Then you accuse him wrongly,' said Nicholas. 'How could he be in two places at the same time? I slept near the door. Anyone going out or coming into the room would have woken me as they passed.'

'In that case, he suborned someone else to do the deed.'

'I doubt that. Who would take on such an office? None that I could name. They hold you in high esteem. Why should they lend themselves to a jest like this?'

'On a promise of reward.'

'Then it came not from me,' said Mussett. 'My purse is empty. I had no money to ensnare an accomplice, Barnaby. Look elsewhere.'

'Or dismiss the incident from your mind,' recommended Nicholas.

'Aye,' said Firethorn. 'That's the best advice. Forget the whole business.' He pointed to the platter of food. 'And put some victuals inside you. We must be away.'

Gill was baffled. Until Nicholas had spoken up for him, he was convinced that Mussett had been responsible for the cruel jest. A doubt had now been put into his mind. It was confusing. Unable to gain retribution, he fumed in silence.

The road to Maidstone took them through some of the prettiest countryside in Kent. It was a fine day but a swirling wind sprung up to bring an occasional shiver to the little cavalcade. Bushes trembled, grass rippled in the fields and trees swayed to the rustling rhythm of their leaves. Clumps of wild flowers shook their petals in complaint. No sooner did a burst of bright sunshine pacify them than the wind strengthened to begin its mischief all over again. Expanses of woodland were interrupted by pasturage for cattle and horses, but the most common sight was acre upon acre of fruit trees, waving to the travellers as they passed. Hops, a new crop to most of them, were also grown, rising high above the hedges and fences that enclosed them. From time to time, they caught sight of a prodigy house, owned by some rich London merchant, or some vast aristocratic estate. Proximity to London made the county an attractive home for the wealthy.

Lawrence Firethorn rode at the head of his troupe like the captain of an army, chatting to Owen Elias, who rode beside him, about the first performance on their tour and wishing that they were not hampered by the presence of Barnaby Gill. Both men wore swords to deter any highwaymen from attack. Bringing up the rear was Edmund Hoode, a lone figure on a donkey, looking less like a member of a theatre company than a pilgrim on his way to a distant shrine. While others studied the changing landscape around them, Hoode's mind was elsewhere, grappling with a scene in the new play that he was writing and wondering when and how he would find the time to commit his thoughts to paper.

Giddy Mussett again diverted the occupants of the first wagon with his jests and anecdotes, endearing himself even more and winning their confidence completely. He then plied them with questions about the company, wanting to know as much detail as he could about the affray at the Queen's Head. They had been trundling along for an hour when he moved to sit on the driver's seat beside Nicholas Bracewell.

'Let me take a turn with the reins, Nick,' he volunteered.

'Have you handled two horses before?'

'Two and four, Nick. Here, let me show you.'

Nicholas gave him the reins, happy to have a rest from keeping the wagon on a fairly straight line while avoiding as many potholes as he could. Mussett was as good as his word. He was an experienced coachman who handled the horses well. Nicholas was able to relax. He was also glad of the opportunity to speak to Mussett alone.

'Who did play that trick on Master Gill last night?' he asked.

'I wish I knew.'

'I hope that you were not involved, Giddy.'

'How could I be?' asked Mussett. 'You saw me fast asleep.'

'I saw what I *thought* was you but the room was fairly dark.'

'It was me, Nick, I dare swear it. I was too tired to pester Barnaby though I would love to shake the hand of the man who did lock him in the privy.'

'It was nobody in the company. Fear would hold them back.'

'Fear of being caught?'

'Yes,' said Nicholas, 'and fear of facing me afterwards. They know what I would say. We are bound together in this enterprise. Good fellowship is the only thing that will carry us through. Fall out with each other and we are doomed.'

'I've never fallen out with anyone in my life,' attested Mussett.

'What about Conway's Men?'

'Ah, that was different, Nick. They fell out with me.'

Nicholas smiled but he still had nagging doubts about the clown. Though he had settled into the company with apparent ease, Mussett needed to be watched. There was an unpredictability about him that was worrying. It stopped Nicholas from trusting him too much. Mussett tugged on the reins to guide the horses around a large dip ahead of them then he threw a glance at his companion.

'Dick Honeydew was telling me of the affray,' he said.

'It robbed us of ten days at the Queen's Head.'

'Was there no way to quell it?'

'None,' said Nick. 'It caught us unawares.'

'I've been on stage myself when fighting broke out and I always used it to my advantage. The last time it happened,' recalled Mussett, 'I tossed a bucket of water over the men who were brawling and dampened their spirits. It amused the other spectators and brought to fight to an end. Laughter is the best way to control wayward lads. Could not Barnaby have contrived it somehow?'

'He had no chance, Giddy. They mounted the stage and assaulted him.'

Mussett smirked. 'Was his performance *that* bad?'

'No,' chided Nicholas, 'and you know it only too well, Giddy. The fault lay not with him nor anyone else in the company. We were up against a dozen or so, paid to halt our play and drilled in the best way to do it. They caused such a disturbance that the whole yard was in turmoil. We were lost.'

'Dick mentioned a spectator who was killed.'

'Murdered where he sat.'

'Who was the poor man?'

'Part of Lord Westfield's circle. A harmless fellow, by all accounts.'

'Dick Honeydew did not know his name.'

'There's no reason why he should,' said Nicholas, dropping his voice so that the apprentices behind could not hear him. 'The lads were shaken enough, as it is. I saw no point in upsetting them again with details of a killing.'

'So what was he called?'

'Why do you ask?'

'Simple curiosity,' said Mussett. 'I'm grateful to him. His death helped to give me life. If it had not been for the riot at the Queen's Head, I'd still be in that torture chamber of a prison. I'll not forget it in a hurry, Nick. While Barnaby and this other fellow suffered, I was the benefactor.'

'The name will mean nothing to you.'

'How do you know?'

'Because even our patron could tell us little about it. Master Hope had not been in London long enough to win a place among Lord Westfield's closest friends.'

'Master Hope?' asked Mussett, his interest quickening.

'Yes, Giddy.'

'Would that be Fortunatus Hope, by any chance?'

Nicholas was surprised. 'The very same. You've heard of him?'

'Heard of him and met him, Nick.'

'When?'

'Less than a year ago.'

'What can you tell me about him?'

'More than Lord Westfield, I suspect.'

'And you actually *met* Master Hope?'

'Three or four times,' said Mussett. 'It must be the same man because there cannot be two with that name. Besides, nothing pleased him more than to watch a play. That's when our paths crossed, you see. During my time with Conway's Men.'

Maidstone was the shire town, built at an attractive point on the River Medway and containing something close to two and a half thousand inhabitants. Its bustling market drew in people from a wide area, swelling its population and bringing a noise and vibrancy to the heart of the community. Its long main street consisted largely of inns, shops and houses, all well maintained and giving the impression of neatness and civic pride. As Westfield's Men came down the hill towards High Town, the first sight that greeted them was the prison, where the quarters of some traitors were set up on poles to act as a warning. Giddy Mussett looked over his shoulder at the apprentices.

'Mark them well, lads,' he said. 'Those belong to actors who gave a bad performance and were executed for it. You'll have to be on your mettle.'

Following Lawrence Firethorn, who now led the way alone, he drove the first wagon along the High Street until they came to the Star Inn, a large and commodious hostelry with more than a faint resemblance to their home in London. It had the same shape and disposition as the Queen's Head with each storey jutting out above the one below and with its shutters daubed with the same paint. What set it apart from the inn that they had left was that this one had no melancholy landlord with an intense dislike of actors. Jonathan Jowlett, their host, a beaming barrel of a man in his fifties, came into the yard to give them a cordial welcome. Alive to the benefits of having a theatre company in town, he was also fond of plays and had an almost reverential attitude towards those who presented them. Jowlett identified the leading actor at once.

'You can be none other than Lawrence Firethorn, sir,' he said.

'I answer to that name,' replied Firethorn grandly.

'Your reputation precedes you.'

'Is that why you have locked your womenfolk away?' asked Owen Elias.

Jowlett rubbed his flabby hands nervously together. 'The Star is at your disposal, sir. Let us know your needs and they will be satisfied at once.'

'Thank you,' said Firethorn.

Ostlers and servants were summoned to take care of the horses and to help to unload the wagons. The visitors were glad to stretch their legs. It was only mid-afternoon but they seemed to have been travelling for days. Having lain in the same position for hours, Barnaby Gill was especially stiff and it made him fractious. George Dart had to endure constant criticism as he tried to assist the older man out of his wagon. Nicholas Bracewell made sure that Mussett was kept well away from his rival. When he saw how Gill hopped across the yard, Jowlett showed his compassion.

'Can he put no weight on the other leg?' he asked.

'Not for some weeks,' said Firethorn.

'Then it would be a cruelty to give him a bedchamber at the top of the inn. Here's my suggestion, Master Firethorn. We have a room on the ground floor that we use for storage. It could easily be cleared so that your friend could lay his head there.'

'Barnaby would be most grateful.'

'The room is small, I fear, not fit for more than one person.'

Firethorn grinned. 'This gets better and better,' he said. 'None of us will have to put up with his bad temper and his snoring.'

'My wife has a cure for snoring, sir,' confided Jowlett.

'Does she?'

'Every time I snore, she tips me out of bed. Nan would soon cure your friend.'

'Barnaby has a complaint that no woman can remedy,' said Firethorn, winking at Nicholas. 'Let's go inside and inspect the rest of the accommodation.'

'Follow me, good sirs.'

Jowlett guided them into the building and along a narrow, twisting passageway until they came to the taproom. The welcoming smell of strong ale lifted the spirits of the newcomers. Several customers were enjoying a drink and there was an atmosphere of jollity. Mussett looked round in wonder as if he had just stumbled on his spiritual home. Firethorn was more interested in the buxom wench who was carrying a tray of food across the room. Gill was too busy complaining at Dart for trying to hustle him along too fast. It was left to Nicholas to discuss prices with the landlord. Rooms were then chosen and Nicholas selected the groups who would occupy them, ensuring that Mussett and the apprentices shared their accommodation with him.

When the actors went upstairs to leave baggage in their respective rooms, Nicholas and the landlord escorted Gill to a tiny chamber at the rear of the premises. An assortment of small barrels stood on the floor while poultry hung in hooks from the low ceiling. Gill was not enamoured of his temporary home.

'God have mercy!' he cried. 'I'll not sleep in a storeroom.'

'It will be emptied at once,' promised Jowlett.

'What am I supposed to do – lie on the floor or hang from a hook like a dead duck? A pox on the place! I'll have none of it.'

'A mattress can easily be brought in, sir,' said the landlord.

'Save yourself the trouble.'

'Would you rather climb three flights of stairs to the attic?' asked Nicholas. 'This spares you that labour. Most of us would relish the notion of a room alone. It would be a rare treat. And something else should recommend it to you.'

'The stink of beer?' said Gill sardonically.

'An open window will soon dispel that. No,' said Nicholas, pointing to the door. 'There is a stout bolt. That will keep out any unwelcome visitor.'

It was an argument that weighed heavily with Gill. In his present condition, he was a sitting target for Mussett and feared an outrage like the one that had been perpetrated at the Shepherd and Shepherdess. He still believed that the other clown was somehow involved in his earlier incarceration. Safety was paramount.

'If the rascal so much as shows his face in here, I'll crown him with my crutch.'

'You'll take the room, then, sir?' asked Jowlett hopefully.

'Empty and clean it first before I decide.'

'Yes, yes. At once.'

Gill hopped off with the aid of his crutch and left the two men alone. Nicholas felt obliged to apologise for the ill-tempered behaviour of his colleague.

'Forgive him, sir,' he said. 'The broken leg has taken his good humour away.'

'We'll do our best to recover it for him.'

'That may be beyond both of us. Let me repair Master Gill's omission and thank you for offering this room for his use. It solves more problems than you can know.'

'Then I'm pleased to give it to you.' Jowlett broke off to call for a servant before turning back to Nicholas. 'Yours is a larger company than we have had here in the past.'

'We tour with as many players as we can afford.'

'Our last troupe was barely half the size of yours.'

'When did they stay here?'

'No more than ten days ago. Unlike you, they have no home in London and no chance to play before large audiences. They are on the road throughout the year. It was a source of great regret. They spoke with such envy of Westfield's Men.'

'Did they?'

'Envy and bitterness.'

'I am sorry that we provoke bitterness,' said Nicholas. 'Who were they?'

'Conway's Men.'

Chapter Six

Westfield's Men settled quickly into the Star Inn. Most adjourned to the taproom to sample the ale, others decided to snatch an hour's sleep after the rigors of their journey, a few chose to explore Maidstone on foot and Edmund Hoode found a quiet corner in which to work on a scene in his new play. Giddy Mussett spent an improving hour with Lawrence Firethorn, being patiently instructed in the roles he would play. Nicholas Bracewell was dispatched on an important errand. Before the company could perform in the town, a licence had to be obtained and that task invariably fell to the book holder. He set off towards the town hall, glad that they had arrived safely and certain that Maidstone would prove a rewarding place to visit.

After the teeming streets of London, the town seemed curiously empty and Nicholas found that a welcome relief. It enabled him to saunter along and appraise their new home at his leisure. He soon passed a sight that was very familiar in the capital. Seated in the stocks, a forlorn individual was raising both arms to protect himself from the rotten fruit and clods of earth being thrown at him by mocking children. Set out in front of the malefactor were some loaves of unwholesome bread and Nicholas realised that he was looking at a baker who had sold mouldy produce and who was being punished accordingly.

When he got to the town hall and introduced himself, he was immediately shown in to meet the mayor, a tall, stooping man with an alarming battery of warts on his face. Lucas Broome was surprised to hear that the troupe had already arrived in town.

'We did not expect you for a matter of weeks,' he said.

'Our hand was forced,' explained Nicholas. 'We had to quit London sooner than planned. I hope that we are still able to find an audience here.'

'No question but that you will, my friend. I've been waiting a long time to see so illustrious a company as yours visit Maidstone. Whenever I've been in London, I've made the effort to call at the Queen's Head.'

'What have you seen of ours?'

'Nothing that failed to delight me. The last time it was *Mirth and Madness*. Before that it was *Vincentio's Revenge*. Another play that I remember,' said Broome, exposing a row of small, uneven teeth, 'is *Cupid's Folly*. It made me laugh so.'

'We expect to offer it again during our tour.'

'Your clown was worth the price of entry on his own.' He scratched his head. 'Now, what was his name?'

'Barnaby Gill.'

'That was him,' said Broome, snapping his fingers. 'Barnaby Gill. I trust that you have brought him to Maidstone with you?'

'Master Gill is with us,' said Nicholas, 'but unable to take an active part in our work. A broken leg makes him a spectator on our tour. But have no fear,' he went on, seeing the disappointment in the mayor's face. 'His substitute is just as skilled in the arts of comedy. They are two of a kind and you will not tell the difference between them.'

'I long to see the fellow.'

'Grant us a licence and you will do so.'

'Westfield's Men are welcome at any time.' Nicholas reached inside his jerkin to take out some documents but Broome waved a dismissive hand. 'No need to prove who you are, my friend. I know and respect your patron. Those who wear his livery stand high in my esteem.'

'Do you not wish to see our licence to travel?'

'The quality of your work gives you that. My wife has oftentimes heard me talk of my visits to the Queen's Head. Now she can enjoy the same pleasure herself.'

'When and where shall we play?' asked Nicholas, slipping the documents back inside his jerkin.

'The Lower Courthouse will be yours for one performance,' decided Broome, 'and it will be filled to the rafters. Of that I can assure you, my friend. However, you will have to wait a couple of days until the assizes come to an end.'

'That will suit us well, sir. We will need that time to

rehearse our new clown into his roles. You have a liking for *Cupid's Folly*, you say?'

'Why, yes, but I'll not prescribe your choice. Give me something that I have never seen before and I'll be equally pleased. Meanwhile, we'll voice it abroad that you have come to town and bring in a wider audience for you.'

'The landlord wishes us to play at the Star Inn as well.'

'Then so you shall. That will give us two chances to savour your art.'

'We are indebted to you, sir.'

'And we to Westfield's Men.'

Nicholas was thrilled with his reception at the town hall. Having been on tour before, he knew that other towns were not always so welcoming and other mayors not so fond of theatre that they sought it out in London. Lucas Broome was a keen admirer of their work. He and his wife would assuredly be there with other civic dignitaries to watch the first performance. Before he left, Nicholas asked if he might have a brief glance at the Lower Courthouse to see how best it could be adapted to their needs. Broome conducted him there in person and they soon found themselves in a long, low, rectangular room with light flooding in from windows along both sides. Two doors in the far wall made that the obvious place where the stage could be set. Having taken note of the proportions of the room, Nicholas thanked his guide.

'Is this where Conway's Men performed?' he asked.

'Yes,' said Broome, 'and they made good use of it. They gave but one performance in the town and fortune decreed that it took place here.'

'Why? Was the weather unkind?'

'A torrent of rain fell throughout the whole day. Had they tried to play at the Star, they'd have been washed away.'

'We'll pray for sunshine when we take over their yard.'

'I'll join you in your prayers.'

Nicholas took his leave. Instead of returning directly to the inn, he had a second errand to run and it was of a more personal nature. Anne Hendrik had given him a letter to deliver to a cousin of her late husband's. Well over a hundred immigrants had come to the town, driven from the Netherlands by persecution and bringing to Maidstone their skills in the manufacture of cloth, Spanish leather, pottery, tile, brick, paper, armour and gunpowder. Pieter Hendrik was one of them and he had hired a house in Mill Street where he had set up two looms. Nicholas found the place without difficulty. Hendrik was a big, hulking man in his forties with a head that seemed too small for the massive body. Both of the large wooden looms were in use inside the house and the noise made conversation difficult so he took Nicholas into the garden at the rear of the property. Hendrik's mastery of English was not yet complete.

'A frient of Anne's, you are?' he said, peering at Nicholas.

'Yes,' replied Nicholas, handing him the letter. 'Anne sent this for you.'

'Thenk you, thenk you. Please to excuss me, ha?'

He opened the letter and slowly read its contents, a fond smile on his lips as he did so. When he had finished, he let out a throaty chuckle.

'Anne speak fery vill of you, Niklaus.'

'I'm pleased to hear it.'

'The work, it is fery gut.'

'Yes,' said Nicholas. 'Anne has carried on where her husband left off. They never lack for customers. People from all over London wear hats made by one of her men. Preben van Loew is a master at his trade.'

'Preben, I know,' said Hendrik, folding up the letter. 'A gut man. I not sin him since Jacob's funeral. Jacob, my cussin, I miss. Togither, we grow up. Loffly man.'

'Anne has told me all about him.'

'She write nice litter. You tek what I write bek?'

'With pleasure,' said Nicholas. 'I'll be in the town for a few days yet. If you want to reply, I'll carry the letter with me though it may be some time before I can put it into Anne's hands. She'll be delighted to hear from you.'

'Gut, gut.' He looked quizzically at Nicholas. 'So why you to Medstun come?'

'I travel with a theatre company called Westfield's Men. We stay at the Star Inn and mean to perform two plays in the town. I hope that you will come to see us.'

Hendrik's face clouded. 'Mebbe, Niklaus, we see.'

'Do you object to plays?'

'No, no. That not risson.'

'I know that some of your countrymen do.'

'Not me. I like.'

'Then why were you so uneasy when I mentioned the theatre company?'

'It nothing. No fault from you.'

'Fault?'

'I haf little trouble, that all.'

'With a theatre company?'

'Yis.'

'Then it must have been Conway's Men,' said Nicholas, his curiosity aroused. 'They were here not long ago, were they not?'

Hendrik nodded. 'Conway's Men,' he said ruefully. 'They here.'

'Did you see them play?'

'Yis. Fery gut. I laugh a lot.'

'Then why are you so wary of theatre companies?'

'I deal with menegar. You know the fillow?'

'Only by reputation. His name is Tobias Fitzgeoffrey.'

'That him.'

'What kind of dealings did you have with Master Fitzgeoffrey?'

'Bad ones, Niklaus.'

'Oh?'

'We mek fustian, grogram and other cloth. Best in Medstun. This man, Fissjiffry, he come to buy from us.'

'He probably wanted it to make new costumes or repair old ones.'

'This what he say.'

'How much did he have from you?'

'Lot, Nicklaus. But no money. Fissjiffry, he say he pay me nixt day. When I call at Star Inn for money, they gone. It no mistake. They liff at dawn with my cloth. No pay,' said Hendrik, wounded by the memory, 'Conway's Men, thieves.'

* * *

'It sounds a fine play,' said Giddy Mussett with admiration. 'Yet another worthy piece from Edmund Hoode?'

'*A Trick To Catch A Chaste Lady* did not come from Edmund's pen,' said Lawrence Firethorn. 'It's the work of a younger playwright, Lucius Kindell.'

'I do not know the name.'

'You soon will, Giddy. He gets better with each play. Lucius came to us to write tragedies but he tried his hand at comedy as well.'

'And a clever hand, it is. If the other scenes are as rich as the ones in which I appear, then the play is a certain success.'

'It worked well at the Queen's Head until this last performance. The piece was never allowed to run its course then. When we reached the point where the clown does his jig, the hounds of hell were unleashed upon us.'

'We'll not have that vexation again.'

'I hope so, Giddy. With all my heart, I do.'

The two men were in an upstairs room that overlooked the yard of the Star Inn. Firethorn was taking his new clown through the plays that they would perform in Maidstone, explaining the plot of both in detail so that Mussett had some grasp of how his part related to the whole drama. It was when he handed the clown a scene to read aloud that Firethorn encountered an unexpected problem. Mussett was almost illiterate. He pleaded poor eyesight but it was evident that he could make out only one word in four and he could hardly get his tongue around that. To his credit, however, he had a quick and retentive brain. When

97

Firethorn read the lines out to him, Mussett memorised a number of them instantly. At one point, he repeated an eight-line speech without a fault.

'Which play do we stage first?' asked Mussett.

'That depends on where we perform it,' explained Firethorn. 'If it is to be here, then *Cupid's Folly* is the better choice. If we play indoors, then we'll introduce them to the chaste lady. We must wait for Nick to come back.' He looked down through the open window and saw the book holder entering the yard. 'Talk of the devil! There he is.'

'Nick promised to school me in my roles.'

'And he'll do it better than me, Giddy.'

'Am I free to go now?'

'As long as you do not join the others in the taproom,' warned Firethorn sternly. 'Remember your contract. No drunkenness, no women, no fighting.'

'Would you have me become a monk?'

'I would have you aim higher than that – at sainthood.'

Mussett cackled. 'My hopes of that have already been lost,' he said. 'But I'll not go astray. You have my word on that. I mean to take a walk to remind myself what sort of town Maidstone is.'

'You've been here before, then?'

'Some years ago, when I was with the Earl of Rutland's Men.'

'Why did you part with them?'

'To become a holy anchorite.'

Mussett cackled again and let himself out of the room. Watching him go, Firethorn gave an indulgent smile. It was hard to dislike a man so relentlessly cheerful as the clown. He might lack Barnaby Gill's education but he had other gifts to bring to his work. Firethorn turned to the window again and noticed that Nicholas Bracewell was looking at something through the door to the stables.

'Nick, dear heart!' called Firethorn.

Nicholas saw him at the window. 'All is well,' he said, waving a hand.

'Wait there until I come down.'

Firethorn went through the door and down a rickety staircase. When he came out into the yard, he saw that Nicholas was still peeping into the stables. Firethorn strode quickly across to him.

'What have you found, Nick?'

'Something that may turn out to be a blessing.'

'Where's the blessing in horse dung?' asked Firethorn, seeing the manure that was piled in a corner. 'Is that what caught your attention?'

'No,' said Nicholas, pointing. 'Look there.'

Firethorn's gaze fell on a wooden wheelbarrow that had been dumped against the side of a stall. Its wheel was missing and one of its handles had been snapped off. The timber was stained by years of usage. Firethorn was bewildered.

'I think that I'd rather look at the horse dung,' he said.

'The wheelbarrow has been abandoned.'

'It deserves to be, Nick. It's outlived its time.'

'Not if it's repaired with care,' said Nicholas.

'And why should anyone bother to do that? The only

use is has now is to serve as firewood. I'm surprised it has not already gone up in smoke.'

'That may be to our advantage. Find a new wheel, make a new handle, wash it out thoroughly and we bring it back to life.'

'To what possible end?'

'A certain person might be able to move about with less pain.'

'Barnaby?' said Firethorn with a laugh. 'Sitting in a wheelbarrow? Moved around like so much dung? He'd never countenance it.'

'He might if we used some clever carpentry,' said Nicholas, 'and I'd undertake that. I need to make it more comfortable and build something to support his back. We could surely woo him with the notion then. Walking is a trial for him. George Dart could push him around with more speed and far less pain.'

'You may be right, Nick,' conceded Firethorn, taking the idea seriously at last. 'Let's speak to the landlord first and see if we can have the wheelbarrow. If you can mend it, as you say, we'll tell Barnaby he travels on an imperial couch from now on.'

'I'll leave you to coax him into it.'

'I may need to hitch up two of the horses to do that.' They shared a laugh then Firethorn rubbed his hands together. 'How are we received?'

'Better than we could have desired.'

Nicholas described his visit to the mayor and told Firethorn about the place in which they would perform.

The fact that they would have two days to prepare made the actor sigh with relief. Clicking his fingers, he reached an immediate decision.

'We'll give them *A Trick To Catch A Chaste Lady*,' he announced.

'That would be my choice.'

'It's a pity that Lucius Kindell is not here to see his play take wing again.'

'After the riot at the Queen's Head, he may not be too eager to view it. Lucius was there when the affray broke out,' said Nicholas, 'and he still thinks that his play provoked it in some measure. It grieved him.'

'We'll offer it to the good people of Maidstone instead, and play it through to the end even if an invading army tries to stop us.' He slapped Nicholas on the shoulder. 'We have two reasons to celebrate now. The town wants us here and,' he added, indicating the broken wheelbarrow, 'you have found a chariot in which to drive Barnaby.'

'I'm not sure that George will relish his office but someone must take it on.'

'George will do as I tell him,' said Firethorn grimly 'But what kept you, Nick? You've been gone above an hour and I thought we'd lost you.'

'No,' said Nicholas. 'When I left the town hall, I had to honour a promise to Anne. She has a relative here, one Pieter Hendrik, a cousin of her husband's. I delivered a letter on her behalf and am glad that I did so.'

'Why?'

'Pieter is one of many Walloons who settled here when

they were driven out of their country. He's a weaver by trade and has already made his mark here. He was happy in his work until he had dealings with Tobias Fitzgeoffrey.'

'That scourge of our profession!' cried Firethorn. 'He's a disgrace to the name of actor. Tobias should be driven from the stage with whips of steel.'

'Pieter Hendrik would be ready to wield one of those whips.'

'Why? Did he have to endure one of the man's fearful performances?'

'No,' said Nicholas. 'He enjoyed the play that Conway's Men offered. That was not his complaint. Tobias Fitzgeoffrey had bought a large amount of cloth from him and promised to pay him the next day. Instead of that, he and his company left at dawn and Pieter was left out of pocket.'

'Nothing surprises me in that. Conway's Men would stoop to anything.'

'Including murder?'

Firethorn hesitated. 'Even they might draw back from that.'

'I wonder,' said Nicholas. 'According to Giddy, they are a law unto themselves. He has tales that accord with what Pieter Hendrik told me. They take what they can get wherever they can. Fortunatus Hope once consorted with their patron. Could it be that the two men parted in anger?'

'Lord Conway is a spiteful old devil. He'd not have been pleased to see a close friend sitting beside our patron instead. He hates us almost as much as Tobias.'

'Do either of them hate us enough to cause that affray at the Queen's Head?'

'I think so.'

'Would they also hire an assassin to kill Master Hope?'

'Who knows, Nick?'

'Only time will tell,' said Nicholas. 'If they are touring Kent ahead of us, we may well cross paths with them at some stage. I promised Pieter Hendrik that I'd ask them why they failed to pay him.'

'And I'll ask Tobias Fitzgeoffrey why he dares to strut a stage when he has no skill as an actor. No wonder London has kept Conway's Men at bay.'

'That's their main cause of resentment. Giddy told me that it rankles with them.'

'He did well to shun the company.'

'How has he fared this afternoon?' asked Nicholas.

Firethorn grimaced. 'We had a desperate start, Nick.'

'Why?'

'Did you know that the fellow is unable to read?'

'I saw that he cannot write when he tried to sign that contract for us. If reading is beyond him as well, he must have found ways around the disability.'

'He has,' said Firethorn. 'His mind is like a bird that picks up every crumb. Teach him a couplet and he knows it at once. Speak a line and he repeats it like an echo. Giddy is yours now, Nick. Take him through *A Trick To Catch A Chaste Lady*.'

'I will,' agreed Nicholas, 'and I'll make sure that he does not catch any other kind while I am at it.'

'My decree has been impressed upon him. No drink, no whoring, no fighting. Giddy is a changed man,' said Firethorn confidently. 'He'll not disobey me.'

Bess Roundel was a jovial, red-headed woman in her thirties with a bosom and buttocks of generous proportions. She lay on the bed with her skirt up, giggling with joy as a half-naked man thrust away energetically between her thighs, pausing from time to time to take a swig of ale from a flagon. Giddy Mussett was starting to enjoy his visit to Maidstone.

'There you are, Bess,' he said, swallowing another mouthful of ale. 'I promised to come back to you one day. And here I am!'

Barnaby Gill was beginning to regret his decision to travel with Westfield's Men. His broken leg was both a huge impediment and a source of continual pain, and his forced retirement from performance made him the outsider in the company. What irked him most was the way in which Giddy Mussett had been accepted so readily by the others. While they ate their supper in the taproom on their first evening, the actors shook with laughter at Mussett's endless supply of anecdotes. Owen Elias, in particular, seemed to have a real affinity with the new clown. Watching it all from the other side of the room, Gill became increasingly jealous of his rival. He took out his anger on George Dart.

'George!' he snapped.

'Yes, Master Gill?' said Dart, scurrying across to him.

'You are supposed to look after me.'

'I wanted to listen to Giddy's story about—'

'Forget him,' snarled Gill, interrupting him, 'and attend to my needs instead.'

'But the tale was so merry.'

'I've no stomach for merriment and no wish to hear anything that that interloper has to say. Now, get me up off this seat,' he ordered, reaching for his crutch. 'I've had enough of this jollity. Take me to my bed, George.'

Dart helped him up and supported him across the room. As they passed the table where the others sat, Elias grinned and warned Dart to be careful when he was alone in a room with Gill. More teasing followed but Mussett took care not to get involved in it.

'Good night, Barnaby!' he said. 'Sleep well.'

'How can I do that when I'm under the same roof as you?' retorted Gill.

He struggled out and made his way towards the little storeroom that had been cleared for his use. A mattress had been brought in along with a stool, a jug of water and a bowl. The considerate landlord had even provided a chamber pot. After helping him into the room, Dart was dismissed and ran swiftly back to the others. Gill began the laborious process of getting ready for bed and lowering himself by degrees onto the mattress. He slept fitfully, unable to get comfortable and wondering how many days it would take before the pain in his leg began to ease. At cockcrow, he was already awake. Abandoning any hope of sleep, he hauled himself up on his crutch to see what sort of day it was, opening shutters that had been locked throughout the night to ensure his privacy.

The weather was fine, the temperature warm. Gill was about to turn away when he saw a figure emerging from a door nearby to stroll across the yard. Nicholas Bracewell disappeared into the stables, leaving Gill to speculate on what made the book holder get up at that hour and why he had been carrying so much timber in his arms.

Lawrence Firethorn wanted to make full use of the day for a rehearsal and he insisted that everyone rose early for breakfast. Seated at the head of the table, he explained to the company what lay ahead of them.

'Today we will rehearse *A Trick To Catch A Chaste Lady* with particular attention to the scenes in which the clown appears so that Giddy can take full measure of the part.' He looked down the table. 'Where is the fellow?'

'He left the room before I did,' said Owen Elias. 'I expected him to be here.'

'I hope that he's not causing any mischief.'

'No, Lawrence. Giddy will have gone off to start the day with a good deed. He's probably letting Barnaby out of the privy.'

'This is no jest, Owen,' said Firethorn, silencing the sniggers with a raised hand. 'I prefer to have Giddy where I can see him. If he has been bothering Barnaby in any way, it will go hard with him.' He picked out the smallest figure at the table. 'George.'

'Yes, Master Firethorn?' Dart piped up.

'Have you seen Barnaby this morning?'

'Yes, Master Firethorn.'

'Were there any incidents during the night?'

'None,' said Elias, 'for Barnaby's splint kept getting in the way.'

'This is a serious matter, Owen,' said Firethorn. 'Well, George?'

'I called on Master Gill earlier,' he said, 'to see if I could bring him breakfast in his room, but he chose to have it with the rest of us. He has not slept at all but it is not Giddy's doing. There was no mention of him.'

'I'm pleased to hear that. So where is Giddy now?'

'I do not know, Master Firethorn.'

'Nick was supposed to keep an eye on him,' recalled Elias. 'You must ask him.'

'But he's not here either,' said Firethorn with exasperation. 'Where on earth is everyone *hiding* this morning?'

'I am not hiding, Lawrence,' declared Barnaby Gill, making a sudden entrance and pausing in the door for effect. 'I've come to take my rightful place in the company.' He ran his eye down the table. 'Has Giddy Mussett absconded yet?'

'No, no, Barnaby.' Firethorn beckoned him over. 'Come and sit next to me.'

Dart moved across to help the newcomer but Gill waved him away, using the crutch with skill and hopping over to the table. Elias moved along the bench to make way for him. Gill's arrival served to dampen everyone's spirits and conversation among the actors was more muted. When he had eaten his first mouthful of bread, Gill remembered what he had seen earlier.

'What is Nicholas doing in the stables?' he asked.

'Is that where he is?' said Firethorn.

'I saw him walk past my window.'

'When?'

'Shortly after dawn. He had some wood in his arms.'

'Ah! So *that's* what he's doing!'

'I am none the wiser, Lawrence.'

'Let me explain,' said Firethorn, lowering his voice to a persuasive purr. 'What is the thing that annoys you the most, Barnaby?'

'Having that drunken rascal, Giddy Mussett, in the company.'

'But for your broken leg, he'd not be here. That is the root of your trouble, man. You've been in great pain ever since the accident occurred.'

'It was no accident. I was flung to the ground.'

'Be that as it may, you are now hopping around on one leg and taking an age simply to get from one side of the room to the other.' He leant in closer. 'How would you like to move with more speed?'

'Why? Do you intend to carry me on your back?'

'Lawrence has already been doing that for years,' said Elias, unable to resist the jibe. 'But tell us how it may be done, Lawrence. Is there some means by which Barnaby can be made to fly like a bird?'

'No, there is another way. It was Nick Bracewell's idea.'

Gill bristled. 'Then it will certainly not appeal to me.'

108

'Hear me out. Nick must be working on the notion right now.'

'Why? Does he mean to board me up in the stables?'

'No, Barnaby,' said Firethorn, 'he intends to do you a great favour. We found an old wheelbarrow that could be mended in order to move you from place to place.'

'A wheelbarrow!' protested Gill. 'You expect *me* to sit in a wheelbarrow? Am I no more than a pile of earth to be carried around then dumped?'

'This wheelbarrow was used for horse dung.'

'There you are, Barnaby,' said Elias, chuckling. 'You'll feel at home.'

'I'll hear no more of it!' shouted Gill, banging a fist on the table but unable to stem the general laughter. 'I have high standards.'

'Wait until you see what Nick has done,' advised Firethorn.

'What he has done is to come up with the most insulting idea that I've ever heard in my life.' Righteous indignation turned his cheeks bright red. 'Ride in a wheelbarrow? I'd sooner crawl on all fours.'

'We were only trying to help you.'

'You were trying to turn me into a figure of fun.'

Elias grinned broadly. 'Nature has already done that for us.'

'Be quiet, Owen,' admonished Firethorn. 'How can I prove to Barnaby that we have his interests at heart if you keep breaking in?'

'Say no more, Lawrence,' asserted Gill, quivering

with anger. 'You've wounded me enough already.'

'But I've not told you what Nick intends to do.'

'I've no wish to hear. Nothing on God's earth would ever get me to lower myself in that way.' He wagged a finger. 'Keep your wheelbarrow away from me.'

At the very moment when he spoke, the door to the taproom was flung open and Nicholas Bracewell entered with the results of his endeavours. The wheelbarrow had been transformed. Having made and fitted a new wheel, Nicholas had added a stout board to support the back and a piece of wood that jutted out horizontally over the front of the wheelbarrow. Its purpose was clear. While Nicholas pushed him around the room, Giddy Mussett lay in the wheelbarrow with a lordly air, reclining on the cushions with which it had been filled and resting the leg he had put in mock splints on the piece of wood that protruded over the front. The wheelbarrow came to a halt beside Gill.

'You're too late, Barnaby,' announced Mussett. 'I want it for myself.'

Chapter Seven

As soon as breakfast was over, the rehearsal began in earnest. Having no room on his premises that was large enough for their purposes, Jonathan Jowlett was happy to give them free use of his yard, provided that they did not hold up the normal running of the inn. Whenever travellers arrived by cart or on horseback, the actors had to break off to allow them free access to the stables. They also had to endure the goggling eyes of the ostlers, servingmen and tavern wenches as they honed their art in the open air. The company approached *A Trick To Catch A Chaste Lady* with some caution. Its previous performance had been disastrous and their superstitious natures made them uneasy about the piece. Another cause for discomfort was the fact that one of the main roles – that of Bedlam, the clown – was being played by someone who had no real acquaintance either with the play or with the people acting in it. Giddy Mussett was an affable companion but that did not mean he would be a worthy substitute for Barnaby Gill. When word of Mussett's illiteracy spread, the company became even more restive.

It was Nicholas Bracewell who helped to restore their confidence. Not only did he show Mussett where to stand and when to move in each scene, he repeated the clown's lines over and over again until Mussett had committed them to memory. The others were amazed at the speed with which their new colleague was mastering the basic elements of his role. What he lacked was Gill's familiarity with the part and his ability to invest each line with a comic slant. His jig, however, was equal to that of his predecessor and his facial contortions made the onlookers break into spontaneous laughter. Gill was less than amused. Still outraged at the proposition that he should be carried around in a wheelbarrow, he had retired to his room to sulk. He was now watching the rehearsal through the window with a mixture of sadness and pique, dejected because he was unable to take part and nettled that his role had been given to a man whom he loathed so much. Each laugh that Mussett gained was like a dagger through Gill's heart.

When the company paused for refreshment, Lawrence Firethorn sought the opinion of the two people he trusted most, Edmund Hoode and his book holder.

'Well?' he asked. 'How do you judge him?'

'Giddy has done well,' said Hoode. 'He has a better memory than any of us. Whether it will stand up to the hazards of performance is another matter. I'd have preferred a week at least in which to rehearse him.'

'We do not have a week, Edmund.'

'Nor do we need it,' said Nicholas. 'Give me time to work with him privily and I'll have him ready for the good citizens of Maidstone.'

'What of *Cupid's Folly*, Nick?' asked Firethorn.

'We'll look at that as well.'

'The clown holds the whip hand over all of us in that play,' noted Hoode. 'Would it not be sensible to choose a drama that puts less weight on him? There is so much for Giddy to learn.'

'That will not disturb him.'

'No,' added Firethorn. 'When I told him about his other role, he could not wait to play Rigormortis.'

'There are other reasons to choose the play,' said Nicholas. 'This yard will be an ideal place in which to stage it and the piece is a favourite of the mayor's. He would not dare to miss it. Where he leads, many others will follow.'

Hoode was worried. 'I still feel that we ask too much too soon of Giddy.'

'Someone must take the role of Rigormortis.'

'Not if we select another play.'

'We have the costumes and scenery for *Cupid's Folly*.'

'And for *Vincentio's Revenge*.'

'This is no town for tragedy, Edmund,' said Firethorn. 'Let's brighten their day with happy laughter. There'll be rustics in the audience, brought in from miles around. The soaring verse of *Vincentio's Revenge* will be wasted on them. We'll play it later in the tour to more discerning spectators.'

'I agree,' said Nicholas. '*Cupid's Folly*, it shall be.'

Hoode pursed his lips in doubt. 'I hope that it does not prove *our* folly.'

'You saw this morning how quickly Giddy can learn.'

'Yes, but I'd feel safer if Barnaby were able to help. He has delighted an audience as Rigormortis well above thirty times. He should be the one to instruct Giddy in the way that the part should be played.'

'You ask the impossible,' said Firethorn. 'The only thing that Barnaby would consent to teach Giddy is how to take his own life.'

'Besides,' argued Nicholas, 'it would be wrong for one clown to school another. We do not want a pale replica of Barnaby. Giddy must give his own performance.'

'Can he possibly do it in a mere two days?' wondered Hoode.

Mussett supplied his own reply. Stepping out onto the gallery that ran around three sides of the yard, he struck a pose and declaimed the opening lines from the prologue to *Cupid's Folly*.

> '*Come friends and let us leave the city's noise*
> *To seek the quieter paths of country joys.*
> *For verdant pastures more delight the eye*
> *With cows and sheep and fallow deer hereby,*
> *With horse and hound, pursuing to their lair,*
> *The cunning fox or nimble-footed hare,*
> *With merry maids and lusty lads most jolly*
> *Who find their foolish fun in Cupid's Folly.*'

'Dear God!' said Firethorn with delight. 'He has mastered the prologue even though he does not have to speak it in the play. Giddy is a true marvel.'

Nicholas smiled. 'That's why I suggested his name.'

'I cast off all my worries,' said Hoode. 'He may yet outdo even Barnaby.'

Gill heard him and felt salt being rubbed enthusiastically into his wounds.

Two days later, they were finishing their rehearsal in the Lower Courthouse in readiness for their performance that evening. Their stage had been set up at the far end of the room in a position that had been occupied by the assize judges. Scenery was artfully used to create a rural setting and both doors were concealed behind skilfully painted trees that stood on bases of solid wood. One door led to the tiring-house where the costumes and properties were arranged in order, the other to an antechamber that was used for storage but which was connected by a door to the larger room that had become their tiring-house. When they were not acting in the play, the musicians sat on a platform that was raised above the level of the stage. Having rehearsed the piece outdoors, they had to make a number of adjustments. Voices that had rung around the yard at the Star Inn had to be modified in a more confined space. Movements had to be changed as they went along. Effects that had always been successful at the Queen's Head proved much more difficult indoors and had to be adapted accordingly. It made for a long and testing rehearsal during which many mistakes were made. Owen Elias began to have serious doubts. When they finished their work, he drifted across to Nicholas Bracewell.

'Was it really as bad as it felt, Nick?' he asked.

'I have seen it better performed,' said Nicholas.

'How can we lose so much of our spark?'

'The surroundings are unfamiliar. You need to find your feet.'

'Feet, hands, head and body,' said Elias. 'We lost them all.'

'You are too harsh, Owen. A rehearsal is a time to explore and that always leads to errors. When you have an audience in here, it will be very different.' He glanced down the room at Barnaby Gill, who sat motionless on a chair with his arms folded. 'All that you had was a lone spectator.'

'That's what unsettled us. Barnaby made us feel that we were on trial.'

'His eyes were not on you. Only one performance concerned him.'

'I know,' said Elias. 'He came to gloat over Giddy's errors but they were too rare to notice. Barnaby will have been disappointed. Instead of letting us down, Giddy was the best of us.' He looked across at Mussett. 'How long can he keep it up, Nick?'

'Until we have our own clown back again.'

'I did not mean his work on stage. It is this peculiar change that's come over him. We've been in Maidstone for three days and I've not seen him once drink ale, chase women or lose his temper.'

'Those were the conditions under which we employed him.'

'*I* could not keep to such a contract,' admitted Elias. 'Lechery is natural to any red-blooded man. Strong drink merely helps it take its course. We have a duty to take our pleasures where we find them.'

'You follow inclination more than your duty,' said Nicholas with a grin. 'Giddy is the dutiful one. His pleasure consists in proving to Barnaby that he is the better clown. He needs a clear head to do that.'

'Can he *keep* that clear head?'

'If he does not, then we are all lost.'

It was a sobering thought. *A Trick To Catch A Chaste Lady* was a play that relied heavily on its clown. Lawrence Firethorn took the leading role but Mussett's support was crucial. On the following day, he would be taking on an even more demanding role. It would increase the burden on him. If Mussett faltered in either piece, the whole play would crumble around him. Nicholas was alive to that danger.

'Do you know why he left Conway's Men?' asked Elias.

'He told me that the quality of their work was too inferior.'

'That's not the story I had, Nick. According to Giddy, he stole a woman right from under Tobias Fitzgeoffrey and let her warm *his* bed instead.'

'Master Fitzgeoffrey has his own skill at stealing,' said Nicholas. 'Conway's Men have not only filched plays that do not belong to them, they bought cloth from a weaver here in town and rode off without paying him.'

'Why does he not bring an action against them?'

'How can he when he has no idea where they are?'

'The company is touring Kent.'

'Then we must be the magistrates here, Owen,' said Nicholas. 'If we chance to catch up with them, they can be arraigned on three charges. Theft is one. Inciting an affray at the Queen's Head may well be another.'

'What is the third?'

'Conspiring in the murder of Fortunatus Hope.'

Barnaby Gill was in a quandary, not knowing whether to watch or spurn the performance that evening. Loyalty to Westfield's Men made him wish them success but hatred of Giddy Mussett induced a hope of failure. He could not bear the notion of seeing his rival cheered to the echo by an audience. At the same time, however, he was so possessive about the role that he had created that he did not want to miss its appearance on a stage. On the way back to the Star Inn, his mind was in turmoil. There was a practical problem to be faced as well. He had ridden to the Lower Courthouse in the wagon that carried the scenery but he had to walk back. Even with George Dart's assistance, it took him almost twenty minutes to reach the inn, leaving him with a bare half-hour before he would have to set off again for the performance. It was a painful journey. The crutch dug into an already bruised armpit and his broken leg ached every time he swung it forward. Dart offered a tentative solution.

'Would it not be easier to use that wheelbarrow, Master Gill?' he asked.

'Never!'

'I could move you to and fro much faster in that.'

'But without a shred of dignity,' said Gill.

'Nick Bracewell has disguised it so well. It does not *look* like a wheelbarrow.'

'It does to me, George, and I'll have none of it.'

Dart knew better than to pursue the discussion. When they reached the inn, he was dismissed and went off to seek refreshment with the others. Gill felt out of place in the taproom, especially as everyone was saying kind words to Mussett about his performance during the rehearsal. Exhausted by the walk, Gill made his way to his room, questioning the wisdom of attending a play that would commit him to another arduous journey. The wagon might bring him back after the performance but he would still have to get to the Lower Courthouse on foot. It was a frightening prospect. Common sense urged him to remain at the inn that evening in order to spare himself the agonising walk and the discomfort of watching someone else play the role of Bedlam.

Still unable to reach a decision, he let himself into his room. A shock awaited him. Standing beside his mattress and taking up much of the space was the wheelbarrow that Nicholas Bracewell had mended. Gill was incensed. His first instinct was to call the landlord to have the object removed but something made him pause. When he looked more closely at the wheelbarrow, he saw how artfully Nicholas had fashioned it. The board would offer good support for his back and, as he had seen, provision had been made to hold up the leg that was in splints. A large piece of fustian had been draped over the cushions to add more comfort and to disguise the outline of the wheelbarrow. Only the wooden wheel proclaimed its earlier function. Gill's objections began to weaken. He was even tempted to try sitting in it.

What held him back was the fear that Mussett might be playing a trick on him. If the wheelbarrow had been tampered with, he might get into it then find that it collapsed. Yet it seemed sturdy enough when he shook it and it looked more inviting with each moment. Gill put the crutch aside. Using a hand to steady himself against the wall, he lowered himself into the wheelbarrow and sank back into the cushions. When he lifted his broken leg onto the piece of wood that had been put there for the purpose, he felt strangely comfortable. Gill smiled for the first time since they had left London.

Lucas Broome had not exaggerated. A large audience squeezed itself into the Lower Courthouse, excited by the notion of watching a celebrated London theatre company at work. Wearing his mayoral robe and regalia, Broome sat in the front row with his wife, surrounded by members of the town council with their respective spouses. Three rows of chairs gave way to several rows of benches with standing room at the rear for those arriving too late to secure a seat. It was early evening with ample natural light for the performance, though candles had been set out in case they were required later. There was a buzz of anticipation as the spectators awaited *A Trick To Catch A Chaste Lady*, a title that was already provoking amusement in some quarters. Convinced that they were about to witness a remarkable event, Broome settled back complacently in his seat.

Behind the scenes, there was far less confidence. Instead, there was a gathering sense of doom. Giddy Mussett had failed to return from the Star Inn. Lawrence Firethorn was close to panic. Eyes blazing, he turned to his book holder.

'Where the devil is he this time, Nick?' he demanded.

'I wish I knew.'

'You were supposed to watch him at all times.'

'Yes,' said Nicholas, 'but I stayed here while the rest of you went back to the inn. There were some repairs I had to make to the scenery for the last act. I asked Owen to keep watch over Giddy.'

'And so I did,' said Elias defensively. 'Giddy was as anxious as the rest of us to get back here on time. But when we set out, he remembered something that he forgot and ran back to the inn to fetch it.'

'Did you not think to go with him?' asked Firethorn.

'No, Lawrence. He said that he'd catch us up within minutes.'

'This was some device.'

'I blame myself for being taken in,' confessed Elias. 'When we got here and Giddy failed to appear, I hurried all the way back to the inn to search for him.' He spread his arms in a gesture of helplessness. 'The bird had flown.'

'That may not be the case,' said Nicholas.

'What else can explain his absence? Giddy has deserted us.'

'At a moment to embarrass us the most,' observed Firethorn. 'We cannot stage the play without Bedlam or it will turn into Bedlam itself. Listen to those people out there. They *want* us. What will they think when they hear that the performance will not take place? There'll be uproar.'

'Think back, Owen,' suggested Nicholas, keen to find an explanation for the disappearance of their clown. 'Could he have been taken ill? Did he eat something that may have upset him? What did Giddy drink at the Star?'

'There was nothing wrong with his health, Nick.'

'Then he may have been prey to sudden fear.'

'That's *my* prerogative,' said Firethorn sourly. 'I shake with terror. Call off the play and we lose any money the mayor will give us. It will also limit our numbers at the Star tomorrow. Who will want to see a theatre company that lets its audience down?'

'Yes,' said Elias, 'and how could we even dream of offering *Cupid's Folly* without the man who takes the leading part? Giddy has ruined our visit to Maidstone.'

'They'll probably drive us out of town with stones.'

'Giddy would not let us down without a good reason,' insisted Nicholas.

'It's in his nature,' said Firethorn darkly, 'and that is reason enough.'

'Could he have lost his way here?'

'*We* are the ones who lost our way when we employed the rogue.'

'Yet he has worked so hard to master his part. Why would he do that?'

'To lead us astray,' concluded Elias. 'Giddy Mussett won our friendship in order to fend off our suspicions. He meant to betray us from the very start. The one consolation is that Barnaby is not here to see our humiliation.'

'Why not?' asked Firethorn.

'When George Dart went to fetch him from his room, he had fallen asleep in the wheelbarrow. George thought it best to leave him there.'

'What was the wheelbarrow doing in his room?'

'That was my invention,' said Nicholas. 'I hoped he might come to appreciate its worth if he could see it properly. My stratagem may have worked.'

Elias was grateful. 'At least, it kept Barnaby from crowing over us out there. He warned us that something like this would happen.'

Firethorn gritted his teeth. 'Let's not delay the anguish, Nick,' he decided. 'Go out on stage and find as pretty an excuse as you can to explain why we are unable to play here this evening. We were fools to trust a proven rascal like Giddy.'

Nicholas took a deep breath and headed for the door, blaming himself for foisting Mussett on to the company and vowing to track the man down. Before he could step out on stage, however, there was an outburst of laughter from the audience. Peeping around the tree that covered the entrance, Nicholas saw what had caused the noise. Giddy Mussett, dressed in the costume he would wear as Bedlam, was turning cartwheels down the length of the room before stopping in front of the mayor and somersaulting backwards on to the stage. He acknowledged the applause before scuttling towards the exit. Nicholas grabbed him and took him into the tiring-house. Mussett gazed happily around the startled faces of the actors.

'Well?' he said jocularly. 'Shall we teach them a trick to catch a chaste lady?'

The performance surpassed all expectations. Horrified at the thought that they would have to abandon the play and sneak ignominiously away, Westfield's Men were so delighted at the appearance of the missing clown that they put more zest and bite into their work. *A Trick To Catch A Chaste Lady* took flight in a way that had never quite happened before. Firethorn was supreme as Lackwit, Elias ranted magnificently as his rival, Hoode introduced a quieter humour with his portrayal of a dithering parson and Richard Honeydew was so convincing as the heroine of the play's title that half the audience firmly believed that the company had broken with tradition and employed a young woman as their chaste lady. Even George Dart, impressed against his will into a minor role, managed to get a laugh in the correct place.

Giddy Mussett began slowly, feeling his way into the part. When he forgot lines or missed cues, other actors covered for him so expertly that none of the spectators noticed the slight mistakes. Throughout the play, his performance grew until it even threatened to overshadow Firethorn's brilliant

Lackwit. It was when he came to his jig that Bedlam really took command, dancing with comic verve and keeping the audience in a state of helpless laughter. Nobody appreciated his comic genius more than Lucas Broome. As the play surged on to its climax, he had forgotten all about Barnaby Gill. The name on his lips – and on those of countless others – was Giddy Mussett, a clown whose mobile features and sprightly antics were a positive joy to behold.

When the play was over, Firethorn was the first to congratulate the newcomer, slapping him on the back and telling him that he had saved their reputation. It was a different matter when he led out his troupe to take their bow. The applause was long and loud but it was not directed largely at Firethorn this time. Accustomed to being the centre of attention, he was dismayed when most pairs of eyes were fixed on Mussett. Even the young women in the hall seemed to prefer Bedlam to Lackwit. It made Firethorn resolve to make certain changes to the play before it was staged again. He was too vain an actor to allow a complete newcomer to steal the plaudits away from him. Instead of being the company's saviour, Mussett could turn out to be Firethorn's personal nemesis.

Back in the tiring-house, the other actors crowded around their clown to shake his hand in admiration. The sight made Firethorn seethe even more. But it was Nicholas Bracewell who took a more considered view of the performance. Biding his time until the general excitement had died down, he took Mussett aside for a private word.

'You did well, Giddy,' he said.

'Thank you, Nick.'

'Better than we could have hoped.'

'It is a wonderful part,' said Mussett, 'and I mean to make it my own.'

'You'll not do that if we have any more of your cunning tricks.'

'Tricks?'

'Yes,' said Nicholas sharply. 'You went missing on purpose. You kept us waiting until the very last moment before you deigned to appear. That was both cruel and unnecessary. You made us suffer, Giddy, and that was unforgivable.'

'The others have forgiven me,' said Mussett blithely.

'I have not.'

'Come, Nick, you must. My performance made amends for everything.'

'Nothing can excuse the way you treated your fellows, Giddy. I thought better of you. When I came to you in prison,' Nicholas reminded him, 'you swore to abide by any contract that we could devise. You broke it on the very day of departure, making us think that you would not turn up then falling from that window to gain a few easy laughs. You did not impress me then and you did so less this evening.'

'The play was a success. What more do you ask?'

'Loyalty from every member of the company. I've yet to see it in you.'

'I've worked hard for Westfield's Men,' said Mussett with a disarming smile, 'and I deserve some reward. Leave off this carping, Nick. We have a triumph to celebrate.'

'Remember the terms of your contract.'

'Can we not forget them for one night?'

'Keep the celebrations within the bounds of reason.'

'I always do.'

'And no more of your tricks,' warned Nicholas. 'Show some respect for the feelings of others. Turn up when you are told and stop seizing all the attention for yourself. I'll not tell you again, Giddy.'

Mussett's smile vanished. Hands on hips, he stood in an attitude of defiance.

'I rescued Westfield's Men this evening,' he asserted.

'Only after you'd first caused us fear and upset.'

'I did that for a reason, Nick.'

'To have another laugh at our expense.'

'No,' said Mussett. 'To show you how much you missed me. Without your clown, the play would have been cancelled and you would have been humiliated. I taught you a lesson this evening. You *need* me, Nick. Take Giddy Mussett out of the company and see what calamity follows. I'll hear no more threats from you,' he went on, thrusting out his chin. 'Westfield's Men would not survive without me. That gives me power.'

When Barnaby Gill awoke in his room, he was utterly bewildered. What was he doing in a wheelbarrow that was filled with cushions? It took him a full minute to gather his thoughts. Fatigue had clearly got the better of him. Wearied by a night without much sleep and taxed by the effort of using a crutch, he had succumbed to tiredness in the comfort of the wheelbarrow. His body had made the decision that he had been unable to reach and kept him away from the performance. Torn between relief and exasperation, he vowed to berate George Dart for not waking him up and at least offering him the chance to return to the Lower Courthouse. Gill had no idea how long he had dozed but, when he glanced though the open window, he could see that the sky was just beginning to darken. The play might well be over already. He longed to know how it had been received.

It took some effort to haul himself out of the wheelbarrow but he eventually succeeded. Reaching for his crutch, he looked back at the place where he had enjoyed such undisturbed slumber. It was softer and more easeful than either the bed in his lodging or the mattress with which the landlord had provided him. In spite of himself, he felt an upsurge of gratitude towards Nicholas Bracewell. The book holder had gone to great trouble to convert the wheelbarrow so that it met Gill's particular needs. It might yet have wider uses for the invalid. Summoning up his strength, he hopped his way towards the taproom to see if the others had returned yet. His timing could not have been better. As he entered the room by one door, three of the actors came bursting in through another. Owen Elias was in the lead.

'Barnaby!' he called, seeing the other. 'Come and join us, old friend.'

'How did the play fare?' asked Gill.

'Wonderfully well. We are famous throughout Maidstone.'

128

'Yes,' said James Ingram, 'and the best news is that the mayor was so pleased with us, he is to pay five pounds for the chaste lady.'

'Much of that should go to Giddy,' said Elias, sitting at a table, 'for he was the chief delight this evening. He even put Lawrence into eclipse.'

'Giddy was Bedlam to the life.'

'So was I, James,' insisted Gill, hitting the floor with his crutch. 'Edmund wrote that part for me and I am the only actor who can play it properly.'

'Oh, I agree,' said Ingram tactfully. 'You made the role what it is.'

'I hope that you all remember that.'

'We do, Barnaby,' said Elias. 'You first played the role but Giddy added to what you did. His dances were inspired, his vigour remarkable. Ask anyone who saw him. He was beyond compare.'

'You speak the truth, Owen,' said Rowland Carr. 'I never thought to see the day when someone could match Barnaby.'

Gill sneered. 'Mussett is but a pale shadow of me.'

'You did not watch the performance.'

'Why not?' asked Ingram. 'I thought that you were eager to measure yourself against our new clown. What kept you away, Barnaby?'

'I had more important things to do.'

'Is anything more important than cheering on your fellows?'

'Do not look to me to raise a cheer for Mussett. He's a

counterfeit clown, a sham, a mere pretence, a low, dishonest creature that steals from others what he could never achieve by himself, a rogue, a villain, a monster of deceit.'

'That is not how we find him. After this evening, he is a dear friend.'

'More to be honoured than vilified,' said Elias. 'Sit down with us, Barnaby. Share our joy. Giddy will be here soon. Take him to your bosom as we have done.'

'I'd sooner roll in a pit of vipers!'

'He is one of us now.'

'Then you are fools to think so, Owen, and I'll not stay to see you fawning upon him.' He started to move away. 'I bid you all good night!'

They called him back but he ignored them and hopped out of the room moments before Giddy Mussett entered it with Edmund Hoode. The actors gave their clown a rousing welcome. Ale was ordered and Mussett was the first to seize a tankard.

'Are you allowed to drink that?' said Elias.

'What man here will try to stop me?' replied Mussett with a cackle.

'None here, Giddy,' said Ingram. 'You've earned it.'

'What kept you back?' wondered Carr.

Mussett smirked. 'The mayor wished to introduce me to his wife.'

'A comely woman, as I recall.'

'Plump and delicious, Rowland. Did you hear what the mayor said? He told me that I was the finest clown he had ever set eyes upon and he has seen Barnaby as well.

That was sweet music in my ears,' he confided. 'The town loved me, the mayor worshipped me and his wife was so consumed with lust for me that her marriage vows were in danger.' He raised his tankard. 'Here's to other conquests along the way, my friends.' They joined in the toast with alacrity. 'Victories on the stage, victories in the bedchamber and, most of all,' he added with a malicious glint in his eye, 'victory over Barnaby Gill.'

The news had been worse than he had anticipated. Having seen the endless mistakes made during the rehearsal, Barnaby Gill could not believe that the play had been such a success. Still less could he accept that a man who had never even heard of the piece until a few days ago could give a performance in it that drew such unstinting praise from the other actors. It was galling. When he reached the safety of his room, he was panting for breath and pulsing with rage. He was also deeply hurt that friends like Elias, Ingram and Carr could forget the long years of service that Gill had given Westfield's Men as its clown and acclaim instead an unworthy intruder. Hundreds of signal triumphs lay behind him yet they were obliterated by two hours in the Lower Courthouse in Maidstone. An event in a building devoted to justice left Gill squirming with a sense of injustice.

He lowered himself into the wheelbarrow again and brooded in silence. It was too late to turn back now. Having elected to travel with the company, he was doomed to remain with them and watch his rival win more approval with each performance. Mussett had to be stopped in some way. Gill was still trying to work out how when he began to feel drowsy. He tried to shake himself awake. It was too early to retire to bed. He had neither undressed nor closed the shutters. Comfortable as he found it, he did not intend to spend the whole night in a wheelbarrow. Yet somehow he lacked both the strength and the willpower to move. His eyelids became heavy, his body sagged. Even the sound of merriment from the taproom could not keep him from dozing quietly off. The wheelbarrow that he had once derided was now a snug and consoling bed.

Hours later, he was still asleep, snoring up to heaven and dreaming of a time when his art was unrivalled and he was spoken of with awe. The dream did not last. Through the open window came a shape that merged with the darkness until it landed on Gill's chest. Sharp claws suddenly dug into his flesh and the creature let out a fearsome shriek. Gill came awake to find himself wrestling with a large black cat that seemed to be trying to scratch him to death. It was a desperate encounter. The struggle only ended when he managed to grab the animal by the nape of the neck and hurl it out through the window. As soon as he got his breath back, Gill spat out the name of his tormentor.

'Giddy Mussett!'

Chapter Eight

Nicholas Bracewell was heartened by the response from the company. Although they had celebrated into the night, the actors were up the next day to eat an early breakfast before helping to erect their stage in the yard of the Star Inn. The scenery and properties needed for rehearsal had to be unloaded from the wagons. Since *Cupid's Folly* involved a dance around a maypole, they had to practise setting up the pole in the swiftest and safest way. Even the principal members of the company took their turn with the various duties. Touring with a theatre troupe abolished distinctions between sharers and hired men. All were expected to take on whatever tasks were required of them, however menial they might be. Edmund Hoode, playwright and actor, made no complaint as he set out benches in the galleries. Owen Elias thrived on physical labour. Of the sharers, only Lawrence Firethorn was missing from the work party.

Nicholas was pleased to see the enthusiasm with which Giddy Mussett was going about his tasks. While he had joined the others in the taproom the previous night, he had neither drunk to excess nor become belligerent. A notorious lecher, he confined himself to a teasing remark to a tavern wench. There was no hint of the defiance that he had shown earlier to the book holder. Mussett was as buoyant as ever and his cheerfulness rubbed off on the others. A busy couple of hours seemed to fly past.

When the preparations were complete, Nicholas sent them off to take a rest before the rehearsal began. He was alone in the yard when the visitor arrived.

'Good morrow, Nick!' called a voice. 'Do you remember me?'

'Sebastian!' said Nicholas, turning to see a tall, thin, well-dressed man with an air of quiet prosperity about him. 'How could I forget the finest scrivener we ever had?'

'My hands are not as deft as they once were, I fear. Age takes its toll.'

'It has been kind to you.'

'And even kinder to Nick Bracewell.'

They shook hands warmly then stood back to appraise each other. Sebastian Frant was in his early fifties, slight of build and shy of manner. When he lived in London, he had worked for Westfield's Men for a number of years, copying out their plays with a meticulous skill so that their prompt books were both accurate and easy to read. Frant was a true friend to the company, supporting them whenever they played. Nicholas and the others were disappointed when he retired to Kent.

'Where do you live now, Sebastian?' asked Nicholas.

'In a tiny village not far from Dover.'

'We play in Dover in due course.'

'You've also played here, I learn,' said Frant. 'Had I known, I would have come to watch you. I will certainly hope to see *Cupid's Folly* for, judging by the maypole, that is the comedy you intend to present here.'

Nicholas smiled. 'How did you guess?'

'I copied out every word of the play, including its songs.'

'And earned my undying thanks. No hand is clearer or neater.'

Frant flexed his fingers. 'If only that were still the case!'

'What brings you here?'

'What else but the news that Westfield's Men are in Maidstone? My daughter and I are staying with some friends in Bearsted, close by the town.'

'I did not realise that you were married.'

'Nor am I any longer,' said Frant sadly. 'My wife died three years ago.' He smiled fondly. 'But I have my daughter to comfort me now. She is a joyous companion. Thomasina is truly a gift from God.'

'How old is she?'

'Barely nineteen.'

'Will we get to meet the young lady?'

'Thomasina will insist upon it,' said Frant. 'We arrived too late to watch your performance last evening but will not miss *Cupid's Folly*. How long will you stay in Maidstone?'

'Until tomorrow.'

'Whither will you go?'

'First to Faversham,' said Nicholas, 'then on to Canterbury. From there, we travel to Dover where you may chance to see us again.'

'I'll hope to watch you before then, Nick. I've a brother in Faversham whom I've not seen for a while. He may well find that he has guests for a day or two.'

'It will be comforting to have a good friend in the audience.'

'Westfield's Men make friends wherever they go.'

'Not of your quality, Sebastian. You understand our work.'

'I understand how difficult it is,' said Frant, 'because I've seen how much effort goes into each performance. What I do not understand is how you can so willingly bind yourselves to such an uncertain occupation, at the mercy of things over which you have no control. Winter exiles you from your inn yard theatre, plague can expel you from London altogether. And there are other perils to face at every turn.' He gave a polite shrug. 'Why do you do it, Nick?'

'I wish I knew.'

'Do the rewards outweigh the hazards?'

'Most of the time.'

'I admire you all,' said Frant seriously. 'You take risks that I would not even dare to consider. I chose a quiet, safe, dull, uneventful life. I am too cowardly to do what actors do, Nick. You show true bravery.'

Nicholas gave a wry smile. 'Is it bravery or folly?'

'The two are closely allied.'

'We've learnt that, Sebastian. But come and meet the others,' he added, patting Frant on the arm. 'There are many in the company who still remember you.'

'Edmund and Lawrence, I hope.'

'Westfield's Men would die without them.'

'And Barnaby. If you play *Cupid's Folly*, you must travel with Barnaby Gill.'

'He's here,' said Nicholas, 'but not to play Rigormortis. An affray at the Queen's Head sent us out on the road. Barnaby's leg was broken in the commotion.'

Frant was alarmed. 'A broken leg?' he repeated. 'What a cruel blow to a man with such nimble feet. How did it happen?'

'Let him tell you the story himself, Sebastian.'

'I long to hear it.'

'First, be warned. Barnaby is in a truculent mood.'

'A broken leg would make anyone truculent.'

'It is not the leg that irks him but a black cat.'

'A black cat?' echoed Frant. 'Is not that a sign of good fortune?'

'Not in this case. That's his complaint.'

'This is not a request, Lawrence. It's a demand. Giddy must be dismissed forthwith.'

'When he has proved himself such a boon to us?'

'He's no boon to me,' growled Barnaby Gill. 'He's a curse.'

'Everyone else loves the man.'

'They have not been entombed in a foul privy!'

'Calm down, Barnaby.'

'They have not been attacked by a wild cat in the middle of the night. If Giddy Mussett had done either of those things to *them*, they'd take a different view of him.'

'But he did neither of those things to *you*,' said Lawrence Firethorn.

'He did, he did.'

'Nick Bracewell swears the man is innocent.'

'Then he conspires against me.'

'Giddy shared a room with Nick and Edmund. At the time when a cat came in through your window, Giddy was fast asleep.'

'Only after he'd tossed the animal in on top of me.'

'How could he? Nick vouches for him. He never left their room.'

'Then Nick is lying through his teeth.'

'I beg leave to doubt that, Barnaby,' said Frant, standing in the doorway. 'Nick Bracewell is as honest as the day is long. He would not lie to anyone.'

'Sebastian!' cried Firethorn, pounding him on the shoulder by way of a welcome. 'It's good to see you again after all this time. What brings you here?'

'I've come to defend Nick against vile accusations.'

'I can do that for myself,' said Nicholas, who had entered the taproom with him. He turned to Gill, who was seated in a chair. 'You have my sympathy for what happened last night. It must have been a shock to you. But do not blame Giddy Mussett.'

Gill was still enraged. 'I blame the pair of you.'

'Then you must blame Edmund, Dick Honeydew and the other apprentices as well for all of them shared the room with Giddy. The six of us will take our Bible oath that he did not stir from his mattress.'

'He must have. Who else would hurl a cat on top of me?'

'Could not the cat have jumped in on his own?' suggested Nicholas. 'They are famed for their curiosity. An open window was an invitation he could not refuse.'

'There,' said Firethorn. 'That's your answer, Barnaby. This cat took a liking to you and wished to sleep in your arms. Enough of your protests, man. Do you not recognise an old friend standing here?'

'I am sorry to hear of your plight, Barnaby,' said Frant pleasantly.

'Which one?' replied Gill. 'They come upon me daily.'

'Nick talked of an affray at the Queen's Head.'

'It was more than that, Sebastian. It was vicious assault on me. When they could not take my life, they broke my leg instead. I believe that Giddy Mussett may have been behind that outrage as well. He had me removed so that he could usurp my place.'

'This is lunacy,' said Firethorn. 'Ignore him, Sebastian. When the riot broke out, the man Barnaby accuses was locked up in the King's Bench Prison.'

Frant was interested. 'Tell me more. Who caused the affray?'

'My enemies,' wailed Gill.

'It was not simply an attack on you, Barnaby,' scolded Firethorn.

'Then why is my leg in a splint?'

'We were all victims that day,' said Nicholas. 'Westfield's Men were robbed of their home and a murder was committed in the gallery.'

'Murder?' gasped Frant.

'During the tumult, a friend of Lord Westfield's was stabbed to death.'

'Can this be true? A spectator *killed* while watching a play?'

'Felled by an assassin who was biding his time.'

'These are dreadful tidings. Who was the man?'

'His name was Fortunatus Hope.'

'Newly come to London and part of our patron's circle,' said Firethorn.

'Before that,' added Nicholas, 'he was an acquaintance of Lord Conway's.'

Frant shook his head. 'He was much more than an acquaintance, Nick,' he explained. 'Conway's Men have played in Dover a few times and I have met their patron more than once. I am sure that he introduced me to a Fortunatus Hope last year. It is not a name that one forgets.'

'And you say that he is much more than an acquaintance?'

'Yes,' said Frant. 'He was Lord Conway's nephew.'

Rehearsals of *Cupid's Folly* took up all of the morning and most of the afternoon. The performance was not due to begin until early evening when people had finished their work for the day and could allow themselves some entertainment. The play was a staple drama in the repertoire of Westfield's

Men and that was one of the arguments in favour of staging it at the Star Inn. So familiar was it to the actors that many scenes needed scant rehearsal. The bulk of the time could therefore be devoted to the sections that involved Giddy Mussett. Aided by Nicholas, he had conned the part well but his grasp on the character was still unsure. Rigormortis was a longer and more complex role than that of Bedlam and, while there were shared values between them, there were also significant differences. It was left to the book holder to explain what those differences were.

One aspect of the play was mastered instantly by Mussett. Shunned by Dorinda, a beautiful shepherdess, Rigormortis urged his suit again and chased her around the stage so wildly that he blundered into a conical beehive. Immediately, he was attacked by a swarm of angry bees. In an effect devised by Nicholas, he knocked over the hive, tossed a handful of black pepper into the air to suggest the swarm, then jumped, twitched and smacked himself as the bees, apparently, stung him all over. The actors had seen Barnaby Gill play the scene so often that it had ceased to divert them but Mussett's version made them hoot and clap. Once again, Gill did not share their approval. He watched from his room, writhing with a mixture of envy and regret.

They were emotions experienced by Lawrence Firethorn as well. Even from casual observers who wandered into the yard, Rigormortis was getting more response than Lord Hayfever, the role taken by Firethorn. He envied the clown's capacity to amuse with a gesture or gain a laugh with a facial expression, and he began to regret the selection of a play that cast him in a subordinate role for once. At the same time, he was forced to admire Mussett's extraordinary skills. For a man who had never seen the play before, he was making exceptional progress. It remained to be seen if he could sustain that progress in front of an audience.

The success of *A Trick To Catch A Chaste Lady* brought spectators flocking to the inn. Lucas Broome and his wife were among them but this was no formal occasion for the civic worthies and their families. The warm, dry evening lured people from all levels of society. Gatherers had been hired to take money at the door. The mayor and his party were allowed in free but everyone else was charged and they paid willingly. Most of those who came were happy to stand in the yard in front of the stage. By paying extra, people could also occupy the benches in the gallery and make their stay even more comfortable by hiring a cushion. Refreshments were on sale, carried around on trays by servingmen. The beaming Jonathan Jowlett, who took his own seat in the gallery, stood to make a handsome profit from the performance.

Westfield's Men were delighted with the huge audience that they attracted. It was almost as if they were back at the Queen's Head. That was their natural home. They had performed at The Theatre and The Curtain, the two playhouses in Shoreditch, and they had trodden the boards at The Rose, the new Bankside theatre, but they preferred their inn yard to all other venues. The Star Inn suited them much more than the Lower Courthouse. Given the number of country folk in the audience, *Cupid's Folly*, with its pastoral setting and rustic humour, was an ideal choice. Up in the gallery, Sebastian Frant explained the plot to his daughter, Thomasina, but took care to give nothing away that would spoil the recurring surprises that made the piece so popular. Thomasina, who had inherited both her father's intelligence and his reserve, was an attractive young woman in a pale blue dress, who sat upright with her hands folded in her lap. Like everyone else in the yard, she was gripped by a sense of anticipatory pleasure.

Cupid's Folly did not let them down. From the moment he entered as Lord Hayfever, the pompous landowner, Firethorn held sway over the spectators. Females of all ages craned their necks to get a closer look at the striking figure in his finery. There was abundant romance as well as humour and Edmund Hoode, in a part he had written for himself, was very touching as a lovesick shepherd. It was a role that mirrored a private life that was littered with rejection and unrequited passion. Owen Elias shone as a rapacious farmer while James Ingram was the dashing hero who elopes with the farmer's daughter and rescues her from parental tyranny. The rest of the company supported the principals loyally.

Rigormortis was the only disappointment. Mussett collected plenty of laughs and his encounter with the beehive earned him an ovation but he was tentative with his lines and uncertain about his movements. It was only when he was on stage alone, dancing, singing or jesting with the audience that he really blossomed. The play concluded with a spirited dance around the maypole that had been set up in the middle of the stage. All the characters joined in and the collisions between Lord Hayfever and Rigormortis were a source of continual hilarity as their respective ribbons became hopelessly intertwined. When Firethorn brought the play to an end with a rhyming couplet, applause reverberated around the yard. This time, he knew, his position as the star had not been threatened by the clown. Mussett had been merely good where he might have been superb. Conscious that he would once more be the cynosure, Firethorn was lavish in his praise.

'You excelled yourself, Giddy,' he said, as they left the stage.

'I made too many mistakes.'

'Nobody noticed a single one of them.'

'I did,' said Mussett, 'and I'm sure that Barnaby did as well.'

'Let's go back out and drink the sweet nectar of applause.'

As Firethorn swept out on stage the whole cast followed to bask in the acclaim. Mussett smiled as broadly and bowed as low as any of them but he was not content.

'I need something stronger to drink than this,' he murmured.

Nicholas Bracewell had controlled the performance from behind the scenes but his work was not over when the play had run its course. While the actors changed out of their apparel in the room that was used as their tiring-house, Nicholas had to gather up the properties, put the costumes back in their baskets and, with the help of George Dart, clear the stage. Once that was done, and when the crowd had dispersed, they could begin the process of dismantling it. Nicholas was heaving one of the boards off its trestle when a shadow fell across him. He turned to see the bulky frame of Pieter Hendrik standing there. The weaver was still chuckling at what he had seen.

'Fery gut, Niklaus,' he said. 'Fery funny.'

'Thank you for coming.'

'The pleasure, it is mine. I like it more than the others.'

'Is that because we did not steal your cloth like Conway's Men?'

'No, no. Wistfield's Men is gooder than them. I like fery much.'

'I'll pass on your comments to Master Firethorn.'

'Ah, yis,' said Hendrik, his memory jogged. 'Something else you pass on, please.' He took a letter from his pocket and handed it to Nicholas. 'This you give to Anne, will you?'

'When we get back to London,' said Nicholas. 'And if we do catch up with Conway's Men, I'll be sure to mention your name.'

'Yis, yis. They owe much money. Thank you.'

After shaking Nicholas's hand, Hendrik ambled off with happier memories of a theatre troupe. *Cupid's Folly* would make him smile all the way back to Mill Street. As one contented playgoer left, two more came over to the book holder. Sebastian Frant introduced his daughter then gave his own verdict.

'You could not have chosen a better play for the occasion, Nick,' he said.

'That is what we felt.'

'I expected to miss Barnaby Gill but your new clown filled his place admirably. The man was familiar. Did I not see him once with Conway's Men?'

'With them, with Rutland's Men, with Banbury's Men, even with Viscount Havelock's company, for a short time. Giddy has played with them all.'

'I'm glad that he's added Westfield's Men to his list.'

'As are we, Sebastian,' said Nicholas. He smiled at Thomasina. 'I hope that you enjoyed the performance as much as your father.'

'Yes, I did,' she said demurely.

'Who caught your eye? Rigormortis? Or did you prefer Lord Hayfever?'

'I like them both, sir, but I loved the shepherd even more. He sighed so.'

'That was Edmund Hoode,' said Frant. 'You must meet him, Thomasina.'

'I would like that, Father.' Her eyes flicked to Nicholas. 'I am told that you are the most important person in the company.'

'Oh, no,' replied Nicholas, 'that is too gross a claim.'

'Not in my opinion,' said Frant. 'The actors would be helpless without you behind the scenes. You all but run the company. Who pays the rent to the Queen's Head on behalf of them? Nick Bracewell. Who employs a scrivener like me to produce a neat copy of a new play? Nick Bracewell. Who keeps all the play books safe? Who collects all the money from the gatherers at the door? Who devises many of the tricks that are used on stage? And who spreads contentment among the others simply by being there?'

Nicholas was modest. 'Your father overstates his case,' he said.

'I think not,' she said. 'He was close to Westfield's Men at one time.'

'It was a sad day when we had to lose him, Miss Frant.'

'Come,' said Frant. 'There are plenty of scriveners in London.'

'But none with anything to rival your experience, Sebastian. Before you came to us, you held an exalted position.'

Frant gave a wan smile. 'Hardly that, Nick! I was secretary to the Clerk of the Privy Council. Have you any idea how tedious it is to copy out edicts and statutes and memoranda? I all but died of boredom,' he went on. 'Working for a theatre company was excitement itself after that. When I first set eyes on *Cupid's Folly*, I could not stop laughing, and that was before it ever graced a stage.'

He broke off as Firethorn and Elias came striding out of the tiring-house. Both had changed out of their costumes but they still cut an impressive figure. Holding a position in the middle of the stage, Firethorn gazed at Thomasina.

'Where have you been hiding this divine creature, Sebastian?' he asked. 'This surely cannot be your daughter. She is too beautiful to be sired by humankind.'

Thomasina blushed. 'Thank you, sir,' she said, bowing her head.

'Well,' said Elias, staring at her. 'Introduce us to this angel, Sebastian.'

Frant did as he was bidden and both men claimed the privilege of kissing her hand. Nicholas observed how unused she was to flattery. Some of their fulsome comments brought a fresh tinge of colour to her cheeks. He stepped in to fend off any further embarrassment for her.

'I think that you have not watched a theatre troupe very often, Miss Frant.'

'Not at all,' she confessed. 'I did not know what to expect.'

'Why have you neglected your daughter's education, Sebastian?' asked Firethorn. 'You should have taken her to every play that you could.'

'Opportunities to do that are few in number,' said Frant. 'Conway's Men have been to Dover but they are nothing beside you. I'd not make Thomasina sit through their barren performances.'

'Giddy Mussett has a low opinion of them as well,' noted Elias.

'So does Pieter Hendrik,' said Nicholas. 'A weaver in the town who supplied them cloth that they took without paying.'

Frant nodded. 'They've made many enemies in Kent, I fear.'

'Unlike your lovely daughter,' said Firethorn, inclining his head towards her in a token bow. 'Thomasina will only ever leave admirers in her wake.'

After praising the performances of both men, Frant decided that it was time to leave but he promised to watch the company perform in Faversham, and his daughter was eager to see them again as well. As the visitors walked out of the yard, Nicholas waved to their old scrivener. All that his companions could see was the daughter.

'*Diu!*' exclaimed Elias. 'Have you ever seen such a lovely face as hers?'

'Forget her, Owen,' warned Firethorn with a grin. 'Thomasina is *mine*.'

'Edmund was her choice in the play,' Nicholas told them.

Firethorn was aghast. 'What? A lovelorn shepherd is preferred over me?'

'At least, it was not Rigormortis,' said Elias with a laugh. He looked around. 'By the way, where is Giddy? We need to celebrate.'

'Was he not in the tiring-house with you?' asked Nicholas.

'No, Nick. He left some time ago. I thought he came out here.'

Nicholas sensed trouble. Mussett was on the loose.

The Black Eagle was a tavern that was situated down an alley that led off the High Street. It was a low, ugly, lopsided building with an air of dilapidation about it. Even in broad daylight, the interior was dark and gloomy. There was a musty smell that was intensified by the tobacco smoke that curled up from a dozen pipes. Yet when Giddy Mussett stepped over the threshold, he breathed in deeply as if inhaling fresh air. The fetid atmosphere of the Black Eagle was like the breath of life to him. The taproom was almost full, every table occupied by shadowy figures playing with dice or cards. Mussett ordered a tankard of ale and quaffed half of it in a single guzzled mouthful. Then his eyes became accustomed to the fug. Having slaked his thirst, he wanted pleasure. He went through into the smaller room at the back and saw Bess Roundel, sitting beside a bearded man who was playing familiarly with her hair. Mussett strolled over to them.

'Good even, Mistress Roundel,' he said, raising his tankard to her.

'Giddy!' she cried with delight.

'Get rid of that foul toad beside you.'

'Who is this?' demanded the bearded man, glaring at Mussett. 'Bess is mine for the night and I'll stand no interference.'

'If you'd interfere with Bess, then I'll interfere with you, sir.'

'Away with you, you pie-faced rogue.'

Mussett tossed the remains of his ale in the man's face then struck him on the head with the tankard. Before he could recover, a flurry of punches hit him from all angles and the man slumped off his chair and on to the floor. A ragged cheer went up from the others in the room. Bess looked alarmed but Mussett cackled in triumph.

'Come,' he said, grabbing her by the hand. 'He'll not be needing you now.'

'I can see why Sebastian never mentioned his daughter before,' said Firethorn. 'He wanted to keep the girl away from temptation.'

'*You* sound like the one who is tempted, Lawrence,' remarked Edmund Hoode.

'As never before.'

'Is this the moment to remind you that you are a married man?'

'Marriage vows dissolve in the face of so much beauty.'

'Sebastian is our friend,' said Nicholas. 'For his sake, you must not even consider such a thing. The girl is young and innocent.'

'Youth, innocence and beauty. Thomasina has all three.'

'So did Margery when you first met her,' Hoode reminded him.

They were sitting in a corner of the taproom in the Star Inn, enjoying a drink as they reflected on the performance they had just given and looked forward to the one they would next offer. Barnaby Gill would have sat in on such a discussion as a rule but he had withdrawn to his room once more.

'Who *did* throw that cat on to Barnaby's chest?' wondered Firethorn.

'Not me,' said Hoode. 'Barnaby has endured enough as it is.'

'Are we certain that it was not Giddy?'

'Yes. Nick and I retired to the room with him. He did not leave it at all.'

'He's nimble enough to have climbed through the window,' said Firethorn. 'We all saw that fall he pretended to have at the White Hart.'

Nicholas was not persuaded. 'I locked the shutters

myself. They creaked with age. Giddy could not have opened them without rousing the whole room.'

'Well, someone did the deed. Barnaby had scratches on his face.'

'What hurts him more are the scratches on his reputation.'

'Did he watch us this evening?' asked Hoode.

'Yes,' said Nicholas, 'but it was more punishment than pleasure for him. The sight of Giddy as Rigormortis must have curdled his blood but he had some compensation. Good as he was, Giddy came nowhere near Barnaby in the role.'

'That's why I think we should let the people of Faversham see the play,' said Firethorn, pleased at the way he had dominated the performance. 'It will soothe Barnaby's feelings. However many times he dances around the maypole, Giddy will never threaten him as Rigormortis.'

'He will as Bedlam,' argued Hoode. 'Giddy even put *you* in the shade at the Lower Courthouse. I say that we play *A Trick To Catch A Chaste Lady* again.'

Firethorn looked at Nick. 'You be the judge.'

'Neither would be my choice,' said Nicholas.

'Why not?'

'Because both place such a mighty weight on Giddy.'

'He has carried it lightly in both cases.'

'The effort is bound to tell on him. I'd choose a play that did not rest so much upon our clown. *Vincentio's Revenge* is one such piece. *The Loyal Subject* might be even better for our purposes.'

'But Giddy has already conned two parts,' said Hoode,

running a hand across his smooth chin. 'Why force him to learn a third?'

'We cannot offer a mere two plays, Edmund.'

'Even when they work so well?'

'We have a reputation to protect. Do you want the people of Kent to think of us as capable of nothing more than low comedies? Think of yourself. Do you wish to be remembered solely as the author of *Cupid's Folly* when we have finer dramas of yours to set before an audience?'

'Nick is right,' said Firethorn, adding more wine to his cup from the jug. 'We must be bold enough to show the very best of ourselves. *Vincentio's Revenge* enables us to do that. Giddy will have only a small part beside mine.'

'But he is a jewel we should polish up,' said Hoode.

'He'll have his chance to sparkle.'

'Yes,' said Nicholas, 'we have a long way to go yet, Edmund.' He sipped his wine. 'I wonder when we shall overtake Conway's Men.'

Firethorn inflated his chest. 'In all that matters, we overtook them years ago.'

'Sebastian said they had played in Dover and Rye.'

'And here in Maidstone,' said Hoode.

'Where does that leave? Rochester, perhaps? Faversham? Canterbury?'

'There's not room for two companies in one town.'

'Then we'll drive them out like dogs,' said Firethorn.

'Not until we have put some questions to them,' said Nicholas. 'I still feel they were implicated in the affray at the Queen's Head. Even if they were not there in person, they could have incited those young rascals. Then there is the murder to consider. Their patron's nephew betrays them by going over to Westfield's Men. I do not think Lord Conway would have sent best wishes to Fortunatus Hope.'

'Conway's Men are scoundrels!'

'But they'd stay their hand at murder, surely?' said Hoode.

'I'd believe anything of Tobias Fitzgeoffrey.'

'We need more proof,' said Nicholas solemnly, 'or our accusations are empty. Sebastian knows the county better than we. Let's ask him to find out where the company will next be. Then we can stalk them.'

Firethorn gave a ripe chuckle. 'I'd rather stalk Sebastian's daughter.'

'She's old enough to be your *own* child, Lawrence,' said Hoode.

The comment went unheard. Into the taproom had come three men, bearing the body of a third. They did not stand on ceremony. After flinging their burden down on the floor, they stamped out again. Nicholas was the first on his feet, horrified at what he saw. Lying flat on the floor, covered in blood, caked in filth and positively reeking of ale was Giddy Mussett. He raised himself up on one elbow.

'Who wants a fight?' he challenged.

Then he passed out.

Chapter Nine

When they set out early next morning, Westfield's Men were downcast. Maidstone had been kind to them. It had enabled them to stage two highly successful performances that had brought in the money that would help to pay for their tour. The Star Inn had been an amenable hostelry and they had warmed to the town itself. Yet they left the inn yard in a state of despondency. One reckless act threatened the future of their work. In the space of a couple of hours, Giddy Mussett had changed from being the saviour of the company into its potential destroyer. Having seen him at his best on stage, they now had a glimpse of Mussett at his worst. A drunken evening in the arms of a prostitute ended with a tavern brawl that he had almost certainly started. When he was dragged unceremoniously back to the Star and dumped in their midst, the actors were reminded how slender was the thread from which their continued success hung. On the slow journey to Faversham, their new clown provided no laughter.

Nicholas Bracewell was afflicted by pangs of guilt. He was the one who had advised that Mussett be employed and he had promised to keep the latter under control so that he would not indulge his well-known vices. Nicholas had failed in his duty. Mussett had sneaked off when the book holder's back was turned. He had been so badly beaten at the Black Eagle that he could not even make his own way back to his friends. It had fallen to Nicholas to clean the blood from his face and bind his wounds. A strip of linen around his head, Mussett now dozed in the back of the leading wagon, surrounded by George Dart and the four apprentices, who stared with horror at the bruised face and the hideously swollen lip. The clown was not the man he had once been. They felt that they had lost a friend in exchange for a troublesome stranger.

As if to match the mood of the travellers, steady drizzle was falling, moistening the backs of the horses and making the occupants of the wagons huddle together. Mussett was oblivious to it all, still trying to sleep off the effects of the beating. Every time that Nicholas glanced over his shoulder, he saw that the man lay in the same position with a weary smile on his battered face. What had happened at the Black Eagle on the previous night was not yet clear. While he was being doctored, Mussett was too inebriated to give a coherent account of events and Nicholas was determined to drag the truth out of him in due course. He had also come to an agreement with Owen Elias and Edmund Hoode that each of them in turn would keep their clown under observation. They could not risk another escapade like the one in Maidstone.

There was one source of consolation for Nicholas. After refusing even to consider the notion of using the wheelbarrow, Barnaby Gill had become reconciled to it. Except as an alternative bed, Gill had not actually used it but he consented to have it loaded on to the wagon with the rest of the baggage. Nicholas had every hope that he would soon agree to be moved about in the wheelbarrow, making it much easier for Dart to transport him from place to place, and, more importantly, keep him apart from his rival. Gill was the one person to derive pleasure from Mussett's fall from grace and he predicted that it would only be the first of many such lapses. Most of the actors were inclined to agree with him. It was largely up to Nicholas to confound the prophecy.

When Mussett finally opened his eyes, he looked up to see a lattice-work of branches above him as they passed through a small wood. The drizzle had stopped but not before it had bathed and soothed the wounds on his face. He saw the anxious eyes of the apprentices, staring down on him, and tried to give them a reassuring smile but his bruised jaw ached and his swollen lip throbbed violently. It was minutes before he worked out where he was and what had occurred during the preceding night. His conscience pricked him mercilessly. As soon as could summon up enough strength, he hauled himself up and clambered onto the seat beside Nicholas. They were back in open countryside now, wending their way along a twisting track that climbed a hill.

'Good morrow, Nick,' began Mussett.

'Ah,' said Nicholas. 'You have awakened at last.'

'And wished that I had not. I am in such pain.'

'So are we, Giddy. And the fault is yours. You brought disgrace upon us.'

'I know,' admitted Mussett. 'I owe you a thousand apologies.'

'They will not atone for the damage you have done,' said Nicholas pointedly. 'We rode into the town as one of London's leading theatre companies and we ride out with our reputation blemished. Instead of remembering us as the players that gave them *A Trick To Catch A Chaste Lady* and *Cupid's Folly*, they will always think of us the troupe with the drunken clown. You were fortunate not to spend the night behind bars.'

'I was attacked, Nick.'

'Where?'

'At the Black Eagle.'

'Had you been with us at the Star, no harm would have befallen you.'

'I needed to get away to celebrate.'

'By getting drunk and picking a fight?'

'No, Nick,' said Mussett. 'I thought to spend an hour with a friend, that is all. Bess is good company. I love you all but I miss the touch of a woman. So it was that I sought Bess out and rescued her from some bearded oaf with groping hands. When I came back downstairs, he was sitting there with friends, calling me foul names and hurling insults that could not be borne. I knocked him from his chair.'

'In other words, *you* started the brawl.'

'His lewd taunts did that.'

'Your hot temper was to blame, Giddy.'

'His friends set upon me, all three of them.'

Nicholas turned to him. 'What encouragement did you give?'

'None beyond a few remarks.'

'Taunts and curses, more like.'

'They did not frighten me, Nick. I had to show them that.'

'So you provoked them instead,' said Nicholas. 'No wonder they assaulted you. If you punch their friend and call them vile names, what do you expect?'

Mussett forced a smile. 'I expected to win.'

'You are lucky that you survived, Giddy. Others might have left you for dead or hurled you into the river. And how did they know where you were staying?' asked Nicholas, eyes back on the road ahead. 'My guess is that this friend of yours must have told them.'

'Yes, I think she did. When they stopped kicking me, I heard Bess mention the Star.' He winced aloud and felt his side. 'My ribs are wondrous sore this morning.'

'It's no more than you deserve,' said Nicholas coldly.

'Am I to have no sympathy at all?'

'It's reserved for Westfield's Men. The landlord thought us welcome customers until you were brought in like that. It changed his opinion. Jonathan Jowlett was glad to see the back of us today. I daresay he was relieved that you started the brawl elsewhere and not at the Star Inn.'

'That bearded rogue was to blame.'

'No,' said Nicholas firmly, '*you* were. And it's not the first time, is it?'

'It's the first time since I joined Westfield's Men.'

'First and last, Giddy.'

'I swear it!'

'Your word is easily given, and just as easily forgotten.'

'Fists and feet reminded me of that last night,' said Mussett with contrition. 'Because I forgot my oath to you, I was justly punished. My face is on fire and my body aches as if a herd of cattle trample over it.' He put a hand on Nicholas's arm. 'Forgive me, Nick. I'll make amends.'

'How?'

'By taking a vow of abstinence that I mean to keep.'

'That will not wipe away the memory of last night.'

'Then I'll do more.'

'What more is there?'

'There must be *something*,' said Mussett, casting round for a way to regain his approval. 'Something that will prove to Westfield's Men how much I value what they did for me. I have it!' he announced, smacking his knee. 'I'll help you to find the killer of Fortunatus Hope. Only I can do that, Nick. If Conway's Men are involved in any way, I can tell you for sure.'

Nicholas was interested. 'Go on.'

'We know that they are in the county and may not be far away.'

'Sebastian Frant has offered to find out where they are.'

'When he does,' said Mussett, desperate to impress, 'send me off to them. Tobias would hate to see me again but I still have friends among Conway's Men. One, in particular, owes me a great favour. He has no love for Tobias Fitzgeoffrey. If there is scandal to report, I'll hear it from him.'

'We could never trust you enough to let you out of our sight.'

'Then come with me, Nick. Or give me another companion to watch over me. If you seek the truth about Master Hope's death, this is the best way to find it.' He gave a crooked smile. 'Will this win back your good opinion of me?'

'No,' said Nicholas bluntly, 'but it will prove that you are in earnest.'

Lawrence Firethorn called a halt near a large pond so that they could have a rest and water the horses. Edmund Hoode's donkey was the first to trot to the edge of the pond, its loud bray scattering the ducks that had been floating around in search of food. Now that the drizzle had abated, the sun peeped grudgingly through the clouds to show the travellers what beautiful countryside they were passing through. Apple orchards stood off to their left. On a farm to their right, pears, plums and cherries were grown. The soil was rich and the climate benevolent. Kent was a truly county of abundance. Like other visitors from London, Westfield's Men felt that the cows were much larger, the poultry much finer and the sheep much fatter than those raised on the fringes of the capital. Unwilling to leave the Queen's Head, they were finding that travel had its compensations.

After leading his horse to water, Firethorn had a quiet word with Nicholas.

'What does he have to say for himself?' he asked.

'Giddy is full of penitence.'

'He was too full of ale last night. There's nothing penitential about that.'

'I taxed him with his folly.'

'What of his injuries?'

'Good fortune attended him,' said Nicholas. 'Nothing was broken, apart from his promise to us, but he'll be in pain for some time. Giddy is a strong man. Others would not recover so quickly from such a beating.'

'He'll get another from me if he lets us down again.'

'You'll not lack for helpers.'

Nicholas looked in Mussett's direction. Squatting at the edge of the water, he was dabbing a wet cloth gingerly on his face. Everyone else had turned away from him. There was no happy banter. It was as if the others were pretending that he was not there.

'He'll not play Bedlam in that condition,' said Firethorn.

'Nor Rigormortis. Those dances are well beyond him. His legs are black with bruises and make him stagger rather than walk.'

'Our choice is made for us, Nick. *Vincentio's Revenge*, it shall be in Faversham.'

'Or *The Loyal Subject*,' argued Nicholas. 'It gives him less to learn.'

'Watch him closely.'

'I will.'

'Acquaint him with the degree of my anger,' said Firethorn.

'I think he knows that.'

'Then keep him out of my reach or I'll not be able to reign in my temper.'

'That was Giddy's offence. He was too choleric.'

'I like drink and women as much as any man,' confessed Firethorn. 'And, yes, I can be choleric on occasion. But I'd never let my weaknesses put Westfield's Men in danger. For that is what he did.'

When they set off again, Nicholas relinquished the lead to the wagon that bore Barnaby Gill and some of the other actors. He was content to bring up the rear, letting someone else control the pace and direction for a change. Mussett kept trying to ingratiate himself with the apprentices but they were on their guard against him. Even Dart, who had giggled ridiculously before at all of the clown's jests, was wary of him. Nicholas drove the wagon and chatted to Hoode, who rode alongside him on his donkey. They were no more than a dozen yards behind the wagon in front of them.

The road to Faversham was full of undulations. The ascent of a hill might slow them down but they quickened on the long descent. When they crested yet another rise, they saw a stream at the bottom of the slope. Fringed with trees and bushes, the fast-flowing water rippled over a stone bed and glistened in the sunshine. The only way to cross the stream was by means of a ford. It was no more than twenty feet wide but it was surprisingly deep, as Firethorn discovered when he spurred his horse across. Water reached above the animal's knees. To get the wagons across, the load had to be lightened. All but Barnaby Gill and the driver jumped out and waded behind the first wagon, putting their shoulders to it to help it over the uneven surface. Rocked and bounced across the stream, Gill complained bitterly about the pain in his broken leg.

Two wagons got safely across and continued on their way. Since he was much heavier than the clown, Nicholas asked Mussett to take over the reins so that he could lend his strength to that of the others as they shoved from behind. Hoode rode alongside and exhorted them to greater efforts. They were in the middle of the stream when the ambush occurred. Without warning, three hooded figures suddenly came out of the bushes on horseback. Splashing through the water, they headed straight for the wagon. Two of them brandished swords but the third had a rope that he was twirling in the air. The donkey was so alarmed by their approach that it bucked wildly and dislodged its rider. Hoode was still flailing around in the water as the attackers closed in.

Nicholas drew his sword and stood protectively in front of the apprentices. As one of the men thrust his weapon at him, the book holder parried it skilfully before jabbing hard to open a small wound in his arm. Furious at the resistance, the rider brought the flank of his horse around to buffet Nicholas then lashed at him with renewed vigour. As he fought one man off, Nicholas kept an eye the other two. They had ridden straight for Mussett, one trying to dislodge him from his seat by throwing the rope around him while the other hacked at him with his sword. Mussett shed all of his stiffness. Faced with a battle for his life, he proved as lithe and cunning as ever. He dodged the rope and leapt into the rear of the wagon, grabbing a stool from among the stage properties to fend off the flashing sword, and somehow keeping his balance as the wagon continued to bump its way through the water.

One of the attackers was soon put to flight. When Nicholas parried a second thrust, he responded so swiftly with his own that he slit his adversary's wrist and forced him to drop his sword. Abandoning the field, the man wheeled his horse round so that he could splash his way out of the water and gallop off along the road to Maidstone. His confederates were not far behind him. The noise of the ambush had roused Firethorn and Elias into action. Pulling out their swords, they kicked their horses into a canter to come to the aid of their friends. The attackers saw that their cause was hopeless. In a last vain attempt to strike at Mussett, the man with the rope took out a dagger and hurled it at him but the clown was ready, lifting the stool as a shield and letting the point of the weapon sink into it. As his assailant tried to escape, Mussett hurled the stool at him and caught him a glancing blow on the side of the head.

The ambush was over. Before Firethorn and Elias

reached them, the two hooded figures fled in the direction of their accomplice. The apprentices were shivering, Dart was whimpering and Hoode, who had finally regained his feet, was spitting out water and wondering what had happened to his donkey. By the time that Firethorn and Elias had established that nobody was hurt, it was too late to go in pursuit. Mussett was grinning with exhilaration, feeling that his prompt action would earn him some admiration. Nicholas was puzzled by the fact the attackers had made for the clown.

'Who were they?' asked Elias.

'The three rogues who beat me at the Black Eagle,' said Mussett, retrieving the stool from the water. 'They came to finish what they started last night.'

'Is that what happened, Nick?'

'I am not sure,' replied Nicholas. 'But one thing is certain.'

'What is that?' said Firethorn.

'Someone does not wish us to play in Faversham.'

After travelling by a different route and at a faster pace, Sebastian Frant and his daughter arrived in Faversham well before the actors. They first called at the cottage where Frant's brother and his wife lived, and where they were given a cordial welcome. David Frant, a frail old man with a tonsure of snowy hair, now retired from a lifetime's involvement in the manufacture of gunpowder, was in poor health. He was surprised and delighted to see his younger brother and his niece. Not having met for over six months, they all had much gossip to trade but Frant eventually excused himself. Leaving Thomasina with her uncle and aunt, he went off into the town to make some enquiries on behalf of Westfield's Men. By the time that the three wagons finally rolled into the town, he had the information that Nicholas wanted. He met the company in the square.

'Welcome to Faversham!' he said.

'Thank you, Sebastian,' replied Firethorn, dismounting from his horse. 'We are fortunate to get here unscathed. Highwaymen attacked us not five miles away.'

Frant's face puckered with concern. 'Highwaymen?'

'Three of the villains.'

'What did they take?'

'They seemed to be after blood rather than money. They went away with neither.'

'Thank heaven for that!'

'Nick Bracewell and Giddy Mussett were the heroes. They fought them off.'

'I rejoice to hear it,' said Frant. 'Kent is a lovely county but it has its share of highwaymen, alas. No road is entirely safe. Thomasina and I travelled with a larger party to get here. We would never dare to ride such a distance alone.'

Firethorn beamed. 'How is that pretty daughter of yours, Sebastian?'

'Very well. She stays with my brother and his wife.'

'I trust that we'll have the pleasure of seeing her again.'

'Yes, Lawrence. She was much taken with the play last evening. Thomasina will want to see anything that you present here.'

'I long to know her better.'

Other members of the company had now dismounted or climbed out of their respective wagons. Those who knew him came to exchange greetings with Frant. He recommended an inn where they could stay and where he had already established that sufficient accommodation was available. Before they set off, Nicholas contrived a word alone with their former scrivener.

'Do you hear any word of Conway's Men?' he asked.

'Yes, Nick.'

'Were they in Faversham?'

'Barely a week ago,' said Frant. 'They are now settled in Canterbury and mean to stay there for a few days more.'

'This is excellent news, Sebastian. I had not hoped they'd be so close.'

'A good horse will get there in an hour or so.'

'We'll need two for Giddy Mussett will come with me.'

'Giddy?'

'He played with Conway's Men and still has friends in the company.'

As Nicholas was speaking, Mussett came round the angle of a wagon. Frant saw the bruises on the clown's face and the bandage that poked out from beneath his cap. He also noted the wet attire.

'What a sorry sight!' he said. 'Is that the highwaymen's work?'

'No,' said Nicholas. 'Giddy brought that upon himself. He started a tavern brawl in Maidstone and came off worst. He is in disgrace with us.'

'I thought that Lawrence called him a hero.'

'His bravery is not in question, but it does not excuse his drunken behaviour.'

'He looks contrite enough now.'

'Giddy abused our trust. He knows how much we need him, Sebastian. He and Lawrence are the twin pillars on which all our plays rest. That gives him power and Giddy let that power overwhelm his other senses last night.'

'You'd certainly be lost without him,' said Frant. '*Cupid's Folly* would be empty indeed without its clown to dance his way to glory. But I hold you up,' he went on, seeing the others climbing on to the wagons. 'Go with them, Nick. You deserve refreshment after your journey. And Giddy Mussett looks as if he needs a long sleep.'

'That's more than we will get,' said Nicholas with a smile. 'From now on, we mean to watch him twenty-four hours a day, like misers poring over their gold.'

Faversham was an attractive town. With over four hundred houses, it was a thriving community that derived much of its prosperity from the fact that it was sited on a navigable branch of the River Swale. There was constant activity at the creek, where several ships and smaller vessels were moored. Goods of all kinds were imported while grain, shellfish and oysters were the major exports. On marshy land to the west, gunpowder was made, using imported saltpetre and sulphur along with charcoal from local woodland. Townsfolk like David Frant had helped to build up a proud reputation for the trade over the years. Fear of a Spanish invasion had not vanished with the defeat of the Armada a few years earlier. All of the larger towns in Kent were required to keep a ready supply of arms and ammunition so that any further naval attack could be repulsed. As a result, the demand for Faversham's gunpowder never flagged.

Nicholas Bracewell was pleased that they were staying at the Blue Anchor. Its nautical character appealed to someone who had spent his most impressionable years at sea. Situated close to the creek, the inn was large and full of a gnarled charm. The river and the nearby oyster-pits provided its kitchen with a range of fresh food. Nicholas once again decided where the various members of the company would sleep, reserving the best rooms, as always, for the sharers. Firethorn took charge of the apprentices so that Nicholas could occupy a small bedchamber with Owen Elias, Edmund Hoode and Giddy Mussett. With three of them watching over the clown, it was felt, his opportunities to go astray would be removed altogether. Mussett did not object to the new regimen. If anything, he seemed to welcome it. Injured during the brawl in Maidstone, he was also feeling the effects of the desperate struggle at the ford. At the earliest opportunity, he took to his bed.

It was early evening when Nicholas set out. Leaving his two friends to guard the sleeping clown, he went in search of a licence to perform in the town. Though he was in time to see the mayor, he was given nothing like the reception that he had enjoyed in Maidstone. Reginald Gilder had none of Lucas Broome's passion for the theatre. He was a stout man of middle height with a face that rarely lost its sour expression. Before he would even consider Nicholas's request, he demanded to see the company's patent and their licence to travel, complaining that they had already had a troupe in Faversham only a week before and they did not really need another. Patient and tactful, Nicholas argued their case and the mayor agreed to grant them permission to play. However, only one performance was allowed and that would not take place for a couple of days. When he left the town hall, Nicholas was resigned to the fact that Westfield's Men would be paid less than half the generous sum of five pounds that they had been given in the shire town.

He was about to report back to the Blue Anchor when he noticed two people whom he recognised. Sebastian Frant and his daughter were talking to a man farther down the street. It was only when they broke away that they saw Nicholas walking towards them. Thomasina was pleased to meet him again and eager to hear what the company intended to perform in Faversham.

'The decision has not yet been taken,' he said, 'but it will be neither of the plays that we offered in Maidstone.'

'I would willingly sit through *Cupid's Folly* again,' she said.

'So would I,' added Frant. 'Even though I know every last line of it.'

'Father says that you have many plays from which to choose.'

'Yes,' said Nicholas. 'We travel with costumes and scenery that can be used in a variety of ways. Comedy has been in request so far but I feel that tragedy may take the stage in Faversham.'

Thomasina smiled nervously. 'A tale of murder and intrigue?'

'With darker passions at work.'

'Then you have brought such a play to the right place,' observed Frant.

'Why?'

'Have you not heard tell of Arden of Faversham?'

'He that was killed by his wife and her lover? Yes,' said Nicholas. 'Everyone knows that story even though the case must be forty years old by now.'

'Almost exactly that, Nick. Walk with us down Abbey Street and I'll show you where the crime took place. Thomas Arden was once the mayor of the town.'

'I hope that he was a more affable one than the man who now holds the office.'

'Were you given short shrift by him?' asked Frant.

'Our work has had warmer embraces.'

'That does not surprise me. My brother, David, does not speak well of the new mayor. The man is too full of self-affairs. Still,' said Frant, indicating the direction, 'let us go this way.'

The two men walked along with Thomasina in between them. Though he was very interested to view the site of a notorious murder, Nicholas sensed reluctance on the girl's part. Eyes down, she had withdrawn into her shell. Abbey Street was a main thoroughfare that ran south from the square. It contained many of the finest houses in the town, some stone-built and others with timber frames, all combining to give an impression of unobtrusive affluence. Thomas Arden's house stood at the gateway of an abbey that had contained the tomb of King Stephen until the building perished during the Dissolution of the Monasteries. It was not a large property but its pleasant, half-timbered façade and its prime position suggested wealth and taste.

'Lust and gain,' noted Frant. 'Those were the evils that led to his murder.'

'He was obviously a rich man,' said Nicholas.

'Few in the town were richer, Nick. Not only was he involved in the distribution of confiscated church property such as the abbey that stood here, Thomas Arden was also Commissioner of Customs at the port here.'

'A lucrative post for a respected man.'

'It is a pity that his wife did not share that respect.'

They discussed the crime for a few minutes but Thomasina remained silent. As her father related the details of the murder, she seemed to be mildly distressed. When he glanced at her, Nicholas was shocked. There were tears in her eyes.

Giddy Mussett was revived by his nap. When he joined the others in the taproom of the Blue Anchor, he had regained some of his natural exuberance. Edmund Hoode, who had watched over him while he slept, was glad to be relieved of that particular duty. He could now relax with his friends. Mussett did his best to make his peace with the actors, openly admitting that he had been at fault and that they had every right to despise him for it. His apparent sincerity won them over slowly but there was one member of the company who stayed as hostile towards him as ever. Barnaby Gill began to taunt his rival.

'You should be grateful to those men,' he suggested.

'Grateful?' said Mussett. 'Because they gave me a sound beating?'

'They improved your face greatly with their fists. It is nowhere near as ugly as it was before. Strive to keep that appearance, Giddy. It becomes you.'

'Goad me and I'll improve *your* ugly visage, Barnaby.'

'Nothing could improve my face.'

'Except a mask.'

'Keep those two apart,' said Firethorn from the other end of the table. 'They are fellows in the same company, not fighting cocks with spurs on.'

'Let's watch the feathers fly,' urged Elias. 'My money rests on Giddy.'

'And mine on Barnaby,' said James Ingram.

Mussett shrugged. 'It's not a fair contest. I'll not fight with a man whose leg is broken and whose reputation is in tatters.'

'My reputation is impregnable,' said Gill, tossing his head.

'You did not see *A Trick To Catch A Chaste Lady*.'

'Giddy speaks true,' said Elias. 'His Bedlam was a magical creation.'

'The mayor told me that I was a finer clown than you.'

174

Gill curled a lip. 'What do country bumpkins know of such things?'

'Master Broome has seen you at the Queen's Head whenever he was in London. His judgement is above reproach. That's why he chose *me*.'

'You were never a true clown, Giddy. You are a vagabond.'

'I wear that title with pride.'

'All you could offer was the false lure of novelty.'

'That was preferred to the decaying skills of an old man.'

'I am not old!'

'Your body may still have vigour, but your mind has aged beyond recall.'

'At least, I *have* a mind,' responded Gill. 'You lack anything that might be taken as a brain. Dumb animals show more sense than you, for which of them would drink themselves into a stupor so that three men could beat them for sport?'

'I left my mark on them as well,' boasted Mussett.

'You've left one on this company and it's a hideous stain.'

'Do they still snarl at each other?' said Firethorn with annoyance. 'Knock their heads together, Owen, and let's have some harmony.'

Mussett raised both palms. 'No need of that,' he said, producing a broad smile that brought a stab of pain to his swollen lip. 'The fault is mine. Barnaby deserves my respect. And I think he needs it badly, for he'll get little of it elsewhere.'

Gill choked back a reply, angry that the others were now siding with Mussett. Earlier in the day, none of them would speak a civil word to him yet now he was winning their regard. It was aggravating and Gill could no longer bear it. He looked around the taproom for his beast of burden.

'George!'

'Yes, Master Gill,' replied Dart from a bench in the corner.

'Take me to my room.'

'The wounded dragon retires to its lair,' mocked Mussett.

'No more of that, Giddy,' scolded Hoode. 'You gave a promise to behave.'

'And so I have, Edmund.'

'Until the next contemptuous act,' said Gill, using the crutch to get upright. 'What will provoke it this time, Giddy? Female flesh, strong drink or your bellicose nature?'

'None of them, Barnaby. I am reformed.'

'Ha! You'll tell me next that the Thames has run dry and that the Archbishop of Canterbury has turned highway robber. Reformed, are you?' he asked, hopping out with Dart's assistance. 'You look the same pox-ridden botch of nature you've always been!'

Everyone expected Mussett to respond to the gibe but he put back his head and laughed aloud. Tension eased considerably with Gill's departure and Hoode was relieved. An altercation between the two clowns was something that had to be prevented. Apart from anything else, it encouraged the company to take sides and that would breed more antagonism. Hoode really wanted to believe that Mussett had now reformed. Watching the man carefully, he saw how abstemious he was. The others were drinking heavily but Mussett refused to touch any ale, contented simply to be back into the fold again and determined to honour his promises. When the book holder returned, Hoode would have good news to give to Nicholas Bracewell. He had done his duty. Going to the other end of the table, the playwright had a first glass of Canary wine with Firethorn. It had a delicious taste.

When he reached his room, Barnaby Gill flicked Dart away without a word of thanks. Once again the clown was housed on the ground floor. Seeing his predicament, the landlord of the Blue Anchor had cleared out a room at the rear of the property for him and put in a truckle bed, a chair, a small table and a chamber pot. The wheelbarrow was also part of the furniture, standing incongruously below the single window. The room had once been a scullery and it preserved many aromatic memories of its former use. As he sank into the wheelbarrow, Gill was no longer aware of its compound of smells. He was preoccupied with a question that blocked out all else. How could he get rid of Giddy Mussett? How could he expose the man as the impostor he felt him to be? Gill had hoped that Mussett might save him the trouble by making himself such a liability to the company that they would oust him of their own accord. Evidently, that would not happen. Had any other hired man been guilty of Mussett's reprehensible behaviour in Maidstone, he would have been dismissed instantly yet the obnoxious newcomer had been retained.

The person to blame, he concluded, was Nicholas Bracewell. Blind to the fact that he was reclining in a moveable couch that the book holder had worked hard to create for him, Gill persuaded himself that Nicholas was in league with Mussett against him. Who had brought the vagabond into the company even though it meant paying his debts in order to get him out of prison? Who had proclaimed Mussett's innocence when someone trapped Gill in the privy of a wayside inn? Who had absolved the clown for the second time when he was accused of tossing a cat through Gill's window? Nicholas Bracewell. Both outrages bore the hallmark of Giddy Mussett yet he was called to account for neither. That would only encourage him to inflict further humiliations on Gill. It was time to get his revenge. If nobody else would hound Mussett from the company, then Gill would have to do it himself. He began to speculate on the best means of doing it.

Deep in thought and simmering with anger, he was deaf to all sound. When the door inched open behind him, he was still devising harsh punishments for his rival. The attack was swift. A sack was dropped over Gill's head then a rope encircled his chest. Before he had stopped spluttering with shock, he found himself tied securely to the support at the back of the wheelbarrow. When he tried to yell for help, a handful of sack was pushed into his mouth and bound into position by a piece of cloth. Worse was to follow. Unable to move or protest, Gill found himself being wheeled out of the room and down a couple of stone steps. He was being abducted from the inn.

Nicholas Bracewell was away for much longer than he had anticipated. Having met an old friend and his daughter, he was pressed by Sebastian Frant to meet the scrivener's brother. Curiosity took him to the cottage but fascination kept him there. Though David Frant was a sick man, his memory was still tenacious. He talked about the changes he had seen over the years in Faversham and remembered how appalled the whole town had been at the murder of Thomas Arden. Forty years on, the crime still had a resonance.

What intrigued Nicholas most was the description of the port's naval history. David Frant was well-informed. When he heard that Nicholas had once sailed with Drake on the circumnavigation of the globe, he was only too eager to furnish him with details of the town's past. Though not one of the designated Cinq Ports, Faversham was a corporate member, being a limb of Dover and therefore charged with responsibilities of naval defence. Nicholas learnt that, two years before the Spanish Armada sailed, the town had fitted out a ship of fifty tons at a cost of four hundred pounds, supplementing it in Armada year itself with the *Hazard*, a vessel of forty tons.

Sebastian Frant was sorry when Nicholas finally bade them farewell. His brother invited him to come back at any time he chose. Impressed by Nicholas's record as a sailor, Thomasina joined her father at the door to wave their friend off. With his mind still bubbling with naval history, Nicholas walked back towards the Blue Anchor. His route took him along the bank of the creek. He was strolling happily along when he saw an alarming sight. Drifting towards him on the evening tide, and spinning helplessly to and fro, was a rowing boat with a most unusual passenger. He was sitting upright in a wheelbarrow, trussed up with a sack over his head. The man's body was writhing madly as he fought to escape his bounds and attract help. Nicholas felt the searing pain of recognition. It was Barnaby Gill.

Chapter Ten

It was no time for hesitation. In trying to struggle free, Barnaby Gill was in grave danger of turning over the boat and, although there were a few curious onlookers on both banks of the creek, none of them seemed inclined to go to the rescue of the man in the sack. Nicholas Bracewell did not pause to goggle at the strange sight. Peeling off his jerkin, he dived into the water and swam powerfully towards the boat. As if suddenly awakened to the peril of the situation, the people watching shouted encouragement to Nicholas and urged the occupant of the boat to stop rocking it. Even if he heard it, Gill paid no attention the advice, twisting and turning in a futile attempt to get free and making the boat rock so much that it began to take in water. When Nicholas reached it, the vessel was bobbing about wildly. He took a firm grip on the stern and gave his command.

'Sit still!' he yelled. 'You'll turn the boat over.'

Recognising his voice, Gill obeyed at once and stopped moving. The boat ceased to rock so violently but it dipped towards the stern as Nicholas hauled himself aboard. Water dripped off him in rivulets. Spreading his feet to maintain his balance, he used his dagger to slit through the rope and through the gag that had silenced Gill so effectively. Nicholas lifted the sack carefully up to reveal a man on the verge of collapse. Wide-eyed and red in the face, Gill was too shaken even to speak. He blubbered incoherently. Nicholas put a comforting arm around him and assured him that he was now safe. Gill slowly calmed down.

The boat was still drifting downriver. When he was satisfied that his passenger was not seriously hurt, Nicholas slid the oars out from under the wheelbarrow and fitted them into their rowlocks. He soon established control over the vessel and was able to turn it around and row back in the direction of the Blue Anchor. Soaked to the skin, he ignored his own discomfort in favour of Gill's needs. The man was deeply shocked. It was important to get him back on dry land where he could recover from his ordeal. To his credit, Gill's first words expressed his gratitude.

'Thank you, Nicholas,' he said, still shivering with fright. 'You saved my life.'

'We'll soon be ashore.'

'I might have ended up in the water and drowned.'

'That was my fear,' said Nicholas. 'I thank God that I reached you in time.'

'I've never known such horror.'

'Who did this to you?'

'Who else?' sneered Gill. 'Giddy Mussett.'

'Can you be certain?'

'As certain as I am of anything.'

'Did you *see* Giddy?'

'I had no time to see anyone,' complained Gill. 'The rogue came up behind me and threw that sack over my head. What they kept in it, I know not but it had a foul smell. Before I could resist, I was tied and gagged then wheeled out of my room.'

'By one person?' asked Nicholas. 'Or was someone else involved?'

'I only heard one pair of feet.'

'And you think they belonged to Giddy?'

'I *know* that they did, Nicholas! He tried to kill me.'

'I beg leave to doubt that.'

'You saw the way I was trussed up,' said Gill, pointing to the rope. 'Once in the water, there would have been no hope for me. He wanted me to drown.'

'It looks as if someone may have had that intention,' conceded Nicholas.

'Yes – Giddy Mussett.'

'But I left Edmund and Owen to watch over him.'

'Then they failed in their duty.'

'I find that hard to believe. Giddy might elude one pair of eyes, but not two.'

'I want him arrested.'

'We need proof that he was the culprit first.'

'He is Giddy Mussett,' cried Gill, 'and that is all the proof that you need. I want him arrested, Nicholas. Arrested and charged with attempted murder!'

By the time that the two of them reached the jetty, a small crowd had gathered. There was a smattering of applause for Nicholas and some shouts of congratulation. He had displayed true bravery in rescuing Gill from his plight. Willing hands helped to steady the boat and moor it to an iron ring. The wheelbarrow was too heavy to lift with its occupant in place so Gill had to be eased gently ashore by Nicholas. When the wheelbarrow was pulled out of the boat, Gill was still so jangled that he agreed without protest to get back into it. Someone had brought the jerkin that had been discarded on the bank. After thanking the man for returning it to him, Nicholas put it around Gill's shoulders before wheeling him off. He squelched his way towards the Blue Anchor.

As they approached the inn, they were seen from the window and several members of the company came rushing out to meet them. When he noted that Mussett was among them, Gill went berserk, pointing a finger and screeching abuse. For his part, Mussett was a picture of innocence. Lawrence Firethorn was the first to step forward.

'What happened, Nick?' he asked.

'Giddy set me adrift in a boat,' replied Gill, shaking a fist at his rival. 'If Nicholas had not come to my aid, I would surely have drowned.'

Firethorn turned on Mussett. 'Is this true?' he growled.

'No,' said Mussett. 'On my honour.'

'You *have* no honour,' snarled Gill.

Nicholas took control. 'There is no point in arguing out here,' he said. 'Master Gill has been through a harrowing experience and needs rest. Take him to his room, George, and fetch some wine to soothe him.'

'All that will soothe me is the sight of Giddy, hanging from the nearest tree!'

'Do as I say, George.'

'Yes,' said Dart, grabbing the handles of the wheelbarrow to push it away.

'Look at the state of you, Nick,' said Firethorn.

'Someone had to dive in.'

'Change into dry clothing and we'll hear the full story.'

'I long to hear it myself,' said Nicholas, throwing a suspicious glance at Mussett. 'I sincerely hope that the tale does not involve you, Giddy.'

Mussett was defensive. 'This is the first I've heard of Barnaby's ordeal,' he said. His face split into a grin. 'But I tell you this. Had I known what straits he was in, I'd have come out here to enjoy watching him.'

'No more of that talk!' snapped Firethorn, grabbing him by the throat. 'Barnaby is in great distress. If I find that you had a hand in it, I'll be judge, jury and executioner. Do you understand, Giddy?'

'Yes, yes.'

'Then hold your peace.'

Firethorn pushed him away then walked back towards the inn with Nicholas and the others. Ten minutes later, the book holder had dried himself off, changed into fresh attire and joined the actor-manager in his room. Giddy Mussett was also there along with a crestfallen Edmund Hoode and an embarrassed Owen Elias. Having failed to frighten a confession out of him, Firethorn stopped trying to browbeat Mussett.

'You talk to him, Nick,' he said with exasperation, 'and I hope you have more success than I did. I can get nothing from Giddy. It's easier to get blood from a stone.'

Mussett hunched his shoulders. 'I never touched Barnaby.'

'We'll look into that in a moment,' said Nicholas. 'First, I want to hear from Edmund and Owen. They were meant to keep you where they could see you.' He looked at the pair of them. 'Is that not what happened?'

'Yes, Nick,' said Elias, shifting his feet. 'I did my share.'

'And I, mine,' said Hoode, 'until I went into the taproom.'

'What then?' asked Nicholas.

'I thought that Owen would take over from me.'

'Nick asked *you* to stand guard, Edmund,' said Elias.

'Only while Giddy was asleep.'

'Yet you came into the taproom with him.'

'And you should have done *your* share of the work then, Owen.'

'Wait,' said Nicholas, interrupting them. 'Are you telling me that one or both of you allowed Giddy out of your sight?'

'It was Edmund's fault,' said Elias.

Hoode flared up. 'Owen is to blame.'

'They're both at fault, Nick,' said Firethorn, 'and so am

186

I, for all three of us shared a cup of wine together. One minute, Giddy was there; the next, he was gone.'

'For how long?' wondered Nicholas.

'It's difficult to say.'

'Did no one search for him?'

'I did,' said Elias, jabbing his chest. 'No sooner did I step outside the taproom than I saw Giddy coming towards me. He might only have been away for a moment.'

Nicholas turned to the clown. 'Where did you go?'

'Nature called,' replied Mussett.

'How long were you away?'

'How long do such things take *you*, Nick?'

'Do not jest with me, Giddy.'

'It was no jest. I am in deadly earnest.'

'Can you swear that you did not go to Barnaby's room?'

'On the biggest Bible in Christendom.'

'You've lied to us before,' said Nicholas. 'Why should we believe you now?'

'I'm not asking you to believe *me*,' replied Mussett, 'because I know that my word will be doubted but you may believe someone else. I have a witness.'

'A member of the company?'

'No, Nick. Yet someone who will prove my innocence.'

'Can you produce this person?'

'Instantly,' said Mussett, moving to the door. 'Have I your permission?'

'Let me go with him,' suggested Elias, trying to make up for his earlier lack of vigilance. 'We want no more of his trickery.'

'He can go alone,' said Nicholas. 'Be quick about it, Giddy.'

Mussett left the room and closed the door behind him. Firethorn was worried.

'I think he's guilty,' he decided.

'Let's hear his witness first.'

'I doubt if there is such a person, Nick. This has to be Giddy's doing. He and Barnaby were jousting earlier on. I had to part them. Barnaby's tongue was dagger-sharp enough to draw Giddy's blood. It may have goaded him to take revenge.'

'Even Giddy would surely not go that far,' reasoned Nicholas. 'He would never expect to get away with it. If he wheeled Barnaby down to that boat, he would certainly have been seen. There were people around the creek.'

'Do you feel that he's innocent?' asked Hoode, 'or do you hope that it is so?'

'Both, Edmund.'

'Then you have to answer another question.'

'I know,' said Nicholas. 'If Giddy was not guilty of this, then who was?'

Elias sighed. 'He was the only one who left the taproom.'

'That does not put the halter of blame around his neck, Owen. He was accused of locking Barnaby in that privy, of hurling a cat in through his window. I was with Giddy when both those things occurred. He did neither.'

'No,' said Firethorn. 'He was saving himself for a more serious assault.'

'I wonder. Giddy was himself the victim of assault on

the road here. Back at the Queen's Head, it was the whole company who suffered. Do you not see a pattern here?' asked Nicholas, thinking it through. 'Someone is trying to destroy our work. First, they have us turned out of our home. Then they ambush our clown. And now, they try to dispatch Barnaby to a watery grave. We have an unseen enemy.'

'Tobias Fitzgeoffrey?'

'Someone connected with Conway's Men, perhaps.'

'How would they know when to attack Barnaby?' said Elias.

'Because they were more alert as sentries, Owen. They watched Giddy more carefully than you and seized their chance when he left the room. There's craft at work here,' concluded Nicholas. 'Suspicion was thrown on to Giddy.'

'I still hold that he did the deed,' declared Firethorn.

Elias nodded. 'And I side with you, Lawrence.'

'I prefer to reserve my judgement,' said Hoode. 'Nick could be right.'

'For Giddy's sake,' said Nicholas, 'I hope that I am.' There was a tap on the door. 'Here comes the witness. Now we'll hear the truth.'

The door opened and Mussett entered with a tall, stringy woman in her thirties with a roguish look in her eye. Over a plain, crumpled, food-stained dress, she wore a large apron. Mussett had his arm wrapped around her shoulders.

'This is Kate,' he announced. 'We met last year when I visited Faversham with Rutland's Men. Kate worked at the

189

Ship then, in the kitchen. To my delight, she now works at the Blue Anchor.'

'Gentlemen,' she said, dropping what she took to be a curtsey.

'I understand that you can help us, Kate,' said Nicholas pleasantly.

'Yes, sir. I believe that I can.'

'What have you to say?'

'Well,' she replied, licking her lips before continuing. 'When Giddy left the taproom earlier, it was to see me. We are old friends, as he says. One look between us was all it took, sirs. We met in the storeroom to . . .' She giggled with undisguised glee. 'To talk to each other alone.'

Mussett savoured the look of surprise on the faces of his interrogators.

'As I told you,' he reminded them. 'Nature called.'

It took Firethorn an hour to placate Barnaby Gill and a further hour to persuade him that Mussett was not responsible for his ordeal. When he heard about the tryst with Kate, he was thoroughly disgusted, finding yet another reason to detest his rival. Fearing a second attack, Gill insisted on an armed guard and Firethorn had him carried to a room upstairs so that George Dart could sit beside him with a sword across his lap. When news of the arrangement reached the others, they burst into laughter, wondering if the sword was for Gill's protection or that of Dart. Oddly, Mussett did not join in the fun.

Nicholas, meanwhile, had searched the creek for anyone who might have seen the wheelbarrow leaving the inn. Most of those who had been there earlier had drifted away but he did find one old man who remembered the incident. Mending a net as he talked, the fisherman had the weathered face of a sailor and the cold eyes of someone who had seen too many unusual sights in his time to be surprised by one more.

'Yes,' he croaked. 'I see them both.'

'Both?' repeated Nicholas. 'There were *two* men wheeling him?'

'No, sir. One in the wheelbarrow, one pushing him along.'

'Can you describe him?'

'He were covered by a sack.'

'Not the man in the wheelbarrow,' said Nicholas patiently. 'The other one.'

'Oh, ah, I remember him.'

'Well?'

The fisherman spat on the ground. 'It were some distance away, mark you.'

'Just tell me what you saw.'

'A servingman, pushing someone down to the jetty in a wheelbarrow. When he got them in the boat, he cast off and set it adrift. Then he ran back to the Blue Anchor.'

'And you think he was a servingman?'

'He must have been, sir. He wore a cap and a leather apron.'

'Was he tall or short? Young or old?'

'All I know is what I've told you,' said the fisherman. 'Except that he could run fast. Look for him in the Blue Anchor. That's where he went.'

Night passed without incident but Nicholas Bracewell achieved only a few hours sleep. The events of the previous day preyed on his mind. Both clowns belonging to Westfield's Men had been attacked and he was convinced that it was no mere coincidence. Barnaby Gill had earlier been the target at the Queen's Head, singled out on purpose. Those who interrupted the performance could have done so at any point in the afternoon but they chose to strike when Gill was alone on stage. During the ensuing affray, others in the company had received cuts and bruises but only the clown sustained serious injury. Nicholas wondered why Gill had been picked out. Another name also kept floating into his mind, that of Fortunatus Hope. Gill had survived, albeit with a broken leg. Hope had perished. For what reason, it was not yet clear. Nicholas explored every possible motive in his mind but none seemed entirely satisfactory.

Events at the creek continued to puzzle him. He could not decide whether Gill's ordeal was intended as a prelude to death or simply as a means of humiliation. If the former were the case, why had someone risked being seen when he could have killed his victim in the privacy of his room? If it was a cruel jest, had it been the work of the same person who had locked Gill in a privy and thrown a snarling cat onto his chest as he lay in his room? Nicholas was perplexed. Westfield's Men were being stalked by an unknown enemy.

It was only a matter of time before he struck again.

Sheer fatigue eventually claimed Nicholas but, as soon as the first finger of light poked through the shutters, he came awake with a start. Owen Elias nudged him.

'Have no fear, Nick,' he said.

'Why?'

'He'll not escape *me* to answer a call of nature.'

Elias pulled back the blanket to reveal the piece of cord that was twisted around his hand. The other end was tied to Mussett's ankle. The clown was quite unaware that he was tethered to the Welshman. It was ironic. While two of his guards had a disturbed night, Mussett slept like a baby.

Lawrence Firethorn was not happy to lose both his book holder and his clown for some hours but he accepted the necessity of it. If the danger came from Conway's Men, then it needed to be identified as soon as possible, and there might never be a time when they were quite so close to their rivals. Firethorn gave the expedition his blessing. The absence of Nicholas and Mussett would impede the rehearsal but it removed one thorny problem. Barnaby Gill would not be able to taunt the man who had replaced him against his will. When he watched the others at work, he would have no excuse to carp or cavil.

Undeterred by dark clouds, Nicholas Bracewell and Giddy Mussett set out after breakfast on borrowed horses. Both were armed with sword and dagger, confident that they could either beat off any attack or outrun any highwaymen. In fact, it proved an uneventful journey. After maintaining a steady canter until they reached Boughton-under-Blean, they slowed to a trot that made conversation easier.

'Did you not think her a fine woman?' asked Mussett.

'Who?'

'Kate Humble. My witness.'

Nicholas was amused. 'Is that her name? I saw no humility in her.'

'No, Kate has too much spirit for it to be cowed.'

'She seemed very fond of you, Giddy.'

'With every reason.'

'You must have given her sweet memories.'

'Oh, I did,' said Mussett with a cackle. 'But I own that I was worried.'

'Why?'

'You've seen my face, Nick. It's so ugly that I dare not look in a mirror. I feared that Kate would not even recognise me. Or, if she did, that she would be so scared that she'd not let me touch her.'

'Your fears were unfounded, then.'

'Oh, yes. It was not my face that mattered to her.' He let out another cackle. 'Kate loved me for something else.'

They quickened their pace and rode on until they saw Harbledown Hill rising before them. It was a long climb but the reward more than justified the effort. When they paused at the summit, they got their first view of Canterbury Cathedral, spearing the sky with its soaring magnificence and dominating the city with Christian certitude. Encircled by a high stone wall, Canterbury had a dignity that set it apart from the other places they had so far visited. Maidstone might be the shire town but here was the acknowledged seat of government of the whole Church of England. It exuded real significance. As they descended the hill, their eyes never left the cathedral, using it as their guide. When they entered the city through Westgate, however, it was lost behind intervening buildings.

It was market day and the streets were filled with people. Nicholas was reminded of the daily bustle in Gracechurch Street except that everything here was on a much smaller scale than in London. The haphazard line of stalls had narrowed an already limited space. With Mussett behind him, Nicholas elbowed his way gently through the crowd in St Peter's Street, taking stock of his surroundings as he did so. When they crossed the little bridge over the river, he turned to his companion.

'Where will we find them, Giddy?' he asked.

'Close by The Mercery.'

'Is that where they will rehearse?'

'No,' said Mussett. 'Tobias is too lazy to rehearse as early as this. He'll still be abed with a warm woman, if I know him. We'll head for the Crown.'

'Will Conway's Men stay there?'

'I doubt it, Nick. The inn is far too small to hold them. They'll sleep elsewhere, at the Three Tuns, most like. But the Crown sells the finest ale in the city so that is where I expect him to be.'

'Who?'

'My good friend, Martin Ling.'

'An actor with the company?'

'More important than any actor,' said Mussett with a grin. 'As you should know, if anyone does. Martin's their book holder.'

Picking their way past the various stalls, they walked on up the High Street until they came to The Mercery, a lane to their left that was lined with shops and houses. So narrow was the thoroughfare, and so much did each story of a building jetty out above the one below, that it was possible for occupants of attic rooms to reach out and touch the fingertips of their neighbours opposite. Silks, satins and other rich fabrics were on sale in the shops and business among merchants was brisk.

Nicholas thought of Pieter Hendrik, the weaver, who dealt in much simpler materials. He would never aspire to such commercial heights. When they reached the end of the lane, they were confronted by the sheer majesty of Christ Church Gate, the main entrance to the cathedral precincts. Nicholas paused to admire the sculptured beauty of the stone work, and to study the coats of arms above the gate, but Mussett went across to the Buttermarket. He waited outside a small inn until his friend caught up with him. Nicholas looked up at the golden crown emblazoned on the sign above their heads.

'Is this the place, Giddy?'

'I got to know it well when Rutland's Men were in the city.'

'Let's go in.'

'No,' said Mussett, restraining him with a hand. 'This is work for me alone. Martin is as close as the grave. I'll not get much from him, if I'm seen with a stranger.'

'What if he's not inside?'

'Then we'll search elsewhere for him. Mingle with the crowd and wait out here.'

'I want you where I can see you,' said Nicholas.

'Learn to trust me.'

'After what happened in Maidstone? How can I?'

'You have no choice, Nick.'

With a mischievous grin, Mussett darted in through the door of the inn. Nicholas was annoyed but there was little that he could do. He retreated to the gate so that he could watch the inn from a short distance away. It was a popular hostelry. Customers went in at regular intervals. Those who tumbled out had the happy look of people who had enjoyed the Crown's ale. Nicholas waited patiently. It was only when the cathedral bell chimed again that he realised how long he had been there. Suspicions began to gnaw at him. Was Mussett really talking to a friend at the inn or had he surrendered once again to the lure of strong drink? Could it be that the clown was not even inside the building? Mussett was closely acquainted with a woman in Maidstone and with another in Faversham. Had he slipped out of the rear of the Crown for an assignation with a third female friend?

Nicholas went back to the inn and peered in through the window. The taproom was packed with customers but Giddy Mussett was not among them. Chiding himself for trusting the man, Nicholas hurried down an alleyway to the rear of the property. The Crown had a small garden with a bay tree at its centre and some of its patrons had spilt out into the fresh air. Mussett was there. Sitting on a wooden bench, holding a tankard in his hand, he was talking to a bedraggled individual of middle years with unkempt hair sprouting out from the edges of his cap. Nicholas came to a halt. If the man was Martin Ling, he was visible proof that a touring company like Conway's Men paid their book holder far less than could be earned by someone with a London troupe. Nicholas was suddenly grateful to be employed by Westfield's Men. He had seen lean times with them but had never endured the kind of suffering that was etched on Ling's face. Chastened, he withdrew quietly to his former vantage point near the gate.

When Mussett finally emerged from the inn, Nicholas beckoned him over.

'Was your friend there, Giddy?' he asked.

'Yes,' sighed the other. 'Martin is older and sadder than ever.'

'What did he have to say?'

'Nothing good of Tobias Fitzgeoffrey. The man is a tyrant.'

'Then why does the book holder stay with him?'

'Why do *you* stay with Westfield's Men when you have a tyrant called Lawrence Firethorn in charge and a monster of vanity like Barnaby Gill to irritate you?'

'I love the company.'

'Martin loves to hate his. And he has nowhere else to go.'

'Did you find out anything of interest?'

'I found out that they have been struggling their way

around Kent all summer, and with poor results. We earned five pounds in Maidstone. The mayor only gave them eighteen shillings for their pains.'

'What of the attacks upon us?'

'Martin knew nothing of those,' said Mussett. 'Tobias does not confide in him. There exists a kind of truce between them but I doubt that it will last much longer. There was one nugget that I dug out of my old friend, however.'

'Oh?'

'It concerns the day that you last played at the Queen's Head.'

'Go on.'

'Tobias Fitzgeoffrey left his troupe in Kent and went off to London that day.'

'Why?'

'He wanted to see the work of a particular rival,' said Mussett. 'When he came back, Martin told me, he was all smiles for a week afterwards, as if he was celebrating a private triumph. Do you know what play he saw when he was in the capital?'

'I think that I can guess.'

'*A Trick To Catch A Chaste Lady.*'

The decision to stage *The Loyal Subject* in Faversham made it possible to rehearse many of its scenes. While the role of the clown was important, it was not as critical as in the plays so far performed in Kent. Firethorn had the title role, ably supported by Richard Honeydew as a regal Duchess of Milan. The play's author, Edmund Hoode, took the part of the judge who condemned Lorenzo, the loyal subject, to an undeserved death. The rehearsal took place in an upstairs room at the Blue Anchor. It was a little cramped for their purposes but it was all that the inn could offer. Rain was now falling outside. A rehearsal in the yard was impossible.

Though not directly involved, Barnaby Gill insisted on being there, sitting in his wheelbarrow, propped up on cushions like an eastern potentate and making summary judgements on performances. During a break, Firethorn tried to persuade him to leave.

'You've no need to be here, Barnaby,' he said.

'Where else can I be? Alone in my room, at the mercy of another attacker?'

'You unsettle us. Your comments are too harsh.'

'Honesty is all that I offer,' said Gill.

'A bruising honesty that causes too much pain. Not to me,' added Firethorn with a touch of arrogance. 'My skills fortify me against your gibes but it is not so with the others. They lack my armour. You even upset Edmund.'

'He needed to be upset.'

'What purpose did it serve?'

'It made him strive harder.'

'I'll not have you here when Giddy Mussett returns.'

'But that is when I most want to watch,' insisted Gill. 'He takes my role in the play, Lawrence. I wish to see how badly he mangles it.'

'Your only wish is to distract him, and I'll not allow it.'

'I have certain rights.'

'Not when you sit in your wheelbarrow. I can have you moved at will.'

'They are back!' called Elias, looking through the window. 'Nick and Giddy have just ridden into the yard.'

'At last!' sighed Firethorn.

'They look wet and weary from their travels.'

'It matters not if they are safe returned.'

'Let me stay, Lawrence,' said Gill, almost pleading. 'I swear I'll not interfere.'

'There'll be no opportunity for you to do so.'

'I'll sit in the corner and be as silent as the grave.'

'Your very presence would speak volumes.'

'I may be able to help.'

'You do that best by being absent,' said Firethorn peremptorily. He snapped his fingers. 'George!' he called. 'Come here.'

'Yes, Master Firethorn,' said Dart, trotting over.

'Wheel Barnaby into the other room and stay with him for company.'

'My place is here,' argued Gill. 'With my fellows.'

'We can spare you. George, do as I bid.'

Dart moved to the wheelbarrow. 'Yes, Master Firethorn.'

Taking it by the handles, he wheeled the protesting Gill out of the room and along the corridor. The atmosphere suddenly cleared. With their lone spectator out of the way, everyone began to relax. Gill had been far too censorious. The actors had even more cause for delight when Nicholas Bracewell came in a minute later, his hat, jerkin and face moistened by the light rain. Everyone greeted him warmly but it was Firethorn who took him aside for a private word.

'Where is Giddy?' he asked.

'Stabling the horses. He'll join us soon.'

'Was the visit a profitable one?'

'I think so. Giddy spoke to their book holder, Martin Ling, an old friend with a lasting grudge against Conway's Men.'

'Anyone who has seen them perform will have a lasting grudge against them!'

'Giddy talked at length with him.'

'What did he learn?'

'Many things,' said Nicholas. 'Lord Conway holds our own patron in disdain. He was shocked when his nephew, Fortunatus Hope, fell out with him and fell in with Lord Westfield. It was an insult that rankled more each day.'

'That spurred him to take revenge on his nephew?'

'It may have done.'

'What evidence is there?'

'Tobias Fitzgeoffrey was at the Queen's Head that day.'

Firethorn was astonished. 'When we were halted by the affray?'

'Yes. He was in London for that purpose.'

'What brought him to us? Did he wish to learn from me and see what a great actor can achieve with an audience? Or was he there to steal ideas that he could use behind our backs with Conway's Men?'

'I believe that he may have been sent by his patron,' said Nicholas.

'To slide a dagger between the ribs of the nephew?'

'Or to hire an assassin to do the deed. Why else should he be there?'

'The whoreson rogue!'

'His company is on tour yet he found the time to ride to London for one particular event. I call that strange,' observed Nicholas. 'Giddy's friend remembers his return. He was in such good humour that he bought them all a drink, so rare an event that they were quite amazed.'

'Fitzgeoffrey is as mean a man as any in Creation.'

'So what made him spread his bounty? And where did it come from? They have had bare rations here in Kent. Eighteen shillings was all they raised in Maidstone and even less elsewhere. Yet, suddenly, he has money to spare.'

'Blood money!'

'That was my guess.'

'He was paid for his villainy by that goat-faced patron of his.'

'It is more than possible.'

'By heavens, Nick,' said Firehorn. 'We've enough to hang the pair of them.'

'More proof is needed yet.'

'We'll cudgel it out of Tobias Fitzgeoffrey.'

'We have to find him first,' said Nicholas. 'Giddy and I searched for him all morning but he was nowhere to be found in Canterbury. One of the actors we met said that he had gone to see Lord Conway.'

'To plot another crime!'

'We cannot be certain of that.'

'It is as plain as the nose on my face.'

Nicholas was cautious. 'We suppose much more than we know.'

'What more proof do we need?' asked Firethorn. 'On the very day that a play was halted at the Queen's Head and a man stabbed to death, Tobias Fitzgeoffrey is there to enjoy it all. Who else but he was behind that ambush on the road? Who else would try to drown Barnaby in the creek? Do you not see, Nick? He's bent on destroying us.'

'We need to be on guard. That much I agree.'

'I spy their purpose. They mean to replace us in London.'

'That will never be.'

'Not while *I* have breath in my body,' vowed Firethorn.

'Conway's Men stay in the city for a few days. I'll go to Canterbury again soon to see if Master Fitzgeoffrey has returned. He holds the key to the mystery.'

'Will you take Giddy with you?'

'Yes,' said Nicholas. 'I must. Without him, I would be lost.'

Giddy Mussett unbuckled the girth and removed the saddle from the second of the two horses. Having put Lawrence Firethorn's stallion into a stall, he turned his attention to the bay mare that he had borrowed. The animal had been ridden hard and deserved his gratitude. Patting her as he worked, he talked quietly to the mare. When he had put the saddle away, he led the animal into a stall then started to take off the bridle. Freed of her tackle, the mare whinnied then shook her mane to dislodge some of the moisture.

'Hold still!' said Mussett with a laugh. 'I'm wet enough, as it is.'

He collected some hay from the corner and stuffed it into the manger. The mare moved eagerly across to it. Both horses were soon eating contentedly. Mussett went in search of a wooden bucket so that he could give them some water. The farther he went into the stables, the gloomier it got. All he could pick out at first were the outlines of other horses as they shifted their feet in the straw. When he thought he saw an upturned bucket in a corner, he bent down to retrieve it.

The man moved in quickly. Clapping one hand over his victim's mouth, he pushed the dagger between his ribs and into his heart. It was over as simply as that.

Chapter Eleven

Owen Elias was still standing beside the window of the upstairs room, gazing down idly at the yard below. The rain had stopped now and a burst of afternoon sunshine was making the cobbles glisten. His interest quickened when an attractive young woman came out of a door and he leant out to catch her attention. His cheerful wave was not returned. After giving him a blank look, she crossed the yard and went into a storeroom. Elias's first instinct was to follow her but he knew that the rehearsal would soon begin again. He felt thwarted. Nicholas Bracewell joined his friend at the window.

'Is there no sign of Giddy yet?' he asked.

'Not unless he is wearing a green dress and a white bonnet.'

'He should be here by now. It does not take this long to unsaddle two horses.' Nicholas was about to move away. 'I'll see what keeps him.'

'No,' said Elias, detaining him with a hand. 'That's my office. You've travelled enough for one day. Let me fetch Giddy.'

'Scold him for keeping us waiting.'

'I hope that the wretch has not sneaked away,' said Lawrence Firethorn, coming across to them. 'We have to stop him hearing that call of nature.'

'He's still in the stables,' Elias assured him. 'I'd have seen him leave.'

'Is there no back way out?'

'None,' said Nicholas. 'I checked that before I left him alone.'

'Then where is he?'

'I'll chase him out, Lawrence,' said Elias, heading for the door. 'The ride has tired him, I daresay. Giddy is probably asleep in the straw.'

Eager to make amends for his earlier failure, the Welshman clattered down the winding oak staircase and went along a stone-flagged passageway. As he came out into the yard, the young woman he had seen earlier was retracing her steps with a small sack in her arms. He gave her a respectful bow this time and collected a half-smile. It was progress. Since she worked at the Blue Anchor, it would be possible to make her acquaintance in time. It gave Elias something to build on. Mussett's intimacy with a kitchen maid was now common knowledge. Elias wanted his own conquest.

'What have you got there?' he wondered.

'Vegetables, sir.'

'Will you save some for me?'

'If you wish.'

'When shall I come to collect them?'

He gave her a frank grin and she coloured slightly, but she looked back over her shoulder when she reached the door. Elias was encouraged. He blew her a kiss.

When he got to the stables, he paused at the door and peered into the gloom.

'Giddy!' he called. 'What are you doing in there?'

There was no reply. He took a few steps inside and called again.

'Where are you, man? Lawrence wants you for the rehearsal.'

All that he got by way of response was a neigh from one of the horses and a rustling in the straw. There was no sign of Mussett. Elias became mildly alarmed, worried that the clown had somehow slipped past him once more. Yet he had never taken his eyes off the yard. Nobody could leave the stables without being seen. Elias decided that Mussett was playing a game, hiding in one of the stalls to fool him. The Welshman began a thorough search, walking along the line of stalls and expecting Mussett to jump out at any moment. But the clown did not appear. If he had found a hiding place, it was a good one. Elias glanced up, wondering if the agile Mussett had climbed up into the roof by way of a jest.

He was still gazing along the beams when a noise from the rear of the stables alerted him. Something fell to the ground with a small thud that was not muffled by straw.

Elias became circumspect. Narrowing his eyelids to stare into the shadows, he moved slowly forward.

'Is that you, Giddy?' he said. 'What trick are you up to this time?'

Only the movement of horses could be heard. Elias walked on, heading for the corner from which the noise had seemed to come. A shape was gradually conjured out of the gloom, a large, round lump on the floor against the back wall. Elias swallowed hard.

'Giddy?' he cried, hurrying forward. 'What happened?'

Mussett was in no position to tell him. As soon as he touched his friend, Elias knew that he was dead. His hand brushed against the dagger that was sticking out from Mussett's back.

'*Iesu Mawr*!' he exclaimed. 'Who did this to you?'

By way of an answer, a cudgel struck him hard on the back of his head. Unable to stop himself, Elias plunged forward, landing on Mussett and forcing the dagger even deeper into his unprotected back.

While appreciating the value of the visit to Canterbury, Firethorn was concerned that valuable rehearsal time had been lost. *The Loyal Subject* was a complex drama that dealt with a number of themes. Everyone else in the company knew the play well and had mastered their roles. The newcomer who most needed to rehearse was the one actor who had not been there. Firethorn consulted his book holder.

'Can he learn yet another part in such a short time, Nick?'

'I am sure that he can.'

'You will have to feed the lines to him on a spoon.'

'I'll be happy to do so,' said Nicholas. 'I've already told Giddy the plot of the play and talked about his role. He's not entirely unprepared.'

'If only we had not brought Barnaby with us!' sighed Firethorn.

'Does he still complain?'

'Complain, chastise, censure and condemn. Nothing pleases him. He made so many unkind comments during the rehearsal that I had him wheeled away. This room is too small to have both Barnaby *and* Giddy Mussett inside it.'

'We have neither at the moment,' said Nicholas, moving back to the window. 'What is holding Giddy up? He could have unsaddled half a dozen horses by now.'

'Owen should have grabbed him by the scruff of his neck.'

'Why this delay?'

Even as he spoke, Nicholas was given an explanation. Elias came stumbling out of the stables with a hand pressed against the back of his head to stem the blood from his scalp wound. He used his other arm to beckon Nicholas.

'Come quickly!' he yelled. 'All is lost!'

Nicholas did not wait to hear any details. Taking Firethorn with him, he rushed down the stairs and out into the yard. Elias was still dazed from the blow. He swayed on his feet as he pointed to the stables.

'Giddy is inside,' he said. 'Stabbed to death.'

'Murdered?' cried Firethorn.

'See for yourselves.'

Nicholas lent him a supportive arm so that he could take them to the spot where Mussett lay. They crouched beside the body and checked for signs of life. It was the second time that Nicholas had seen the handle of a dagger protruding from a victim's back. Firethorn was aghast.

'Who could have done this?' he gasped. 'We are done for!'

'Let's hear what Owen has to say first,' suggested Nicholas.

Elias shrugged. 'I've little enough to report. I called out for Giddy when I got here but there was no answer. I thought he was playing one of his tricks on me so I came in search of him.' He indicated to the body. 'This is what I found in the shadows. Before I could raise the alarm, someone struck me from behind. My head is splitting. He must have had a powerful arm.'

'We'll dress the wound for you.'

'Forget me, Nick. I still live. Giddy is beyond any help.'

'And so are we!' wailed Firethorn.

'Think back, Owen,' said Nicholas. 'You saw us arrive at the inn. You stood at the window all the time that Giddy was in here. Did you see anyone else come in or out?'

'I did,' replied Elias. 'One of the ostlers, a young lad, came out and went into the kitchen. A little later,' he recalled, 'a man came out of the taproom and walked across to the stables. A bearded man, with something of your build. I paid no heed to him.'

'Did he go into the stables?'

'Yes. I thought he was going to fetch his horse.'

'But you never saw him again?'

'No,' said Elias, rubbing his head. 'He saw *me*.'

'You were lucky that you were not stabbed as well,' said Firethorn.

'Giddy was the only target,' decided Nicholas. 'I suspect that the man who killed him was part of that ambush at the ford. They were after Giddy then but we beat them off. One of them came back to finish the task.'

'And to finish *us* at the same time. Our clown is dead. That leaves a hole so large that it can never be filled. Westfield's Men are victims here as well.'

'It was Giddy who paid the greater penalty. He only joined us to help us out.'

'True,' said Elias, gazing down at the body. 'And we could not have asked for a livelier companion. Giddy had his faults but they were outweighed by his virtues.'

'This man you saw,' said Nicholas. 'Was he wearing a leather apron and a cap?'

'No, Nick. Doublet and hose. Why do you ask?'

'I thought he might have been the one who set Barnaby adrift in the creek.'

'We are all adrift now,' moaned Firethorn.

'I am looking for similarities,' explained Nicholas. 'The company has been attacked by means of its clowns. Barnaby was set upon at the Queen's Head and here in Faversham. Giddy was murdered at the second attempt.'

'What does this tell us, Nick? Do we search for a man with no sense of humour?'

'I think not. Yet there is one thing we do know about him.'

'What's that?' asked Elias.

'He has a ready supply of daggers,' said Nicholas, pulling the weapon from Mussett's back. 'This matches the one I found lodged in the body of Fortunatus Hope. I believe that we are dealing with the same assassin. What worries me is this,' he went on, turning to the others. 'How many more daggers does he possess and where are they destined to end up?'

News of the murder caused fear and consternation at the Blue Anchor. Those who worked there were horrified, those staying there were shocked and local people who came into the taproom were so nervous that they kept looking over their shoulders with apprehension. The crime was reported and constables took charge of the dead body. When his scalp wound had been bathed, Owen Elias gave a statement to a magistrate about the circumstances in which he had found Mussett. Nicholas Bracewell, meanwhile, turned his attention to the landlord of the inn. Without realising that he might be looking at an assassin, Elias had seen a man leave the taproom and go into the stables at a time when Mussett was inside. Nicholas hoped that the landlord could give a better description of the man but he added little to what the Welshman said. All that he could remember about the customer was that he sat with a tankard of ale beside a window that looked out on to the yard. There had been other people there at the time but, when Nicholas questioned them, they could only echo the landlord. The bearded man was a stranger to whom they paid scant attention.

The rehearsal had been abandoned and most of the actors chose to subdue their grief in the taproom. Now that he was dead, they came to see just how much they had liked Giddy. His fall from grace in Maidstone was completely forgotten. What remained in the mind was an image of an affable, vigorous, gleeful man who was a natural clown. Even Barnaby Gill, his old enemy, was moved to admiration.

'Giddy was truly gifted,' he admitted. 'I envied his talent far more than I hated the man himself. He was a vagabond clown and I'll miss him.'

'Not as much as we do, Barnaby,' said Firethorn, downing another cup of wine.

'Yes,' agreed Edmund Hoode. '*The Loyal Subject* is impossible without him. You were right to call off the rehearsal, Lawrence. There is no point in working on a play that we cannot present. Giddy would have given it his own particular glow.'

'I, too, can impart a glow, Edmund.'

'We know, Lawrence,' said Gill. 'You can blaze like a beacon. But you are no clown. Giddy Mussett was. We are a rare breed, you see.'

'You sound like a species of sheep,' said Firethorn.

'If I am, then I mourn the black member of our flock.'

Gill lifted a cup of wine in honour of the dead man. The three of them were sitting at a table in the taproom, still stunned by the blow that had befallen them and having little idea what to do best. When Nicholas joined them, they were almost maudlin.

'You must speak to the mayor, Nick,' said Firethorn.

'He'll have caught wind of the murder by now,' said Nicholas.

'But he will not understand its effects. Tell him our play must be abandoned. It's out of the question to perform *The Loyal Subject*. The town of Faversham will have to forego the delight of seeing Westfield's Men on stage.'

'Why?'

'Why else, man? We have lost our clown.'

'Then we have to replace him.'

'In the space of a day or so?' asked Firethorn. 'It would take a miracle.'

'Common sense will suffice,' argued Nicholas. '*The Loyal Subject* may be beyond us because Giddy would have danced his way through it, but we've other plays to offer an audience.'

'Not if we lack a clown, Nick.'

'But we have one. He sits beside you.'

Gill was astounded. 'Do you look at *me*?'

'Yes,' said Nicholas.

'I am an invalid. My leg is broken.'

'Your talent is still in good repair.'

'This is folly, Nick,' said Hoode. 'How can Barnaby perform with his leg in a splint? He is unable to walk, let alone dance a jig.'

'Then we make a virtue of necessity, Edmund. You'll see to that.'

'What do you mean?'

'Change a play to suit our circumstance,' said Nicholas. 'The wheelbarrow comes to our aid here. Our clown may not caper, but he can be moved at will about the stage. Much comedy can be gleaned from that.'

'Why, yes,' said Firethorn, latching on to the idea at once. 'This may be the answer, Barnaby. When we first offered you the wheelbarrow, you turned up your nose at it because it would make you a figure of fun. That is what we wish you to be. A figure of fun upon the stage.'

Gill sniffed. 'The notion offends my dignity.'

'Think of your purse, man. Would you rather leave Faversham unpaid?'

'Nick has hit the mark,' said Hoode, seeing the possibilities. 'I can easily write scenes that turn the broken leg into a source of rich comedy. Where Barnaby cannot dance, he shall sing instead. It could be done.'

'But it will not be,' said Gill, folding his arms defiantly.

'With you in the cast, we could even play *The Loyal Subject*.'

'I have another suggestion,' said Nicholas. 'Let's put a tragedy aside and give them homespun humour instead. After the dark deed in the stables, our fellows need a comedy to lift their spirits. *The Foolish Friar* meets all objections. It's a light piece on a serious subject. Our friar will look even more foolish if the only way that he can move about is in a wheelbarrow.'

'The perfect play,' said Hoode. 'It lends itself to change and variation.'

'Not on my account,' affirmed Gill. 'I am too unwell to act.'

'Then we harp on that,' said Nicholas. 'Give the foolish friar a whole array of ailments, Edmund. To his broken leg, add a bad back, a diseased liver, a sore throat, a high fever and a choleric disposition.'

Firethorn laughed. 'Barnaby already has that!'

'I'll not be a foolish friar,' said Gill.

'You'll be a foolish friar, a wise virgin or a statue of Venus, if we ask it. You have a contract with us,' said Firethorn, 'and it obliges you to act what we decide. There is no mention of a broken leg anywhere in its terms. Were you stricken down with sleeping sickness, we could still enforce the contract.'

'Besides,' said Hoode, adopting a softer approach, 'you would not let us suffer the humiliation of having to cancel a performance. Think how your fellows would welcome your return, Barnaby? They'd be eternally grateful to the man who came to our rescue. Our reputation is in your hands.'

'One thing more,' said Nicholas. 'Giddy must be borne in mind. Though he was with us such a short time, he left his imprint on the company. For his sake, we must not abandon a performance. Giddy would have expected us to go on. It would be a way to honour his memory.'

Gill was weakening. '*The Foolish Friar* is a good play. I like it.'

'Share that pleasure with an audience.'

'Who would push me in the wheelbarrow?'

'Anyone you choose. George Dart, perhaps?'

217

'No, not on stage,' said Gill. 'He's too weak and clumsy for that. I need someone strong enough to move me around without bumping into the scenery.'

'Owen Elias, it shall be,' said Nicholas. 'Strong and sensible.'

Hoode's mind was racing. 'We'll have a song that the pair of you can sing together,' he said, 'for Owen has the best voice of us all. And in place of your dance, he can spin you around the stage to music. That wheelbarrow is a godsend.'

'Well, Barnaby,' asked Firethorn. 'What do you say now?'

'It might work,' said Gill pensively.

'You'd become our hero.'

'Which would you rather do?' said Nicholas. 'Sit on a bench to watch a play or ride in a wheelbarrow and take part in it?'

Gill smacked the table. 'I'll do it!'

The landlord of the inn was saddened by what had happened. Murder on his premises would leave its taint for a long time. Like the people he employed, he went about his chores with far less enthusiasm that evening. Most of them did not know Giddy Mussett well enough to grieve for him, but they felt the effects of his death. Some customers were drawn to the Blue Anchor by ghoulish curiosity but the murder frightened many regular patrons away. It was the actors who kept the cooks and the servingmen busy, eating to assuage their appetites and drinking to relieve their sorrow.

There was one person who knew the deceased well. Kate Humble had a special place in her heart for Mussett. A friendship that had begun on his previous visit to the town had been revived instantly when she saw him, even though his face had been battered in a brawl. In their brief moments together, he had given her more pleasure and amusement than she had enjoyed in a whole year. Unlike the other kitchen maids, Kate could not simply work on as if nothing had happened. Pleading sickness, she withdrew to the tiny attic room that she shared at night with three others. There she could give free reign to her emotions, remembering the times she had enjoyed with Mussett and savouring some of the things he had said to her. Treasured memories made her smile through her tears. It pained her to think that she would never see him again.

Kate was still weeping copiously when there was a knock on the door. Fearing that it might be the landlord, she dried her tears with her apron. There was a second tap.

'Come in,' she said, biting her lip to hold back another fit of weeping.

The door opened and Nicholas Bracewell put his head around it.

'I was told that you were ill,' he said. 'I came to see how you were.'

She was touched. 'That's very kind of you, sir.'

'Giddy was a friend of mine. I know that you loved him, too.'

'He was the best man in the world,' she said as fresh

tears flowed. 'Forgive me, sir. I cannot help it. The thought of how he died distresses me so much.'

'And me, Kate.'

'Who but a madman could want to kill Giddy?'

'I mean to find out,' he assured her.

'He spoke well of you,' she said, wiping away her tears once more. 'Nick Bracewell let me out of prison – that's what he told me. I know that he did bad things sometimes, sir, but think well of him.'

'I always will.'

She studied him through moist eyes as if trying to decide if she could trust him. Nicholas caught a whiff of guilt that was mingled with fear. He sensed that she had something to tell him but he did not rush her. He gave her a consoling smile.

'Is there anything we can do for you?' he asked.

'Oh, sir, You do not have to bother about me. I am just a kitchen maid.'

'Giddy thought you much more than that.'

Her face brightened. 'Yes, he did. That's why I loved him.'

'Were you surprised to see him back in Faversham again?'

'No,' she said proudly. 'He promised me he'd come back to see me one day. Though he did not tell me that his face would be quite so bruised.'

'Did he say how he came about his injuries?'

'By falling down some steps when he was drunk.' She laughed merrily. 'Giddy was always too fond of his ale but I did not hold that against him.' Kate brushed away a last tear with a knuckle then met his gaze. 'Can I trust you, sir?' she asked.

'I hope so, Kate.'

'If I tell you something, will you promise me I will not get into trouble?'

'That depends what it is.'

'Giddy made me do it.'

'Do what, Kate?'

There was an awkward pause. 'Lie for him,' she confessed.

'What sort of lie did you tell?'

'You will be angry when you know, sir.'

'No,' said Nicholas quietly. 'If it concerns Giddy, I'll not be angry. I know he had his vices, Kate, but they made him what he was. I'll bear him no ill will.' He took a step closer to her. 'Tell me about this lie.'

'He did do it, sir,' she said, blurting the words out. 'He did put a sack over that man's head and wheeled him to the creek. I found him the sack in the kitchen. I also got him an apron and a cap so that Giddy looked like a servingman. There was no intent to harm the man,' she insisted. 'All that Giddy wanted to do was to frighten him. There were people about and he was sure that someone would rescue him. In the end, you were the one who did it. Giddy was glad of that.'

'Did he say *why* he put Master Gill in that boat?'

'It was but a jest, sir, like the others.'

'Others?' repeated Nicholas.

'Giddy told me what he did. In one place, he paid an

ostler to lock Master Gill in the privy. In Maidstone, he bribed a lad to throw a black cat in through the window where his enemy slept. Giddy had an excuse each time.'

'*You* were his excuse here at the Blue Anchor.'

'And I was glad to be it,' she said. 'Until now. Are you angry, sir?'

'No,' said Nicholas. 'I'm not angry, Kate.'

'But I lied to you and the others.'

'You were protecting a man you loved, that is all. The important thing is that the truth has now come out. To be honest, I am relieved.'

'Because Giddy played a trick on Master Gill?'

'In a sense, yes,' said Nicholas. 'I thought it might be the work of another man and that alarmed me. It was a cruel jest that could have led to serious harm. Giddy was wrong to do such a thing. But I do not hold it against you, Kate.'

'Thank you, sir,' she said, clutching at him. 'You are so kind.'

'I just wish to find the man who killed him. That's why I'm grateful for any information that helps me to do that. What you've just said has been very useful. It explains things that puzzled me.' He squeezed her hands in gratitude. 'Giddy was not a rich man, as you know. He leaves a poor bundle of things behind.'

'He was rich in the things that mattered, sir.'

'I know,' said Nicholas. 'We have no use for his belongings but there may be something there that you could have as a keepsake.' Her face lit up again. 'Would you like to take something of your choice?'

'Yes, please!' she said with alacrity.

Bursting into tears again, she flung herself into his arms.

Sebastian Frant sat in the parlour of the cottage with his brother. Supper was over and both Thomasina and her aunt had retired early to bed. The two men were alone. David Frant lit a pipe and puffed away at it before speaking.

'It is so good to see you both, Sebastian,' he said.

'We should have come to Faversham long before now.'

'You must visit us, brother, for I am not able to travel to Dover.'

'What does the doctor say?'

'That I'm afflicted with an incurable disease. It is called old age.'

'You are not that much older than me, David.'

'I never enjoyed your rude health.'

'You did,' said Frant, trying to cheer him up. 'And whatever the doctor says, you'll last many years yet.'

'I doubt that, Sebastian.'

Privately, so did Frant. He had been distressed to see how much his brother had declined since his last visit. His condition could not be ascribed solely to the passage of time. Some malady was slowly eating him away. David Frant had hollow cheeks, lacklustre eyes and a body that seemed to have shrunk in upon itself. When he had a sudden fit of coughing, it was minutes before he was able to speak again.

'Forgive me, Sebastian,' he said at length. 'This tobacco will ruin me.'

'It gives you pleasure and that is all that matters.'

'I get little of it elsewhere, I know that.'

A knock on the door made both men sit up. The servant girl went to see who it was and voices were heard in the passageway. A visitor was then shown into the parlour. Nicholas Bracewell was profuse in his apologies for intruding at that time of the evening but both men were pleased to see him. Frant pumped his arm in greeting. His brother indicated a chair and Nicholas sat down.

'Do you wish to hear more about the history of Faversham?' he asked.

'Another time,' said Nicholas. 'I come on an errand to see Sebastian.'

'What kind of errand?' asked Frant.

'A sad one, I fear.'

Nicholas lowered his voice and told them about the murder of Giddy Mussett. David Frant was dismayed but his brother, who had seen Mussett on stage, was quick to gauge the loss involved.

'But the fellow was a genius, Nick,' he said. 'Thomasina and I laughed at him until we were in pain. This is a terrible blow for Westfield's Men.'

'We are still dazed by it, Sebastian.'

'What will you do?'

'That is what I've come to tell you. We need your help.'

'How can I be of any assistance?' said Frant. 'I can be a fool at times, as David here will tell you, but I'm no clown. Do not look to me to replace Giddy Mussett. I doubt if any man in England could do that.'

'Happily, there is such a person.'

'Who?'

'Barnaby Gill.'

Frant was amazed. 'But he has a broken leg.'

'That will not hold him back in our hour of need.'

Nicholas explained how they proposed to overcome Gill's disability and drew approving comments from both men. David Frant was so amused by the notion of a foolish friar in a wheelbarrow that he resolved to see the play himself. His younger brother was still bewildered.

'What must I do, Nick?' he said. 'Push the wheelbarrow?'

'A pen is all that we ask you to push, Sebastian. Thus it stands,' said Nicholas, taking some sheets of paper from inside his jerkin. 'Edmund has written a new scene for the play and a couple of new songs. His hand still shakes with grief at the loss of Giddy. You'll see how he scribbles. We'd prefer a scrivener to make the words legible.'

'But I do not know this play. What is it called?'

'*The Foolish Friar*. A harmless comedy.'

'One of Edmund's pieces?'

'No, Sebastian. It's the work of another playwright but he is not here to make the changes that we require. Edmund will do that. He is a master cobbler.' He held up the sheets of paper. 'It has taken him only a few hours to produce these.'

'You must help them, Sebastian,' urged his brother. 'They need you.'

'And we'll gladly pay you for the work,' said Nicholas.

'I'd not dream of charging you a penny,' replied Frant, taking the papers from him to glance through them. 'It will take me far less to copy these songs than it took Edmund to create them. Thank you for calling on me. I'm delighted to aid you.'

'That's what I told the others.'

'It would have been impossible for me to refuse.'

'Why?'

'Because I have a daughter to answer to,' said Frant. 'When we heard that Westfield's Men were in Maidstone, I promised Thomasina that she would see the finest clown who ever appeared on a stage. She was disappointed to learn that Barnaby Gill was unable to take part even though he had a worthy substitute.'

'Barnaby will now substitute his own substitute,' said Nicholas.

'Quite so. What would Thomasina say if I did not assist him willingly?' He held up the papers. 'I'll deliver these to the Blue Anchor tomorrow morning with a set so crystal clear that even a blind man could read them.'

The rehearsal that morning went badly. Conway's Men were never less than competent on stage but never more than entertaining. They seemed to lack commitment and went about their work with a sense of obligation rather than dedication. As they rehearsed the play that they would perform in Canterbury that afternoon, they fell short of even their own modest standards. Tobias Fitzgeoffrey was sarcastic.

'Do you dare to call yourselves actors?' he said, addressing his whole company. 'A herd of cattle would give a better account of themselves on stage. And, at least, they would provide the audience with something to drink. All that you will do is to send them to sleep. It is shameful.'

He berated them for several minutes then sent them off in disgrace, confident that his scathing comments would sting them into giving a better performance. Martin Ling, the book holder, was not impressed by the actor-manager's tirade.

'You are as much to blame as anyone, Tobias,' he said.

'How can you say that when I was the only one to remember my lines?'

'The play needed more rehearsal.'

'That's my decision, Martin.'

'I only tell you what the others feel,' said Ling. 'You disappeared for the whole day yesterday when you should have been here to work on the piece.'

'I had important matters to attend to,' said Fitzgeoffrey.

'What is more important than offering decent fare to our spectators?'

The actor-manager rounded on him. Tobias Fitzgeoffrey was a tall, broad-shouldered man in his early thirties with handsome features and a commanding presence. Towering over his book holder, he looked down at him with utter contempt.

'If you do not like the way I run this company, Martin,' he said with scorn, 'you are welcome to leave. We'll happily spare you.'

'That thought has crossed my mind,' admitted Ling. 'But I'll not go until you pay me the money that you owe.

I'm not the only member of Conway's Men who is waiting for a debt to be settled.'

'All in good time.'

'How often have I heard you say that, Tobias?'

'Listen, you idiot,' said Fitzgeoffrey vehemently. 'When I went off yesterday, it was for the benefit of everyone. I had to perform a service for our patron and was duly rewarded. That money goes straight into our coffers.'

'When will it come out again to pay us?'

'When I am good and ready.'

Ling turned away to hide a sneer and began to gather up the properties that had been used during the rehearsal. Fitzgeoffrey remembered something. He crossed the room to block the other man's path.

'I heard a rumour that Giddy Mussett was in Canterbury yesterday,' he said.

'Did you?' replied Ling.

'What did he want?'

'Who knows?'

'You'd be the person he'd first seek out. Is that what he did, Martin?'

'He may've done.'

'Was he alone or did he bring someone else?'

'I cannot remember.'

'Did he tell you that he'd joined Westfield's Men?' asked Fitzgeoffrey. 'They must've been mad to engage someone like him.'

'You thought him worth his wage at one time, Tobias.'

'That was before I knew his true character. No matter.

All that is past now. Well,' he went on with a knowing smile. 'I hope that you enjoyed your talk with him.'

'Why?'

'Because I don't think that you'll ever see Giddy Mussett again.'

The Foolish Friar was a happy choice. It made few demands on a company that was still in a state of dejection after the murder of their clown. The two actors who had to work hardest were Barnaby Gill and Owen Elias, learning new lines and practising endlessly with the wheelbarrow. It became a weapon as well as a means of transport. Elias was able to sweep people off their feet by pushing the wheelbarrow into them, or leave it in places where they would trip inadvertently over it. Gill's early doubts were soon removed. Confined to his moveable couch, he could still extract the full comedy from his role. If anything, the wheelbarrow enhanced the humour by its originality. No friar had ever rolled on stage quite like that before.

Pleased with the way that the rehearsal had gone, Nicholas Bracewell was nevertheless anxious to get away. He took Firethorn aside to state his case.

'Let me go back to Canterbury again,' he said.

'We need you here, Nick.'

'But that's where we'll solve the murder of Giddy Mussett.'

'That will have to wait,' insisted Firethorn. 'Your duty is to stay here with us. The company is uneasy when you are away. George Dart can hold the book at a rehearsal but he will never be a Nick Bracewell. In any case, it's too dangerous for you to ride off alone and I can hardly spare anyone else to go with you.'

'I'll take my chances on the road.'

'It's a risk I'm not prepared to share. What happens if you are waylaid? It is bad enough to lose Giddy. If you went, we would be crippled indeed.'

Nicholas was earnest. 'We owe it to Giddy to catch his killer.'

'We owe it to our audience to serve them up a tasty dish.'

'What is to stop us solving a hideous crime as well?'

'Lack of time, Nick,' said Firethorn. 'Lack of time and shortage of people. Ride off to Canterbury and the rehearsal will slow to a halt. You were the one who made that wheelbarrow. Who else but you would have thought of using it on stage and coaxing Barnaby back into work? Westfield's Men *need* you here.'

'I have obligations to Giddy as well.'

'So do we all.'

'Then let me discharge them.'

'In due course.'

Nicholas gave up. Torn between duty to the company and an urge to avenge a crime, he had become increasingly frustrated. But he knew that Firethorn was right. The book holder's presence was crucial. As well as advising Edmund Hoode how *The Foolish Friar* could be amended to their advantage, he had engaged Sebastian Frant as their scrivener, made further important adjustments to the wheelbarrow, and inspected the place where they would perform so that he could take dimensions and decide where best to set the stage. Nicholas had also been a calming influence on the apprentices, all of whom had been overwhelmed by the murder of their clown.

'Take heart, Nick,' said Firethorn, reading his mind. 'I, too, would like to saddle up and gallop to Canterbury but we must discharge our obligations here first. Besides, I think that you are forgetting something.'

'What's that?' said Nicholas.

'The villain has struck twice and may do so again. It behoves us all to stay close together for our own protection. If you leave, you weaken our defence badly. Do you hear what I'm saying?' he asked, slipping an arm around the book holder. 'We may not need to go in search of the killer. He will come to us.'

Chapter Twelve

Given the circumstances, the performance of *The Foolish Friar* was an extraordinary achievement. Westfield's Men were beset by all kinds of problems. Their new clown had been murdered at the Blue Anchor and it left them in the state of cold fear. Coming, as it did, in the wake of the ambush at the ford, the crime made them feel highly vulnerable. Most of the actors just wanted to creep away from Faversham. Their old clown, Barnaby Gill, forced to step into the breach, was nursing a broken leg and could only take the title role if changes were made to the play that permitted its foolish friar to be moved around the stage in a wheelbarrow. To make up for the lost dances, additional songs were written. To master the new scenes that Edmund Hoode had provided, intensive rehearsal was necessary. Owen Elias, in particular, was put under immense pressure. He was called upon not only to learn a different role at short notice but, as a fellow friar, had to wheel Gill around in his wheelbarrow and, at the height of the action, sing a duet with him. Mistakes came so thick and fast during rehearsals that they despaired of ever getting the play in a fit state for an audience.

Yet somehow they succeeded. Staged before the citizens of Faversham in their town hall, *The Foolish Friar* was a glorious romp that was played to the hilt by the actors. None of the spectators would have guessed that the actors were mourning the death of Giddy Mussett, stabbed to death less than forty-eight hours earlier. Grief was hidden beneath joyous abandon. Gill surpassed himself in the role of a cunning friar with so much charm and guile that he was able to exploit the people of a small town for bed, board and money. Pleading poverty, he nevertheless contrived to become the wealthiest man in the town. His folly consisted in overreaching himself. Not content with living off the townspeople, he tried to collect sexual favours as well, assuring the young women in question that he would absolve them of any sin that they committed with him.

Lawrence Firethorn played the local magistrate, taken in at first by the friar's plausible tales and allowing him and the other friar to live under his own roof. It was only when the magistrate's daughter – Richard Honeydew at his most enchanting – aroused the lust of the lecherous friar that their guest was revealed in his true light. Using his supposedly broken leg as a means of gaining sympathy, the friar had no disability once he had enticed his prey into a bedchamber.

To expose the man, and to get his revenge, the magistrate encouraged his daughter to agree to an assignation and then, at midnight, went to the friar in her place. Firethorn had made his name playing tragic heroes but he proved that he could disguise himself as a woman just as effectively as any of the apprentices. Donning a cloak and covering his beard with a veil, he worked the friar up into such a passion that the man confessed his base desires. It was left to the magistrate to beat him, arrest him and push him swiftly around in circles in the wheelbarrow before tipping him into the river.

The splash that the audience heard was nothing more than a bucket being dropped offstage into a barrel of water by Nicholas Bracewell but it was so well timed that it sounded very convincing. Instead of being tipped out, the friar was, in fact, lifted from his wheelbarrow by Elias and Hoode, who were stationed behind the scenery for the purpose. It was only one of many effects that the book holder had devised and, like all the others, it worked remarkably well. The audience went into ecstasies. A comedy with darker undertones, *The Foolish Friar* was hailed as something that was infinitely superior to the play given earlier by Conway's Men. Even the mayor was impressed. He still had reservations about the whole notion of drama but they did not prevent him from joining in the laughter with everyone else.

Nicholas was relieved that the performance had gone so well and congratulated Gill on his ability to improvise so brilliantly. Firethorn actually embraced the invalid and everyone in the company agreed that the foolish friar had been hilarious. Gill was happy at last. He was the undisputed clown once more. It appealed to his vanity that the person the mayor first wanted to meet was the friar. Firethorn, for once, did not bristle with jealousy. The reputation of Westfield's Men had been upheld and that is what mattered most to him. They had also earned some money in the process. He was very conscious of the main reason for their success. He took his book holder aside.

'We owe it all to you, Nick,' he said.

'It was a victory for the whole company.'

'Only because you suggested a play that could entice Barnaby back on stage.'

'I've never seen him better,' said Nicholas.

'Nor I. Perhaps we should keep him in that wheelbarrow in perpetuity. That device gained more laughs than *I* did,' he complained good-humouredly. 'You'll have to make one for me as well, Nick.'

'Barnaby would prefer to have two good legs rather than a single wheel.'

'He's back with us and for that blessing I must thank you.'

'Edmund did his share, so did Sebastian Frant.'

'Yes,' said Firethorn. 'It was good to have our old scrivener back again. I must go and speak to him – and to that beautiful daughter of his.' He gave a ripe chuckle. 'I'm sure that Thomasina would prefer a handsome magistrate like me to a foolish friar with his leg in splints.'

He left the room that they had been using as their

tiring-house and went out into the hall to receive plaudits from all sides. Most of the audience had dispersed but a number of spectators still lingered. When he followed the actor-manager, Nicholas was touched to see that Pieter Hendrik was waiting to see him.

'I did not expect to see you here in Faversham,' said Nicholas in surprise. 'Did you enjoy the play?'

'Fery much,' replied Hendrik, grinning broadly. 'The friar, he make me laugh. But ver is the other man, the one I see in Medstone?'

'Giddy Mussett was unable to appear today, I fear.'

'Fery sorry to hear that.'

'What brings you to Faversham?'

'Vork, my friend. I hev customers here so I deliver what they buy. Then I hear that these actors will put on a play, so I stay to vatch.'

'I'm glad that you did,' said Nicholas.

Hendrik's grin vanished. 'Ver is Conway's Men?'

'Still in Canterbury, I hope. We travel there tomorrow morning.'

'You speak to Master Fizzgoffrey?'

'Oh, yes,' promised Nicholas. 'Tobias Fitzgeoffrey and I have more than one thing to discuss. Your bill is among them. I'll remind him of the money that he owes.'

'Fery good, I thenk you. Give my luff to Anne.'

'I'll give her your letter as well.'

'Ah, yes,' said Hendrik, waving a farewell. 'That, I forget.'

Nicholas watched him go then switched his gaze to

236

Firethorn, who was being introduced to David Frant and his wife. While lapping up their praise, the actor's chief interest was in Thomasina and he took her hand to kiss it. Nicholas could see that she was not sure how to react. He went to her aid.

'A whole bevy of Frants,' he observed. 'We are honoured.'

Frant smiled. 'We came in force to support you, Nick.'

'You did more than that, Sebastian. You provided me with the only pieces of the play that I could read clearly.' He turned to Thomasina. 'Your father claims that his hand no longer has its former neatness but that's not true.'

'I know,' she said fondly. 'Father has lost none of his accomplishments.'

'What are *your* accomplishments?' asked Firethorn, smiling at her 'Apart from a lovely face and a graceful carriage, that is. What hidden talents do you have?'

'None, Master Firethorn.'

'Come, come. I'll not believe that.'

'Thomasina is too modest,' said Frant with paternal pride. 'She has many accomplishments. She sings well and plays upon the virginals. But her greatest talent lies in the way that she looks after her father.'

'I'd love to hear you play something,' said Firethorn, catching her eye. 'I, too, have a keen interest in the virginals.'

The remark embarrassed Thomasina and made her father wince slightly. David Frant and his wife did not seem to notice Firethorn's double meaning. They looked at him in awe, still dazzled by the wonder of his performance.

'Did you enjoy the play?' Nicholas asked them.

'Oh, we did,' said David Frant. 'We've never seen anything like it.'

'What about you, Sebastian?'

'You know my opinion of Westfield's Men,' said Frant affably. 'They are the King Midas among theatre companies. Whatever they touch, they turn to gold.'

Firethorn gave a token bow. 'Thank you, Sebastian.'

'Do you agree with your father?' asked Nicholas, turning to Thomasina.

'Yes,' she replied.

'You have seen us twice now. Which of the plays did you prefer?'

'*Cupid's Folly*, I think.'

'Why?'

'I liked its merriment.'

'But there was merriment in *The Foolish Friar*,' argued Nicholas, 'and a sharper edge to its plot. Did you not approve of the play?'

'Yes, yes,' said Thomasina brightly.

'I sense a reservation.'

'There is none. It was truly wonderful.'

Though she spoke with enthusiasm, Nicholas somehow did not believe her.

The funeral of Giddy Mussett was held on the following morning. After the heady success of the previous afternoon, the actors were brought back down to earth again, reminded that their substitute clown had been killed by an assassin and that they themselves might now be under threat. As they gathered at the little church, they were racked by anguish and troubled by superstition. Every member of the company attended, including Barnaby Gill, who made some gracious comments about his former rival. It seemed a fitting end for a vagabond like Mussett that his bones should be laid to rest during a tour of a county far removed from the place in which he had been born. When the earth was tossed upon the coffin, the actors bade farewell to a remarkable man who would leave a trail of vivid memories behind him.

Kate Humble was among the mourners, holding back tears until the moment when they all moved away from the graveside. When he observed her slipping behind some yew trees to weep in privacy, Nicholas went after her to offer some consolation. As soon as she saw him, she went gratefully into his arms. He waited until her sobbing ended.

'I have something for you, Kate,' he said, releasing her.

'You've already let me choose a keepsake from Giddy's belongings.'

'This is not a keepsake.'

'Then what is it?'

Nicholas put money into her hand. 'His wages.'

'Oh, no,' she said, shaking her head. 'I'll not take his money.'

'Giddy would have wanted you to have it.'

'But he told me that he had to repay a debt to you for getting him out of prison.'

'That debt was settled by his death. Take the money.'

Kate stared at the coins. 'This is more than I can earn in a month.'

'Then use it to buy something that will remind you of Giddy.'

'Oh, I will, sir. I will. Thank you.'

'Thank *you*, Kate. In telling me the truth about what happened at the Blue Anchor, you were a great help to me. It was good to know that it was Giddy who set Master Gill adrift in the creek.'

'I told a lie,' she confessed. 'Master Gill will be furious with me.'

'No,' said Nicholas. 'That incident was buried with Giddy. I've said nothing to Master Gill or to anyone else. There is no reason for them to know.'

After heaving a sigh of relief, she leant forward to kiss him on the cheek before hurrying off on her own. Nicholas rejoined the others as they walked back to the Blue Anchor. Wheeled along by George Dart, Gill was explaining to all who would listen why Mussett was such a worthy rival of his. The untimely death allowed Gill to speak of him with a measure of respect and even a degree of affection. Nicholas did not wish to change that benign view of the dead man by telling Gill who had been responsible for the three cruel jests at his expense.

When they got back to the inn, they found Sebastian Frant waiting to wave them off. Firethorn was disappointed to see that Thomasina was not with him.

'Where's that divine creature you call a daughter?' he asked.

'Thomasina is at the cottage with her uncle and aunt.'

'I was hoping for a farewell kiss.'

240

'Then do not expect it from me, Lawrence,' said Frant with a smile. He looked around the sad faces. 'Was the funeral distressing?'

'Very distressing,' confided Firethorn. 'Giddy was a rare fellow. I've not known anyone make such a lasting impression in such a short time.'

'He certainly made an impression in *Cupid's Folly*.'

'He'd have done so in any play, Sebastian. He's a huge loss.'

'But it was swiftly repaired when Barnaby came to your aid.'

'That was Nick's invention. Like most things of consequence in this company.'

'He even pressed me into service again.'

'You can be our scrivener at any time you choose.'

'A tempting offer,' said Frant, holding up a palm, 'but one that I must refuse. I am retired, Lawrence. I'm learning the joys of not having to work for a living any more.'

Firethorn grimaced. 'If only *I* could do that, Sebastian,' he sighed. 'But there's no release for me. I must go on and on until I expire on stage.'

'That will never happen. You will act for all eternity.'

'Save me from that – *please*!'

After shaking his hand, Frant went off to say goodbye to his other friends in the company. Gill, Hoode and Elias were especially sorry to take their leave of him. They appreciated the value of a meticulous scrivener. The last in line was Nicholas Bracewell. There was a warm handshake.

'When do you set off, Nick?' asked Frant.

'Within the hour.'

'Glad to shake the dust of Faversham from your feet, I daresay.'

'No,' said Nicholas. 'There were happier memories along with the one that has cast a shadow over today. We had our success with *The Foolish Friar*.'

'It was more than a success, Nick. It was a triumph.'

'Your daughter did not seem to think so.'

'Thomasina liked it as much as I did.'

'That was not the feeling that I had,' said Nicholas. 'Was there something in the piece that offended her?'

'How could there be? It was harmless fun.'

'Did she find it too bawdy, perhaps?'

'Not a whit. The fault was not in the play, Nick. Thomasina had something else on her mind, as did I, and it came between us and full enjoyment. The doctor called to see my brother yesterday,' he explained, 'and I managed a word with him alone. The news is not good. According to the doctor, David has less than three months to live.'

Nicholas was upset. 'I'm truly sorry to hear that. I so enjoyed meeting him.'

'It made me feel guilty. I've neglected my brother shamefully. If it had not been for the fact that Westfield's Men were coming to Faversham, I might not have seen him this time.' He hunched his shoulders. '*That* is why Thomasina was distracted yesterday. Her thoughts were with her uncle.'

'She strikes me as a compassionate niece.'

'Oh, she is. Thomasina always puts others first.'

242

'How long will you stay in Faversham?'

'Until tomorrow,' said Frant. 'There's a party travelling to Dover and we'll join them for safety. We have commitments at home or we'd stay longer with David. So, my friend, we must part.'

'Meeting you again was a happy accident.'

'The happiness is all mine, Nick. I wish you well in Canterbury.'

'Thank you,' said Nicholas. 'Shall we see you when we reach Dover?'

'Yes, Nick. Thomasina and I will be there to watch you.'

'We'll count on you.'

'Tell that to Lawrence,' said Frant, glancing at Firethorn. 'He looks as if he is in need of cheering news. When you play in Dover, you will have at least two spectators.'

Westfield's Men set out from Faversham with some trepidation. With its uncomfortable memories, the Blue Anchor was an inn that they were glad to leave but the open road held even more danger for them. One assault on them had already taken place. They feared that a second, more deadly attack might come. Firethorn did his best to dispel their anxiety by riding at the head of the column with his sword in his hand. Armed and alert, Owen Elias brought up the rear on his horse. At Nicholas's suggestion, the wagons kept much closer together than before so that one of them could not be picked off with such ease. The book holder drove the first wagon, carrying the apprentices and some of the baggage with him. Seated beside Nicholas was Edmund Hoode, who felt too exposed on his donkey so he had tethered the animal to the wagon.

It was a cloudy day but there was no imminent threat of rain. They rumbled along the well-worn track that pilgrims had taken in earlier days. Hoode took note of that.

'How many feet have come this way, Nick?' he wondered.

'Far too many to count.'

'The shrine of St Thomas was the most popular in England.'

'Rightly so, Edmund.'

'There are tales of wondrous miracles being performed there.' He looked nervously around. 'We could do with one ourselves.'

'What sort of miracle did you have in mind?'

'One that put us safely in the middle of Canterbury.'

'We'll get there in due course,' said Nicholas.

'But will we arrive in one piece?'

'I am sure that we will. There are too many of us to tempt highwaymen and we are too vigilant to be caught in an ambush again. Rest easy.'

'Someone has a grudge against us, Nick.'

'Someone did,' said Nicholas. 'That is why Giddy was killed. But our enemy may have been satisfied by his death and quietly withdrawn.'

'Do you still think that Conway's Men may be involved?'

'Not so much the company as its patron. He certainly bears a grudge. So does Tobias Fitzgeoffrey. He is eaten away with envy at what Lawrence has achieved.'

'With the help of others,' said Hoode.

'I was not forgetting actors like Barnaby Gill, Owen Elias and James Ingram. Then there are these clever young apprentices curled up behind us. They all helped Lawrence to become what he is – as did a certain playwright called Edmund Hoode.'

'Add your name to that list, Nick.'

'I am only a small link in the chain.'

'Away with this modesty! There are times when you *are* the chain.'

They paused for refreshment near Boughton-under-Blean then pressed on at a slightly faster pace. Once past the halfway point, the company felt more secure and there was even some light-hearted banter in the wagons. Firethorn sheathed his sword, Elias yielded his horse to Rowland Carr so that he could take his turn at driving a wagon and Hoode felt confident enough to ride his donkey. Occasional rays of sunshine pierced the clouds. The dejection they had felt since the funeral slowly began to fade away.

Still driving the first wagon, Nicholas was glad of Richard Honeydew's company. The fair-haired young apprentice with the angelic face clambered on to the seat beside him and watched the two horses as they used their tails to flick away bothersome insects. Honeydew was still worried.

'The others say that we are cursed,' he began.

'Do not listen to them, Dick.'

'We've met one setback after another.'

'That's not unusual in this profession,' said Nicholas resignedly. 'Acting is a perilous road to follow. Only the brave and the sure-footed ever survive.'

The boy shuddered. 'I'm not at all brave.'

'Yes, you are. It took bravery to act the way that you did yesterday in *The Foolish Friar*. The whole company showed courage. I was proud of you, Dick.'

'Were you?'

'You set an example to the other lads.'

Honeydew lowered his voice. 'Do you know what they are saying?'

'What?'

'They think that we are damned.'

'That's silly talk.'

'I told them that but Stephen claimed there was clear proof.'

'Proof?'

'Yes,' said the boy. 'Giddy was our friend. He could make us laugh without even trying. He was much nicer to us than Barnaby, we all agree on that. Stephen says that he knew we were damned when it was Giddy who was murdered and not Barnaby.'

'He should be ashamed of such a thought!' said Nicholas angrily.

'That's what I told him.'

'I'll speak to him myself.'

'You'll only get me into trouble with Stephen if you do that.'

'I won't have anyone saying such things, Dick. We've had ill luck, that is all. Giddy must be mourned but we must be very grateful that Barnaby is still with us.'

'He was his old self in *The Foolish Friar*.'

'Remind the others of that.'

Nicholas was disturbed by the news that Stephen Judd, one of the apprentices, could make such an observation about the rival clowns in the company. It showed him how unpopular Gill was with the boys in spite of his attempts to befriend them. That they should actually wish him dead instead of Giddy Mussett was alarming. It was something that needed to be discussed fully with them.

'Who is doing it, Nick?' asked Honeydew.

'Doing what?'

'Trying to destroy Westfield's Men.'

Nicholas gritted his teeth. 'I am hoping to learn that in Canterbury.'

The road ahead curved slowly round to the right between two high, grassy banks. Until they reached the crown of the bend, there seemed no cause for alarm. Then a small avalanche descended from the top of one of the banks, hurtling down the incline to strike at the wheels of the first wagon and litter the ground with a pile of sharp stones. The suddenness of the attack spread instant fear. Firethorn's stallion bolted, Hoode's donkey threw him from the saddle again and the horses pulling the first wagon were so terrified that they broke into a gallop. Nicholas tried hard to control them but they raced on regardless with the wagon bumping and lurching violently. The apprentices were thrown from side to side and most of the baggage was tossed out of the wagon altogether. The horses had charged over two hundred yards at a reckless pace before Nicholas finally managed to pull them to a halt.

The four apprentices were in tears, bruised and lacerated after their headlong journey. Scattered on the road behind them were various properties and pieces of scenery, some of it smashed to pieces. After checking that nobody in the wagon was seriously hurt, Nicholas jumped down and went to calm the horses, stroking their necks as he talked to them. It was only when they stopped rolling their eyes that he felt they were soothed. Honeydew was the first of the apprentices to recover, hopping down from the wagon to see if he could be of assistance. Nicholas asked him to hold the bridles of the horses so that he could take stock of the damage. It was extensive. The wheel that had been struck hardest by the stones had lost a couple of spokes and another had shed its iron rim when they hit a deep pothole at speed. Something had snapped underneath the wagon so that it tilted at sharp angle. Without repairs, it was impossible to continue.

Having mastered his horse at last, Firethorn cantered up to them.

'Is anyone hurt?' he enquired, reining in his mount.

'No serious injuries,' said Nicholas.

'Thank goodness for that.'

'What about the others?'

'More frightened than hurt, Nick.'

'Then it could have been far worse.'

'This is bad enough,' said Firethorn angrily, pointing to the wagon and to the trail of baggage in its wake. 'I hoped that we might be safe but we have not seen the last of them, after all. They want more blood.'

* * *

Adversity bonded them together. With the single exception of Barnaby Gill, who claimed that the avalanche had been directed solely at him, everyone did his share without complaint. The stones were removed from the road so that the other wagons could catch up with the first one. They camped in a semi-circle while the repairs were undertaken. Skills from other occupations were brought into action. During his time at sea, Nicholas had learnt a great deal from the ship's carpenter and he put that knowledge to good effect. When the horses had been unhitched, the first wagon was propped up firmly so that the book holder could remove the wheel with the broken spokes. The actors watched in admiration as Nicholas fashioned some temporary spokes out of the oaken staffs that were used in *The Foolish Friar*. Once they were fitted, the wheel could be replaced.

It was Firethorn who took charge of the other wheel. The son of a blacksmith, he had not entirely forgotten what he had been taught in his father's forge. The cracked rim was retrieved, a fire was lit and the actor-manager was able to show them how practised a wheelwright he was. Two daggers bound tightly together had to serve as tongs but that did not hold him up. When the fire was red enough, he plunged the rim into it in stages so that the metal slowly expanded. Aided by Nicholas, he got the sizzling rim back on the wheel then used a hammer to tap it into position. It all went so smoothly that Firethorn earned a round of applause. With the wheels now mended, Nicholas could concentrate on the broken struts underneath the wagon.

Slow, laborious work was made easier by the frequent shouts of encouragement from the others. Not all the actors were spectators. While most of them stayed behind, two of them – Owen Elias and James Ingram – had ridden on to Canterbury. Valuable hours would be taken up by the repairs to the wagon and they were anxious to speak to the mayor during his working day so that they could secure a licence to perform in the city. Firethorn had also instructed them to seek out a suitable inn for the company. When the actors returned, Nicholas was still flat on his back, hammering a new strut into position beneath the wagon. He crawled out to hear what they had to say.

Wearied by the ride, the Welshman acted as their spokesman.

'Bad tidings,' he announced.

'Why?' asked Nicholas.

'They'll not grant us a licence.'

Firethorn was outraged. 'They refuse to let us play in the city?'

'No, Lawrence,' said Elias. 'If we return in a week or two, they will be happy to see us perform. Tomorrow, it seems, they start a religious festival that takes over the whole city for days. Even Westfield's Men could not outdo their grand pageants. In brief, we must take our art elsewhere.'

'What of Conway's Men?' said Nicholas.

'That was the other problem,' replied Ingram. 'Conway's Men staged a tragedy there only yesterday. The mayor thought it unwise to have one troupe hard on the heels of another. He felt that a distance should be put between them.'

'There *is* a distance between us and Conway's Men,' declared Firethorn. 'It is a vast chasm. We are real actors while they are mere pretenders. But the mayor speaks sense. I do not wish to tread the boards immediately after Tobias Fitzgeoffrey and his vile crew. We must wait for the stink to clear first.'

'Take me back to London!' ordered Gill. 'I'll not stay in this barbarous county.'

'You'll do as I wish, Barnaby.'

'It would be an act of suicide, Lawrence. We were ambushed on the road to Faversham. Giddy was murdered at the Blue Anchor and I was fortunate not to follow him into the grave. That avalanche was caused in order to crush me to death and now,' he went on, pointing in the direction of Canterbury, 'they have the gall to turn us away from the city like beggars. Let's cut our losses and go home.'

'Kent *is* our home for the time being,' said Firethorn.

'Yes,' said Nicholas. 'If one place spurns us, we simply go to another. Let's stay the night in Canterbury while we make our plans then set off again tomorrow.'

'Well said, Nick!'

'There are inns aplenty in the city,' noted Elias. 'We can drink to our escape.'

'And keep our eyes peeled for further attacks,' warned Nicholas. 'But what else did you learn of Conway's Men, Owen?'

'Only that their play was not well received.'

'Are they still in the city?'

'No, they left at dawn.'

Nicholas was disappointed. 'Tobias Fitzgeoffrey is no longer there?'

'No,' said Elias. 'He and his company have quit Canterbury.'

'Where were they headed?'

'Nobody seemed to know.'

The Three Tuns was a commodious inn that looked particularly inviting after the trials of their journey from Faversham. Once they had settled in, Westfield's Men took advantage of the light evening to explore the city while they could. Conscious of possible danger, the actors went off in small groups so that nobody was isolated. George Dart, however, much to his disgust, was given the unenviable task of remaining at the inn to stand guard over Barnaby Gill, who refused to venture out. Nicholas Bracewell was in charge of the four apprentices. Firethorn and Hoode walked with them in the direction of the cathedral. As they strolled along, Nicholas took the opportunity to detach Stephen Judd so that he could have a private word with the lad. He scolded him for even thinking that Gill's death would have been preferable to that of Giddy Mussett and impressed upon him how much Westfield's Men owed to the talents of their clown. By the time that the book holder had finished with him, Judd was duly cowed and penitent. Nicholas was pleased to see that, when they entered the cathedral, the boy went off to kneel down and beg forgiveness.

The visitors spent an hour admiring the magnificent interior of the building and reading the inscriptions on the various tombstones. It was when they came back out through Christ Church Gate that Nicholas was seized by an impulse. Sending the others on ahead of him, he walked across to the Crown, the small inn that Giddy Mussett had recommended for its ale. Nicholas was not there in search of drink but in the faint hope that a certain person might still be there. A cursory glance around the busy taproom told him that he was wasting his time and he was about to leave. Then he caught sight of a dishevelled individual, sitting alone in a corner and staring into an empty tankard, half-hidden by three customers who stood directly in front of him. Nicholas felt the thrill of recognition. It was Martin Ling, the discontented book holder from Conway's Men.

After buying two tankards of ale, Nicholas went over to Ling and sat down.

'Have a drink with me, my friend,' said Nicholas.

Ling looked up. 'Who are you?'

'My name is Nicholas Bracewell.'

'I've heard of you. Giddy Mussett mentioned your name. You hold the book for Westfield's Men. God bless you for this!' he said, lifting the tankard to sip from it. 'It comes when I most need it.' He regarded Nicholas through watery eyes. 'So you have reached Canterbury, have you? Why did you not bring Giddy with you?'

'He's no longer with us, alas.'

'Fallen out with you already?'

'Fallen out with everything,' said Nicholas sadly, taking a first sip of his own ale. 'Giddy is dead. He was murdered at the inn where we stayed in Faversham.'

Ling was so shocked by the news that he had to take a long drink before he could even speak. Nicholas gave him a brief account of what had happened, making no mention of the other attacks on the company. Ling's haggard face was creased into folds of sympathy.

'Who could have done such a thing?' he asked, shaking his head with incredulity.

'I wish we knew.'

'Giddy made enemies as easily as friends but I can't believe that anyone hated him enough to want him dead. These are dreadful tidings.'

'Why did he leave Conway's Men?'

'For the same reason that I did,' said Ling with rancour. 'He could not stomach Master Fitzgeoffrey. The fellow is mean-spirited and vindictive. I only stayed with him for the sake of the others but he pushed me beyond my limit. Tobias Fitzgeoffrey abused me once too often,' he went on, baring a row of blackened teeth. 'When they set off this morning, I stayed behind. Let him find another book holder.'

'You say that he's vindictive?'

'He'll harbour a grudge for a decade.'

'Did he have any grudges against Giddy?'

'Dozens.'

'Of what nature?'

'The chief one was the most obvious,' said Ling. 'Giddy stole his thunder during a play. Master Fitzgeoffrey would not allow that. He cut the clown's lines and took out two songs to bring Giddy to heel.' He gave a hollow laugh. 'It made no difference. The next time we staged that play,

Giddy put in a jig that he invented and won the love of the audience. But he got no love from Tobias Fitzgeoffrey.'

'Where is the company now?'

'Searching for a book holder and wishing that they still had me.'

'What's their next port of call?'

'Walmer.'

'I know it,' said Nicholas, noting that Conway's Men would not be far from Dover. 'How long will they stay there?'

'Walmer is too small to provide them with an audience,' explained Ling. 'They are to perform at a house nearby that's owned by a friend of our patron.' He pulled a face. '*Our* patron, do I say? He's mine no longer, thank heaven!'

'What manner of man is Lord Conway?'

'As full of spite as Master Fitzgeoffrey. They are twin fangs of malice.'

'One last question,' said Nicholas.

Ling smiled. 'Buy me more ale and you can ask all the questions you wish.'

'Did you ever meet a man called Fortunatus Hope?'

'Why, yes. A number of times. He was Lord Conway's nephew.'

'Tell me about him.'

'There's not much to tell,' said Ling, scratching his chin. 'He was an amiable fellow, that I do remember, and a generous one as well. Once, when we played in Hythe, he bought us all a meal to celebrate the performance.'

'A wealthy man, then?'

'More free with money than his uncle, I know that.'

'Why did the two of them quarrel?'

'You said there was only one more question,' complained the other.

'Here,' said Nicholas, putting some coins on the table. 'How many answers will that purchase?'

'As many as you ask,' said Ling, scooping up the money gratefully. 'But, first, let *me* pose a question. Why are you here?'

'I'm trying to track down the man who killed Giddy Mussett.'

'It was not Master Hope, I can assure you of that.'

'I know,' said Nicholas. 'He, too, was stabbed in the back.'

Ling gaped at him. 'He's *dead*?'

'Felled, I believe, by the same hand that killed Giddy.'

'They were both such friendly souls.'

'When did you last see Master Hope?'

'It must have been some months ago,' said Ling, noisily draining his tankard. 'We were touring in Essex, walking at the cart's arse from town to town. Lord Conway came to see us play in Colchester and Master Hope was part of his circle. Something happened to drive the two men apart but I know not what it was. All I can remember is that our patron was seething with rage.'

'How close is he to Master Fitzgeoffrey?'

'They are two yoke-devils.'

'That is what I imagined,' said Nicholas, about to rise. 'Well, thank you, my friend. You have given me food for thought.'

Ling grabbed his arm. 'Do not leave now,' he pleaded. 'We've so much to talk about. Book holders like us should stick together.' He grinned obsequiously. 'Dare I ask if you have room in your company for another hired man?'

'Alas, no. We had to shed some of our fellows before we even set out.'

'It was ever thus. Touring is a means of torture.'

'We've had our share of that,' admitted Nicholas. He removed Ling's hand and got up from the table. 'Pray excuse me. They'll be wondering where I am.'

'You've barely touched your ale.'

'Drink it for me. I think you've earned it.'

'But I haven't told you about Master Fitzgeoffrey yet.'

'Told me what?'

'It's only just popped into my mind,' said Ling, pulling the other tankard across to him. 'He heard that Giddy had come to see me here in Canterbury. He was not pleased about that. Then he told me something that I thought strange at the time.'

'And what was that?'

'He said that I'd never see Giddy Mussett again.'

Finding the man at the Crown had been a stroke of good fortune but Nicholas felt that he deserved one after all the reverses he had suffered. Martin Ling was a pathetic character, working for a man he loathed until he could no longer bear his insults, then abandoning the company for an uncertain future. Even if there had been a vacant place among Westfield's Men, Nicholas would not have advised anyone to offer it to Ling. Iron had entered the man's soul and drink had corrupted his judgement. He was an example of a man who had been broken on the wheel of his profession. Nevertheless, he had been able to give Nicholas some valuable information. When he left the Crown, he had plenty to reflect upon during the walk back.

Even allowing for Ling's prejudices, Tobias Fitzgeoffrey sounded like a nasty and objectionable man but that was not conclusive proof that he was capable of murder. His presence at the Queen's Head on the fateful afternoon of the affray was something that Nicholas thought highly significant. Why else would the man be there if not to relish the confusion into which a rival company was thrown? Fitzgeoffrey would hardly have been in the audience by chance. To get to London, he had left his company languishing in Kent, unable to perform without him. When money was in such short supply for Conway's Men, why had their manager passed up the opportunity of a performance in favour of a visit to the capital? More surprisingly, why, on his return, was a man who was reputed to be stingy with money, suddenly overtaken by a spirit of generosity?

Nicholas decided that the crucial relationship was the one between Fitzgeoffrey and his patron. Until he could meet one or both of them, he could not reach a firm verdict but evidence was slowly piling up against them. In causing the affray, Nicholas reasoned, they hoped to bring to an end the occupation of Gracechurch Street by Westfield's Men. When the company travelled to Kent, their new clown was first ambushed, then killed, as a means of bringing the tour to an end. But the troupe was too resilient to be quashed. Since it dared to soldier on, another attack was made on it during the journey to Canterbury. Firethorn's prediction was true. They wanted more blood. The enemies of Westfield's Men would not stop until they had halted the company in its tracks.

Absorbed in his thoughts, Nicholas strode through the streets alone without any fear for his own safety. It was only when he reached the door of the Three Tuns that he chose to look over his shoulder. A man dived quickly into the shadows. It was a sobering reminder. Nicholas had been followed.

Chapter Thirteen

Before they could set out next morning, repairs had to be made to the wagon that was damaged by the avalanche. A new wheel was bought to replace the one that Nicholas had mended sufficiently well to get them to Canterbury, and lengths of stout timber were used to strengthen the makeshift struts beneath the wagon. The local wheelwright employed to help was full of praise for the way that the rim had been put back on the other wheel and his comments fed Lawrence Firethorn's vanity. The actor boasted aloud about his skills as a blacksmith. It was Barnaby Gill, reclining in his wheelbarrow, who pricked the bubble of his conceit.

'You should have stayed in the trade, Lawrence,' he said waspishly.

Firethorn blenched. 'And deprive the stage of my genius?'

'I think that your skills are more suited to the forge.'

'At least, I *have* skills of some sort, Barnaby. Unlike you.'

'You would have made an excellent blacksmith.'

'Had you been my anvil, I'd have enjoyed the work.'

'Barnaby *is* your anvil,' said Edmund Hoode wearily. 'You strike sparks off him whenever you meet.'

'I've yet to see any spark in his acting,' said Firethorn.

'That is because you are too busy looking at yourself,' countered Gill. 'An audience is nothing more than a set of mirrors in which you preen yourself.'

'*You* are the Narcissus in this troupe, Barnaby.'

'I strive to look my best, that is all.'

'And you do look your best in that wheelbarrow,' teased Firethorn. 'I'd be more than happy to tip you onto my garden to enrich the soil.'

'Even with a broken leg, I can outrun you on stage.'

'But you only go in circles.'

The rest of the company had gathered in the yard for departure but they were too accustomed to the banter between Firethorn and Gill to pay much attention to their latest squabble. When the baggage had been loaded, they climbed into their respective wagons. Owen Elias led his horse out of the stables and went over to the first wagon.

'Are we ready to leave, Nick?' he asked.

'Yes,' said Nicholas, checking the harness. 'We must head for the Dover Road.'

'I hope that we can have one journey without an ambush.'

'I'm sure that we shall, Owen.'

'What makes you so certain?'

'Wait and see.'

Nicholas clambered up into his seat and took the reins. When Gill and his wheelbarrow had been lifted into the second wagon, it was time to go. They rolled out of the inn yard and into the busy streets of Canterbury. Firethorn rode ahead, as usual, and Elias brought up the rear with Hoode and his donkey for company. The procession made its way towards Ridingate. There was a distinct mood of apprehension. In view of the earlier attacks, Westfield's Men were understandably nervous. Sensible precautions had been taken. Even the apprentices had been given daggers and taught how to defend themselves. Trained in the art of stage fights, the actors all knew how to handle weapons but there was a world of difference between rehearsed combat and fight for their lives with an enemy who could select the time, place and means of an attack. The moment they left the comparative safety of the city, they began to feel uneasy. Richard Honeydew gave an involuntary shiver. He climbed onto the seat beside Nicholas.

'I wish that we could have stayed in Canterbury,' he said.

'The city was not ready for us, Dick.'

'The open road frightens me.'

'When you have all your friends around you?'

'The others are as worried as me,' said Honeydew. 'You've given us daggers but what use are they against an avalanche?'

'No use at all,' agreed Nicholas, 'but we are unlikely to be attacked in that way again. If enemies still lurk in wait, they will not use the same device because they know that we will be more circumspect. Besides, the avalanche inflicted no injuries. It merely delayed us for a few hours.'

'Why do they *want* to injure us, Nick?'

'I believe that envy is at work.'

'Is that reason enough to kill?'

'They seem to think so.' He flicked a glance over his shoulder. 'I spoke to Stephen yesterday. Has he said anything to you?'

'Yes, he mumbled an apology to me as we left the cathedral.'

'There's an end to it then. The others will learn from him.'

'Stephen thinks the same as me now,' said Honeydew. 'We do not like Master Gill as much as Giddy, but we'd hate to lose him. Or to lose anyone else.'

'We'll take steps to make sure that it doesn't happen.'

They had gone barely a mile along the Dover Road when Nicholas called a halt beside a winding track. Firethorn brought his horse alongside the leading wagon.

'Why have we stopped, Nick?'

'I think that we should turn down there,' said Nicholas, pointing.

'But this is the most direct way.'

'That's why they'll be waiting for us somewhere along the route.'

Firethorn unsheathed his sword. 'I'll be ready for the rogues.'

'They'll not give you the courtesy of a fight. Their

strategy is to strike hard when we least expect them before fleeing at speed. They'll not attack unless they can escape.'

'Leave the main road and we add pointless miles to the journey.'

'We also gain a degree of safety.'

'You puzzle me,' said Firethorn, sheathing his sword. 'Last night, I heard you ask the landlord which road we should take to Dover and he named all the villages we'd pass on the way. Why bother to seek that information if it is of no consequence?'

'But it was of consequence.'

'In what way?'

'It misled them,' explained Nicholas. 'When I walked back to the Three Tuns last night, I was followed by a man.'

Firethorn was disturbed. 'Why did you not say?'

'Because I did not wish to spread alarm. The chances were that he'd slip into the taproom at some point. It was so full with custom that we'd not have picked him out. The man who killed Giddy Mussett bided his time from inside the Blue Anchor, remember. Unbeknown to us, we rubbed shoulders with the assassin in Faversham and may have done so again last night at the Three Tuns.'

'I'll rub more than his shoulder!' vowed Firethorn.

'That's why I questioned the landlord so openly.'

'To throw anyone listening off the scent.'

'Yes,' said Nicholas. 'The conversation that nobody overheard was the one I had in the stables with the wheelwright. He taught me another way to Dover.'

'Then let's take it, Nick. Your judgement is sound.' He

gave a chuckle. 'If they *are* lying in wait for us on this road, what will they do when we fail to turn up?'

Nicholas smiled. 'They may become angry.'

It was a perfect place for attack. The bushes that ran along the ridge gave them ample cover. The two men chose a spot that brought them closest to any traffic on the road below. As they lay in the undergrowth, both had loaded muskets at their side. The man with the beard was writhing with impatience.

'They should have been here hours ago,' he complained.

'Perhaps they were delayed,' said the brawny young man with the scarred face.

'By what?'

'Who knows? An accident?'

'*We* are their accident,' growled the bearded man. 'We'll stop them for good. Put a couple of musket balls into Nicholas Bracewell and Westfield's Men will fall apart.'

'You said that when you killed Giddy Mussett.'

'Hold your noise!'

There was a long pause. 'Shall I ride up the road to see if they're coming?'

'No.'

'Why not?'

'Because it would be a waste of time.' The bearded man hauled himself to his feet and picked up his musket. 'A plague on them!' he exclaimed. 'They tricked us.'

The first thing that they noticed as they approached Dover was its massive fortress. Perched on the top of the hill, it was like a town in itself, well fortified with high walls and solid towers, gazing out fearlessly across the English Channel. Having followed a serpentine route that twisted its way past countless hamlets and farms, Westfield's Men entered the town from the north-east, passing in the very shadow of the castle. From their high eminence, they had a good view of the sheltered harbour below, protected by the Pent, a massive wall built of cliff-chalk, forty feet wide at the top. Dozens of vessels lay in the harbour. A three-masted ship was just setting sail for France. Travellers were milling around a second vessel as they waited to board it.

The castle was an intimidating structure but the steep incline that now confronted them was equally breathtaking. With the sea to their left, they had to descend the long road that curved down to the town itself. Nicholas ordered them to lighten the load by walking down the hill. Only Gill remained in the rear of a wagon. Like the other two drivers, Nicholas led his horses by hand so that he had more control over them. Hoode walked beside him with his donkey braying in fear at the sight of the precipice nearby.

'I hope they'll let us play here, Nick,' he said.

'There's no reason to suppose that they will not,' replied Nicholas. 'We know that we must perform at least once at the castle.'

'Yes, but only when Lord Westfield is present. He was adamant about that. We are days ahead of him. He'll not expect us here this soon.'

'Then we'll have to send him word of our arrival.'

'As soon as we may,' said Hoode. 'Where shall we stay?'

'Sebastian Frant spoke well of the Lion. It has sixteen beds to offer.'

'Not all may be available.'

'Then we'll have to make other arrangements,' said Nicholas. 'We've been spoilt so far, Edmund. Last time we toured, some of us slept in the stables.'

Dover was a flourishing community, its population swelled by the large numbers of travellers who came to and fro. Twenty sea-going ships made regular voyages to Calais and other ports on the Continent, giving employment to over four hundred sailors and providing the inns around the harbour with plenty of custom. The newcomers were impressed by the size of the crowds but they also noticed a slight air of decay about the town. A number of churches were in ruins and some of the civic buildings had seen better days. The once imposing St Martin Le Grande was so dilapidated that its stone was being pillaged for use in the construction of sea defences.

Westfield's Men were back in their wagons by the time they turned into the yard at the Lion. The ruse advised by Nicholas had been successful. In choosing an alternative route to Dover, they had avoided any further incidents. It gave them a new confidence. They were delighted that the inn could accommodate them all. While they unloaded their belongings, it was left to Nicholas to obtain a licence to play in the town and to send word to their patron of their early arrival. By the time that the book holder returned, Firethorn was seated in the taproom with Hoode and Gill. None of them could read the expression on Nicholas's face.

'Well,' said Firethorn. 'Good tidings or bad?'

'Good, for the most part,' replied Nicholas. 'We have a licence to play at the Guildhall in two days and there is a possibility that we may be able to give a second performance there.'

'This is cheering news.'

'Let me finish. Our fee, alas, is only thirteen shillings and fourpence.'

'So little for such magnificent fare?'

'It's the same amount that Conway's Men received.'

'That's even more insulting,' said Firethorn testily. 'Our fame surely entitles us to more than that undisciplined rabble.'

'We've played for less in the past,' Hoode reminded him.

'Played for less and deserved much more.'

'The fee has been accepted,' said Nicholas, 'and we could make more by a second performance. Even if we pay for the hire of the Guildhall, there should be a profit in the venture.'

'What of the letter to our patron?' said Gill. 'When Lord Westfield reaches the town, we can look to a third performance with the largest audience yet.'

Nicholas gave a nod. 'Fortune favours us. I told the mayor that I needed to send word to our patron and he offered his help. His own courier travels to London with a string of correspondence so our letter will be in his saddlebag as well.'

Firethorn was content. 'Three performances in all. That augurs well.'

'Provided that we choose the best plays, Lawrence,' said Gill with an arrogant gesture of the hand. 'One must surely be *The Foolish Friar* so that I can conquer yet another audience.'

'Learn to conquer your outrageous pride instead.'

'Who else could dominate the stage from a wheelbarrow?'

'You did not even dominate the wheelbarrow itself, Barnaby.'

The two men started to argue about which plays should be performed, each nominating those in which he felt he would have the commanding role. Nicholas caught Hoode's eye and a silent pact was made. Excusing themselves from the debate, they went out to inhale the fresh air of a fine evening.

'Which plays would you suggest, Nick?' asked Hoode.

'Our choice is limited by that avalanche, Edmund. Some of our scenery was destroyed and several of our properties damaged. I do not have the time or the means to repair them all. However,' he continued with a wry smile, 'one thing that did survive was the executioner's block so we can still offer *The Loyal Subject*.'

'That would be on my list as well. Put it forward.'

'Let's wait until this latest skirmish between Lawrence and Barnaby is over. Until then, neither of them will listen to what we have to say.'

They decided to go for a walk and their steps took them in the direction of the harbour. It was no accident. The son of a West Country merchant, Nicholas had gone to sea at an early age and developed an abiding love for it. He could not stay in a port like Dover without wanting to see what ships were moored there. Hoode was happy to bear him company, enjoying the stroll and the chance to be free of the others for a while. The smell of the sea soon invaded their nostrils. When they got close to the first of the ships, Nicholas stopped so that he could appraise it at his leisure.

'Do you miss being a sailor?' said Hoode.

'Sometimes.'

'Have you never wanted to go back to sea?'

'In the past,' admitted Nicholas wistfully, 'the temptation was very strong. Then I met Anne.'

'Ah, yes. Anne would be a firm anchor for any man.'

'Westfield's Men also help to keep me ashore.'

'Even when we expose you to peril?'

'There's no peril greater than a tempest at sea, Edmund.'

'Then I'll keep two feet firmly on dry land.'

As they sauntered along the line of ships, Nicholas pointed out their salient features. The vessel around which a crowd had formed now started to let its passengers aboard. They carried their baggage up the gangplank and had their passports checked before they stepped on deck. The two friends paused to watch them, wondering where all those people were going and what was taking them there. Nicholas was still speculating on the ship's destination when he caught sight of someone out of the corner of his eye. He turned to see a sailor walking briskly past. A slim, sinewy man of middle height, he wore clothing that had been patched too often and a cap that was pulled down over his forehead. Yet there was something about his gait that was arresting. Putting the man's age around thirty, Nicholas started to make some calculations. Hoode became aware of his interest in the sailor.

'Do you know the fellow, Nick?'

'I begin to think that I do.'

'Go after him, if you must.'

But it was already too late. Before Nicholas could even move, the man was swallowed up in the crowd. Nicholas went off to search for him but it was a futile exercise. The man had vanished from sight. Hoode caught up with the book holder.

'Who is he?'

'A friend,' said Nicholas. 'An old and dear friend.'

Lawrence Firethorn did not believe in wasting time. Since the Guildhall had been put at their disposal for rehearsal, he assembled his company there shortly after breakfast and worked them hard. Three comedies had been performed on tour so far. To introduce variety, and to give Firethorn the role of a tragic hero, *The Loyal Subject* was chosen as the play to set before their first audience in Dover. With its clown, Malvino, confined to a wheelbarrow, radical changes had to be made so that Gill could still offer some comic relief in an otherwise serious and, on occasion, solemn play. Songs replaced dances and the fluent pen of Edmund Hoode created new soliloquies for Gill. Owen Elias was once more engaged as the man who pushed the wheelbarrow around the stage.

Though showing the signs of age, the Guildhall was

ideal for their purposes with a balcony that could be used by the musicians, and where some of the more intimate scenes could be played. The stage was erected beneath the balcony, thereby making use of two doors in the back wall as exits. Light was more than adequate and the indoor venue rescued them from the dependence on the weather that made performances at the Queen's Head such a risky proposition. The long, low, rectangular hall was also kind to their voices. By midday, Westfield's Men had shrugged off most of their fear and dejection. They had good accommodation, an excellent arena in which to perform and the possibility of staging three different plays in the town. They felt wanted.

Nicholas Bracewell was as industrious as ever. Before the others had even risen for breakfast, he was up to repair some of the scenery that was needed in the play. Holding the book throughout the morning, he also suggested many of the changes and devised a series of new effects. As always, he was put in charge of rehearsing the stage fights, drawing on skills he had learnt while sailing with Drake many years earlier. Yet even at his busiest, Nicholas was still troubled by the memory of the man he had glimpsed at the harbour. If it had been the person he thought it might be, then his friend had fallen on hard times. He looked tired and shabby. Nicholas could not dismiss the image from his mind. When the rest of the company went off to the Lion early that afternoon, therefore, he decided to forego a meal in favour of a return to the harbour.

It was as busy as ever. A ship had arrived from France

and passengers were disembarking in a stream. Another vessel was being loaded with cargo, a third was about to set sail. Fishermen brought in the morning catch, surrounded by gulls whose cries added to the general tumult. Nicholas felt at home. Inhaling the salty tang, he picked his way along and searched the faces in the crowd. But there was no sign of the sailor he had seen the previous evening. Even when he peeped into the taverns by the harbour, Nicholas could not find him. Eventually, he gave up, deciding that he had either been mistaken as to the man's identity or that his friend had already sailed on the tide. He strolled down a quay and watched another fishing boat coming into the bay.

This time, it was the other man who recognised Nicholas.

'Is that you?' he asked in disbelief. 'No, it cannot be.'

Nicholas swung round to look at him. 'John?' he said. 'John Strood?'

'The very same, Nick.'

They embraced warmly then stood back to study each other more carefully. But for the coarse skin and deep furrows on his brow, Strood would have been a handsome man. Nicholas sensed disappointment and setback in his friend's life but he was still overjoyed to meet someone with whom he had circumnavigated the world on the *Golden Hind*. John Strood had been a fresh-faced youth then, unable to fend off the attentions of another member of the crew. Nicholas had taken the lad under his wing and a lasting friendship had developed. Strood could not stop grinning.

'Nick Bracewell!' he said, slapping him on the arm. 'I never thought to see you here. What business do you have in Dover?'

'I work with a theatre company in London. We are on tour.'

Strood was impressed. 'A theatre company?'

'Lord Westfield's Men.'

'Have you played before the Queen?'

'Several times.'

'I knew that you'd make something of yourself, Nick.'

'I'm only the book holder with the troupe,' said Nicholas modestly. 'It's the actors who have gained us our reputation. But what of you, John?' he went on, running his eye over his friend's attire. 'I'm glad that you've not deserted the sea.'

'I've not had the chance. You are educated, I'm not.'

'You're a good seaman. That puts you high in my esteem.'

'Thank you, Nick,' said the other. 'I wish that others thought as well of me.'

'You've no need to worry about my good opinion.'

'That means so much to me. You were the best shipmate I ever had.'

'Sailing around the Cape of Good Hope together binds us for life.'

'I always think of it as the Cape of Storms.'

'So do I, John. An ordeal for any sailor.'

'What I remember best is the day we boarded the *Cacafuego* and found all the Spanish treasure aboard. I still have dreams of that wonderful moment.'

While they traded memories, Strood's face shone with delight as if recalling a time when he was truly happy. Nicholas could see that darker days had followed.

'Which is your ship, John?' he asked.

'The *Mermaid*,' replied Strood without enthusiasm.

'Where is she?'

'Out in the bay.'

Nicholas looked in the direction to which Strood was pointing. He understood why his friend was slightly embarrassed. Lying at anchor in the bay, the *Mermaid* was not a vessel that inspired admiration. It was a two-masted ship that looked old, neglected and in need of repair when compared with the trim vessels all around it. Strood clearly took no pride in the *Mermaid*.

'Where do you sail?' asked Nicholas.

'Here and there,' said Strood evasively.

'With cargo or passengers?'

'Both, Nick.'

'What age is she?'

'Too old for comfort.'

Nicholas pressed for more detail but Strood was unwilling to give it, preferring to talk about the work that Nicholas was involved in. When he heard that *The Loyal Subject* would be staged at the Guildhall, he promised to go and see it. They parted with another embrace. As he walked back to join his fellows, Nicholas was thrilled that he had met John Strood after an absence of so many years but sad that his friend had made such little progress in the world. He also wondered why Strood volunteered so little information about the ship that gave him his living.

The performance at the Guildhall was an unqualified success. *The Loyal Subject* touched on themes of fidelity and betrayal that struck a deep chord with a patriotic audience. Gill rode to another triumph in his wheelbarrow but it was Firethorn, as Lorenzo, executed in the final scene, who gave the most memorable portrayal. Westfield's Men not only kept them enthralled for over two hours, they played with such unexampled brilliance that the mayor insisted they offer a second drama at the same place. They had earned both their fee and the opportunity to add substantially to it. There was more good news. A letter had arrived from their patron, saying that he would soon travel to Dover. It meant that Lord Westfield would reach the town in time to see them perform at the castle.

Because the Guildhall would not be used by anyone else for a few days, they were able to leave their stage in position. The scenery had to be dismantled, however, and the properties removed and stored. By the time that Nicholas had finished his work, there were still plenty of people in the hall, talking about the play or listening with interest to one of its leading actors. What everyone wanted to ask Firethorn was how he could still be alive when his head was visibly severed from his body on stage. Firethorn would not give away any secrets. In fact, the execution had been devised by Nicholas, who used a waxen likeness of

Lorenzo's head in the scene. When the executioner's axe fell, the head appeared to be hacked from the body and it rolled across the stage, drawing gasps of surprise and horror from the spectators.

As Nicholas walked past him, Firethorn was still basking in the adulation of the mayor and his family. Gill, too, had an admiring circle around him and Hoode, the author of the piece, was being congratulated both on his play and his performance as the stern judge who sentenced Lorenzo to death. Hoping to see John Strood again, Nicholas was unable to find him and decided that he had not turned up after all. However, another old friend had been in the audience.

'Nick!' said Sebastian Frant, bearing down on him. 'Welcome to Dover!'

'Thank you.'

'I did not expect you for some days yet.'

'Canterbury turned us away while a religious festival is on.'

'What is more religious than *The Loyal Subject*? It has a priest and two cardinals in the cast. You could have been part of the festival.'

'We chose to come to Dover instead, Sebastian.'

'Nobody is more pleased by that than I.'

Nicholas looked around. 'Is your daughter not with you?' he asked.

'No, Nick. Thomasina is still at home. It was only by chance that I came into the town. When I heard that you would perform here, I was determined to come.'

'It's a play that you must have recognised.'

'Most of it,' said Frant, 'for I was your scrivener when it was written. I copied it out from Edmund's foul papers. But there were several changes I noticed, the most obvious being that there was no wheelbarrow when the play was first staged.'

'That was forced upon us, alas. It was the only way to involve Barnaby.'

'Malvino was crucial to the action, and a joy to watch. There were tears of laughter all around me. But tell me what happened since we last met,' he said, dropping his voice. 'I hope that you met with no more setbacks when you left Faversham.'

'None that we could not overcome,' said Nicholas, not wishing to talk about the avalanche. 'And we reached Dover without any problem.'

'That news gladdens my ear. What of your patron?'

'He'll be here in a few days to watch us at the castle.'

'Lord Westfield must be very proud of his company.'

'We like to think so. But I'm glad to see you again,' said Nicholas. 'You may be able to help me. Conway's Men, as we hear, stay in Walmer. Their patron has a friend who lives nearby and they are to play at his house. Can you hazard a guess at whom that friend might be, Sebastian?'

'He lives close to Walmer?'

'So it seems.'

'Then it must be Sir Roger Penhallurick.'

'That's a Cornish name.'

'He lives a long way from Cornwall now.'

'Where is the house?'

'Not three miles distant from the town. Sir Roger has a large estate.'

'I may pay it a visit.'

'Do not waste your time watching Conway's Men perform. It would be a tedious exercise. They have nothing to teach you, Nick.'

'My interest is in their manager, Tobias Fitzgeoffrey.'

'Now, he *does* have talent,' confessed Frant. 'Master Fitzgeoffrey is a true actor, worthy enough to appear with any company in the land.'

'And on close terms with his patron, I believe.'

'The two are hand in glove.'

'Where is Lord Conway now?'

'Staying with Sir Roger, I daresay. If his company is playing at the house of a dear friend, I doubt very much if he would miss the occasion. The chances are that Tobias Fitzgeoffrey and his patron will be under the same roof.'

Nicholas was pensive. 'How would I find the house?' he asked.

Barnaby Gill was so pleased with the success of the performance that he was in a benevolent mood for once. As they supped at the Lion that evening, he bought wine and ale for the actors, and even rewarded George Dart for taking on the thankless task of wheeling him around. What delighted him most was that the play chosen for their second appearance at the Guildhall was *A Trick To Catch A Chaste Lady*, a drama that held a particular significance for him. It was during the performance of the play at the Queen's Head that he had sustained his broken leg. When the comedy was staged in Maidstone, fatigue kept him away from it but everyone praised the way that Giddy Mussett had taken the role of the clown. Gill now had the chance to reclaim the part of Bedlam for himself. While he could not dance any of his celebrated jigs, he was still confident that he could win over an audience from his wheelbarrow.

Inevitably, some alterations had to be made to the play. Nicholas retired to a room with Edmund Hoode so that they could discuss the changes needed and see how best to promote the character of Bedlam. Much of the comic action that had been used in *The Foolish Friar* could easily be transposed to a different play, as could some of the songs. The real problem lay in creating a new role for Owen Elias, who would once again be in charge of the wheelbarrow on stage. Hoode sharpened his goose quill in readiness.

'Fate works against me, Nick,' he said with a sigh of resignation. 'I had hoped to write scenes for my new play, but I spend all my time cobbling old ones instead.'

'You've been a master shoemaker, Edmund. Without your skills, Barnaby would never have been able to appear with us. The wheelbarrow may have got him on stage but you were the one whose words gave him a fresh purpose in each play. Does not that bring you satisfaction?'

'Great satisfaction.'

'You helped to save us,' said Nicholas. 'And by making it possible for Barnaby to act again, you've turned a peevish spectator back into a wondrous clown. When we set out from London, he did nothing but carp and bicker. Look at him now. He is so pleased to be back in harness that he showed true generosity this evening. Can you remember the last time when that happened?'

'No, Barnaby is apt to keep his purse to himself.'

'He's doing what he does best once more. That's the cause of this happiness.'

'But how long will it last, Nick?'

'As long as you can provide plays in which he can act.'

'We cannot stay in Kent forever,' argued Hoode. 'What happens then? Return to London and we have nowhere to play. Barnaby and the rest of us will have to look elsewhere for work. This tour may be the death of Westfield's Men.'

'Someone certainly intends that it should be.'

'That's my other fear. Will we all live to get back to the capital?'

'Yes, Edmund.'

'Our enemies may have other ideas.'

'Then we must keep one step ahead of them,' counselled Nicholas. 'As to the Queen's Head, all is by no means lost. Alexander Marwood drove us out but he may be just as eager to lure us back once the takings in his taproom fall. Westfield's Men bring in much of his custom. The landlord may hate us but the promise of money will make him smile upon us once more.'

'That may be a vain hope.'

'I reason from experience. He has exiled us before, only to welcome us back with open arms. But I've asked Lord

Westfield to lend his influence as well. When I wrote to advise him of our arrival in Dover, I requested him to make overtures to the testy landlord on our behalf. He may bring cheering news on that account.'

'The one man who could charm Alexander Marwood is our patron.'

'Let's pray that he's done so.'

'He may bring other news from London,' said Hoode. 'While we have been on the road, the law has been looking closely into the murder of Fortunatus Hope. Who knows? It may even be that the crime has been solved.'

'No, Edmund, put away that thought.'

'Why?'

'Because the man who killed Fortunatus Hope – and, I believe, Giddy Mussett – is not in London at all. We are the only ones who can catch him,' said Nicholas, 'for he is somewhere close at hand.'

Rehearsal of *A Trick To Catch A Chaste Lady* began in earnest on the following morning with special attention being paid to the new scenes written for the character of Bedlam. Lawrence Firethorn was delighted with the changes made to the play. Barnaby Gill took every opportunity to seize attention as Bedlam but he posed nothing like the threat to Firethorn's dominance that Giddy Mussett had offered. Lackwit was in command of the stage and the actor-manager exploited the fact. For most of the cast, however, the play revived unpleasant memories. Gill had been seriously injured when he took the role of Bedlam and the man who replaced him had been murdered. In spite of soothing words from Nicholas Bracewell, they were bound to be wary of that particular drama. George Dart made the mistake of voicing the opinion, within earshot of Firethorn, that the piece might be cursed.

Firethorn exploded. 'Any play that contains *you* is cursed.'

'It was only a suggestion, Master Firethorn.'

'Keep your suggestions to yourself. They offend my ear.'

'Yes, Master Firethorn.'

'They also insult the intelligence of any sane man. *A Trick To Catch A Chaste Lady* is a fine play. We've staged it before without the slightest trouble, even though you have been in the cast. No more of these wild accusations.'

'I withdraw them at once,' said Dart, wilting before his anger.

'Dover deserves to see my Lackwit and so they shall.'

'It's a role that's worthy of you, Master Firethorn.'

'Yet the name is more worthy of you,' said Firethorn, glaring at him. 'Who in the company lacks wit so painfully as George Dart? You lack wit, wisdom, common sense and everything else that separates man from beast.'

'That's unjust,' said Nicholas, stepping in save Dart from further abuse. 'George made a foolish remark and I'm sure that he regrets it bitterly.'

'Oh, I do, Nick,' said Dart. 'I do, I do.'

'Then no harm has been done. I think that we should remember all the valuable work that George has done for us instead of picking on his one incautious comment.'

'Keep the idiot away from me,' grunted Firethorn. 'That's all I ask.'

'Off you go, George,' said Nicholas, easing him away. 'You have to wheel Master Gill back to the Lion. We'll be close behind you.'

'Yes,' said Dart, glad of the excuse to get away from the Guildhall.

Rehearsal was over for the morning. The actors drifted back to their inn for dinner while Nicholas remained behind to discuss with Hoode a few refinements that could be made to the play. Firethorn stayed long enough to approve the suggestions before setting off alone. Leaving the Guildhall, he stepped out into bright sunshine. For the first time since they had come into Kent, he felt inspired. He filled his lungs with the keen air. Firethorn was convinced that their visit to Dover would redeem their tour. It would make up for the mishaps in Maidstone and the tragedy in Faversham, not to mention the hazards they encountered on the road. All that was past. In Dover, at least, they would be seen at their best and win new admirers of their art.

His mind was still dwelling on future triumph when he was accosted by a young man, wearing the neat attire of a servant. The stranger was polite and well spoken.

'Master Firethorn?' he asked.

'Yes?'

'I was told that I might find you at the Guildhall, sir.'

'What business do you have with me?'

'I am enjoined to deliver this,' said the young man, handing him a letter.

Firethorn glanced at the missive. 'Our patron's hand.'

'It was Lord Westfield who sent me. I'm to await a reply.'

'Then you shall have one,' said Firethorn, breaking the seal to read the contents of the letter. 'Dear God!' he exclaimed. 'This news lifts my heart. He is already arrived in Dover and requests me to join him for dinner.'

'Lord Westfield stays at the Arms of England.'

'How close is that?'

'No distance to speak of, sir,' replied the messenger. 'Let me escort you there before returning to the Lion to tell your fellows where you are.'

'An excellent notion, my young friend. Lead on.'

Thrilled to hear of the arrival of their patron, Firethorn followed his guide with alacrity. Within minutes, they came in sight of the Arms of England, a comfortable hostelry that was somewhat smaller than the Lion but with the better reputation for its food. The thought of a free meal helped to whet Firethorn's appetite.

'When did Lord Westfield reach Dover?' he wondered.

'Less than an hour ago.'

'Does he travel alone?'

'No, sir. He has brought some friends with him.'

'I hope that he brings good news from London as well.'

'This way, sir,' said the young man, taking him to the rear of the inn. 'Your patron has a private room upstairs.'

Firethorn went into the inn and climbed the steps behind him. When they came to the first door, the messenger tapped on it three times before standing back to usher the visitor forward. Composing his features into an ingratiating smile,

Firethorn opened the door and went in to greet his patron. But there was no sign of Lord Westfield. The man who stood by the window had a grizzled beard and a dark glint in his eye.

'Where is Lord Westfield?' demanded Firethorn.

'Do not trouble yourself about him,' said the man.

'But I was summoned to meet him here.'

'Then it looks as if he has let you down, Master Firethorn.'

Suspecting a trap, Firethorn reached for his dagger but the man concealed behind the door moved too fast for him. He cudgelled the actor to the floor then struck him repeatedly until Firethorn lost consciousness. The bearded man locked the door.

'Tie him up,' he ordered. 'We'll move him later.'

Chapter Fourteen

The disappearance of Lawrence Firethorn did not at first become apparent. It was only when Nicholas Bracewell and Edmund Hoode returned to the Lion that the first tiny hint of danger came. The rest of the company was in the taproom, enjoying a hearty meal before the afternoon rehearsal, delighted with the way that Dover had responded to their work and oblivious to the fact that their actor-manager had been lured away. Barnaby Gill had been helped out of his wheelbarrow and into a chair so that he could eat his food in comfort. Nicholas and Hoode joined him at his table.

'Where is Lawrence?' asked Nicholas.

'I thought he was with you,' replied Gill.

'No, he came on ahead of us.'

'Well, I've seen neither hide nor hair of him.'

'Perhaps he went up to his room for something,' suggested Hoode.

Gill smiled sardonically. 'When Lawrence goes into a bedchamber, it is usually for one reason only. He'll no doubt join us when he's had his sport with the wench.'

'Even Lawrence wouldn't begin a dalliance now, surely.'

Nicholas rose from his seat. 'I'll see if he's upstairs.'

'Remember to knock first,' warned Gill, 'or you'll see much more of him than you wish. My guess is that it will be that rosy-cheeked creature from the kitchens.'

Ignoring the jibe, Nicholas left the room and ascended the staircase to the landing. His search was brief but thorough. Firethorn was not in his bedchamber, nor was he in any of the other rooms. Nicholas conducted a search of the entire building and even poked his head into the stables, but it was all to no avail. Firethorn was not there. When the book holder questioned them, ostlers and servants all said the same thing. The actor-manager had not been seen at the Lion since breakfast. Hiding his concern, Nicholas strolled casually back into the taproom to rejoin the others.

Hoode looked up inquisitively. 'Well, where is he hiding?'

'Lawrence is not here,' said Nicholas.

'He must be.'

'I've looked everywhere.'

'Only an assignation would make him miss his dinner,' observed Gill drily.

'I'm going to search for him in the streets.'

'Let me come with you, Nick,' offered Hoode, clearly worried.

'No,' said Nicholas, easing him back into his seat. 'If we both leave, everyone else will realise that something is

288

amiss. There's no need to spread unnecessary alarm. Our fellows have had enough to contend with, as it is. I'll walk back towards the Guildhall. It may just be that he stopped to talk to someone on the way.'

'Then we'd have seen them as we passed.'

'Not if she lifted her skirt for Lawrence in an alley,' said Gill.

'This is serious, Barnaby,' scolded Hoode. 'Enough of these silly jests.'

'Wait here until I come back,' advised Nicholas. 'And try to carry on as if nothing untoward has happened. I'll be as quick as I can.'

'What if someone asks after Lawrence?'

'Invent some excuse to explain his absence.'

'Excuse?'

'Nobody in this room has a more fertile imagination than you, Edmund,' said Nicholas, patting him on the shoulder. 'You'll think of something.'

He slipped out quietly through the rear door. Nicholas walked back in the direction of the Guildhall, looking down every street, alley and lane on the way. He found it difficult to believe that Firethorn had come to any harm in broad daylight. Raised in a blacksmith's forge, the actor was a powerful man whose bustling energy would make any attackers think twice before taking him on. As many had discovered in the past, his skill with sword or dagger made him a doughty adversary. Nicholas tried hard to convince himself that there was a simple explanation for the disappearance of Firethorn, but the further he went, the less persuaded he became that all was well. Hoping that the missing man might somehow have doubled back to the Guildhall, he hurried on to the building and went inside. His search was fruitless. Firethorn was nowhere to be seen.

Nicholas was determined to relieve his anxiety by positive action. He set out on the route that Firethorn should have taken, going back over his own footsteps and stopping to ask people whom he passed along the way if they could remember seeing the distinctive individual whom he described to them. Nobody could help him. Even the most sharp-eyed shopkeepers had not been able to pick out Firethorn in the crowds that drifted constantly past them. Nicholas widened his search, walking down each and every street that branched off the main thoroughfare, peering into shops, inns and ordinaries without success. It was when he turned down towards the harbour that he was brought to a halt. Walking towards him, in the company of a much older woman, was the last person he expected to see emerging from the huddle of people along the sea front.

It was Thomasina Frant.

From her attire and manner, Nicholas guessed that her companion must be a maidservant. He waited until Thomasina caught sight of him. Her face brightened with recognition and she tripped across to him. The maidservant stayed apart from them.

'Good day to you,' she said pleasantly.

'I did not expect to find you here at the harbour,' he observed.

'Ordinarily, you would not have done so. I came to bid farewell to a friend who sails for Calais today. Margaret came with me,' she said, indicating her companion. 'It's not wise for a woman to be alone in this part of the town.'

'I wonder that your father did not escort you.'

'Father has business elsewhere in Dover.'

'I thought that Sebastian was retired.'

'He is,' she replied, 'but old acquaintances petition his help and he's too soft-hearted to refuse. That was ever his fault.' Her eyes sparkled. 'But I hear that Westfield's Men are in Dover and have already given one performance.'

'Your father was in the audience.'

'So he tells me. Should you play again, I intend to sit beside him.'

'Then you must repair to the Guildhall tomorrow afternoon,' counselled Nicholas, 'for we are to stage a comedy called *A Trick To Catch A Chaste Lady*. It was the play that you missed in Maidstone.'

'In that case, I'll make every effort to be there.'

'I think that it will be more to your taste than *The Foolish Friar*.'

'But I liked that play, Master Bracewell.'

'I sensed that it displeased you in some way.'

'Then you were deceived,' she assured him. 'Father will tell you how much I laughed at Master Gill in his wheelbarrow. Will he be your clown again tomorrow?'

'Yes, he'll be there.'

Her face clouded. 'I was sad to learn what happened to your other comedian.'

'We were all shocked by his death.'

'It must have come as a fearful blow.'

'It did,' conceded Nicholas. 'We are still reeling from it.'

'Yet you are able to continue with your tour. That shows great courage.'

'Master Gill has shown most, for he is in constant pain from his broken leg. It takes both courage and skill to play any role in his condition, let alone one that is so important. We are indebted to him.'

'He is fortunate to have such fine actors around him.'

'None better.'

'Especially the renowned Lawrence Firethorn.'

'A gift to any theatre company.'

'He's without compare,' said Thomasina with polite enthusiasm. 'My father warned me that Master Firethorn was a very Titan of the stage. Every role he takes, he makes his own. I trust that he'll be there tomorrow.'

'Yes,' replied Nicholas, concealing his disquiet behind a bland smile. 'Lawrence Firethorn will certainly be there.'

He could neither see, nor speak, nor move. All that he could feel was the searing pain at the back of his head and the dull ache in his limbs. As he regained his senses, Firethorn was slow to realise what had happened to him. Gagged and blindfolded, he was tied to a stout chair that scraped along the floor when he struggled to get free. He had been duped and that fact only served to increase his discomfort. Firethorn was annoyed that he had let down both himself and his company. Anger built steadily inside him. When it reached its peak, he made a supreme effort to break free of his bonds, twisting violently and straining at the thick ropes.

Someone grabbed his beard and held the point of a dagger at his throat.

'Sit still!' ordered the man. 'Or I'll send you where I sent Giddy Mussett!'

It was impossible to keep the news from them indefinitely. Westfield's Men had to be told the truth. Nicholas Bracewell waited until the whole company assembled in the Guildhall. Then, after consulting Hoode and Gill, he made his announcement.

'Grim news, friends,' he said, looking around their faces. 'Master Firethorn is missing.' There was a general murmur of disbelief. 'He's not been seen since he left here after the morning rehearsal. Somewhere between the Guildhall and the Lion, he vanished. I've searched high and low for him but he's nowhere to be found.'

'God help him!' cried James Ingram, speaking for all of them. 'Has Lawrence been stabbed in the back as well?'

'I can only tell you what I know, James. He's not here.'

'Where else could he be?'

'I wish that I knew.'

'Only death would keep him away from a rehearsal.'

'Or an attack of pox,' said Gill, still unwilling to believe the worst. 'I think that Lawrence wandered off into the stews and lost track of time.'

'He would never do that, Barnaby,' said Hoode

mournfully. 'The ugly truth has to be faced. He's disappeared. The likelihood is that he was ambushed.'

'Never!' shouted Owen Elias. 'An army would not dare to ambush him in the middle of a town. He'd fight them all off, and create such a din in doing so that there would be scores of witnesses to tell us what occurred.'

'There are none,' said Nicholas. 'I've spoken to dozens of people.'

'Are they all blind? They must have seen *something*.'

'If only they had, Owen!'

The Welshman squared his shoulders. 'I think we should go out in search of him,' he said firmly. 'Let's turn Dover upside down until we find him.'

'Yes,' agreed Ingram.

'Why stand here and do nothing?' asked Frank Quilter, another of the actors. 'We should be out there now, looking for Lawrence.'

'Wait,' said Nicholas, holding up both hands. 'Do not be so rash. We do not even know if Lawrence is still in Dover or if – God willing – he's still alive. The question we must ask ourselves is what he would want us to do.'

'Rescue him!' asserted Elias.

'Yes,' said Quilter. 'And punish those who dared to touch him.'

Ingram was keen to leave. 'Let's track him down,' he urged.

'Nicholas has already tried to do that,' argued Hoode, 'and we all know how thoroughly he would have gone about the business. Bear this in mind. We came to Dover to display our work. Are we going to let someone prevent us from doing that?'

'How can we perform any play without Lawrence?' asked Gill.

'How can we perform one without Barnaby Gill?' countered Nicholas. 'It is simple. We hire Giddy Mussett as a substitute. And when Giddy is removed from our ranks? How do we manage then? By changing our plays to make room for a clown with a broken leg. There's always a way out.'

'Not this time, Nick,' sighed Ingram.

'It's hopeless,' decided Elias. 'Who could possibly replace Lawrence?'

Nicholas smiled. 'You could, Owen.'

'Me?'

'Your brain is agile enough to learn the part in time.'

'I'm no match for Lawrence.'

'You like to think that you are,' said Nicholas, 'and this is your chance to prove it. For whatever reason, someone is determined to drive us from the stage. They thought to do it by killing Giddy Mussett but they failed. Their next target, as it seems, is our leading actor. Are we going to let them achieve their end?'

'No,' said Quilter. 'We'll get Lawrence back from them.'

'All in good time, Frank. First, we must make a decision. Do we abandon the performance here tomorrow? Or do we honour our commitment and show that Westfield's Men will not be frightened out of their occupation?'

There were no immediate answers. Everyone needed a

few moments to reflect on the dilemma facing them. Their first impulse was to institute a search but Nicholas's words made them pause. There was no certainty that Firethorn was still alive. If someone had been clever enough to lead the actor astray, they would know how to conceal his whereabouts. Combing the town of Dover might relieve their sense of frustration but it would make it virtually impossible to present *A Trick To Catch A Chaste Lady* on the following afternoon. Forced to make changes to their play, they needed some serious rehearsal. Nicholas suggested a compromise.

'Let's divide our forces,' he said calmly. 'The scenes we have to work on most are those that involve Lackwit and Bedlam. In short, only half of you will be called upon this afternoon. While we stay here,' he went on, indicating Quilter, 'Frank will lead a search of the town. I'll teach him the best way to do that. This covers both our needs. Dover will have a play to watch tomorrow and Lawrence will not be abandoned.'

'We'll find him,' said Quilter confidently.

'I hope so, Frank,' added Hoode. 'But if you fail, the rest of us will lend our eyes to the search when we've finished here at the Guildhall. I say that Nick has hit on the answer to our woes. Is everyone agreed?'

'Yes,' said Elias. 'Nobody will scare *me* from the stage.'

'Are we all of the same mind?' asked Nicholas.

'No,' said Gill, waving a dissentient palm.

'Why not?'

'Because I do not think the play is possible without Lawrence.'

'It is, if Owen takes his part.'

'But who will take Owen's part?' said Gill, nodding towards the Welshman. 'He was to have been my legs, wheeling Bedlam around the stage. Everyone else has a role of his own to play. Nobody is left, Nick. How can we even contemplate a performance when I have no strong hands to push me to and fro?'

'I had already thought of that,' said Nicholas.

'There's no remedy.'

'Yes, there is.'

'Who will be in charge of my wheelbarrow on stage?'

Nicholas put a hand to his chest. 'I will,' he said.

The rehearsal went badly. Unnerved by the loss of their manager and confused by a change to the play's main character, they stumbled from one scene to another. Elias felt his way uncertainly into his new role, Gill was at his most petulant and George Dart, deputising for Nicholas whenever the latter was on stage, had great difficulty following the play from the copy that he held in his trembling hands. Too quiet and too late, his prompts were often directed at the wrong actor. It took Nicholas almost three hours to establish a semblance of control over *A Trick To Catch A Chaste Lady*. His own role as Bedlam's companion was the only one played with a measure of confidence. He wheeled the clown around the stage at breakneck speed, drawing loud protests from a dizzy Gill yet managing to produce from everyone else the few laughs of the afternoon.

When the long catalogue of mistakes finally came to an end, Elias was agitated.

'That was truly a nightmare!'

'Our minds were on other things,' said Nicholas.

'We cannot present a play in that state.'

'Nor will we, Owen. You have a whole evening to master the part and there'll be long hours at our disposal in the morning. At the next rehearsal, you'll see a new play.'

'It wants a new cast as well,' said Elias bitterly, 'for none of us was worthy of it. Least of all,' he added, raising his voice so that Dart could hear him, 'an ass of a book holder who held the book upside down and who could not tell the difference between a prompt and a whisper.'

'I crave your pardon,' whispered Dart.

'George gave of his best,' said Nicholas defensively.

'But I achieved the worst results.'

'You should have let him push the wheelbarrow instead,' decided Elias.

'No, no!' exclaimed Gill. 'Spare me that. It calls for someone with a strong pair of hands. Nicholas at least kept me on the stage. George is so weak and nervous that he'd have tipped me out of the wheelbarrow.'

Dart was distraught. 'I cannot stop thinking of Master Firethorn,' he said.

'It is so with the rest of us, George,' said Nicholas softly.

When they had stored everything away, they were ready to leave the Guildhall. Nicholas sent the four apprentices back to the Lion in the company of Edmund Hoode. Wheeled along by Dart, the peevish Gill went with them. The clown was as disturbed as any of them by the disappearance of Firethorn and his fears expressed themselves in the form of a heightened irritability. Dart suffered a verbal whipping every inch of the way back. Nicholas and the others, meanwhile, met up with some of those who had spent the afternoon hunting for the missing man. He could see from the gloomy expressions of James Ingram and Frank Quilter that their search had so far yielded nothing.

'Where have you been?' asked Nicholas.

'Where you told us to go, Nick,' replied Ingram. 'We've looked under every stone between the Guildhall and the Lion.'

'Yes,' said Quilter. 'We've tried all the taverns and ordinaries but nobody remembers seeing Lawrence, and he's hardly a man you would easily forget. The only place we haven't tried so far is the harbour.'

'Owen and I will scour that now,' resolved Nicholas. 'You and James can start at the other end of King Street.'

Quilter nodded then set off with Ingram. The others turned in the direction of the harbour. It was early evening and the place was still seething with people. Elias noted the tavern at the edge of the harbour.

'Let me try my luck in there,' he said, moving off. 'I'll catch up with you later.'

'Do not get distracted,' warned Nicholas.

'At a time like this, even *I* can stay sober.'

While his friend strode towards the tavern, Nicholas weaved his way along the crowded wharf. His eyes were everywhere, searching each new face, appraising each building and pausing beside anything that might be construed as a hiding place. He was halfway along the harbour when he noticed the ship he had earlier seen at anchor in the bay. Moored behind a larger vessel, the *Mermaid* now stood at the quayside. It looked even more neglected at close quarters, its hull in need of attention and its decks in need of a good swabbing. Nicholas felt sorry that his old shipmate could find no better means of employment. John Strood had been evasive when questioned about the *Mermaid* because he was ashamed of it. After serving under one of the greatest seaman of the day, and sailing around the world with him, Strood was now condemned to routine voyages in a vessel that was as pitiful as the man himself.

Nicholas decided to take a closer look at the ship, walking along the quay from stem to stern then gazing up at the rigging. The *Mermaid* creaked noisily as it rode on the dark green water. Since there was nobody on deck, he went up the gangplank to explore. Even at its best, the ship had never been anything more than serviceable. It was now approaching the end of its days and Nicholas wondered how much longer it would remain seaworthy. He went across to the open hatch and looked down.

'Is anyone aboard?' he called, cupping his hands.

There was no reply. Some of the cargo had already been loaded and covered with a sheet of canvas. Nicholas knelt down to study it. Peeping out from one corner of the canvas was a piece of beautifully carved oak. He wondered what it could be. Before he could even begin to speculate, he heard a harsh voice ring out behind him.

'You're trespassing, sir!' shouted John Strood.

Nicholas rose to his feet and turned. 'It's me, John.'

Strood's manner changed at once. 'Nick?' he said in surprise. 'What are you doing here?'

'Inspecting the *Mermaid*, that's all.'

'It will hardly bear inspection.'

'Curiosity brought me aboard.'

'There's little enough to see.'

'You're carrying cargo on this voyage.'

'Yes,' said Strood. 'We're sailing for Boulogne in due course.'

'Was that furniture I saw in the hold?'

'No, Nick. Merely some timber that we take to France.'

'Then it's timber that's profited from the attentions of a wood-carver.'

Strood gave a dismissive shrug. 'One or two pieces, perhaps,' he said. 'The rest of it is fit for little else but the fire. But why do we stand here when we might be talking about old times over a tankard of ale? Shall we step across to the tavern?'

'Another time, John.'

'Oh, I thought you'd come looking for me.'

'I will do,' said Nicholas, 'I promise you that. But I'm searching for someone else at the moment so you'll have to excuse me.' After exchanging a farewell handshake, he stepped off the ship. Something jogged his memory. 'Boulogne, you say?'

'We often sail there, Nick.'

'I thought that Calais was the more usual destination.'

'It is,' said Strood, 'though some ships call at Nieuport, near Ostend, and a few sail to Dieppe. We've been to both in our time.'

'What was the name of the ship that sailed to Calais on the afternoon tide?'

'That's something I can't tell you.'

'Were you not down here at the harbour?'

'Yes, Nick,' said Strood. 'I was helping to load the cargo. That's why I know there was no ship to Calais. Two arrived from there but no vessel went out to sea this afternoon.' He squinted at his friend. 'Why do you ask?'

'No reason, John.'

'Do you intend to go on a voyage yourself?'

Nicholas laughed. 'Heaven forbid!' he said. 'No, my sea-going days are over.'

Owen Elias stayed so long in the tavern, and spoke to so many people, that the landlord told him either to buy a drink or to leave the premises forthwith.

'I'm searching for a friend,' explained Elias.

'Then do so with a tankard of ale in your hand.'

'Perhaps *you* remember him.'

'I only remember customers who pay their way in here,' said the landlord, a big, bovine character with an unforgiving eye. 'Now, then, what will you buy?'

'He was about my height,' said Elias. 'Strong of build, handsome of face and wearing a bright green doublet. Ah, yes, and with a black beard that he trims every day out of vanity. In all, a striking man of my own age. Did you see such a person?'

The landlord stroked his chin. 'I believe that I did, sir.'

'When?'

'Earlier on. A well-trimmed black beard, you say? He may still be here.'

'Where?'

'Follow me and I'll show you.'

Elias was too excited to realise that he was being tricked. As soon as they got to the rear of the building, the landlord opened a door and pushed the Welshman through it into a little yard. Before Elias could get back into the tavern, he heard the door being bolted. He controlled the urge to enter by means of the front door so that he could confront the landlord because nothing would be served by a quarrel. Firethorn was clearly not in the tavern and nobody inside it had either seen or heard of him. Elias walked around the side of the tavern in time to meet Nicholas Bracewell.

'I thought I'd lost you, Owen. What did you learn?'

'That you should never trust an innkeeper in a seaport.'

'What happened?'

'I overstayed my welcome, Nick. And you?'

'Wherever Lawrence is,' said Nicholas with a sigh, 'it's not here in the harbour.'

'Then where can he be?'

'Who knows? He could be miles away.'

Elias was distressed. 'You think that he could have set sail?'

'No,' said Nicholas. 'That's one fear we can put aside.

303

I spoke to John Strood, an old shipmate of mine. Since the time when Lawrence disappeared, no vessel has left the harbour. He must still be ashore.'

'Where do we look for him next?'

'Nowhere, Owen.'

'We abandon the search?' said Elias, shocked at the notion. 'We must never do that until we find Lawrence.'

Nicholas pondered. 'I think that we are going the wrong way about it,' he said at length. 'Instead of looking for him, we should be trying to find the people who are, in all probability, behind his disappearance.'

'Conway's Men!'

'The evidence certainly points at Tobias Fitzgeoffrey.'

'My sword will point at him when I catch up with the villain.'

'He and his company stay at Walmer, not far from here.'

'Is that where they've taken Lawrence?'

'We're not even sure that he was taken anywhere,' admitted Nicholas, 'though I can find no other explanation that fits the situation. It's hard to believe that he would wander off by himself. That means he has either been kidnapped or killed.' He came to a decision. 'It's time to accost Master Fitzgeoffrey. We've much to talk about with him.'

'Let's straight to the Lion to saddle up. You can take Lawrence's horse.'

'Away, then!'

They walked swiftly in the direction of the inn. Elias was fired by a spirit of revenge but Nicholas was considering a more cautious approach. Impatient for action, the Welshman had a hand on the hilt of his sword.

'What shall we do, Nick?' he asked.

'Try to get him on his own.'

'Do we beat the rogue until we get the truth out of him?'

'No,' said Nicholas. 'We question him about an unpaid bill in Maidstone.'

Still tied to his chair, Lawrence Firethorn tried to work out where he was. He listened with great care. The room in which he was guarded by the two men sounded small. As he leant back slightly, Firethorn's shoulders brushed the wall. His captors seemed to be a yard or so away. When one of them left the room, he took only a few short steps to reach the door. As it opened, Firethorn heard the noise of revelry from below. He decided that he was in the upstairs room of an inn and, since the cries of gulls never ceased outside the window, he knew that he was not far from the harbour. Who had kidnapped him and what did they intend to do with him? How had the messenger got hold of a letter in Lord Westfield's hand? What would the rest of the company do when they discovered that Firethorn was missing? Why had the man who boasted of killing Giddy Mussett not thrust a dagger into his back as well?

Firethorn was still grappling with the questions when the door opened and footsteps came in. Something was put down on a table then a voice he had not heard before spoke. It was lighter and younger than that of the assassin.

'This ale will help to pass the time.'

'I'm sick already of waiting,' grumbled his companion. 'When do we move him?'

'When it's dark enough.'

'There are hours to go yet.'

'I know,' said the man who had threatened Firethorn earlier. 'If it was left to me, he'd be lying in a ditch somewhere. Why the delay? I want to *enjoy* his death.'

Leaving the others to continue their search, Nicholas Bracewell and Owen Elias went off in the direction of Walmer. It was a cool, clear, dry evening and their horses maintained a steady canter along the track. During the ride, Nicholas sifted through all the information that he had gathered about Conway's Men and their actor-manager. In view of his daily commitments to his company, Tobias Fitzgeoffrey could not have been directly involved in the two murders or in the ambush on the road to Faversham but he, in league with his patron, could easily have hired agents to work on their behalf. Their envy of Westfield's Men was long-standing and their urge to secure a base in London was ever-present. If they were responsible for the earlier crimes, then the disappearance of Lawrence Firethorn could also be attributed to them. It was the latest in a series of attempts to bring a rival company to its knees. By the time that Walmer Castle came into sight on the horizon, Nicholas had convinced himself that they were closing in on the culprits.

The village was little more than a straggle of houses that looked out across the sea. There was a church, a couple of inns and a blacksmith's forge but what really gave Walmer its significance was the castle, built in the shape of a Tudor Rose and presenting a stern test to any invaders who had the temerity to land on the nearby beach. Smaller and more compact than Dover Castle, it had an air of permanence about it, even though it had only been constructed during the later years of King Henry VIII's reign, when his abrupt break with the Roman Catholic Church provoked papal outrage as well as the wrath of France and Spain. Had the Spanish Armada succeeded in putting foreign troops on English soil, the castles along the southern coast would have been vital strongholds.

Nicholas and Elias were in luck. When they called at the larger of the two inns, they discovered that several members of Conway's Men were there, drinking in the taproom and complaining about their lot. They were a disconsolate crew with none of the vigour or good fellowship of their competitors from the Queen's Head. Nicholas was relieved to see that the company was not performing that evening. If the majority of them had come into Walmer, then Fitzgeoffrey would only have a handful of his actors around him. Nicholas and Elias would not be hopelessly outnumbered. Following the directions given by Sebastian Frant, they rode towards the estate owned by Sir Roger Penhallurick.

'What if he refuses to see us, Nick?' asked Elias.

'Let's run him to earth first.'

'I could always sneak into the house and drag him out by the throat.'

'There must be a simpler way than that,' said Nicholas.

The estate consisted of three hundred acres of rolling parkland, dotted with trees and fed by a gurgling stream. Herds of fallow deer could be seen grazing but they quickly fled when the two riders approached. Game birds were also plentiful. The most arresting feature of the house was its façade, large, elegant and symmetrical with a stone balustrade along the roof and around the square towers at either end of the frontage. Elias was impressed by the sheer size and opulence of the place. Lord Conway clearly had a very wealthy friend.

Nicholas was more interested in some outbuildings off to the right, noting the two empty wagons that stood outside them. The chances were that they belonged to the visiting theatre troupe. When he drew Elias's attention to them, the Welshman reached the same conclusion. Skirting the house, they made straight for the outbuildings. Loud banging noises greeted them. When they got closer, they saw a thickset young man, using a hammer to repair a wooden throne.

'Good even, friend,' said Nicholas.

The man stopped hammering. 'Good even,' he said pleasantly.

'You must be one of Conway's Men.'

'The lowliest of them, sir. I'm actor, stagekeeper, carpenter and anything else that is needed. As you see, my work is never done.'

'We are looking for Master Fitzgeoffrey.'

'Then you'd best try the house,' said the man, 'for that's

where Tobias dwells. Most of us make do out here with nothing but straw to lie on at night. Only our manager has a soft bed on which to rest his bones.' He looked up at them. 'What business do you have with him?'

'We're from London,' said Nicholas, dismounting from his horse. 'We wish to speak to Master Fitzgeoffrey about a performance in the capital.'

'Indeed?' The man grinned hopefully. 'Conway's Men may play in London?'

'That's something we need to discuss with him.'

'Tobias will be interested, sir, no question of that.'

'Do you think that you could fetch him for us?' asked Nicholas with a disarming smile. 'If we go to the house, we'll have to meet Sir Roger and his other guests. The only person we need to speak to is Master Fitzgeoffrey.'

'I'll bring him to you, sir. May I give him your name?'

'Thomas Christopher.'

The man scampered off towards the house. Elias stared at his friend.

'Christopher? Why did you pluck that name out of the air?' he wondered.

'Because my own might be recognised, Owen. Think on it. St Christopher is the patron saint of travellers and who are we, if not travellers?'

Elias dismounted. 'We are certainly in need of a patron saint!'

'Tether the horses,' said Nicholas, handing him the reins of his own mount. 'I'll be with you in a moment.'

He took a swift inventory of the outbuildings. Costumes,

properties and scenery had been stored in one of them but the others were given over to accommodation. Through an open window, he could see three other members of the company, squatting on the floor as they played cards on an upturned wooden box. They were so engrossed in their game that they did not even look up. No sooner did Nicholas go back to his friend than two figures emerged from the house. Tobias Fitzgeoffrey studied the visitors before beckoning them across with a lordly gesture. The young man who had carried the message trotted back to his carpentry.

When they got nearer to him, Fitzgeoffrey's suspicion was aroused.

'I've seen you before,' he said, pointing a finger at Elias. 'You are one of Westfield's Men, are you not?'

'And proud to be so,' replied Elias.

'I saw you play at the Queen's Head.'

'That's the performance we came to discuss with you, Master Fitzgeoffrey,' said Nicholas. 'I'm the book holder with the company.'

Fitzgeoffrey was contemptuous. 'I've nothing to say to you.'

'I think you have.'

'You brought me out here under false pretences.'

'And we mean to keep you here,' said Elias, brandishing his dagger, 'until we get the truth out of you. Be warned, my friend. Call for help and you're a dead man.'

'What do you want of me?' said Fitzgeoffrey, eyeing the weapon nervously.

'First,' said Nicholas, 'there is the small matter of six shillings and fourpence, owed to Pieter Hendrik, weaver in Maidstone. You had cloth from him that was never paid for. Do you recall the transaction?'

'I had no ready money at the time,' lied the other, 'and meant to settle the debt as soon as we visited the town again. Did he appoint you as his bailiffs?'

'It's an office I willingly embraced. But we'll return to that when we've attended to more serious concerns. Why did you visit the Queen's Head recently?'

'For the same reason as everyone else in the audience.'

'No,' said Nicholas, 'they came to enjoy a play. You were there to witness our humiliation. The performance was halted by an affray.'

'Not before time, in my opinion,' rejoined Fitzgeoffrey with a show of bravado. 'It was a weak comedy that was weakly acted by your fellows.'

'Watch your words,' growled Elias. '*I* was on that stage.'

'Yes, you ranted and raved like a madman.'

'Insults are not required,' said Nicholas, jumping in quickly before Elias lost his temper. 'Our reputation is adamantine proof against your slurs. We would not expect a rival to admire his superiors.'

Fitzgeoffrey wrinkled his nose. 'I know of none.'

'When our performance was stopped that day, the whole audience fled.'

'I was among them and glad to flee from such an abominable play.'

'One spectator was unable to leave,' said Nicholas.

'Fortunatus Hope. During the commotion, he was stabbed to death in the gallery.'

'Yes, I heard tell of that,' said Fitzgeoffrey with a cold smile. 'Do not expect me to mourn for the fellow. He treated my patron shabbily and we are well rid of him.'

'I believe that you and Lord Conway may have incited the murder.'

'That's a monstrous accusation!'

'Then let me add another,' said Elias, holding the dagger on him. 'You had Giddy Mussett killed as well.'

Fitzgeoffrey looked surprised. 'Giddy is dead?'

'Do not give us any counterfeit sympathy.'

'Nor will I. Giddy Mussett was no friend of mine. I came to despise the little devil. When he was neither drunk, nor quarrelsome, which was rare because he was usually both at the same time, he was doing and saying more than was set down for him in a play. Sympathy? Ha!' said Fitzgeoffrey with disdain. 'There were times when I'd gladly have wielded a dagger myself.'

'But you hired someone else to do the deed.'

'No!'

'The same man who dispatched Fortunatus Hope,' said Nicholas. 'The two men were killed with matching daggers. Thanks to the work of an assassin, two enemies of Conway's Men were removed.'

Fitzgeoffrey was defiant. 'I rejoice in the fact!'

'Not if you wish to live,' said Elias, prodding him with his weapon. 'Giddy was a friend of mine. I was the one who found the body and I got a lump on the back of the head for my pains. The man you hired cudgelled me.'

'I hired nobody.'

'Then who caused that affray at the Queen's Head?' demanded Nicholas.

'Some drunken ruffians.'

'How much did you pay them for their ale?'

'Not a penny.'

'Someone set them on,' said Nicholas, 'in order to cause a distraction so that Fortunatus Hope could be killed. If you were not involved, what were you doing there? Why were you in London at all when your company needed you here in Kent?'

'That's a private matter,' replied Fitzgeoffrey.

Elias prodded him again. 'Then we'll have to intrude on your privacy.'

'Tell us,' advised Nicholas. 'Owen is getting impatient with his dagger.'

'*Very* impatient.'

'Stand off!' said Fitzgeoffrey as a jab opened up a slit in his doublet. 'Look what you've done, you Welsh idiot!' Elias became even more menacing. 'Yes, yes,' said the actor, frightened of him, 'I'll tell what you wish to know, if only you'll give me room to tell it.' He turned to Nicholas. 'Keep him away from me.'

'We still await our answer,' said Nicholas. 'Understand that we have some intelligence of what went on. Giddy spoke to your book holder, Martin Ling. So did I when the fellow left your company in disgust.'

'Martin was almost as much trouble as Giddy Mussett.'

'According to your book holder, you returned from London in such a mood of contentment that you spread your money among the company. Is that true?'

'I do not deny it.'

'Then you must also admit you were celebrating our humiliation.'

'It was a pleasure to behold.'

'Your corpse would be a pleasure for *me* to behold, Master Fitzgeoffrey.'

'Let him speak, Owen,' said Nicholas. 'Well?'

The actor took a deep breath. 'I was summoned to London by a letter from a lawyer. An uncle had left a bequest to me. When I learnt how generous that bequest was, I was so pleased that I let a friend persuade me to bear him company to the Queen's Head. And you were right,' he confessed. 'I did not come to enjoy the performance at all. I went to sneer at it and mock the arrogance of Lawrence Firethorn in setting himself up as some emperor of the boards. When the affray broke out, I took some real enjoyment from the occasion, after all. That is why I was in such high spirits.'

'Can any of this be proved?'

'I have the papers from the lawyer with me and I'll gladly furnish you with his name so that my word can be upheld by him. Taking a theatre company around the shires is a labour of Hercules, as you well know. Rewards are few, hazards are many. When I had this sudden stroke of fortune,' he went on, 'I did what anybody would have done in my position. I shared it with my fellows.'

314

Nicholas could see that he was telling the truth. He became acutely aware that they were levelling their accusations at the wrong man. Tobias Fitzgeoffrey had some blatant defects of character and Nicholas could never bring himself to like him, but he was not part of a conspiracy to destroy Westfield's Men. Elias, however, still clung to the belief that Fitzgeoffrey was guilty of the various crimes.

'What have you done with Lawrence?' he said, putting his face close to that of the other man. 'Where is he being kept?'

'How would I know?'

'Tell us – or I'll cut that doublet into a thousand pieces.'

'No,' said Nicholas, easing his friend a pace backward. 'Sheath your dagger, Owen. We have no need of it here. Master Fitzgeoffrey has told us all we need to know.'

'But he hasn't, Nick. I swear that he's hiding Lawrence somewhere.'

'I think not. We must tender him an apology.'

'That's the least I expect,' said Fitzgeoffrey huffily. 'The pair of you should be locked up for your audacity. Now, be off with you, sirs!'

'First, however,' said Nicholas, 'let me congratulate you on your good fortune in inheriting some money from your uncle. It means that you are now in a position to settle the debt you incurred in Maidstone. Pay the six shillings and fourpence that is owed to Pieter Hendrik and I'll see it put into his hands.'

Fitzgeoffrey started to bluster until he saw the glint of determination in Nicholas's eyes. Eventually, he capitulated.

Opening his purse, he counted out the money and thrust the coins into the book holder's palm.

'Thank you,' said Nicholas. 'Come, Owen. We have stayed long enough.'

They collected their horses and rode quickly away. Elias was rueful.

'I thought that we came here to solve some dreadful crimes,' he said. 'And all that we did was to secure payment for a weaver who was too dim-witted to ask for his money in advance.'

'We did more than that,' reasoned Nicholas. 'We learnt the folly of reaching too many conclusions on too little evidence. I blame myself for that. Tobias Fitzgeoffrey was not involved in the crimes that have plagued us. Nor was his patron. They are too busy trying to keep that miserable troupe of theirs together. So our journey was not in vain. We did make some progress.'

'I fail to see it.'

'Since they've been cleared of blame, they will no longer divert us. We can now forget about them and search for Lawrence elsewhere. I *know* that he's still alive.'

Hours of sitting in the same position, with his hands tied behind his back and his body encircled by rope, took their toll on Lawrence Firethorn. Limbs that once ached were now subject to cramp. Pain came in spasms but he did his best to withstand it so that his captors could not see his suffering. When he heard a candle being lit, he knew that darkness was starting to fall outside. Time oozed slowly by.

The men said little but he hung on every word in the hope of learning who they were and why they had abducted him. One of them eventually left the room again and was gone for some while. On his return, he came to stand directly in front of the prisoner. A dagger was slipped in under the rope around his chest. Firethorn sensed that they were going to cut his bonds and he got ready to dive forward by way of attack. The opportunity never came. Before the dagger slit the rope, a cudgel struck him hard on the top of his head and he was too dazed even to move.

'Cut him loose and put that sack over him,' said a voice. 'We move him now.'

Chapter Fifteen

It was dark by the time they got back to Dover and candlelight glowed in open windows. Lanterns were hanging in the stables at the Lion so that the ostlers could see to unsaddle the horses. Wearied by their ride in pursuit of a false scent, Nicholas and Elias joined the others in the taproom. The mood was sombre. Though they had searched the town until nightfall, the actors had found no clues as to the whereabouts of Lawrence Firethorn and they were convinced that he was dead. The arrival of the newcomers destroyed their last faint hopes. Nicholas and Elias had come back empty-handed. All was lost. The company grieved in silence and the taproom was uncannily quiet. Looking around the sad faces, Nicholas began to wonder if the actors would be able to summon up the strength and the dedication that was needed to stage a play in front of an audience. Elias tried to set a good example by retiring to a quiet corner with a tankard of ale and a copy of his scenes from *A Trick To Catch A Chaste Lady*. He was soon repeating lines to himself.

Nicholas sat beside Edmund Hoode, who was morose and withdrawn.

'Where's Barnaby?' asked Nicholas.

'He's gone to his room,' replied Hoode. 'He prefers to be alone. George has been running hither and thither, fetching wine and food for him.' He looked at his friend. 'I begin to have doubts, Nick. Is it wise for us to go ahead without Lawrence?'

'We have no choice in the matter.'

'But we do. We can cancel the performance.'

'When we have already agreed to give it?' said Nicholas. 'Playbills have been printed. Word of mouth has spread our fame afar. Think how our reputation will suffer if we disappoint our audience.'

'It will suffer far more if we offer them the botched piece we saw at rehearsal this afternoon. I was ashamed to be involved in such horror.'

'Then help to turn it into an acceptable performance.'

'Time is against us.'

'I disagree, Edmund. It's our greatest asset. Look at Owen,' said Nicholas, indicating the Welshman. 'He knows how little time he has to con his part and that inspires him to work at it all the harder. It is so with our fellows. I, too, had doubts about them when I walked in here – then I remembered that we have less than sixteen hours to pull the play together. When we get to the Guildhall tomorrow, there'll be no room for grief or anguish. The company will respond as Owen has done.'

'The play will not be the same without Lawrence.'

'We thought it would not be the same without Barnaby yet we gave a rousing performance of it at Maidstone. The mayor loved it. When did we last earn five pounds when we were out on the road? And that's another consideration, Edmund,' he went on. 'Cancel the performance and we lose both face and money. Fill the Guildhall tomorrow afternoon and we stand to replenish our coffers.'

Hoode was despondent. 'That may be so, Nick. But no matter how much we earn, it will not atone for the loss of Lawrence.'

'I grant you that,' said Nicholas, 'but imagine how pleased he will be when he comes back and finds that we have abided by our contract to play and swelled our funds.'

'*When* he comes back? Do you honestly believe that he will?'

'Yes, I do.'

'Then you are the only one of us here that does.'

'I think not. Owen is of the same opinion as me.'

'Even though you drew a blank with Conway's Men?'

'That left us chastened but not downhearted,' explained Nicholas. 'I was too hasty in singling out Tobias Fitzgeoffrey as the culprit. I reason thus. Two people who are linked to Westfield's Men have been murdered. Fortunatus Hope was the first and Giddy Mussett, the second. Both were left where they would be found so that their fates would act as a warning to us. *That* is why Master Hope was killed at the Queen's Head and not in some more private place. It was a visible blow against us.'

'Nothing could have been more visible than Giddy's death.'

'It was meant to frighten, Edmund.'

'It succeeded.'

'Yes,' said Nicholas, 'but how much more upsetting would Lawrence's death be? Suppose that we had found *him* lying in a stable with a dagger in his back? We would all have been distraught. Do you follow my argument?'

'Very closely, and it brings me some relief.'

'Good.'

'Had Lawrence been murdered, his killer would have dangled his body in front of us to cause us real terror. Since that has not happened, there is a chance that Lawrence is still alive.' His brow furrowed. 'But *why*, Nick? Why spare him when his death would throw us into disarray?'

'I can only guess. Whoever kidnapped him thought that his disappearance would be enough to halt us in our tracks. But that is not the case.'

'I know,' said Hoode, suddenly alarmed. 'We are pressing on in spite of his loss. Could that not be dangerous for Lawrence?'

'It is what he would expect of us.'

'Not if it imperils his life.'

'We've no means of knowing that it will.'

'But it's a possibility, Nick. Look at the situation. Lawrence is snatched from us in order to prevent us from playing again in Dover. If we ignore the message, will they not simply kill Lawrence in order to give us a starker warning?'

'It's a risk,' admitted Nicholas, 'but we have to take it.'

'I'm not sure that we should.'

'We must, Edmund. Our intentions have been made clear. Instead of giving up in the face of fear, we struggled on at the Guildhall this afternoon. That will not have gone unnoticed. If our decision endangered Lawrence's life, his dead body would have turned up by now. Yet it has not. He's still *alive*,' he continued, 'and that means we have a chance to rescue him.'

'I wish that I had your confidence.'

'You share my love for the company. Let that carry you through.'

Hoode was reassured. 'You are right,' he said. 'We must perform the play.'

'It will have another virtue.'

'And what is that?'

'It will bring our enemy out into the daylight again,' said Nicholas. 'I think that we've been watched ever since we set out from London. We know that the killer was in the audience at the Queen's Head. I suspect that he's seen every performance that we have so far given on tour. If we take to the boards at the Guildhall tomorrow, he'll probably be hidden away among the other spectators.'

'Wondering who his next victim will be,' said Hoode with a shiver.

'No, Edmund. Realising that he'll not stop us.'

Nicholas stayed long enough to share a light supper with his friend and did his best to still Hoode's apprehensions. As a courtesy, the book holder then went to Gill's room to explain what happened on their visit to Conway's Men.

Before he could even tap on the door, however, he saw George Dart backing out of the room on tiptoe. Dart closed the door behind him and raised a finger to his lips to signal the need for silence. Nicholas took him to the other end of the passageway before he spoke.

'Is he asleep, George?'

'Yes,' said Dart. 'He was very tired.'

'I know that he's in pain.'

'He never shows it in front of the others but it is different when we are alone. Every time he moves his leg, he's in agony. Master Gill drinks wine to deaden the pain.' He smiled hopefully. 'Did you find what you were after, Nick?'

'Unhappily, no. It was a false trail.'

Dart's face fell. 'Like all of the others.'

'We'll keep looking, George.'

'And so will I.'

'Your task is to take care of Barnaby.'

'That does not stop me joining in the search,' said the willing Dart. 'When I wheeled Master Gill back from the Guildhall, I was as vigilant as any of them. And I all but stumbled on a clue that nobody else had found.'

'A clue?' asked Nicholas with interest.

'That's what I thought it might be at the time.'

'And now?'

'I was probably misled by him.'

'By whom, George?'

'It does not matter now. Master Gill told me to forget the man.'

'What man?'

'A beggar in the street.'

'Go on. Tell me what happened.'

'Well,' said Dart, biting at a fingernail, 'the poor wretch looked so miserable, sitting in a doorway like a stray dog, that I took pity on him. I stopped to give him a coin even though Master Gill chided me for doing so. The beggar was very grateful. He asked who I was and what I was doing in Dover. When I told him that I belonged to Westfield's Men and that we were looking for Master Firethorn, he said that he could help me, if only I was to put more money into his palm. But I had none left to give.'

'So what did you do?'

'What I was told to do by Master Gill. He ordered me to wheel him back here and told me that I was a fool to listen to the fellow.'

'Why?'

'Because he was telling a lie.'

'Was that the impression that you got?'

'No, Nick. I felt that he was in earnest. But Master Gill insisted that it was only a ruse to get more money out of me. If I gave the beggar a bag of gold, he said, I'd get nothing but falsehood out of him.'

'Who knows?'

'Master Gill was certain that the man was deceiving me.'

'Yet he *might* have seen something,' said Nicholas.

'Oh, there was no question of that.'

'Why not?'

'The beggar was blind.'

* * *

Lawrence Firethorn had never before had such sympathy for the blind. Deprived of his sight by the piece of material tied across his eyes, he came to understand their plight and their helplessness. Firethorn had the additional handicaps of being tied up and gagged so he could not use touch and taste by way of guidance. All that he could rely on were his sense of smell and his hearing, and they gave him only limited intelligence. It was night. That much was certain. The tumult of the harbour had given way to a cloying silence that was broken from time to time only by the distant barking of a dog or the cry of a drunken man trying to find his way home. Firethorn could smell fish. Indeed, he could smell little else inside the room where he was locked. He decided that he was incarcerated in a warehouse of some sort. The abiding stink suggested that there was no window to admit any fresh air. As time wore on, the atmosphere became increasingly oppressive.

His captors had left him alone. That meant they had no fear that he could escape from his prison. Firethorn was tied to a stout wooden post and, even though he strained every sinew in an effort to break free, he could not budge the timber. He was there for the whole night. What happened then, he could only conjecture. He could certainly expect no sympathy from the two men who held him. When they moved him to the warehouse, they had been rough to the point of brutality, taking full advantage of his inability to defend himself. Firethorn vowed to take revenge on them a hundred times but he was in no position to exact it. Everything depended on other people. Whether or not he stayed alive depended on his captors. Whether or not he was rescued, depended on Westfield's Men.

Firethorn was afraid. When he fell asleep out of sheer exhaustion, the same question was repeating itself inside his mind: 'Nick Bracewell – where *are* you?'

Any fears that Westfield's Men would be unequal to the challenge that lay ahead were swiftly dispelled. When they gathered at the Guildhall early on the following morning, they had shaken off their despair and found a new resolution. Nicholas explained to them why he believed that Firethorn was still alive and they were further bolstered. There was also a strong rumour that their patron would arrive in Dover in time to see them perform. It served to make the actors apply themselves more rigorously. As a result, the rehearsal bore no resemblance to the halting performance of the previous day. Mistakes were still made but they were quickly rectified. Owen Elias's grasp on his character and his lines was now secure. George Dart contrived to prompt audibly at the correct moments. Even Barnaby Gill, normally so peevish at rehearsals, was lulled into a rare state of optimism by the way that the company lifted itself out of its pervading woe. It augured well for the afternoon performance.

While most of the others returned to the Lion for refreshment, Nicholas remained behind with George Dart to put everything in readiness. Scenery was set up for the opening of the play and properties placed on stage. Benches were arranged so that everyone had a good view of the action. Gatherers had to be instructed in their role so that nobody slipped past them without paying an entrance fee. Sunlight streamed in through the windows on both side walls to eliminate any need for candles. When the work was done, Nicholas spared a few minutes to follow up the potential clue that Dart had mentioned. The two of them walked to the exact spot where the blind beggar had sat on the previous day but the man was not there.

'Are you sure that it was here?' asked Nicholas.

'This was the very doorway.'

'I saw no blind beggar when I passed by with Owen.'

'Perchance he moved.'

'Why should he do that?'

'He had money to spend. I gave it to him.'

'Look about for him. Try the streets nearby.'

They split up and went down all the adjacent streets and lanes. Their search was thorough but, once again, completely futile. Nicholas was disappointed. A tiny wisp of hope seemed to have vanished the moment that it appeared.

Impressed by the reputation of Westfield's Men, and lured by the title of the play, a large audience descended on the Guildhall that afternoon. Most paid for a seat but there was also standing room at the rear and a number of sailors had been tempted away from their taverns to watch *A Trick To Catch A Chaste Lady*. The mayor and his wife were there again, as were most of the city worthies. Sebastian Frant brought his daughter this time and they sat near the front so that they would get full value from the performance.

Lord Westfield did not arrive in time but John Strood did, mingling with the standees at the back of the hall and wondering what had drawn his former shipmate, Nicholas Bracewell, into a theatre troupe. It struck him as an odd choice of profession.

Behind the scenes, Nicholas took on a role more usually assigned to Firethorn, that of instilling confidence and spirit into the company. While the actor-manager did it with a hortatory speech, declaimed with characteristic zest, the book holder preferred to move quietly from one person to another so that he could speak individually to them. By the time that Nicholas had finished, everyone knew what was expected of him. The musicians took up their places in the gallery and James Ingram was poised to stride out on stage to deliver the Prologue. The customary buzz of anticipation could be heard from the audience. They were there to enjoy themselves and Westfield's Men were determined not to let them down. Certain that everybody was ready, Nicholas gave the signal. The musicians began to play.

Almost immediately, a lute string snapped with a resounding twang, catching the lutenist on the arm and producing an involuntary yell of surprise. It gained the first unintended laugh. When Ingram swept on stage to deliver the Prologue, his black cloak caught on the edge of the scenery and was badly torn. More laughter followed. It was an inauspicious start but the actors were not distracted. Once the play began, they imposed a degree of control over it that never really slipped. At the same time, however, they failed to inject any of the fire and hilarity that had marked earlier performances of the play. Gill was strangely subdued and it was only Nicholas's frenetic manipulation of the wheelbarrow that produced any sustained mirth. The apprentices were little more than adequate as the female quartet and Rowland Carr, playing a disreputable hedge-priest, was less than reliable. It was not for want of effort. Everybody committed himself wholeheartedly to the enterprise but that soon became a fault. By trying too hard, they fell short of their high standards. They speeded up the action to an almost bewildering pace, their timing was awry and they lost all the subtleties of the play.

It was Owen Elias who lent the piece its real quality. In the leading role of Lackwit, he was so outstanding that they hardly missed Firethorn. The Welshman seized his opportunity to dazzle like a man who had been waiting a whole lifetime for such a moment. He was both hero and clown, winning the sympathy of the spectators yet earning most of the laughter as well. Elias had always been a fine actor with a commanding presence and a powerful voice but nobody had expected him to blossom in the part of Lackwit. Much to Gill's disgust, Bedlam was overshadowed and it spurred the clown on to desperate measures. He inserted comic songs that were not even in the play and made such use of his facial contortions that he appeared to be having some kind of fit. None of it challenged Elias's supremacy. It was he who rescued the play from the mediocrity into which it would otherwise have sunk.

Fortunately, the majority of the audience was unaware of the glaring defects in the performance. Unused to seeing plays on a regular basis, they were not unduly critical and enjoyed every moment. Even with its blemishes, *A Trick To Catch A Chaste Lady* was superior to anything that Conway's Men, or any other touring company, had offered to the people of Dover and they were highly appreciative. The actors, however, knew only too well how much better the play could have been. During the long and generous applause, they took their bow with a measure of guilt, feeling that they did not entirely deserve it. Elias was again the exception. Having carried much of the play on his broad shoulders, he felt entitled to bask in the ovation and he made the most of it. When he led the cast into the tiring-house, he was congratulated by all and sundry. Even Gill had a word of praise for him.

Nicholas was deeply disappointed. In times of adversity, Westfield's Men could be usually be counted on to pull together but it had not happened that afternoon. What had worked so well in rehearsal that morning had faltered during the actual performance. Even experienced actors like Gill, Ingram, Carr and Frank Quilter had signally failed to do themselves justice. Something positive had been achieved. In defiance of the attempt to prevent them from playing at all, they had actually staged the comedy in front of a full audience. Money had been earned and spectators went away happy. But it was not enough to satisfy Nicholas. He was forced to accept the fact that, without Firethorn, the company was not in a fit state to defend their high reputation. Their patron, an assiduous theatregoer, would have been shocked to see how disorganised they had become. He would certainly not allow his company to perform at the castle in front of Lord Cobham.

Suppressing his own anxieties, Nicholas did his best to give encouragement to the others but it was in vain. They were sad and jaded. The performance had exposed their limitations and reminded them just how much they depended on Firethorn. All that they wanted to do – apart from Elias, that is – was to creep back to the Lion and reach for the consolation of strong ale. Gill crooked a finger to call Nicholas over to him.

'That was an abomination,' said the clown.

'It was lacking in some respects,' admitted Nicholas.

'Thank heaven that Lord Westfield was not here to witness it.'

'I, too, am grateful for that small mercy.'

'Spare us from further disgrace, Nicholas.'

'What do you mean?'

'Inform our patron that we are unable to perform at the castle. I'll not be humiliated like that again. Until we find Lawrence, we are but pale shadows of what we should be. Look around you,' said Gill. 'There's hardly a man among us who would dare to take to the boards again. Explain the situation to Lord Westfield. Tell him that we've given our last performance in Dover.'

It took a long time for the crowd to disperse from the Guildhall. Several of the spectators remained in order to add their personal congratulations to the actors as they came out from the tiring-house. Owen Elias was the first to appear, surrounded immediately by adoring young women who quickly discovered that he was nothing like the timid and unworldly Lackwit that he had played. Barnaby Gill was wheeled out by George Dart to a smattering of applause and there was great interest as well in Richard Honeydew, whose portrayal of the heroine had been so convincing that some refused to believe that he was really a young boy. Under the supervision of Nicholas, the hired men began to dismantle the stage. Sebastian Frant and Thomasina came across to the book holder.

'Do you have a moment to spare, Nick?' asked Frant.

'I always have time for your and your daughter,' replied Nicholas, leaving the others to get on with their work. 'It is good to see you both again. I wish that we could have offered you something better than was on display this afternoon.'

'But we enjoyed the play,' said Thomasina with obvious sincerity. 'It was a more cunning and amusing tale than *Cupid's Folly*. Master Gill was a delight and you proved yourself a very able actor.'

'Yes,' said Frant. 'I've never seen you on stage before.'

Nicholas gave a tired smile. 'Nor will you do so again, Sebastian. I was there merely to move the wheelbarrow. I'm not proud of my performance.'

'You should be, Nick.'

'I agree with Father,' said Thomasina. 'You were another clown. But where was Master Firethorn? I thought that you told me he was certain to appear today?'

'He was indisposed, I fear,' said Nicholas.

Her eyes filled with concern. 'I hope that he is not ill.'

'His condition is not serious and we expect him to return soon. Fortunately,' he went on, pointing to Elias, 'we had an able deputy in Owen. He was a true hero on that stage this afternoon.'

'Oh, I know. Pray excuse me while I tell him so.'

Seeing that Elias was breaking away from a group of admirers, Thomasina went over to speak to him. The Welshman was soon lapping up her congratulations. It gave Nicholas the opportunity of a word alone with someone who knew much more about the theatre than his impressionable young daughter.

'Be honest, Sebastian,' said Nicholas. 'What did you really think of us?'

Frant was tactful. 'You've given me more entertaining performances.'

'I asked for an *honest* opinion.'

'Then I have to confess that I was disappointed. Thomasina might not have seen the faults but I lost count of them. Barnaby was curiously weak and Edmund was simply walking through his part. Owen Elias,' he said, nodding towards the Welshman, 'was the only person to bring true worth out of his role. You missed Lawrence sorely.'

'We were all aware of that.'

'Will he be back in time for your appearance at the castle?'

'It seems unlikely,' said Nicholas. 'That being the case, we will have to forego the pleasure of playing here again. Barnaby refuses to countenance the idea and most of our fellows will be of the same mind. Owen apart, they would like to quit Dover at the earliest opportunity.'

'Are they so upset by their performance?'

'They are mortified, Sebastian, and so am I. You've seen us at the Queen's Head. You know what Westfield's Men can do at their best.'

'No rival can even challenge them.'

'We did not feel quite so invincible today.'

Frant was sympathetic. 'Take heart from the fact that you had more spectators here like Thomasina. They loved what they saw and gave you the tribute of their palms.' His daughter rejoined him. 'We must away, my dear. And we must let Nick get on with his work.' He shook hands with Nicholas. 'Give my warmest regards to Lawrence. I hope that he is soon able to take his place on stage again.'

'Yes,' said Thomasina. 'I long to see him once more.'

'It may not be in Dover,' said Nicholas. 'Farewell.'

As he watched Frant and his daughter leaving the hall, Nicholas had his worst fears confirmed. Their former scrivener had been candid. By their normal standards, the performance was extremely poor. Nicholas felt that they had cheated the audience and yearned for the chance to make amends. That chance would not come in Dover unless Firethorn was found and restored to his pre-eminence in the company. It was a sobering reminder. His main task was to continue the search. After instructing the others to load everything into the waiting wagons, Nicholas slipped out of the Guildhall. He did not walk far before someone stepped out to block his way. It was John Strood.

'I was hoping to see you, Nick,' he said, pumping his friend's hand. 'You told me that you were the book holder. I did not realise that you were an actor as well.'

'Only by necessity, John.'

'It was the wittiest play I've ever seen.'

'I'm glad that you enjoyed it.'

'It was such a clever idea to use a wheelbarrow as you did.'

'That, too, was forced upon us,' said Nicholas. 'But it was good of you to come.'

'It was the only time that I could.'

'Why? Are you setting sail?'

'Later this evening.'

'How long will you be away?'

'Several days,' said Strood. 'You'll doubtless have moved on from the town by then. I'm sorry that we were not able to spend more time together.' He shifted his feet uneasily. 'And I'm sorry that you did not find me in a happier station.'

'I was delighted to see you, John, whatever your station in life.'

'The *Mermaid* is an unworthy ship for someone of my abilities.'

'Then find a better one.'

'That is not as simple as you might imagine.'

'Why not?'

'One day, perhaps, I'll tell you.' He embraced Nicholas. 'Adieu!'

'Good fortune attend you, John!'

Strood gave a mirthless laugh and hurried away.

Nicholas was pleased that they had been able to exchange a farewell but saddened by the fact that they were unlikely to meet again. His friend deserved to sail on a much finer vessel than the *Mermaid* yet there was an air of resignation about Strood that suggested he would never do so. Nicholas waited until his old shipmate had vanished into the crowd before he set off in the other direction. His thoughts were solely on Lawrence Firethorn now.

The blind beggar was sitting in the precise spot that George Dart had indicated. White-haired and dressed in rags, the old man was curled up in a doorway to keep out of the sun. A small bowl stood on the cobbles in front of him but it was empty. Nicholas tossed a coin into the bowl and a scrawny hand shot out to retrieve it.

'Thank you, kind sir,' said the beggar.

'How do you know that I'm a man and not a maid?'

'By the sound of your feet. You've the tread of a tall man with a long stride.'

Nicholas crouched down beside him. 'How good is your memory?'

'As good as yours, I think. Try me, sir.'

'A friend of mine spoke to you yesterday, shortly after noon.'

'A young man. I remember him well.'

'Why?'

'Because he dropped a coin in my bowl. Few people do that.'

'He also talked to you,' said Nicholas. 'He told you who

he was and where he worked. When he confided a problem to you, you claimed that you could help.'

'I did,' agreed the beggar, 'but he went away before I could tell him what I knew. He was with another man, older and more irritable, who seemed to be in a small cart.'

'It was a wheelbarrow.'

The beggar cackled. 'Does he have no better means of moving about?'

'His leg is broken and in a splint.'

'Ah,' said the old man, 'then he has my sympathy. He has a burden to carry, like me, and must try to overcome it as best he can.' He reached out a hand to feel Nicholas's arm. 'Who am I talking to?'

'My name is Nicholas Bracewell.'

'Also employed by Westfield's Men, I think.'

'The same.'

'Then you, too, are looking for a certain Master Firethorn.'

'We are desperate to find him,' said Nicholas. 'Anything of help that you can tell me will earn my gratitude.'

'I need more than gratitude.' Another coin was dropped into the bowl. The beggar grabbed it at once. 'Is this all that I can expect?'

'That depends on the intelligence you give me,' said Nicholas. 'Since you were unable to see anything, you must have heard it instead.'

'Oh, yes. My ears can pick up the slightest sound. I hear snatches of a thousand conversations every day yet I can always tell them apart. Age has robbed me of much but left me with my wits.'

'Tell me about Master Firethorn.'

'He was coming from the same direction as you when he was stopped by someone. A younger man, judging by his voice.'

'Where was this?'

'No more than a few yards from where I sit now.'

'Did this other person give a name?'

'No, sir,' said the beggar, scratching at the fleas beneath his armpits, 'but he recognised Master Firethorn and gave him a letter.'

'A letter?'

'I heard the seal being broken.'

'What else did you hear?' asked Nicholas, listening intently.

'The name of the man who sent the letter. It was Lord Westfield.'

'Are you certain?'

'My ears never deceive me. The messenger told Master Firethorn that he was to go to an inn where Lord Westfield was staying. They went off together.'

Nicholas was mystified. 'But our patron has not yet arrived in Dover. How could he send for Master Firethorn when he is not even here?'

'I've told you all I know.' The beggar grinned. 'Except for one thing.'

'And what's that?'

'The name of the inn.'

The scrawny hand was extended and Nicholas knew that he would have to buy the information. How reliable it was, he could only hazard a guess but the beggar had clearly heard enough to convince him that he was telling the truth. He put three more coins into the man's open palm. It closed instantly.

'Where did this messenger take him?'

'To meet Lord Westfield.'

'At which inn?'

'The Arms of England.'

Lawrence Firethorn had lost all track of time. Roused from his sleep, he was untied from the post and hustled out of the warehouse by the two men who had stood guard over him earlier. He was then taken along a quay, helped down some stone steps and pushed into a rowing boat. The point of a dagger was held to his ribs. Firethorn could do nothing but lie in the stern of the boat as it was rowed away. He was bruised and bewildered. He had cramp in his arms and legs. The boat seemed to take a long time to reach its destination and he feared that he was being taken out to sea to be drowned. Then the oars were shipped and he felt the thud of contact with a larger vessel. Ropes were lowered and tied around his chest and under his armpits. Unable to resist, he was hauled upward.

When they lowered him down, he knew that he was in the hold of a ship. It creaked and rolled as it was buffeted playfully by the waves. Firethorn felt sick. His captors came aboard to take charge of him, lugging him along a floor then securing him to some iron rings set in the side of the hold. Where were they taking him? Why did they handle him so roughly? What time was it? Who *were* they? Hours of excruciating discomfort limped slowly past before one of his captors bent over him.

'I'm to offer you food.' It was the voice of the man who had killed Giddy Mussett. 'If it was left to me, I'd sooner throw you overboard but we've been told to keep you alive. Do you want to eat?'

Firethorn's stomach was too unsettled even to consider the offer but he nodded his head nevertheless. Any chance to have his gag removed had to be taken. He could at least ask some of the questions that had been tormenting him.

'Say nothing,' warned the man. 'Cry for help and it will not be heard. We're too far from the shore for that. Do you understand?'

Firethorn nodded again and adopted a submissive pose. His gag was untied.

'I've some cheese for you,' said the other, inserting it hard into his mouth. 'I hope that it chokes you to death.'

Firethorn spat it into his face and roared his defiance. 'I'll kill you one day!'

Something struck him viciously on the side of the head. The blows continued until he sank into oblivion. When he recovered consciousness again, Firethorn learnt that one side of his face was covered in blood and that he was lashed even more tightly to the iron ring. His gag was firmly back in place. There would be no more meals for him.

* * *

The landlord of the Arms of England was a swarthy man of middle years with a face that glowed with geniality. A former sailor, he had tired of life at sea and found an occupation that suited his talents and inclinations. Nicholas Bracewell weighed him up at a glance.

'What's your pleasure, sir?' asked the landlord.

'I'm looking for a friend.'

'Then search about you. Do you see him here?'

'No,' said Nicholas. 'He came in yesterday, not long after midday.'

The landlord chuckled. 'Then you'll hardly find him here now. We've lots of customers who like to drink themselves into stupidity but we always turn them out at the end of the day unless they have hired a room.'

'First, tell me if my friend came in here. He's a man you'd remember.'

'Why is that?'

Nicholas gave him a description of Firethorn and explained that he probably came into the inn with a younger man. The landlord had no difficulty in identifying them.

'Ah, yes,' he said. 'I do recall your friend, sir, and he was with a young man.'

'How long did they stay?'

'I've no recollection of that.'

'None at all?'

'The room had been hired until morning but they left well before that.'

'Room?' repeated Nicholas. 'My friend was taken to a room?'

'One of our finest.'

'Who paid for it?'

'The fellow did not give a name,' said the landlord. 'I took him on trust. He was a seafaring man like myself and that was enough for me.'

'But he's not there now?'

'Neither of them are, sir.'

'There were two of them staying here?'

'Yes, sir. Though the other man was no sailor. I could tell that. When this friend of yours came in, he was taken straight up to their room. It's above my head so I know that they went in there.'

'Is it occupied now?' asked Nicholas.

'No. Why? Did you wish to hire it?'

'I simply wish to look into it.'

'But it's empty, sir.'

'That makes no difference.'

The landlord was cautious. 'I like to oblige my customers but I don't make a habit of showing them into my rooms. I'd need a good reason to do that.'

'I've an excellent reason,' said Nicholas with urgency. 'My friend was tricked into coming here. I've reason to believe that the men you talked about were lying in wait for him. He was kidnapped.'

'Here? Under my roof?'

'That's my suspicion. I'll pay, if you let me confirm it.'

'There's no need for that, sir,' said the landlord, moving across to the stairs. 'I'll take you up there myself. We've lively customers here at times but I never let them get out of hand. And I'd certainly not let them have a room if I thought that they were intending to commit a crime here.'

'We don't know that they were,' said Nicholas, following him up the steps. 'But it strikes me as a strong possibility.'

The landlord opened the door then stood back to let Nicholas go in. It was a small room with a central beam so low that he had to duck beneath it. The bed took up almost a third of the available space. The place looked clean and cosy but Nicholas could discern no sign of recent occupation. If Firethorn had been held there, he had left no mark of his visit behind. Nicholas went around the room with scrupulous care, even getting on his knees to peer under the bed.

'You'll find nothing under there, sir. The room has been cleaned.'

'Had the bed been slept in?'

'No, sir.'

'Then nobody stayed the night.'

'We think that they sneaked away in the dark.'

'Why should they do that?' wondered Nicholas, getting to his feet. 'May I open the shutters to let in more light?'

'I'll do it for you, sir.'

The landlord stepped into the room and lifted the latch. When he opened the shutters, a gust of wind blew in from the sea and achieved what Nicholas could never have done. It dislodged a tiny object that had been missed by the maidservant who had cleaned the room earlier. It was a white feather. Disturbed by the wind, it leapt high into the air and floated for several seconds until Nicholas snatched at it. He held it between a finger and thumb to examine it.

'Have you seen it before, sir?' asked the landlord.

'Oh, yes.'

'Where?'

'It was in my friend's hat,' said Nicholas. 'He was here.'

Remorse set in as soon as they reached the Lion. Ashamed of the way they had acquitted themselves, the actors supped their ale and indulged in bitter recrimination. They felt that they had betrayed their talent at the Guildhall and it left them without any urge to perform again in Dover. Owen Elias raised a lone voice against the general melancholy, arguing that the best way to exonerate themselves was to give a performance at the castle that was truly worthy of them. He was shouted down by the others, who were beginning to resent the way that the Welshman had succeeded so brilliantly on stage when they had so miserably failed. Elias could not even rally support from Edmund Hoode. When he saw Nicholas enter, he hoped that he would at last have someone on his side.

'You agree with me, Nick, I'm sure,' he said, intercepting him to take him aside. 'We must play at the castle.'

'Not without Lawrence.'

'We managed without him this afternoon.'

'And paid a heavy penalty,' said Nicholas. 'You took the laurels, Owen, but the rest of us buckled. Had we given such a performance at the Queen's Head, we'd have been mightily abused by some of our spectators.'

'The mayor and his wife approved. They told me so.'

'Leave them to their own likes and dislikes. I've news of Lawrence.'

Elias was attentive. 'Good news or bad?'

'Something of each,' said Nicholas. 'I know where he was taken and am sure that he was still alive by nightfall. If they meant to kill him, they'd have done so long before then. Those are the good tidings.'

'And the bad ones.'

'I've still no idea where he is now.'

Nicholas told him the story in full, praising the part played in it by George Dart, the least likely member of the company to provide crucial information. When he heard about the letter that was handed to Firethorn, the Welshman shook his head.

'It could not have been genuine, Nick. Our patron only arrived this afternoon.'

'How do you know?'

'Word awaited us when we got back here.'

'Where does Lord Westfield stay?'

'At the castle.'

'Why did Lawrence not realise that?' asked Nicholas, stroking his beard. 'When he was summoned to that inn, he must have known Lord Westfield would not be there.'

'I disagree, Nick. Our patron is as fond of his drink as any of us. After a long ride from London, where else would he go but to a reputable inn like the Arms of England? What drew Lawrence there was that letter.'

'It was a forgery.'

'He did not think so at the time, Nick.'

'That's what puzzled me. Lawrence knows our patron's hand.'

'He should do,' said Elias. 'We've had enough letters from Lord Westfield in the past. If he enjoys a performance, he always has the courtesy to tell us so.'

'Yet Lawrence was still deceived.'

'What does that tell you?'

'Something that I'm loath even to think,' said Nicholas, piecing the evidence together in his mind. 'And yet I must. It has been there under our noses all this time, Owen. Who knew about our life at the Queen's Head? Who asked about the towns that we would visit on tour? Who came to see us perform? And who,' he added, 'was the one man capable of forging our patron's hand with any skill?'

Elias was shocked. 'Only one name answers all that.'

'Then it must be him.'

'But he's a friend of Westfield's Men.'

'Is he?' said Nicholas. 'I begin to wonder. It was he who encouraged our suspicion of Conway's Men in order to throw us off the scent. And he who got close enough to know our innermost thoughts. Let's go and find him, Owen,' he decided. 'It's high time that we learnt if Sebastian Frant is the friend that we thought him.'

Chapter Sixteen

It took them some time to find the house. All that they knew was that Sebastian Frant lived close to Dover, along the Folkestone road, and they set off in that direction. The first people they encountered on the way were unable to help them. Though they had lived in the area for many years, and could recite the names of every village and hamlet for miles around, they had never heard of anyone called Frant. It was almost as if the former scrivener was in hiding. Nicholas Bracewell and Owen Elias rode on until they eventually found someone who gave them some guidance. The man was a local farmer, tending his cattle.

'Frant?' he repeated, shaking his head. 'That name means nothing to me, sirs.'

'He's a tall man,' said Nicholas, 'with fifty years or more on his back. A slim, well-dressed fellow whom some would account handsome.'

'Do not forget his daughter,' added Elias with a grin. 'Thomasina is an angel in human form. A fresh, fair virgin of eighteen or nineteen years at most.'

'Ah,' said the farmer. 'I think I know who you mean.'

'Once seen, Thomasina is not easily forgotten.'

'Do they live far away?' asked Nicholas.

The farmer nodded. 'Little over a mile, sir, but the house is difficult to find. I've seen the pair of them from time to time but never exchanged more than a friendly wave. I did not know their names. They like their privacy.'

Taking careful note of the directions, the two men set off again. They soon reached the wood that the farmer had mentioned and picked their way along a track that twisted and turned for hundreds of yards until it brought them out into open country. The house was not at first visible. Shaded by trees, it was set in a hollow in the middle distance. It was only when they got much closer that they had their first glimpse of it. Elias was astounded.

'Is *that* where Sebastian lives?' he exclaimed.

'It's much bigger than I imagined, Owen.'

'We are in the wrong profession. If this is what a scrivener can afford, I'll quit the stage tomorrow and take up a pen.'

'Sebastian did not buy this place with what he earned from us,' said Nicholas. 'I know what fees he charged because I handed the money over to him. No matter how diligent his pen, he'd not have amassed enough to afford such a house.'

'He must have had private wealth, Nick.'

'Then why did he need to work as a scrivener?'

'Let's ask him.'

They cantered down towards the house, a large, low, rambling structure with a thatched roof that gleamed in the sunshine and walls that had been painted white. It was set in several acres of land, some of it cultivated but most kept for horses to graze. To the side of the house were a stable block and a run of outbuildings, all of which appeared to be in good repair. Sebastian Frant clearly maintained his home well. Tethering their horses at the front of the house, they went up to a door that was made of solid oak and fortified with iron spikes. In response to a knock, a servant opened the door. He was a sturdy young man with darting eyes.

'Is your master at home?' asked Nicholas.

'No, sir.'

'Can you tell us where he is?'

'No, sir,' said the man bluntly.

'In that case, we'll wait until he returns.'

'My orders are to let nobody in the house.'

'Is Thomasina here, by any chance?' asked Elias. A flicker of the servant's eyes betrayed him. 'Ah, in that case, we'll speak with her instead.'

'She may not wish to see you.'

'Tell her that we insist,' said Nicholas. 'We come from Westfield's Men.'

'Yes,' said Elias. 'Thomasina and her father watched us perform this afternoon. I want to give her the chance to congratulate me properly.'

'Wait here,' grunted the man, about to shut the door in their faces.

'Let them in, Daniel,' said a voice behind him. The

servant stood back to reveal Thomasina Frant. She looked at them in surprise. 'What brings you here?'

'We need to speak with you,' said Nicholas.

'Then you had better come in.'

Her manner was pleasant, if not welcoming. She led them into the parlour, a spacious room with low beams, a huge fireplace and some expensive furniture. Nicholas took particular note of an ornate oak chest and a high backed chair that had been exquisitely carved. He was also aware of the fact that the servant was lurking protectively outside the door. Thomasina invited them to sit down but remained standing.

'Father is not here,' she explained, looking from one to the other. 'He's visiting friends and may be away for some days.'

'Let's talk about a friend of yours first,' suggested Nicholas. 'When I met you at the harbour the other day, you said that you'd been bidding farewell to someone who was sailing to Calais.'

'And so I was.'

'No ship left Dover that afternoon.'

'Then the vessel must have been delayed.'

'I begin to wonder if it existed,' said Nicholas, 'along with your friend.'

'Do you doubt my word?' she said with indignation. 'Have you ridden all this way to accuse me of telling lies? I'll call Margaret, if you wish. She'll vouch for me.'

'I'm sure that she will. Margaret is well-trained, like that other servant who is standing out in the passageway as a guard dog. They'll only say what they've been told to say. I'd rather hear the truth from you.'

'You've already done so.'

'We took you for an honest girl, Thomasina,' said Elias.

'This is intolerable,' she retorted with a rare flash of anger. 'What I do when I'm in Dover is my business. I'll not be interrogated like this. Daniel will show you out.'

Nicholas was determined. 'Not until we've discussed a few other things.'

'Other things?'

'Yes,' he said. 'Such as our visit to Arden's house in Faversham. Or the performance of *The Foolish Friar* that upset you so much.'

'I was not upset at all,' she said, folding her arms. 'I liked the play.'

'What did you think of me as a friar?' asked Elias, fishing for a compliment.

'Very little, Owen,' said Nicholas, 'and I suspect that Thomasina thought even less of Barnaby Gill in a habit. She and her father were appalled.'

'Why?'

'Let her tell us.'

She was perfectly calm. 'There's nothing to tell.'

'I believe that there is.'

'You can believe what you wish, Master Bracewell. It's of no concern to me. What does trouble me is that you and Master Elias are guests in our house yet all that you can do is to try to browbeat me. I took you for gentlemen. I can see that I was mistaken.'

'We thought you were a friend,' said Nicholas, 'but we were also mistaken.'

351

'How can you say that? Father has the fondest memories of Westfield's Men. Did we not come to watch you play out of friendship? We saw *Cupid's Folly* in Maidstone and, this very afternoon, we admired Master Elias in *A Trick To Catch A Chaste Lady*.'

Elias beamed. 'Thank you.'

'My interest is in *The Foolish Friar*,' said Nicholas. 'And in that visit we made to a certain house in Faversham. Now I know why that particular place made you cry.'

'The story moved me,' she said. 'That is all.'

'Which story?'

'That which touched on the murder of Thomas Arden.'

'No,' said Nicholas, watching her closely. 'I fancy that it was another murder that produced those tears. Thomas Arden was more than a former mayor of the town. After the Dissolution of the Monasteries, he was involved in the distribution of Catholic property that had been confiscated. Abbey Street no longer has a Catholic abbey, does it? You regard that as a heinous crime.'

Thomasina was dismissive. 'That all happened before I was even born.'

'But not before your father was born. He'd have brought you up in his religion.'

'Discuss the matter with him when he returns.'

'Oh, we've much more than that to discuss with him,' said Nicholas. 'But let's come back to *The Foolish Friar*. It was bold of you to attend a play that you knew would mock the Old Religion. That's why you were so perturbed. Your father hid his feelings because he has had more practise in doing so. Your displeasure showed in your face. You hated a play that held Roman Catholicism up to ridicule.'

'I found it rather barren beside *Cupid's Folly*,' she confessed.

'Barren and insulting.'

There was a long pause. 'I'd like you both to leave.'

'Will you not come to the defence of your faith?'

'It's a purely private matter.'

'Not when it leads to the murder of two people and the kidnap of a third.'

She was genuinely shocked. 'Murder? Kidnap?'

'The kidnap may have become another murder by now,' explained Nicholas. 'When I said that Lawrence Firethorn was indisposed this afternoon, I was concealing the truth. He was abducted in Dover and we've not seen him since.'

'But who could want to abduct him?' she said with alarm.

'I think that you might be able to tell us that.'

'On my honour, I could not!'

'Are you certain?'

'I admire him greatly, as you know.'

'Except when he played in *The Foolish Friar*.'

'I'm truly horrified to learn that he's been kidnapped,' she said earnestly. 'I'd swear as much on the Holy Bible.'

Nicholas got to his feet. 'Would that be a Roman Catholic Bible?'

Her manner changed at once. The polite and reserved young woman revealed another side to her character. Crossing to the door, she snapped her fingers and the servant appeared at her side, holding a musket with the air of someone who had used the weapon before. Thomasina's eyes were cold and unforgiving.

'Escort these gentlemen off our property,' she ordered.

'Yes,' he said, glaring at the visitors. 'Out!'

Nicholas ignored the command. Instead, he walked across to the oak chest and ran his hand over its ornate carving. Then he examined the chair that had been embellished so strikingly by a woodcarver. Nicholas sat down in it and stroked the arms. The servant came over to him and pointed the musket at his chest.

'Get up!' he snarled.

'But it's such a beautiful chair,' said Nicholas, leaning back, 'and of a piece with that magnificent chest. Both were carved by the same man, were they not? I'll wager that I've admired his handiwork before. It was on a lectern I saw in the hold of a ship called the *Mermaid*.' He looked at Thomasina. 'Is that what you were doing in the harbour that day? Sending some church furniture abroad? For that's where this chair and that fine chest came from, I suspect. They're too elaborate for the taste of Protestants. My guess is that they are the work of a Catholic woodcarver.'

Daniel jabbed him in the chest with the barrel of the musket but Nicholas was ready for him. Knocking the weapon upward with his arm, he kicked out both feet to trip the servant up. As the man fell backward, the musket went off and its ball lodged itself harmlessly in the ceiling, sending down a flurry of plaster. Before Daniel could move, Nicholas wrenched the weapon from his grasp and Elias leapt from his seat to hold a dagger at the servant's throat. Nicholas strolled back to Thomasina.

'It's all over now,' he warned. 'Further denial is pointless.'

'I know nothing of murder and kidnap,' she cried.

'I believe you, Thomasina.'

'Nor does my father. He'd never stoop to such things.'

'He may not be the person you think him. Sebastian certainly misled us. And so did you,' he went on. 'I thought you a decent, honest, God-fearing person with pride and self-respect. Yet you are too ashamed of it even to declare your faith.'

'No,' she rejoined vehemently. 'I follow the Old Religion with a dedication that you could never even understand. We've withstood scorn, ignominy and persecution for many years now and we are still unbowed. Yes, Master Bracewell, I *was* upset when we saw that house in Faversham because it was a symbol of the vicious cruelty visited upon the Roman Catholic Church.'

'And *The Foolish Friar*?'

'It was an unjust attack on our beliefs. I hated listening to that raucous laughter at our expense. Father took me there to see what we were up against in the theatre. The friar was held up as an object of derision and loathing. For two long hours I suffered as I watched you sharpening your blades on the only true religion.'

'Only true religion? Not in England.'

'Here and anywhere else,' she said defiantly. 'We'll never be conquered.'

'Then you should not have given yourself away,' said Nicholas. 'Was my guess correct?' he added, glancing at the chest. 'Did that begin life in a church?'

'Yes, and it will be returned to one soon.'

'Where?' asked Elias, hauling the servant to his feet.

'That's something you'll never know.'

'We mean to find out,' said Nicholas, as realisation dawned. 'Come, Owen. We must away. I think I know where Sebastian is. He's waiting to sail to France with a cargo of furniture. We must try to get to him in time.'

Lawrence Firethorn could not understand the kindness that he was receiving. Having been battered to the ground, he was now being cared for by tender hands. Someone was bathing his face to remove the blood from the gash in his scalp. The man said nothing but he was showing true compassion. When the dried blood had been washed away, a strip of linen was tied around the head to cover the wound. Firethorn wished that he was in a position to express his thanks but the ropes, gag and blindfold were severe restraints. He heard voices shouting above and the sound of activity as the anchor was hauled up. When the wind hit the sail, there was a flap of canvas and the *Mermaid* moved forward with loud creaking noises. Firethorn was disturbed.

After a last look at him, Sebastian Frant stifled a sigh of regret and slipped away.

When they reached the harbour in Dover, the *Mermaid* was just beginning to move away from the bay. Elias was dismayed but Nicholas did not give up so easily. With the Welshman at his heels, he spurred his horse in the direction of Dover Castle. Their names were enough to get them admitted instantly to Lord Westfield's apartment. Resting on a couch after his journey, their patron gave them a wave of welcome.

'I bring good tidings from London for you,' he said.

'That's more than we can offer you, my lord,' said Nicholas.

'I had word from the Queen's Head. That imbecile of a landlord has recognised his folly and wants Westfield's Men back again. Break the news to Master Firethorn.'

'We cannot do that until we find him, my lord.'

'No,' said Elias. 'We do not even know if he is still alive.'

Lord Westfield was aghast. 'What's this? Has he disappeared, then?'

Nicholas was succinct. He gave enough detail to show how serious the situation was but did nothing to impede the action that was necessary. Their patron was horrified at what he heard but could not see how he could help.

'This ship has set sail, you say?'

'Yes,' said Nicholas. 'Sebastian Frant is certainly aboard. It may even be that Master Firethorn is there as well. We need to overhaul them, my lord.'

'Even *you* cannot swim that fast,' said the other with a feeble smile.

'A faster vessel must be dispatched. Only my Lord Cobham could sanction that.'

'Then it shall be done!'

'Will you speak with him on our behalf?'

'No, Nicholas,' said the patron, 'you'll do it much better yourself. Acquaint him with the villainy that's taken place and the Lord Warden of the Cinque Ports will be only too willing to oblige you. Lawrence Firethorn kidnapped? Mercy on us! The future of my theatre company is at stake. You shall have your ship from my dear friend.'

'There's another favour I must beg of him, my lord.'

'What's that?'

'I wish to sail in the vessel,' said Nicholas.

Sebastian Frant was not capable of expressing the deep anger that he felt. Instead of being furious with his bearded companion, he sounded merely petulant.

'There was no need to belabour him like that,' he complained.

'He had the gall to spit at me.'

'Then you must have provoked him.'

'No,' said the man. 'I offered him cheese and he spat it in my face. Nobody does that to me with impunity.'

'You might have caused him serious injury.'

'If only I had the chance!'

'Robert!' said Frant reproachfully.

'You are too soft, Sebastian. It's not a fault shared by our enemies.'

'Lawrence Firethorn is not an enemy.'

'You wanted to bring Westfield's Men to a halt, did you not?'

'I did. But not by killing their manager.'

'It would have been the deftest way.'

'Only to someone as bloodthirsty as you, Robert. There's been enough killing.'

'There can never be enough of that!'

Frant was standing on the deck of the *Mermaid* with

Robert Armiger, the bearded assassin who had stabbed two men to death and arranged the kidnap of a third. Because they were sailing into a head wind, the ship was obliged to tack and that slowed them down. Frant peered over the bulwark for the first sign of the French mainland but he could see nothing on the horizon.

'We'll be late,' he decided.

'We should use a bigger vessel,' said Armiger. 'The *Mermaid* has seen better days. She needs to have her hull repaired.'

'She's served us well enough in the past, Robert. Who else would do the kind of work we require and ask no questions? We'll just have to suffer her tardiness.'

'It's more than tardiness. The ship is a disgrace. I was a sailor once and it offends me to use the *Mermaid*. She's not fit for the work.'

'We've crossed without trouble so far.'

'Except from Master Firethorn,' sneered Armiger.

'You keep away from him.'

'He has to be beaten into submission.'

'No, Robert,' said Frant. 'I forbid it. When we get to France, he's to be taken ashore, a long way from the coast, then released. By the time he's found his way back to Dover, it will be too late. The danger will be over.'

'Kill Master Firethorn and there would *be* no danger.'

'You do not know Westfield's Men.'

'I know them well enough to want to destroy them.'

'That's not as easy as we imagined,' said Frant. 'I hoped that Giddy Mussett's death would bring them to their knees but they simply pressed on. They should never have been allowed to stage *The Loyal Subject* here. It was agony to sit through it.'

'Our religion was mocked again.'

'Mocked and vilified.'

'And the chief culprit was the man tied up in the hold.'

'He's paid for it, Robert. He's suffered.'

'Then let me put him out of his misery,' said Armiger, fingering his dagger.

'No! Leave him alone!'

'You may live to regret your weakness, Sebastian.'

'It's not weakness,' said Frant, 'but a debt that has to be paid.'

Armiger scowled and moved away. Frant continued to scan the horizon until a member of the crew walked past. He turned to speak to him.

'How long before we sight land, John?'

'Not long now, Master Frant.'

'This delay irks me.'

'The *Mermaid* was not built for speed,' said Strood with a shrug. 'If you want a fast crossing, choose another vessel. I reckon she'll reach Boulogne ahead of us.'

'Who will?'

'The other ship.'

'Where?'

'Look behind you, sir. We've company.'

Frant crossed the deck to stare over the other bulwark. Half a mile behind them was a small, sleek three-masted galleon under full sail. When he saw the sun glinting off the cannon, Frant became slightly worried.

'Do you recognise her, John?'

'Yes, sir,' said Strood. 'She's the *Mercury* and well-named for her speed. The main and foremast are square-rigged, with topsails, spritsails and top-gallants. When she straightens her line, you'll be able to see the lateen sail on her mizzen. All in all, she must have three times as much canvas as we do.'

'She's carrying guns.'

'The *Mercury* is well-armed with seven cannon on each side as well as smaller ordnance. She's one of the ships kept at Dover to ward off any attacks from Spain.'

'What makes you think that she's heading for Boulogne?'

'She's holding the same course as the *Mermaid*. That means one of two things,' argued Strood. 'She's either bound for the same port as we are.'

'Or?'

'The *Mercury* is following us.'

Owen Elias was an indifferent sailor. From the moment they left the shelter of Dover, his stomach began to feel queasy and his legs unsteady Yet he did not wish to miss out on the action. Instead of going below, he forced himself to stay on deck with Nicholas, who was savouring the exhilaration of a voyage once again. Crossing the Channel might not compare with some of the nautical experiences he had been through with Drake but it could still set his blood racing. Nicholas had been the first to pick out a ship on the horizon and he was thrilled when the tiny dot grew bigger and bigger until it was eventually identified as the *Mermaid*.

'Are we going to catch her in time?' asked Elias.

'No question but that we will.'

'I think that we should blow them out of the water.'

'There's no reason to do that,' said Nicholas. 'We know that Sebastian is aboard and he may even have Lawrence with him. Would you want the pair of them to drown?'

'No, Nick. I spoke in haste.'

'We need to seize the ship while we can. If the *Mermaid* is carrying illegal cargo, as I suspect she is, her captain will be called to account. Sink the vessel and we'd have no idea what was in her hold.'

'I'm just anxious to strike back at Sebastian.'

'We'll not do it with cannon, unless we put a shot across her bows. With luck, nobody will be harmed. Remember that I've a friend in the crew.'

'He may not be too pleased to see you.'

'I doubt that he will,' said Nicholas, feeling a pang of regret. 'If his ship is being used for smuggling, John Strood will not thank me for setting off in pursuit of it. His days at sea may be cut short for a while.'

'What of your friendship?'

'It will perish, I fear.'

'Yes,' said Elias. 'Like our friendship with Sebastian Frant.'

'He has a higher duty, Owen. At least, that is how he and that pretty daughter of his will have seen it. They serve God in their own way and that justifies anything.'

'Even murder and kidnap?'

'Apparently.'

362

'It is so unlike the Sebastian we knew. He was such a gentle creature.'

'Nobody is suggesting that he wielded the daggers himself.'

'No,' said Elias, 'but he gave the order to the assassin.'

'That's what we suppose. I'll be glad to learn the full truth of it.'

'So will I, Nick.'

'Why did he turn against a theatre company that once employed him?' wondered Nicholas. 'Why did he sanction the ambush against us and the death of Giddy Mussett?'

'Lawrence is the person who concerns me.'

'All the victims deserve our sympathy.'

'He's the only one who may still be alive.'

'Pray God that it be so!'

They looked across at the *Mermaid* as it changed tack once again. It was now close enough for them to see the crew on deck, going about their duties. Nicholas could not pick out John Strood yet but he knew that his friend must be there. It would be an uncomfortable reunion for both of them. There was no possibility that the *Mermaid* would outrun them. The old and leaky merchant ship could never compete with a galleon like the *Mercury*. Thanks to their patron, a trim vessel had been put at their disposal. Lord Cobham, Warden of the Cinque Ports, had acted promptly and decisively. The chase across the Channel was now almost over.

'I feel sick,' complained Elias.

'Go below,' advised Nicholas. 'Sit in a quiet corner with a bucket nearby.'

'And miss the chance of a brawl?'

'They'll be fools if they resist, Owen. We outnumber them easily.'

'I want to measure my sword with the killer himself. Will he be aboard?'

'I think it very likely, especially if Lawrence is on the ship. Sebastian would not be able to handle him alone. He'd need a strong man to do that. My guess is that we'll find both master and assassin on the *Mermaid*.'

'Why would they take Lawrence with them?'

'To get him out of the way.'

'Would it not be easier simply to kill him?'

'Yes,' said Nicholas, 'but I feel that Sebastian will stay his hand. He's not entirely beyond the reach of friendship and he'll not decree another murder for the sake of it. He's a devout man. Sin must ever be weighed against necessity.'

'Necessity?' echoed Elias. 'What necessity was there to have a harmless clown like Giddy Mussett stabbed in the back?'

'He was not harmless to Sebastian, or to his daughter.'

'She, at least, does not have Giddy's blood on her hands.'

'No,' agreed Nicholas, 'that's true. Sebastian kept her innocent of that. What she will think when she learns the truth about her father, I do not know, but it might shake her faith in the Old Religion.'

The *Mercury* dipped and rose in the swirling water, gaining on the other ship with every minute. As they drew even closer, Nicholas and Elias caught a glimpse of a lone passenger, standing in the stern of the *Mermaid* and watching them with apprehension.

It was Sebastian Frant.

Lawrence Firethorn was in agony. Still tied up below deck, he was suffering pain in every limb and a pounding headache. The gag made breathing difficult and the rope was cutting into his wrists. Wearied by loss of sleep, and by the beating he had taken, he had no strength left to test his bonds any more. But the mental anguish was far worse than any physical torture. He worried for himself, for his family and for his beloved company. Not knowing what lay ahead for him, he tormented himself by imagining all sorts of hideous deaths. It was his wife and children who occupied his mind most. How would they feel when they learnt that he had vanished across the sea? How would Margery cope on her own? Who would bear the news to her? What would happen to their home in Shoreditch?

He was still wallowing in remorse when he heard distant yells above his head. They did not sound like orders being barked to the crew. One voice was much closer than the other, though the second seemed to come nearer with the passage of time. Firethorn strained his ears to catch what was being said but the noise of the waves and the creaking of the ship made it impossible. There was a long wait, followed by a resounding thud that made the whole vessel shudder. At first, Firethorn thought that they had been rammed and that the *Mermaid* would be holed below the water line. Alone of the people aboard, he would be unable to save himself as the ship sank to the bottom of the sea. Seized by panic, he began to recite his prayers to himself. But no water came gushing in to claim his life and no cries of alarm were heard from the crew. Firethorn gave thanks to God for sparing him the horror of being drowned.

There was another long wait. A mixture of strange sounds came down to him but they only confused Firethorn. He had no idea what had happened beyond the fact that the ship did not seem to be maintaining the same speed any more. Hurried feet then came down the wooden steps. The next moment, someone stood behind Firethorn with an arm under his chin to pull back his head. The cold blade of a dagger was held against his throat. He braced himself for the murderous incision but he was spared yet again. Other people came down into the hold and approached him. Against all the odds, he heard a voice that he recognised and loved.

'Leave go of him, Sebastian,' warned Nicholas Bracewell.

'Keep away!' replied Frant, tightening his grip on Firethorn.

'There's no escape.'

'Take one more step and I slit his throat.'

'Why? What has Lawrence ever done to you?'

'He got in the way.'

'Was that Giddy Mussett's crime as well?' asked Nicholas, his voice deliberately calm. 'Did he get in the way?'

'His death was forced upon me.'

'I think that I can guess why.'

'I doubt that,' said Frant.

'Then perhaps I should tell you that we called at your house earlier on. We spoke to Thomasina and admired the furniture in your parlour. Some similar pieces are stored down here in the hold, are they not? Your daughter told us why.'

'Thomasina would never do that.'

'She was too proud of her religion to deny it.'

'Give me the dagger, Sebastian,' said Owen Elias, 'or I'll take it from you.'

'Not if you wish Lawrence to live.' Frant's hand shook and the blade of the dagger drew a trickle of blood from Firethorn's throat. 'Stay back, Owen. If you value his life, keep your distance.'

'That's sensible advice,' agreed Nicholas. 'Leave him be, Owen.'

The Welshman was perplexed. 'Allow him to get away with this?'

'Sebastian will get away with nothing.'

'That depends on what kind of bargain we strike,' said Frant.

'You are hardly in a position to strike any kind of bargain,' said Nicholas quietly. 'The ship has been boarded and we've a dozen armed men on deck. Do you think that you can defy us all, Sebastian?'

'I'll trade my safety for Lawrence's life.'

Elias was scornful. 'Your safety! You *have* no safety.'

'Let me handle this, Owen,' said Nicholas. 'My only concern is with Lawrence's safety. We should rejoice that he's still alive. Sebastian deserves our thanks for that.'

'He'll get no thanks from me.'

Nicholas turned to Frant again. 'Forgive him, Sebastian. He does not understand. There's only one reason why you spared Lawrence and it was not because you needed him as a means of bargaining, was it?'

'That no longer matters,' said Frant, desperation making his voice hoarse.

'I believe that it does.'

'Lawrence's life is in your hands, Nick.'

'And what about Thomasina's life?' asked Nicholas. 'Have you forgotten her? It's a cruel father who'd save his own skin and leave his daughter to suffer the consequences of his crimes. I refuse to believe that Sebastian Frant is that callous.' He took a step closer. 'Thomasina loves you. She looks up to you. At least, she did until she heard that you were involved in murder and kidnap. Are you going to make her even more ashamed by taking yet another life?'

'Be quiet!' howled Frant, wrestling with his conscience.

'Put the dagger aside, Sebastian.'

'No!'

'Put it aside,' said Nicholas softly, moving in closer. 'We both know that you could not kill Lawrence. You've too much compassion in you for that. You simply wanted him out of the way so that Westfield's Men could not continue. Nothing will be served by his death now.' He held out a hand. 'Let me have the dagger, Sebastian.'

'Stay back!' shouted Frant, pointing the weapon at him.

'Would you kill *me* as well? Then do so,' invited Nicholas, spreading his arms and offering his chest. 'Come on, Sebastian. We know that you can hire an assassin. Let's see if you have the courage to use that dagger yourself.' He took another step forward. 'We were friends once. End that friendship now, if you must.'

Frant raised the dagger to strike then lost his nerve. Opening his hand, he let it drop with a clatter to the floor. Nicholas was on him in an instant, pinioning him so that he could not move. Elias moved with equal speed to cut through Firethorn's bonds. The actor-manager tore off the gag and the blindfold. He blinked up at Frant.

'*You* had this done to me, Sebastian?' he asked. 'I'll strangle you!'

'No,' said Nicholas, using his body to protect Frant. 'We'll take him back to face the rigour of the law.'

'He'll feel my rigour first, Nick.'

'You do not look as if you've any to spare, Lawrence,' said Elias, putting an arm around him. 'Leave him to us.'

'But he was the one who ordered my kidnap.'

'Sebastian did not carry it out himself,' observed Nicholas. 'He'd not soil his Roman Catholic hands with that kind of crime. He instructed someone else to abduct you. Is that not true, Sebastian?' He tightened his grip on Frant. 'Who was the man and where is he now?' Frant's lower lip began to tremble. 'I thought so. The villain is aboard.'

As soon as they were hailed from the deck of the *Mercury*, he knew that they were in severe difficulties. A ship would not be dispatched from Dover to overhaul them unless there was a good cause. Flight was impossible. The only hope for Robert Armiger was to mingle with the crew of the *Mermaid* to pass himself off as one of them. Arrests would be made, the ship would be impounded and the captain would certainly be punished for his smuggling activities. Lowly members of the crew, however, might not suffer undue hardship. Armiger felt confident that Frant would not give him away and there was nobody else to identify him as a killer. Accordingly, he stood close to John Strood under the watchful eyes of the armed sailors who had come aboard from the *Mercury*.

His dream of escape was soon shattered. Nicholas Bracewell came bursting out of the hold with vengeance burning inside him. He looked around the deck.

'Which one of you is Robert Armiger?' he called out.

There was no reply. Crew members exchanged nervous glances but said nothing.

'Where is that killer?' demanded Nicholas. 'Anyone who hides him is guilty of his crimes. I ask again – which one of you is Robert Armiger?'

'He is,' said Strood, pointing to his companion.

It was a dangerous admission. The words were hardly out of his mouth when Strood felt a dagger being thrust between his ribs by Armiger. Letting out a groan, he fell to the deck. Armiger fled from the spot, pushing his way roughly through the other members of the crew. Nicholas ran quickly to Strood to kneel beside him, cradling his head in one arm and trying to stem the bleeding. It was too late. Armiger's thrust had been fatal. With a last smile of apology to his old shipmate, Strood finally escaped the shame of making his living as a smuggler on the *Mermaid*. Nicholas swallowed hard and offered up a silent prayer for his friend. Then he looked for Armiger once more. The man was up on the quarter deck, holding three people at bay with the bloodstained dagger that had just cut down Strood.

'Leave him to me!' ordered Nicholas, running to the steps.

Everyone backed away from Armiger. Having killed once, he was clearly ready to do so again and would not be taken without a fight. What amazed all those who watched was that Nicholas had no weapon of his own. He stood within six feet of Armiger.

'John Strood was a friend of mine,' he said.

'Then I'll send you after him,' retorted Armiger, waving the dagger.

'You've murdered enough people already.'

'One more would give me great pleasure.'

'Your case is hopeless,' said Nicholas. 'We can have you shot down with muskets or run through with swords. Put up your dagger while you may.'

'Then step a little closer,' urged the other man, 'and you shall have it.'

Nicholas did not hesitate. During his years at sea, he had learnt to handle himself in a brawl on deck and had disarmed more than one adversary. Armiger was a skilled assassin but he preferred to stab his victims from behind when they were unguarded. Circumstances had changed. They were on the quarter deck of a merchant ship that was bobbing violently on the water. Nicholas was no unprotected victim. He was strong, alert and brave enough to take on an armed man. It put a tiny doubt in Armiger's mind. As Nicholas came forward, he lunged at him with the dagger then made several sweeps to keep him away. Nicholas eluded the weapon with deft footwork then circled his man as he waited for his moment. It soon came. Armiger lunged again, missed, stabbed the air once more as Nicholas leapt back then hurled the dagger with vicious force. Nicholas ducked and the weapon went harmlessly over his head and into the sea.

Armiger gave a yell of exasperation and flung himself at Nicholas, grabbing him by the throat and forcing him back against the bulwark. They grappled, twisted and turned, then fell to the floor. Nicholas was momentarily dazed as his head struck the stout oak boards but Armiger did not pursue his advantage. Instead, refusing to end his days at the end of a rope, he decided to take his own life and clambered over the bulwark. Before he could jump, he felt Nicholas's arm around his neck. There was another ferocious struggle as the two of them grappled and punched. Armiger would not be denied. With a last burst of energy, he jumped from the bulwark and pulled Nicholas after him. There was a loud splash as the two bodies hit the water. The moment they surfaced, they went for each other's throats again.

Everyone on board rushed to the bulwark to watch the fight. Firethorn and Elias were among them, urging Nicholas on and wishing that they could help him in some way. Intent on drowning, Armiger was determined to take Nicholas with him and they threshed about wildly. A boat was lowered but it could never reach them in time to separate them. Armiger got a grip around Nicholas's neck and forced him below the surface. The two bodies vanished for well over a minute with only a patch of white foam to show where the fight was still continuing. Firethorn and Elias began to fear for their friend but their anxiety was premature. Nicholas's head eventually appeared. After gasping in air, he hauled the spluttering Armiger to the surface.

'He's still alive!' he shouted. 'I saved him for the hangman.'

Lifted by the safe return of their actor-manager, Westfield's Men entered Dover Castle with brimming confidence. They felt that they could conquer with their art a fortress that could not be taken by force. The first surprise that greeted them was the amount of livestock in the grassy courtyard. Over a hundred sheep and a dozen cows were grazing peacefully within the confines of the castle so that fresh milk and tender mutton were readily available. The Great Hall was larger than anywhere else where they had performed in Kent and the number of chairs and benches already set out indicated that a full audience was expected. Nicholas Bracewell had visited the place earlier to take note of its dimensions and to work out where best to erect their stage. All that the actors had to do was to polish a well-tried play. The morning rehearsal went well though Firethorn, still feeling the effects of his ordeal, was careful to pace himself. Refreshment was then served before the company readied itself for the afternoon performance.

William Brooke, tenth Baron Cobham, presided over the occasion. As Constable of the Castle, he held an important post but, as Lord Warden of the Cinque Ports, he also had a ready source of wealth. Governor of the ports of Hastings, Romney, Hythe, Dover and Sandwich, to which Winchelsea and Rye had been added, he was allowed to deduct five hundred pounds from any parliamentary taxation levied on the towns. Several members of his family were in attendance, including his son, Henry, and, significantly, his son-in-law, Sir Robert Cecil. Lord Westfield had brought his own entourage and guests from a wide area came in to swell the numbers. It was a more distinguished and exclusive audience than the troupe had met before in the county. No standees were allowed and no sailors were permitted to wander in from the local taverns.

In view of recent events, *The Loyal Subject* was the obvious choice even though it had been staged earlier at the Guildhall. It dealt with themes that had great relevance for Westfield's Men and gave Firethorn the opportunity to exhibit the full range of his skills. Though set nominally in Italy, everyone recognised that the play was about the dangers that threatened the English throne. The Duchess of Milan was a cipher for Queen Elizabeth and some of her leading courtiers could also be identified with their real counterparts by more perceptive spectators. It gave the piece a sharpness and immediacy that added to its appeal. Richard Honeydew was a beautiful but peremptory Duchess with the other apprentices as his ladies-in-waiting. Having whitened his beard to assume old age, Owen Elias was a Chief Minister who bore much more than a vague resemblance to Lord Burleigh, whose son, Sir Robert Cecil, was in the audience. Edmund Hoode once again took the small but telling role of the judge while Rowland Carr, James Ingram and Frank Quilter all had individual chances to shine as conspirators. Barnaby Gill, a decrepit retainer, was liberated from his wheelbarrow and carried on stage in a chair. Deaf, scatterbrained and querulous, he provided some wonderful humour, his broken leg concealed beneath a long robe and his comic song a special moment in the performance.

It was Firethorn, however, who dominated the stage as Lorenzo. Brave, honest and glowing with integrity, he was a hero whose tragedy touched all who watched. His prompt action saved the Duchess from an assassin's dagger. Yet it was his loyalty that eventually betrayed him and led to his execution. Firethorn used a particular couplet to give the fullest expression to his grief. Manacled by his gaolers and left alone in his cell, he spoke words that were a howl of pain.

> 'Fidelity has always been my cry
> And constant will I be until I die!'

At the close of the play, when the executioner held up the head that he appeared to have struck from Lorenzo's shoulders, there was an outburst of protest from the hall and several of the ladies began to weep. Relief was mixed with gratitude when Firethorn led out his troupe to take their bow and it was seen that the actor was still very much alive. The applause was deafening. After their disappointing performance at the Guildhall, the company had vindicated its reputation in the most striking way.

It was while they were in his apartment with their patron that the whole story began to emerge. Lord Westfield had invited Firethorn, Gill and Hoode to join him as the leading sharers and, because of his involvement in the rescue, Nicholas Bracewell was also there. All five of them were sipping Canary wine of the finest quality. Having been kept at the outer margin of events by his disability, it was Gill who felt that he had missed everything. He pressed for details.

'Sebastian was a friend of ours,' he said. 'Why did he let us down?'

'He served another master,' explained Nicholas, 'and that was the Roman Catholic Church. In time, it made him lose all affection for us.'

'Why was that, Nicholas?'

'You've seen one of the reasons this very afternoon. *The Loyal Subject* is a play that's anathema to those who follow the Old Religion. So was *The Foolish Friar*. In their different ways, both laid bare the iniquities of Popery. When we performed harmless comedies or dark tragedies about revenge, Sebastian Frant was happy enough to act as our scrivener and watch us at the Queen's Head. Then we presented a play that he found so repulsive that he could not bear to stay in our employ.'

'Which play was that, Nick?' asked Firethorn.

'Not one of mine, I hope,' said Hoode.

'No, Edmund,' replied Nicholas, 'the author was Jonas Applegarth.'

'Then it must have been *The Misfortunes of Marriage*.'

'The very same.'

Lord Westfield stirred. 'But I thought it no more than a simple comedy.'

'It had a deeper meaning, my lord,' said Nicholas tactfully, 'and it was not lost on someone like Sebastian. He told me that it was an ordeal to copy out lines that abused the religion to which he had dedicated his life. That was the point at which he left us but it was not to go into retirement. He continued the work that he had always been doing.'

'As a spy,' said Firethorn with disgust. 'We harboured a Catholic spy.'

'He confessed the truth as we sailed back to Dover. It all began when he was secretary to the Clerk of the Privy Council. Secret documents passed before his eyes every day. Sebastian was only required to copy them out but his keen memory retained them so that he could pass on intelligence to French and Spanish accomplices.'

'Thank heaven you caught him, Nick!' exclaimed Hoode.

Gill was puzzled. 'Why choose to act as our scrivener?'

'Because the work interested him,' said Nicholas, 'and it was a convenient mask behind which he could hide. When he quit his post, he needed to remain in London for a time. Westfield's Men were only one of a number who employed him.'

'I wish that we'd never met the rogue,' growled Firethorn. 'Although, I have to admit that he was not entirely without finer qualities. When that ruffian of his beat me aboard the ship, it was Sebastian who bathed my wounds. I thank him for that.' His voice hardened again. 'But it will not stop me cheering when he and Armiger are hanged.'

'Their confederates will also suffer,' noted Nicholas. 'Both have been arrested. One was the messenger who led you astray with that forged letter.'

'I was too easily fooled by that.'

'Sebastian has a cunning hand.'

'Too cunning,' said Lord Westfield. 'When he told that he was to retire, I wrote to thank him for all the work he had done. He would have kept the letter to copy both my hand and seal.'

'His days as spy and forger are over,' said Nicholas.

'What of his daughter?' asked Gill. 'Was she caught up in his nefarious work?'

'To this extent only. Like her father, she kept alive the flame of the Old Religion. They bought furniture that had once belonged in Catholic churches and sold it in France. Sebastian told me that they sometimes brought back Catholic bibles in exchange. That's what led them to use the *Mermaid* as their merchant ship. It was old and decayed but it was known to carry anything for money. When they searched the hold,' said Nicholas, 'they found that church furniture was not the only thing being smuggled. The captain will not be sailing a ship for a very long time.'

'What will happen to Thomasina?' said Hoode.

'That's for the court to decide.'

'So lovely yet so seasoned in deceit.'

'Thomasina had no part in the murders or the kidnap,' Nicholas reminded him.

'Her father did. He instigated all three. Why pick on Fortunatus Hope?'

'That's my question,' said Lord Westfield, leaning forward.

'Then I'll give you Sebastian's answer,' replied Nicholas. 'He and Master Hope were partners in treachery, passing secrets to our enemies abroad. At least, so it seemed to Sebastian. Then he realised that Fortunatus Hope was playing a deeper game as a counterspy. That discovery sealed his fate. Sebastian had him killed to avoid being exposed himself.'

'But why arrange the murder at the Queen's Head?' said Firethorn.

Gill tapped his chest with an indignant finger. 'And why choose my dance as the moment to halt the performance? It was unforgivable.'

'It was pure chance,' said Nicholas. 'Sebastian's orders were to cause sufficient disturbance to distract everyone but the lads he employed went beyond that. They were too drunk to care. Once the affray started, it got completely out of hand. Sebastian wanted it to be a public murder so that it would embarrass us. From the moment that we began to stage plays like *The Misfortunes of Marriage* that ridiculed the Roman Catholic faith, he wanted to get his revenge on us.'

'Is that why he had Giddy Mussett stabbed?' said Hoode.

'It was an attempt to stop us, Edmund. In driving us out of the Queen's Head, Sebastian did the last thing that he intended. He set us out on the road to Dover. When he learnt where we were headed, he did all in his power to bring the tour to a halt, even if it meant killing our clown or kidnapping our manager.'

Firethorn rolled his eyes. 'At least, he spared *my* life.'

'An old affection lingered.'

'There's no affection in being abducted and beaten, Nick.'

'His aim was to stop us reaching here,' continued Nicholas. 'If we got as far as Dover Castle, it was inevitable that our host would learn of the death of our clown and, before that, of the assassination of Fortunatus Hope.'

Lord Westfield rose to his feet. 'I can explain why,' he said, seizing his cue. 'My good friend, William Brooke, Lord Cobham, is a man of consequence who knows the very nerves of state. Had the name of Master Hope been whispered in his ear, he would have realised at once that an English spy had been murdered for political reasons. It would have led him to do what he has now done and that was to order a search of the dead man's papers that were kept at a secret address.'

'A secret address?' repeated Gill.

'Here in Dover,' said Nicholas. 'Lord Cobham knew where it was because Master Hope reported to him from time to time. Sebastian Frant did not. When he believed they were confederates, he sent letters to Master Hope that would expose Sebastian as a spy if they fell into the wrong hands.'

'Now I understand why he did all he could to prevent us playing here at the castle,' said Firethorn. 'Stop the tour and he saved his life.'

'But the truth about Master Hope was bound to emerge in time,' said Hoode.

'Yes,' agreed Nicholas. 'That's why Sebastian had someone searching the town for that secret address. He wanted to destroy those letters before they destroyed him.'

'But how could they, Nick?'

'What do you mean?'

'The letters would have been written in code that nobody but Sebastian and Fortunatus Hope could decipher. Sebastian would have been safe.'

'Would he?' asked Nicholas. 'You've seen that neat hand of his. No matter how clever the code, there would be no doubt who actually wrote those letters. Sebastian Frant was betrayed by his own profession. His hand was wedded to an elegance that no other scrivener could have achieved. It would have been his undoing.'

'*You* were his undoing, Nick,' said Firethorn gratefully. 'When I was tied up in that stinking hold, the last voice I expected to hear was yours. I was sore afraid, I confess it. When Sebastian held that dagger to my throat, I thought my end was nigh.'

'He could not bring himself to do it.'

'I think that I understand why. It was one thing to have a vagabond clown like Giddy Mussett stabbed to death but I posed a different challenge. When it came to it,' said Firethorn, giving his vanity free rein, 'Sebastian was restrained by the memory of all those wonderful performances I gave at the Queen's Head. He could not bear the notion of robbing London of its finest actor. Without me, Westfield's Men would wither away.'

'But that's not what happened, Lawrence,' said Gill contentiously. 'We staged *A Trick To Catch A Chaste Lady* at the Guildhall and won many plaudits. Owen Elias was as masterful in the role as you.'

'It's true,' said Hoode. 'Owen was another Lawrence Firethorn.'

'With more compassion than you could ever muster.'

'And a touch more humour, I fancy.'

'Can this be so, Nick?' asked Firethorn, angered by the remarks.

'Owen was our salvation,' said Nicholas with a quiet smile. 'Most of the company gave a poor account of themselves that afternoon but Owen could not be faulted. I've never seen him conquer an audience so completely. He had them at his mercy. We were horrified when you disappeared but we certainly did not wither away in your absence. In some ways,' he recalled, 'it brought out the best in us.'

'Hell and damnation!' roared Firethorn, waving an arm. 'I expect to be *missed*.'

If you liked *The Vagabond Clown*,
try Edward Marston's other series...

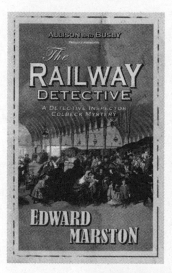

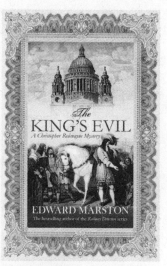

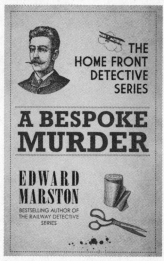

By Edward Marston

EDWARD MARSTON was born and brought up in South Wales. A full-time writer for over forty years, he has worked in radio, film, television and theatre and is a former chairman of the Crime Writers' Association. Prolific and highly successful, he is equally at home writing children's books or literary criticism, plays or biographies.

edwardmarston.com